Tabors Creek

Mona Papoutsis

Mona Papoutsis

ISBN:1721038183
ISBN-978-1721038183
ISBN-978-1983120497

DEDICATION

To my husband, James, my children:
Monica, Chris and Angela

TABLE OF CONTENTS

Tabors Creek

ACKNOWLEDGEMENTS

In this novel I have taken the liberty to write of Tabors Creek, W. Va., where like my father, I was born and lived for the first seven years of my life. Although this is a fictional story, it is based on facts which I remember as a young girl living in W.Va. It was a unique and interesting childhood, one which leaves me with many memories, some wonderful and others not as much.

I am deeply indebted to my friend, Nancy Hoke, for all the assistance and advice she kindly gave to me during and following completion of this novel. She was especially helpful in preparing the work for publishing.

I am also grateful to the dedicated staff on line at Create Space for their professional assistance.

In addition, I want to say thanks to my family and friends who have read and critiqued with professional, exceptional suggestions.

July 1929

I

Ellen Peck wiped a tear from her cheek as she stood in the doorway of the one-room shanty she shared with her mother, Bertie, Ellen's husband, Sherm, and their two children. She looked in the distance toward the small town of Tabors Creek, hopelessly wondering if she could see dust flying, a sure sign Sherm would be driving her direction, on his way home. He had left the home or shanty a couple of hours earlier to peddle his "juice." During this prohibition time, good homemade booze was popular, though very expensive, and knowing someone was an open door to finding it. Here in this part of the country, the Appalachian Valley, however, it wasn't too difficult to find. When you lived here, you knew just where to go.

Bertie, standing behind her, both hands on her ample hips, a concerned look on her face, asked, "What are you looking for, honey?"

"Oh, just wonderin' if Sherm was on his way home yet." She looked as if she might cry, but held it together. "You know how I worry, mama," she said. "Every time he goes to town with his juice, I always wonder if maybe this will be the time he'll get caught. He's been doin' this for about a year already!"

Bertie dropped her hands from her hips, appearing angry but serious, looked straight at Ellen, "and who would care if he got caught?" she answered.

Ellen looked down at the ground, wrung both hands nervously together, holding back tears. She solemnly stared at her mother. "Mama! Please don't even think like that! Don't say it either. What in the world would we do if they caught him? You know they'd take him straight to jail and we'd have nothing at all."

"We don't have much more'n that now, do we," as she walked across the boarded, dirty floor.

"Mama, mama!" Ellen said loudly, with obvious frustration, "no we don't, but at least it's somethin'. He's also the only way we can put food on the table, like him or not. If only I could get a job, I would, but I can't even do that, bein' pregnant like I am!" She held on to her very pregnant stomach, bowed her head a cried a bit. Pointing out the door at the children in the yard, she glanced back at her mother and said, "You know I still have to feed the kids and we have to eat too."

Bertie walked slowly to her daughter, and gently placed her arms around her.

"Don't cry honey. I know how frustrated you feel. We gotta keep our calm, okay? You know he worked that still pretty hard last month. I know he took some extra jugs with him today, so he should bring home extra money this time. I'm hopin' he will anyway." Aware Sherm would keep any extra money if he could, she continued, "Now if he just shares it, we'll be able to get some more groceries. Heaven knows we need them. There isn't much here right now, as you know."

"It seems so hopeless sometimes," said Ellen. "Never enough money. Barely enough to eat. I don't see a future for any of us." She hesitated, placed both hands to her face and bent to place her head in her lap. "I don't know. Guess I'm feeling way down today. Just thinkin' about bringin' another baby into this mess seems so wrong, and even though I'll love this child," rubbing her bulging stomach, five months heavy with child, "we'll still have another mouth to feed." She began to sob uncontrollably.

"Try not to worry, honey. We'll get out of this mess some how, some day. I can't say having another baby makes it easier, but it's comin', like it or not. No matter what, you know we'll love it, money or no money. Now try to stop your worrying. Don't do you or me any good at all. And it sure don't help the kids!"

It wasn't the time to cry, not now. And what good would it do, none at all. Only her mama would notice or hear her. "I'm sure you're right, Mama. Some day, maybe, we'll figure out a way. Today, I just can't see how. I can't see anything but the worst. God surely needs to help us out."

Ellen, feeling defeated, stepped outside to check on the children who were down the bank in front of the house. She lifted her apron to wipe away a tear that rolled down her cheek. Her once exquisitely coiffed, bronze colored hair was pulled into a knot at the back of her head and her feet were bare. The blue, flower-printed, cotton dress she wore, made from a feed sack, had faded from years of washing. Being pregnant, she nearly filled out the dress, which had once been too large, but was now one of only two dresses she could wear.

In the yard, she kicked at the yellow dandelions and mustard plants that grew prolifically along the dirt path that led from the road, up the hill and to the house. *Silly to cry,* she thought. *It doesn't help.* She looked back at the house, a wooden structure of sorts, with a tin roof. It sat slanted on the hill, as if the angry winds had blown it out of shape. The thought of the illegal still behind the house, afforded privacy by the woods in which it was built, ignited the worry she loathed. Sherm had moved to this location solely for his purposes. It provided him with a concealed area rarely traveled by anyone but him.

Ellen could hear the children giggling as they ran up the hill to the house, Charlie chasing Neet. The children were comforting, in spite of hard times. She had to believe that one day she could provide better for them. They deserved a much better life than what she now could provide. She prayed that somehow, some way she could give them a future to look forward to.

Her thoughts were interrupted by the sound of Neet crying. She hurried to her as Neet held out her scratched and dirty hand for her mother to see. Her knee was scraped and bleeding slightly. "Charlie was chasing me and I fell down," Neet cried.

"Charlie, honey, how many times have I asked you not to chase your little sister? You're five years old and she's only three. You know she can't run as fast as you can."

"I'm sorry, Mama. I didn't mean to make her fall."

"I know you didn't, honey, but you need to be careful." She placed Neet on her lap. Looking at Charlie, she said, "I think you need to tell her you're sorry."

"I'm sorry, sis. I didn't mean you to fall." Charlie's eyes pleaded for her forgiveness as he stood watching Neet cry. Tears that fell down his small face washed the dirt from his cheeks leaving a clear path down to his chin. He wore a cotton-knit, short-sleeved, white shirt, obviously smaller than his actual size. With his stretched shorts hanging from his waist by suspenders too large for him, he appeared frail and considerably smaller than he actually was.

"It hurts, Mama," Neet continued to wail.

"It's okay, honey," Ellen said, hugging her daughter. "Charlie didn't mean to make you fall. It's gonna be okay." Taking Neet from her lap, Ellen placed her on the grass. "Sit on the ground here till I get a rag to wipe your knee." Ellen walked to the side of the house where a bench sat with a pan of water for washing hands. She took a rag hanging from a nail on the outside wall of the house and wet it in the pan. Gently, she wiped Neet's knee. Like Charlie, Neet's hands were black from playing in the dirt and her heavily stained, blue pinafore dress hung unevenly where the hem had torn loose. Taking Neet's hand, Ellen walked inside, Charlie, looking very sad, following close behind them. He was trying very hard to keep in control, even though his lips were quivering.

Inside the house, Ellen's mother, Bertie Potter, stood at the table kneading a bowl of bread dough. She could hear little Neet crying outside and her heart felt heavy. She wished Sherm would disappear, anywhere, it didn't matter, just out of their lives. There had to be a way of surviving without him, but she needed to discover what it was. Ellen's pregnancy had put an added burden on her efforts to plan a way to get them away from him. She feared for Ellen's health and safety, as well as the baby she carried. Sherm Peck wasn't worth the dust that God had used to put him together and she longed for the day when she would show him they didn't need him.

Bertie believed he was probably correct in assuming the Feds wouldn't expect to find an operation like his at a place where there was a wife and young children. So Bertie continued to help Sherm with the operation. She mixed the recipe and on occasion bottled some of the juice. She was sure Sherm was hiding some of the money; if ever she found it, it would be their way out and away from him and all of his illegal moonshining and whatever else he did when he was in town.

She finished kneading the bread and placed it in a greased bowl, covered it with a rag and left it to rise.

"This house ain't fit for humans to live in, with the exception of Sherm, and one day he's gonna have it all to himself," Bertie mumbled out loud to herself. Inside she had divided the only room into areas, mainly for sleeping and changing clothes purposes. Most of the floors were just dirt, but one small area which had boards placed across the room. Using her strong arms and a stick she dug holes where she wanted the wooden posts in the bare, dirt floor. From each post, which she placed around sleeping areas, she strung rope and used clothespins to hang blankets for make-shift curtains that afforded some privacy. Two sleeping areas, hers, which had a curtain between the two beds (homemade mattresses), and theirs, took up one side of the room. Sherm's spit bucket sat at the side of his and Ellen's bed just outside the curtain. A chamber bucket sat by the back exit. There was no privacy for that.

On the other side of the room, at the back, the children slept on a mattress, which Bertie and Ellen had made, like hers and theirs, with fabric and goose feathers. The feathers they had collected from a neighbor who lived near them once and raised ducks and geese. The neighbors had washed and dried the feathers so they could use them for the mattresses. There was no charge since Bertie and Ellen were glad to get them and the neighbor was thankful someone would take them. Wooden boxes salvaged from the general store served as the bed on which the mattresses were placed. An ice box, a wood-burning kitchen stove, and a table with four wooden chairs made up the rest of the room. An unpainted door led to the front of the yard. The chairs were placed along the wall, other than meal time, to afford space in the tiny room.

Light could be seen between the bare boards on the wall, except where Sherm had pounded other, smaller boards over the larger cracks. The boards kept some dust out, but very little else. Bugs, flies, and mice were a constant problem. A sticky-paper fly catcher hung from the end of the electric cord holding a bare light bulb which Sherm had rigged in the kitchen area. On the dirt floor, Sherm had strategically placed boards for walking. In the summer, the inside was sweltering hot until the sun went down, then cooled off somewhat when the door was opened. In the winter, it was uncomfortably cold, with the only heat coming from the kitchen stove.

Bertie walked to the door to follow up on the earlier cries of her granddaughter. Seeing her, she asked, "What's the matter with you, Neet?" Pausing, she waited for a reply. "Never mind, I can see. You were runnin' again, weren't you? Didn't Maw tell you to stop your runnin? Now, maybe you'll listen to me. Come here and let me see." Neet walked to her, whimpering more quietly now. Bertie sat down on the wooden bench in front of the house and gently placed Neet on her lap and cuddled her close. She rocked her back and forth, rubbing the child's sweaty, blond hair out of her face. Soon Neet was asleep.

From her vantage point on the hill, Bertie could see the dust flying in the distance on the road below. It had to be Sherm since no one else in the area had a car.

Holding Neet on her lap, Bertie watched the dust until it stopped at the bottom of the hill, confirming Sherm was home. Ellen walked from the small vegetable garden which she and Bertie had planted, to where Bertie sat. She held several tomatoes in her hands. They heard the car door slam, then watched as Sherm climbed the hill to where they waited. He passed by them, ignoring their stares, and headed toward the house.

"Hi Daddy," Charlie called. If Sherm heard him, the greeting was ignored.

Sherm continued on to the house, carrying two empty jugs, one under each arm, when Bertie stood up, Neet still asleep. With Neet in one hand, she held out her hand to Sherm, "well, where's the money?" in a demanding voice. Sherm placed one jug on the ground, reached in his pocket, and then handed her five dollars.

"Where's the rest?"

"They ain't no more, so don't ask. And they won't be any at all from the next batch."

"You took a lot more jugs outta here this morning – oughta be more than this," Bertie retorted. "You can make it up in the next batch."

"'I just told you there'd be none from the next batch, so don't ask. I got some needs too, you know."

"What needs do you have, I'd like to know?"

"Who do you think pays for the jugs and the other stuff to make the juice? You sure in hell don't."

"And what about groceries for to feed this family, Sherm? That's your job, you know?"

"That's what the five dollars is for – take it or leave it."

Bertie glared at him wishing he'd drop dead on the ground, while Ellen, obviously disturbed by the conversation, walked back to the garden and pulled a few weeds.

Ignoring Ellen and the children, Sherm continued to the back of the house, up the small hill and into the wooded area carrying the empty jugs.

"He's a worthless piece of dirt," Bertie announced.

"Mama, please don't say that in front of the kids," Ellen pleaded.

"Can't help it, Ellen. You know the sayin', 'call a spade a spade.'"

II

1929

Activity was almost nil on this early afternoon in Tabors Creek, West Virginia where the air was hot and dry and the cloudless sky promised no relief in sight. Dust flew where folks walked the downtown dirt street. For many it was the Federal era of Prohibition, but not in Tabors Creek. Folks in Tabors Creek had their own laws, abetted by Sheriff Gordon Workman whose motto was: *Ignore what could cost the town money or create work for the sheriff's office.* He figured folks around Tabors Creek had enough problems making a living. No need to complicate it any more. Life appeared somewhat peaceful in this little town with finding ways to beat the heat, or learning how to survive it, everyone's greatest endeavor at the present time.

*****

Skinny Jedd Skeens and Elton Miller sat in tall, straight-back rocking chairs on the wooden slat front porch of Tom's General Store. Skinny Jedd was dressed in a sleeveless, ribbed undershirt and baggy, blue denims, held up with a belt that ran through some belt loops and skipped others. A hand-rolled cigarette hung from his lips. Elton Miller looked somewhat the same in a sleeveless, ribbed undershirt and brown, worn, cotton pants that appeared several sizes too large. Suspenders kept them from falling down. In his hand he nestled a crudely-fashioned corn-cob pipe. Both men sipped on cups of coffee, spots of which they wore on their undershirts. They had no reason to sit there except habit, but they didn't need one. Streets were bare except for one car that could be seen coming in the distance. "Ain't much happenin' today," Skinny said.

"Not unless you call that car comin' down there a happenin'," Elton answered.

They both looked down the road at a car headed toward them in the distance, the dust clouding the air behind it.

*****

Proud of his 1924 Model T Ford, Sherm Peck created a blanket of dust as he sped down the street, disregarding the few walking folks waving the dust from their faces. He felt better suited to a new coupe, but that would have to wait for the time being, at least until he could get rid of the burden of hauling kids, groceries, etc. He was also proud of the good bargain he'd gotten on the car. Originally over two-hundred dollars, with trading and dealing, he had gotten the black, second-hand car for less than half that amount.

After parking in front of the general store, Sherm opened the car door, stepped out, slammed it shut, then looked up and down the street as the dust settled around the car and onto the porch. He reached into the back seat and pulled out some jugs of clear liquid. A tall man, he was 35 years of age, almost handsome with a broad face, sharp features, slightly receding hairline, and a reddish complexion that suggested lasting effects of alcohol and cigarette abuse. A sleeveless undershirt covered over and under the beginning stages of a pot belly and lay tucked inside his belted pants, though the belt was out of sight. His hair was wavy, lying flat at the sides of his forehead, wet with perspiration.

"Damned fool," said Skinny Jedd, as he brushed dust from his face with his hand. "Dang dust. He does it ever time he comes to town. He ain't got no thought of nobody but hisself."

"It's a 'tention gitter, Skinny, don't you know that? He thinks he's purty hot stuff in that fancy car he's got there," replied Elton Miller.

Skinny Jedd glanced at Sherm, then at Elton. "Well, I'd say let him take it somewheres else, except for the apple juice."

"You wanna tell him, Jedd?"

"I ain't telling him nothin, that's fer sure."

Elton raised his left arm, holding on to the corn-cob pipe with the other hand, and answered. "I reckon he's gotta right to feel like he's special. I ain't seen no other body who got a car like his."

Sherm walked up the stairs to the wooden porch, ignoring the two men in the rocking chairs. He entered the general store carrying four half gallon jugs. Owner, Tom Bellemy, looked up from the counter when Sherm entered. "Hi there, Sherm. How many jugs a apple juice you got for me today?"

"Here's four. Didn't git much apples picked this week. Got six more in the car. I'll git maybe ten more tomorrow or next day," he answered as he placed the jugs on the counter.

Tom Bellemy picked up the first of the jugs and placed it under the counter. "Sounds like you been busy, Sherm," he quickly responded.

"Yep, sure have. Lots of work done and lots more to do. I kind of enjoy it though, Tom. Sure glad the Feds don't bother us country folks. I got a family to feed, you know."

"I am hearin' you Sherm. How many kids you got now?"

"Last time I counted we had two and one more a comin." Thinking he was funny, he laughed out loud. As a polite thing to do, Tom laughed with him.

"They'll keep you a hustlin' Sherm. Two will keep you busy, but my God, three! Wow! That's a lot."

"Oh, I got more. I got my great mother-in-law livin' with us too. She's a piece of work for sure."

"How's that workin' for you?" Tom asked.

"About the way you'd think, I'd say."

Tabors Creek

The two of them laughed out loud. Outside Skinny Jed and Elton Miller could hear the laughter. "Wonder what that's all about?" Skinny Jed asked.

"Who knows? Probably nothin' we care about!" Elton answered.

Sherm made two more trips to the car to bring back the other six jugs, while still ignoring the two men in the rocking chairs. He placed the jugs on the counter. "That's it for today, Tom," he stated.

"It's probably all I should have here right now anyway. Only so much room you know. Course it won't last long." He laughed with a loud guttural sound, rubbing both hands across his wide span of stomach. "I git real thirsty sometimes," he continued as he massaged his belly in a circular pattern. "Here's ten bucks and there's more of course, when you bring more juice."

"Sure nuf," Sherm replied, taking the money. Placing the money in his pocket, he walked toward the door.

"Hey Sherm, don't forgit your empties," Tom said, pointing to the jugs sitting on the floor near the door. "Bring 'em back filled though – that's part of the deal." His guttural laughter caused Skinny Jedd and Elton to glance back at the door as Sherm exited. "Love that apple juice," Tom called behind him. "Good for the soul." Laughter continued to ring from the room.

Sherm glanced at the two men sitting in the rocking chairs and acknowledged them with a nod. In a condescending voice, he said, "Don't work too hard now, you hear," then walked down the steps from the wooden porch of the store. He wiped dust from the windshield with his hankie, shook dust from the hankie, then stepped into the car.

"What the hell's that sposed to mean?" Skinny Jedd asked, glancing at Elton.

"I ain't got no idea and I ain't a carin' to git one."

Elton wiped dust from his face with his hankie as Sherm pulled from the store and created more dust. Both men watched as Sherm backed out from the parking place, and continued to watch as he parked the car at Bart's Tavern across the street. "I think I could probably guess what he's after over there," Elton said, with a twisted smile.

Skinny Jedd smiled exposing the gaping hole where teeth had once been. "Probably you're right. None of that stuff for me. Think I'll just git me a jug a juice and go home, I reckon." He rose and walked inside, Elton close behind.

Inside the store Skinny Jedd spoke to Tom, "I'll take one of them jugs of apple juice, Tom."

Placing a jug on the counter, Tom stated, "There you are."

"Yeah, I'll take one of 'em too," echoed Elton.

"You boys a little thirsty, are you?" Tom began his guffawing before he had finished talking. It was a sound Skinny Jedd and Elton were used to hearing.

"Well, my whistle gits real dry, alright – all the dust, you know," Skinny Jedd replied.

Elton added, "That's right. It sure does. A good shot of it'll make you sleep like a baby too, you know, Tom."

Tom placed another jug on the counter. "You betcha it does, Elton. That'll be $2.00 each. And remember, the only juice you buy at the general store is what?"

Elton and Skinny Jedd, in unison, "Apple juice."

"That's what I wanted to hear. We don't need them Feds to git any ideas."

Elton and Skinny Jedd exited the store and walked down the wooden sidewalk in front of the other stores with Tom Bellemy's laugher ringing out the door behind them.

*****

Sherm exited his car in front of Bart's Tavern, exuding an air of undeserved pride in himself. A bead of perspiration fell from his wet forehead onto his sleeveless undershirt as he stepped onto the wooden porch. Running his hand from his chin to his forehead and through his hair, he made a vain effort to freshen his look, but freshen couldn't happen on a hot, sweltering day like this one. "Damn," he cursed, as he opened the tavern door.

Both Edna Fellows, a regular at Bart's, seated at the bar, and Bart Johns, tending bar, turned to look as Sherm banged the door shut clanging the cowbells on the door.

"Hi Sherm," Bart called. "Come in to cool off with some apple juice, did you?"

"It sure as hell is a hot one out there today." Sherm smiled, slammed the door shut, and continued to the bar. He purposely took the seat next to Edna Fellows. "Nothin' better en that juice, now is there? Maybe we oughta give Edna a drink too, Bart," he said, as he looked at her with a wide smile and a knowing wink.

Edna reached for Sherm's chin. Speaking coyly, "You're cute, Sherm."

Bart served a glass of juice to Sherm, then placed one in front of Edna. "Thanks Sherm," Edna said. "Haven't seen you in a few days. Where you been?"

"I been cookin' up a storm, Miss Edna. Got lots of apples out there and a thirsty bunch in here."

"Watch for them Feds, Sherm. They're sneaky bastards, you know. I heard on the radio just last week they was up in Lexington and busted three places. Even one man got shot. So you best be careful."

"Sherm ain't no dummy, Edna," said Bart. "Besides, all we sell here is apple juice, cider, and lemonade. Ain't nothin' wrong with that, so don't you worry your pretty head about nothin'."

Looking at Sherm, Bart continued, "You got any juice today for me, Sherm?"

"Not today, but should have some tomorrow." Sherm sipped on the sweet, but tangy tasting juice, smiled at Edna and stated with cocky assurance, "Bart's right, Edna. Them Feds ain't lookin' for me anymore 'n I'm lookin' for them."

"Stayin in town for a bit, Sherm?" Bart asked.

"Well, for a little bit anyway. Edna and I – we got some things to talk about upstairs for a while. Right, honey?" He placed his arm around Edna's waist as he took another sip of his juice.

Edna, looking as seductive as she could in a red satin, tight fitting blouse that met a white, skin-hugging skirt at her waist, turned to face Sherm. "I can't wait Sherm. It's been too long."

Sherm reached into his right pants pocket taking out a can of Prince Albert tobacco. From his left pocket, he took a small pack of cigarette papers, tore one sheet off, closed the pack and placed it back in his pocket. Like an artisan with years of practice, he poured some tobacco into the paper he held deftly between his thumb and two fingers and began to roll a cigarette.

"How much longer do you think this Prohibition thing is gonna last, Sherm?" Bart asked.

"The way I see it, them Feds are gonna git pretty tired of tryin' to run all over the country findin' people who they think is doin' somethin' wrong. It ain't none of their business anyway. One of these days they'll figure it out and find somethin' else to do. It ain't gonna last Bart."

"I don't know Sherm. I saw the Lexington paper last week and it don't look good. They been goin' in and wreckin' places out in Chicago and some other places, but specially in Chicago," Bart added.

"Yeah, but we're here in Tabors Creek – we ain't in Chicago. They ain't after us little guys. Mark my words."

Sherm winked at Edna, nodded toward the upstairs where a loft with several doors overlooked the barroom. A railing edged the second floor in front of the doors and continued down the open stairway, which led from the loft to the center of the barroom. One of the upstairs doors opened and a middle-aged man walked out combing the sides of his unkempt hair. He placed the comb in his pocket, and buttoned his shirt as he walked down the stairs. A young woman with short brown hair, dressed in a long, flowing, blue robe followed him out of the room and entered the room next door.

Edna pulled her long blond hair all to one side of her face and stepped off the stool, making sure the slit in her skirt came open, revealing her black, mesh stockings. She stood watching Sherm as he took one last drag from the hand-rolled cigarette he held in his hand. He pressed it firmly in the ashtray on the bar extinguishing the lit end then headed toward the stairway. Edna followed. "Hi, John," Sherm said, nodding to the man coming down the stairs.

*****

Sherm walked around his still like a peacock with a secret, holding a smile that expressed his smarter-than-the-Feds attitude. He checked the jugs, pulled some full ones and replaced them with empties, capping the full ones. After a while, he picked up the filled ones and walked out of the woods and headed toward the house.

In the kitchen, at the stove, Bertie placed potatoes in the skillet for frying, cut up an onion into the skillet and added salt and pepper. She worked with the dough on the table, squeezed the dough into biscuit shape, and then placed them on a flat baking pan.

Ellen took down a smoked ham, which had been hanging from a ceiling rafter hook in the kitchen area. She placed it on the table and began slicing it as Sherm walked in the back entrance.

He placed the jugs on the floor by the front door, then pulled back the blanket hanging in front of his and Ellen's bed. He sat down on the bed, and stuffed a piece of chew in his mouth.

Neet lay on a blanket on the floor nearly asleep while Charlie lay beside her looking at a picture book. "Hi Daddy," Charlie called.

"Hi, boy. Ain't you got nothin' better to read than that sissy stuff?" he replied.

"Let the boy alone, Sherm," Bertie replied.

Perturbed, Sherm said, "Shut the hell up, Bertie. How long before supper?"

"You'll just have to be patient. It'll be ready when it's ready. We were busy tendin' the garden today and collectin' wood for the stove before we could cook your supper."

"Well, you had all day, didn't you?"

Bertie glared at Sherm, resisting the urge to tell him what she was thinking. "Well, I didn't see you around liftin' your hand, did I? Where'd you spend your whole afternoon? It wasn't spent workin', now was it? Maybe you had a visit to one of those nice girl halls in town, huh, Sherm?"

"Go to hell, Bertie."

Ellen looked pleadingly at her mother. "Mama, please don't."

*****

Sherm had no choice but to take Ellen, Bertie, and the kids into town to buy the necessary groceries and ice, but he grew impatient as he waited for them to leave the house. "Let's go. I'm leavin' now," he called loudly as he walked out the front door and headed for the car.

"Come on kids," Ellen called. "Let's go. Mama, are you ready?"

"Guess I'd better be," Bertie responded. "The master calls. Might as well get this over with."

*****

Sherm pulled the car into the front of the general store and the family climbed out. Bertie wore one of the two dresses she owned, a small blue-flowered print on white, buttoned up-the-front style, with short sleeves. Short in stature, her amazing strength came from her muscled shoulders and arms. Her braids of hair were wrapped around her head and pinned in place in her desperate attempt to fight the day's heat. On cooler days she wore just one large braid, hanging loose down her back. On dressier occasions, in many years past, she used to wind her hair into a French twist, but that was when she was a single lady, before husband and children changed her life and priorities. Now, her concerns centered on her daughter and grandchildren. She wore brown oxford shoes that laced in the front, her only pair of shoes.

Ellen wore one of her two maternity dresses which Bertie had made for her, a simple A-line made of blue cotton plaid she had purchased at the general store. Her shoes, brown oxfords like Bertie's, were scuffed and worn with deep scrapes on the toes.

Inside the store, Ellen and Bertie looked for groceries while the children hurried to the toys and barrels of candies. Bertie placed eggs, flour, and other items on the counter, while Ellen stood looking at a shelf filled with bolts of material.

"Mama, can I have this?" Neet asked, holding a book of paper dolls. Barefooted, Neet wore a faded green dress, short sleeved, with one button where three used to be.

"Not today, honey. I'll help you make some paper dolls at home. We'll cut them out of the catalogue, okay?"

Pointing into a barrel of candy corn, Charlie called to Neet, "Let's ask Mama for some of these." Charlie too was barefoot. He wore short pants and a short-sleeved, once-white, gray shirt obviously too small for him.

After looking into the barrel, Neet ran back to her mother. "Mama, Mama, can we have some of those?" she asked, pointing to where Charlie stood.

Hearing them, Bertie called, "Now what do you kids want? It's always one thing or another."

"Can we have some of these, please, Maw?" Neet pleaded.

"We'll see. Let's pay for what we have first."

They all stood at the counter while a clerk totaled the cost of the items. "That'll be two dollars and seventy-five cents, Miss Bertie."

"Okay, and we need a block of ice too, and some of that candy corn for the kids – give 'em each a penny's worth."

The children jumped up and down with glee as Bertie paid the clerk. The clerk took a piece of paper from the roll on the counter, and began to get the candy for the children. Ellen watched, smiling.

Bertie walked to the other side of the store where Sherm stood talking to Tom. Pointing to the bin of ice, she asked, "Think you can carry the ice to the car, Sherm? Don't want you to overdo it though."

Sherm glared at her as he walked to where the ice lay. With ice claws, he picked up a 20-pound block of ice and carried it to the back of the car. The rest of the family took their purchases and climbed into the car as Sherm tied the ice to the back bumper.

*****

Sherm strolled through the still operation, filling some partially filled jugs, replacing the filled ones with empties. When he had finished capping and gathering the filled jugs, he picked them up and walked to the house.

Inside the house Bertie was mixing some ingredients for the still. As she measured the yeast to place in the bowl, Sherm stood watching her. "What are you starin' at?" Bertie asked.

"Ain't you done with that yet?"

"Does it look like I'm done? Don't worry yourself. It'll be done soon enough." Pointing to the filled jugs, she continued, "you got enough here to get rid of, so don't worry about what I'm doin'."

Ellen looked at them disapprovingly, "Please stop, both of you." She rubbed her back, and walked to the bed and sat down.

"I'm gonna lay down for a minute Mama, my back is hurting me."

"Well, I'm goin' into town to take my juice in," Sherm announced.

"But you was just there yesterday, Sherm," Ellen sighed.

"Yeah, and I'm goin' again. Gotta feed this bunch, ain't I?"

"Let him go, Ellen," Bertie declared. "Those whores in town need some money too, don't they, Sherm?"

Ellen stood up and glared at her mother. "Mama, stop it. Stop it right now. I can't take it any more!" Sitting back down, her head in her hands, she quietly cried.

Sherm stormed out the front door, grabbing some of his jugs as he walked out.

Bertie walked to the bed and sat down on the edge next to Ellen. She placed her arms around Ellen's shoulder. "Honey, I'm sorry. I just can't help it. He ain't no damned good. You know it and I know it."

"I know, Mama, I know, but he's all we got, you know. Right now, there just isn't a thing we can do. Look at me," as she pointed to her bulging stomach. Her eyes filled with tears, tears that spoke regret and hopelessness.

Bertie held her for a few minutes, trying to sooth her worries. Rubbing her head, she said, "Honey, you need to stop worrying. I know, I know. It looks so helpless, but you know God watches over us all the time, and eventually he will help us get out of this mess. Worrying don't help you nor the baby you're carryin'.

"Of course I know you're right Mama; I just can't stop thinkin about where we're headin'.

Sherm walked back into the house, picked up three more jugs of "apple juice" and walked back to the car. Neet and Charlie followed their daddy outside and waved to him as he walked down the hill, but he never looked around to see them. He was focused on getting into town with the rest of his "juice." Tom would be a waitin' for it.

"We'd be better off without him, Ellen," Bertie continued. "Just wish there was a way outta here now, but you bein' pregnant and all, don't see how we can do it. You deserve so much better than this."

"One day, Mama, the Lord is gonna take things into his own hands. He'll forgive me for getting' myself in this mess and he'll help me. I can feel it. I don't like worryin' like this, and like you said, I need to stop it. You wait and see. Maybe then it won't matter if Sherm ever gets a real job or not. I know this isn't really living. It just exists, but I know we gotta do what we have to right now. Makin' Sherm mad won't help us outta here, now will it? I want my kids outta this mess too. I want them to have a normal, happy life. This isn't happiness, I know that too. We gotta put my mess in God's hands and ask for help, that's all."

Bertie's heart ached for Ellen. She wanted so much more for her. Things she herself never had. If only Ellen had a better life, Bertie would be happier too.

"Sherm ain't never gonna lift a finger to do anything, so long as he can swindle and cheat his way through life, Ellen. You can be sure of that."

"I know. You're right. I know what he is, but it's just so hopeless right now. He's all there is, that's all. We can't do it on our own, so what is there left to do? We just have to wait for the good Lord to tell us what our next step is."

Bertie walked to the icebox and with an ice pick, chipped off a piece of the block of ice and put it in a cup. She poured water on top of the ice from a bucket sitting on the table and gave it to Ellen.

"Here honey, drink this, then get some rest. You'll feel better. You shoulda run away with Sheriff Workman four years ago when he asked you. You know he loved you, Ellen."

"Mama, please don't start that again. You know I couldn't leave. I was married and had a baby."

"Yeah, and he was cheatin' on you back then. When Sheriff Workman saw those bruise marks on you, he pretty near cried, remember that? He told you he'd take care of you and the baby. You know he would have too, just like he said he'd do. He still would if he could. He told you then Sherm was no good and that he'd been runnin' around all the time you two been together."

"It's too late now Mama, so let's don't talk about it any more." Ellen's voice began to quiver and her hands shook at the thought of what she could have done. "Maybe sometime, but not now."

"It ain't never too late, Ellen. Your dream of goin' to nursing school is gonna happen one day if I have anything to say about it. You'd be there if it wadn't for him. You knew better than to get pregnant, especially when you're not married. If he had any sense at all, he'd know that too. He shouldn't have wanted you to give up your nursing trainin.'"

Bertie took the empty cup from Ellen, patted her on the knee and walked to the kitchen. Ellen lay down on the bed.

*****

Standing outside his car, Sherm carefully wrapped the jugs of juice in a blanket, assuring they wouldn't bump each other as he drove the rough, bumpy, and dusty dirt road into town. He placed them on the floor of the back seat and reached for his revolver under the front seat. Assured it was still there, he pushed the short-barreled gun as far under the seat as it would go. Exuding the cockiness of a man who felt totally in control, he smiled as he rolled the ammo shells in his right pants pocket through his fingers several times. From his left pocket, he pulled a pack of cigarette papers, retrieved his Prince Albert tobacco can from the seat beside him, filled the cigarette paper with tobacco, and rolled a cigarette. Licking the paper of the cigarette, he sealed it shut. He rubbed a barn match against his pants twice before it caught fire, then lit his cigarette. Ready to leave, he stepped into his car and shut the door, pushed the electric starter and pulled onto the road. It was a hot, two-mile road into town. Sherm leaned toward the window, anxious for the moving air to help him cool off. With the arrogance of a peacock, he began to whistle as he drove, wishing people could be outside so they could see him.

As he approached the lane to Maggie Sellers' house, he could see her standing on the front porch, watching for him. He turned into the lane.

*****

Stepping out of his car, Sherm tucked his shirt inside his pants and closed his belt. Maggie gave him a hug as he walked to her front porch. She guided him inside the front door, then walked to her tousled bed. As she sat there, clothed in a filmy, short-sleeved robe, she beckoned him to her. "Come on over here, Sherm," she said. Anxiously waiting and wanting to be in her bed, Sherm hurried to her. Sometime later, sitting on the side of the bed next to Sherm, she turned to him, "You don't get anything but better, Sherm," she said.

"All or nothin' for you, Maggie."

"When can we get outta this town, Sherm?"

"Now, Maggie, you can't go rushin' things. I'm gonna get us outta here, just you be patient. We're goin' places, you and me, but when we go, I wanna be sure I can buy you all those fine things you want. We ain't goin' with just a few dollars – we're goin' with a roll, honey. Where you wanna go? We could go to New York, or maybe even Europe – where you wanna go?"

Maggie danced around the room and sang, "New York, New York, here we come, ready or not."

Sherm stood up took her by the hand and led her back to the bed. With a smirk, he said, "what a pretty thing you are, Maggie." He sat back down on the side of the bed, held out his hand for her. "Come back here" Sherm called, perspiration falling from his forehead. "I need to talk to you once more before I run to town. Guess I don't need to hurry after all."

Her robe fell to the floor as she slinked slowly toward the bed, turning to look at Sherm with a come-touch-this look.

*****

Leaving Maggie's house Sherm got into his car. With his ultimate air of arrogance, he spun it around causing dust to fill the air; the car faced the road. With one arm out the window, he waved to Maggie and headed down the lane as fast as he could. Once again, dust filled the air. As he reached the main road, he stopped and waited, his eyes fixed on a car speeding and throwing up dust, coming at a distance from the direction of town. After it passed the lane where Sherm waited, he then pulled onto the road and headed into town. With a grin of amazement, he muttered out loud, "You fellers must be lost, there ain't much out here." The unfamiliar, black Ford headed in the direction of Sherm's house. Suddenly, Sherm had a sudden premonition that just maybe they might be going to check his home. But he was focused on getting to the General Store with his "juice;" and putting that thought aside, Sherm pulled onto the road and headed in the opposite direction, toward Tabors Creek.

*****

Walking inside, Sherm was surprised to see the general store empty. Any time Sherm had been here in the past, there was always at least a couple of people in the store. He looked around and seeing no one, he placed three jugs onto the counter top and called, "Are you back there, Tom?"

Tom came rushing from the back room, obviously very anxious. "Did they come to your place?"

"Did who come to my place?"

"The Feds, the Feds!" he stated excitedly. Running his fingers through his hair, he continued, "They were here in town. They wrecked the Ellis set-up out at his house. Guess they tore everything down and set fire to the stuff he had. Then they stopped at the tavern and seized all of Bart's stash. They didn't know I had anything and the stupid asses didn't even look. Then they got back into their car and headed in your direction. I guessed they was goin' to your house. I thought you'd be there. Sure surprised when you walked in here."

"Goddamn it! I saw them! I saw the sons-a-bitches. I saw them. Goddamn it! I shoulda known it was them." Sherm ran from the store and jumped into his car.

Tom followed him to the porch, and called to him. "Don't do anything stupid, Sherm." Outside and across the street Bart watched from the front of his bar as Sherm ran to his car. As he backed up, the dust flew in the air like a cloud of ash and Sherm quickly headed out of town towards home.

Sherm raced all the way his fury raging like a wind-swept fire as he drove the two miles. "I'll kill the sons-a-bitches. Gotta git there." He kept muttering unintelligible meanderings, which only he could understand. His fixed stare never left the road as he pushed the car with all the power it had. "Come on, you son-of-a-bitch, git me there," he cursed the car. Passing by Maggie's house, for the first time, he never glanced in her direction. A group of straggly, skinny chickens, standing in the middle of the road, scattered to the side and into the ditch barely seconds before they were nearly flattened by the racing car.

When Sherm reached home, the Federal agents' car was parked in front of the house. Sherm reached over and grabbed his shotgun and ran, puffing all the way, up the hill.

Inside the house, Ellen and Bertie watched as he neared the house. Seeing the gun in Sherm's hand, Ellen's quivering voice cried aloud, "Oh my God, what's he gonna do."

"Shut the door and stay right here," Bertie urged her. "Nothin' we can do out there, cept maybe git hurt." She closed the door. Ellen took the children by the hand and led them away from the door and to the bed where they sat down and waited.

*****

Sherm could hear the sound of breaking glass as he neared the edge of the woods. It wasn't the glass he heard, but the crashing of shattered dreams. He wanted to cry; his world was falling apart, but that wasn't possible, not now, not when you wanted to kill at the same time. He was a living, moving, uncontrollable rage. Lost was his ability to rationalize, to consider his own fate. By the time he reached the area where he could see the agents knocking platforms and glass jugs with hammers, he had gone to a place of kill or no return. He aimed his revolver in their general direction in a vain attempt to stop what had already happened. The first shot, which missed both of them, brought the agents around and facing in his direction.

Seeing Sherm with the gun, Agent Frank Coulot yelled to him, "Don't shoot, Sherm. You'll hang if you do."

"You ain't got no right here, you son-of-a-bitch," Sherm answered, pointing his gun at him.

"Listen to me Sherm," Coulot called, holding up his left hand urging Sherm to stop. "You know this is illegal, what you're doin' here." He lowered his right arm, moving closer to his pistol.

Sherm could have heard him, but all he could do was watch as the agent's mouth moved! He wasn't open to really hearing him. "Don't reach for your gun, you bastard," he yelled. With his shaking arms, he maintained his aim with the revolver, pointed directly at Frank Coulot.

"Don't shoot, Sherm. We're just doin' our job here. Don't shoot, please." Sherm shot him once in the chest, then once more in the stomach after he fell on his back.

Sherm stood looking at him, as the other unarmed agent, John Rilling, ran for his life and the car. Sherm wasn't looking at

Rilling. His rage was still centered on Frank Coulot as he stared at him and shot once more. "You wrecked my life. Now we're even, you son-of-a-bitch," he said. After he took a cursory look at the broken still, the helplessness and sinking sensation of his lost dreams brought him to his knees, and for a minute he forgot Agent Rilling. With his head hung low, he began to cry with heaving sobs.

Inside, Ellen sat on the side of the bed. Both children snuggled close to their mother in fear of something they didn't understand.

When Neet heard the shots, she placed her head in Ellen's lap and covered her ears with her dress. "Mama, Mama, what's Daddy doing?"

"Don't you worry. You're okay. Just sit there with Mommie," Bertie said to Neet. She walked to the window and looked outside as Sherm ran down the side of the hill headed toward the car. Charlie stood frozen in the corner of the room. "Go sit wth Mommie, Charlie."

By the time Rilling had reached the bottom of the hill, Sherm's rage had intensified and his thoughts had refocused on the running agent. He rose from his knees and took chase. Sherm could see the agent enter his car as he ran in his direction. Ellen, Bertie, and the kids now stood at the front door watching. After Sherm passed by the house, Ellen ran after him. "Sherm, Sherm," she cried. She stopped at the top of the hill and yelled as loudly as she could, "Sherm, what on God's earth have you done?" There was no answer. "Sherm, stop! Stop, please! Oh, my God. Please stop him. Stop him!"

Sherm had no answer, and without looking back at her, he jumped into his car. He took chase after the agent who was desperately trying to get away in his car. He could see the agent's dust rising in the air a short distance in front of him. "I'll catch you, goddamn you, I'll catch you," he yelled as tears ran down his face and his fist hit the steering wheel.

Tabors Creek

Rain began to fall lightly at first, but soon the ominous looking clouds opened up and poured rain like water from an overfilled bucket. Before long, the yellow clay-like dirt became slippery and driving grew hazardous. The agent slowed down somewhat, but not Sherm. His rage manipulating his actions, he bared down on the agent, ignoring the sliding car on the wet clay. The road narrowed as they neared town and flat land to the right side of the road had been replaced by steep hills by the time they reached the first intersection of town.

Here Rilling was forced to stop as a carriage carrying a man and his wife passed in front of him. Rilling tried desperately to get around the carriage, but the carriage driver had slowed down to a near stop having seen the cars coming faster than normal. Rilling then tried to open the car door and get away. However, before he could get the door open, Sherm had already stopped, jumped from his car and ran to the agent, his revolver in his hand. Terrified, Agent Rilling put his hand in front of his face and pleaded, "Please, don't shoot. Let's talk."

"How does it feel to beg, huh? What did you say, 'just doing my job, wasn't it? Well, I'm just doin' my job, you son-of-a-bitch." Then he shot through Rilling's hand as Rilling's other hand rested on the car door handle.

"You ain't goin' nowheres, you son-of-a-bitch." The agent slumped back into his seat, blood running down the side of his face onto his neck.

Sherm started for his car, but in the distance, near the center of town, he could see Sheriff Workman coming toward him on the back of his gray stallion. To drive out of town, Sherm would have to drive past the Sheriff, which left him but one option. He took off on foot up the side of the hill.

Sheriff Workman reached the dead agent at about the same time Sherm disappeared at the top of the steep hill. Jumping from his horse, he quickly threw the reins around a nearby tree and ran to the agent. He opened the car door, checked the pulse and seeing he was dead, moved him backwards onto the seat, out of view. He turned to the couple who had gotten out of the carriage when they heard the shots and now were at the scene. "Stay here until I get back or till my deputy gets here." He ran up the hill in pursuit of Sherm.

*****

Back inside the house, Ellen and Bertie had watched Sherm leave in the car. Knowing he was gone, Bertie assumed it was safe to go to the area of the still operation. "Stay here and keep the kids inside. I'll be right back." Bertie said to Ellen.

Bertie ran up the hill toward the broken still. The air reeked of the tangy smell of spilled moonshine. As soon as she saw the body of the dead agent lying in a pool of blood in the woods, she stopped and leaned forward, thinking she was about to vomit. She turned and hurried back inside.

"We have to get out of here Ellen."

"He's dead, isn't he?" Ellen sobbed. "Isn't he, Mama?"

Bertie nodded her head.

"Dear God, Mama, what was he thinking? I can't believe he'd do that."

"He ain't never thought, period. How can you think when you ain't got nothin' to think with?"

"What do we do now?" Ellen said, pacing worriedly back and forth and holding her hands together.

"We're gonna pack a bag and git outta here. It's stopped rainin' and since it did rain, it's a little cooler out there. We'll walk – all of us. We can make it."

"I can make it Mama. I have to. But where to?"

"We'll have to figure that out when we get there. Any ole place is better than this one. Sherm won't be back here no ways. If he lives, and they catch him, he's goin' straight to jail, you can bet on that. There ain't much here worth anything, so packin' won't be hard to do. We'll pack up what's here, get started and get outta here. We can take turns carryin' the stuff and take rests on the way. It's only two miles. Sure you can make it okay?" she asked Ellen.

"I can make it," Ellen replied. "There is no more time to wonder how or where. The time I knew would come some day, I think is here. Besides, I don't want to be here when he comes back, if he comes back."

Pausing, Ellen looked around the room as Bertie worriedly watched her. "We need God on our side right now, Mama."

"I'm sure he is, honey. He helped us survive this hell hole for this long, I'm sure he'll help us all survive that last walk outta here. Sheriff Workman will find us a place to stay."

"What about the kids?" Ellen questioned. "Lord, Mama, my kids." Ellen shook her head filled with worry.

"Quit worrying, honey. You worry about the baby you're carrying. I'll help you and the kids. We'll all be okay. It's gonna be tough, but we'll make it," Bertie answered.

"I'm sure we will be. I'll help get our things together," Ellen said. "I'll start with the kids' things."

"Where we goin', Mama? What's Daddy done?" Charlie asked.

"I don't have answers now, Charlie. It's pretty hard to know. Like Maw says, we just need to stop worrying. Right now we need to start walking into town." Ellen put her arms around Charlie's tiny shoulders. "Do you think you're a big enough boy to do that?"

"I can walk, Mama. I'm big now."

"Good. Then I guess we'd better get some things packed, huh?"

Holding up her change purse, Bertie announced, "I got twenty dollars here I been savin'. That'll see us for long enough to find something else. Everything's gonna be okay – you wait and see, all of you."

"Well, I have two dollars in my pocketbook and that's all," Ellen informed Bertie. To the children, Ellen ordered,

"You kids put on your shoes. You're gonna need them and it's also easier than carryin' them."

Into a bag Bertie placed the only clothes the children had, two sets of clothes for each and two pairs of socks, which they shared, when they wore shoes. Ellen gathered the few clothes she owned and toys for the children. Bertie walked to the table and picked up the Bible. She opened it and read an inscription, "To Bertie with love from Mama, June 1890." Tears welled up in her eyes. "I wasn't very old when my mother gave me this. I don't have much, but if I never have anything else, I'll always have this. She had so many plans for me and the rest of the family. If only God had allowed Papa to stay with us just a little while longer. Then losin' your Daddy was just as hard. Makes you wonder why God lets people like Sherm live while them like your Daddy gets taken away."

Bertie wiped her eyes, took a towel from the rack, wrapped it around the Bible and placed it in the bag.

"Don't cry, Mama. Like you said, we'll be okay. Maybe God is gonna help us from above today. We have to stay strong," Ellen said.

Bertie took another towel and rolled up some lace doily pieces and pillow slips, the edges embroidered by her mother, that she had kept in a box by her bed. "These were Mama's too." She held them for a few seconds as past years flowed through her mind; she thought it similar to rain water running through a drain. She hesitantly placed then in the bag.

"Here are your old report cards and some old books you had that I want to use to teach the kids to teach the kids to read. When we get outta here, we can teach the kids at home," Bertie said. They too went into the bag.

Ellen walked to her mother, and putting her arms around her, told her, "I love you, Mama. I'm not sure what I'd do without you. Don't ever leave us, please."

After embracing her mother, Ellen gathered a few more children's books and placed them in the bag.

In a separate bag, Bertie placed some bread and jars of water, along with some apples. She looked around the room to ensure nothing had been forgotten. She picked up the faded apron lying on the chair and tucked it in with the food. Wringing her hands and looking through the room, she said, "Nothin' from nothin' leaves nothin', I guess, wouldn't you say?" Bertie spoke aloud, but when she got no answer, she turned to see that Ellen had already taken the children out the front door.

Neet and Charlie, stood looking back at the door, anxious for the walk to town, with not a hint of the hardships that were to come yet. Their young ages protected them from the reality of what they were facing, but allowed them the pleasure of turning horror into simply an adventure.

"Are you ready?" Bertie called as she stepped into the yard.

"We're ready, Maw," both children replied in unison.

*****

The children ran ahead of Bertie and Ellen, each trying to be the first to reach the bottom of the hill.

"Careful now kids. Don't fall down the hill," Ellen called to them.

"We won't," Charlie answered.

Ellen carried the smaller bag of food, while Bertie carried their possessions in the larger bag.

"We'll stop and rest when the bags get too heavy," Bertie ordered. "So, just be sure to tell me when you're gettin' tired. I know I'm gonna have to take some breaks," she laughed as she held up the bag.

"Well, Mama. Don't know where we're goin', but we're goin'. When you reach the top of a hill and you can't see what's over there, there's got to be somethin' on the other side! And that other side has to be better 'en this side since they ain't nothin' on this side. I'm anxious to find out what we're gonna find."

"So am I, honey, and we gotta come up with a plan in case we see Sherm comin' this way. We don't want him to see us, for sure." She watched the kids running down the hill toward the road as she looked at Ellen and smiled, a look of compassion filling her face. "I say the minute we see a car a comin', we need to hide quickly behind one of them bushes along the road. There's plenty of em'."

"A good idea Mama. We'll do that. I'll explain to the kids to be quiet. I need to make sure they don't give us away."

Bertie answered, "I'll help you."

Ellen and Bertie walked while the children ran and played in front of them. For entertainment, they played tag, kicked stones or chased each other. The sun became brighter as they walked and the further they went, the hotter it grew. The humidity closed in on them with a fierce intensity. They were near Maggie's house when Ellen knew she needed to take a rest. "I'm gonna have to stop for a little bit, Mama. I'm really hot and my legs are tired. The kids need a drink too I'm sure and so do I."

"Yeah, let's stop. I'm pretty tired too. I was just waitin' to see when you wanted to rest." Bertie opened the bag and pulled out a jar of water. Seeing her with the water, both Neet and Charlie turned around and ran back. Neet ran to hug her mother who sat on the side of the bank. Bertie passed the jar around.

Spotting Maggie seated on the front porch of her house, Ellen questioned, "Is that woman over there the Maggie that we saw at the store the other day?"

"Yeah, that's her alright." Although Bertie knew or had heard that she was one of Sherm's conquests that he'd won, she had spared the hurt from Ellen. She didn't need to hear that. But now seemed an appropriate time. "One of Sherm's very own pros....." Both children heard the discussion and were curious who the lady was. They waited for Bertie's response. Seeing they were listening, she stopped in mid-sentence, "You know."

"What, Maw?"

"Just nothin', Charlie. Don't worry about it," Bertie answered as she patted him on the shoulder with hands that appeared to be red and probably ached. They also seemed to be bruised and swollen.

Ellen, watching and listening to them, hung her head. Bertie could see the dread of her situation seeming to take over Ellen's body, and she knew Ellen was painfully soaking in a picture of Sherm and his philandering. She regretted her own outspoken, derision of Sherm to Ellen, but her hatred of him was a driving force at times that overwhelmed her. The day when he was out of their lives, dead or alive, would be a glorious day for all of them, she reasoned.

Maggie stood up to better view the group on the road, as well as to be seen by them. "Miserable woman," Bertie commented. "Don't think she can tell who we are from there though. I'll bet she's a wonderin' though. If Sherm stops in there, she can't tell him she saw us."

As quickly as she had sat down, Ellen stood back up, her head held high. "Enough," she said. She stretched her arms wide, a motion, a stance, like a flower opening to the day's first sunrays. "Let's go, kids, Mama. No more tears, no more feelins, no nothin'. Just let's keep movin'."

"I'm on your side, honey, just like always," Bertie replied.

Both smiled at each other and began the rest of the walk. The children ran in front of them as a rabbit scurried across the road. They both took chase as the rabbit ran into the brush, leaving them peering into the woods at the spot where the rabbit disappeared.

On the porch Maggie stood staring at them. The women chose to pretend she wasn't there as they walked past her lane without a glance in her direction, nor a word spoken.

They continued to walk and talk stopping along the way to take short periods of rest, tear off some bread and share with the children, take a drink of water, and move on. When they neared the edge of town, they could see two cars on the side of the road ahead of them. There were several people standing by the cars.

"That's Sherm's car I believe," Ellen said.

"There's another car too," replied Bertie. "I guess it's probably the Feds' car."

"God, I wonder what else has happened," Ellen spoke quietly, holding her hand over her mouth as if the sound of her voice might announce Sherm's guilt.

"I can't say, but you know Sherm ain't gonna get outta this mess as easy as he usually does." As they neared the two cars, Bertie walked ahead. "Keep the kids back here a little bit. Let me see what's happened before they get any closer." She continued toward Sherm's car, turning back to look at Ellen and assure she and the children were not within viewing distance. As Bertie neared the two cars, she noted Sherm's was empty, but she could see blood was splattered on the inside of the windshield of the agent's car. On the seat she could see the partially hidden body of the agent laying on his side. Turning toward Ellen, she motioned for her to take the children around the vehicles and away from where they could view the cars. Ellen understood. She headed the children far enough around the cars so that they couldn't view anything inside. She was thankful herself to be able to avoid what must be a horrific scene. At a distance the children spotted a dog playing with another child. They ran ahead to play with them. Following the children, Ellen waited for Bertie on the other side of the intersection and away from the deadly scene.

Deputy Sheriff John Bell greeted Bertie. "Hello, Mrs. Potter."

"Hello, Sheriff. I see what's happened. Where's Sherm?"

"He's taken off up that hill, right there," pointing up the steep hill. "Sheriff Workman is on his tail and we're waiting for him. Couple of volunteers took off behind the Sheriff, just in case he needs any help bringin' Sherm in. We got to take care of this body before I can go anywhere. Sure hope to hell they get him."

"Well, I'll take Sherm's car outta the way here. That'll be one less thing for you to worry about," Bertie said.

"Can you drive it?"

"Oh, I can drive it alright," Bertie said with belied authority. She hoped he couldn't detect the trepidation that was slowly moving in. Aware of every step she took, her feet seemed to be floating in space until she reached the car. It seemed like all eyes were on her. What to do once inside the car, she would face when she sat down behind the wheel. She'd watched Sherm drive. She could do it, sure that her helpless feeling would subside, once she started the car. But, could she drive it? She'd have to; there was no time for failure now.

Sheriff Bell followed Bertie to the car and watched as she looked for the starter. He grinned, in spite of the horror of the situation. "You ever driven this before, Mrs. Potter?" he asked. Not waiting for an answer, he reached into the car, pointed to the electric starter and waited for her reaction.

"Oh, that's right. Guess I'd forgotten. It's been a while, you know."

"Yes, it's been a while. I can see," he replied, then began to walk away.

Bertie pushed the starter, causing the car to jump. Sheriff Bell returned to the car. "You gotta shift, Mrs. Potter. Hold your left foot on the pedal, push it all the way in, and your right foot on the gas pedal. Now when you start, you have to let out the clutch slowly as you give it some gas. The pedal in the middle is the brake. That's to stop, you know," he grinned.

"Yes, I know. I'll get it. Just a bit rusty, you know."

"Yeah, I know that too," he smiled.

With the car jerking forward, and gears grinding as she shifted, Bertie managed to move the car near Ellen and the children. Ellen moved the children well off the road until Bertie had stopped the car. "Get in," Bertie called.

"Maw, do you know how to drive this car?" Neet asked.

"Why sure I do, honey. Just get in. You'll see."

Charlie and Neet giggled as they climbed into the back seat and sat down.

Ellen took the front seat next to her mother. "Hang on, everybody, I'm not too good at this yet," Bertie informed them. With that the car jerked and slowed, then jerked again as Bertie shifted gears and moved slowly ahead.

"Whoa," Charlie called when the car leaped forward. Neet giggled again.

"This is a horse I think," Charlie said as he giggled aloud.

"Alright now kids. Just relax. I'm just gettin' used to this car, that's all," Bertie said.

"Where we goin', Maw?" Charlie asked.

"Outta here, Charlie, where the rest of the world lives and life can begin for us too," Bertie answered him.

"Mama, where we goin?" Neet asked.

"Like Maw said, we're going where there's life, honey. We'll get there. You kids just sit back and look out the window."

Charlie and Neet pushed back into their seats leaving their short legs to reach the edge of the seat as the car moved forward and onto the dirt road that led out of town and toward Kentucky.

Leaving town, Bertie turned to the children, "you kids, look back at what's behind you and say 'goodbye' cause we ain't never comin' back."

The children, not understanding, but curious, looked back to see what they were missing. Charlie looked at his sister, shrugged his shoulders, not knowing what he was to look at. "Maw, you look funny driving," Charlie said. They both giggled. "What is that?" Charlie asked.

*****

A short time later Charlie looked at Neet and with a wide grin, looked down at the seat and rubbed the soft seat with his hand. There was no tension riding with them today, not like when Sherm drove them to town, which was the only time they rode in the car. The freedom of the day created an atmosphere for delight and play. Not realizing why, Neet began to giggle, which made Charlie giggle. They played hand tag for a bit, looked out the window some, and soon Neet was getting sleepy.

Looking at Bertie, Ellen stared until Bertie glanced sideways at her. "Whatcha' thinking about, honey?" Bertie asked.

"Oh, just wonderin'."

"About what?"

"Oh, about money and how we're gonna' get by, that's all," Ellen replied.

"Stop your worryin' now. I told you I got us enough to git us goin' with and we'll find us a place. You gotta have this baby, then you can find some kinda work too. We'll make it. You're even gonna get in nursing school, you'll see," Bertie assured her.

"I know we'll make it, Mama. Getting in nurses training isn't gonna be easy though, workin', a new baby and all."

"We'll take it slow – baby steps, you know. First though, we gotta get where we're goin' – Lexington, I hope," Bertie answered. "That's where your daddy thought we'd eventually move to. You probably don't remember that."

"No, fraid I don't," Ellen said, even though the question was directed to the children.

"He always wanted to move to the city, especially Lexington. You and your sister were his little prince and princess. He worked hard on the farm and was doin' really good till he got sick. He thought that farm was gonna make us a lot of money, and it probably would have too. That consumption got a lot of people back then, includin' your sister."

"Oh, I remember that, Mama. I'll never forget it."

"Neither will I, honey. Losin' your daddy and your sister was nearly the end of the world for me. If I'd lost either or both of you too, I couldn't have made it, I don't think."

"We gotta think of the future now though, Mama. Okay?"

"Yep, you're right, honey. Look out future, here we come!" She began to dance in her seat.

Ellen began to giggle at her mother's antics. "Thanks, Mama. I needed that."

In the back seat, Charlie nudged a sleepy Neet. "What?" she asked.

Charlie pointed to a string sticking out from under the back of Ellen's seat. They giggled first, then erupted into raucous laughter.

"What's so funny back there?" Ellen asked.

"Your seat is tied up," Charlie replied, giggling as he spoke.

"You are Mama. We're not kiddin.' Right there," Neet chimed in, pointing to the floor behind Ellen's seat. Climbing from her seat, Neet jumped to the floor of the back seat and pulled on the string. The string was a tie to a small, white, muslin bag, which had been obviously hidden under the seat. "See," she said, holding it up to where Ellen could see it.

"Let me see", Ellen said, reaching for the bag.

Taking the bag in her hand, Ellen asked, "Wonder what this is," speaking out loud, to no one in particular. She cautiously opened the drawstring on the bag, half afraid of what might be inside.

"Oh, dear God", Ellen cried. Looking in the bag with disbelief, she cried, "Mama, it's money, it's money. Can you believe? Surely God has heard our prayers. I can't hardly believe this."

"Count it, Ellen, count it," Bertie added.

Ellen sat staring into the bag, still in shock.

"Count it, Ellen," an exasperated Bertie insisted, pointing her finger at the bag.

Ellen began to count, stopping to wipe the tears streaming down her face. "There's twenty $50 bills here, Mama that I just counted and there's a whole bunch more. Can you believe this? There's also a lot of smaller bills. I'll count everything later.

There's probably about seven or eight thousand dollars here, I bet." She wiped her face on the skirt of her dress. She didn't know whether to laugh or cry, so she did both. Laughter for finding Sherm's money and escaping the hell that had been theirs for the past several years. Tears for the men who had died today, for the fear of Sherm, and for whatever else she wasn't quite sure. But this could be their new beginning, the one she prayed for, and the money would help start it.

"Is that Daddy's money, Mama?" Charlie asked.

"Daddy left it for us, Charlie," she replied. "He knew we'd need extra money to get to Lexington."

Satisfied, Charlie sat back in the seat watching Neet fall asleep. Soon he followed.

"I think Sherm was probably saving this money to get away from us, don't you think, Mama?" Ellen asked her mother.

"He woulda been gone by the end of summer when the weather got cold and he didn't want his ass to get cold makin' stuff to sell. Guess he waited just a little bit too long, huh?" Bertie asked, with a spiteful grin..

"Do you think he'll try to find us?" Ellen asked.

"He'll try to find us alright." Bertie responded. "We got his car and now his money. He'll be madder than two wet cats when he finds out we're gone. Yeah, I think he'll try to find us. I think there's too many people in Lexington for him to track us down though, even if he knew we was there. Even so, I don't think he's got the good sense to figure we'd get that far without him. Not with the big feelin' ego he's got."

In the back seat, both children were asleep, Charlie leaning against the window and Neet leaning on Charlie. Looking in the back seat, then at Bertie, Ellen pointed to the children and noted, "Oh look at them, Mama. It's almost like they know it's gonna be better."

Bertie nodded her head. "Yeah, they do," she said. "They can feel it too. The tension is gone." She kept driving, looking straight ahead as the wind whipped at her face and her lips formed a smirk. "I knew the bastard was holding back, Ellen," Bertie quietly said.. "He did us all a favor though. He just doesn't know it yet. Yeah, he was planning to run with that money, for sure. Losin' a game is hard, but losin' at your own game is gonna' make him see fire."

*****

Bertie had been driving for what seemed a week instead of a day. Her eyes were heavy from lack of sleep and she longed for some rest. The last 20 miles had been the hardest with every bump in the road vibrating her already bruised and aching body. It was another day filled with justifiable reason to hate Sherm Peck. He put Ellen in this position, although he may have unwittingly just gotten her and the rest of them out of it. *He'll be a raging bull when he finds out*, she told herself, but put that thought aside to concentrate on her next, more immediate step, stopping to rest.

The sun was setting on the horizon and darkness was near. Spotting a gas-for-sale road sign, Bertie pulled the car off the road. A one-room, one-pump gas station sat in front of several small rental cabins. One small cabin next to the rental cabins boasted a sign overhead that read, Country Kitchen. In the window sat another sign that read, OPEN. She pulled to the gas pump and waited for help. Ellen stepped from the car to stretch. She opened the back door and motioned for the children to step out.

"Can I help you, ma'am?" the attendant asked.

"Yeah, you sure can. We're needin' some gas and a place to stay for the night," Bertie answered. "We're all pretty hungry too," she said with a sigh and half a smile.

"I'll get your gas and then we'll find you a cabin, if you want it. Gas is cheap, but the cabins ain't. They'll cost you $2 a night. There's plenty of food right there in the restaurant," he said, pointing to the end cabin.

"How far from the city are we?" Bertie asked.

"Well, you're about 100 miles from Lexington."

"We'll take one of them cabins for tonight and we'll be on the road in the mornin'."

"Where you headed?"

"We're hopin' to make it to Lexington." She spoke with some authority; though she had no idea how far away that might be until now. Where they were going wasn't nearly as important as just getting as far away from Tabors Creek as possible. Getting her daughter and grandchildren away from Sherm Peck was all consuming. Lexington made sense since it gave them a big enough place to hide, in the event Sherm was out of jail and wanted to find them.

The attendant stared at Bertie for a minute. Bertie waited for the question, which she could see in his face, hoping he didn't ask anything personal. She had no answer should he ask why they were going to Lexington. Where they had come from, she couldn't answer either, except to lie and she had no lie good enough to try right now. She felt a slight relief when he stated, "Get up early in the mornin' and get goin' and you should be there by supper time - tomorrow evening. It's a pretty big city. Been there before?"

"No, can't say we have."

"I think you'll like it. Nothin' like livin' here, you know." The attendant finished filling the gas tank, then wiped off the windshield. "That's a real big city there. You ladies on your own, are you?"

"Well, we're on our own just temporarily," Bertie lied. "We'll be okay, I'm sure."

"Okay, ma'am. That'll be $1.50 for gas and $2 for the cabin – total of $3.50. You'll take the number two cabin, down by the restaurant. Go ahead and get your family some supper while we put an extra cot or two in there for them kids to sleep on. You can pay for your cabin in the restaurant. I'll bring you the key to the cabin."

"Thank you kindly. We'll be doin' that right away – we're pretty hungry." Bertie replied.

Bertie parked the car in front of the cabin while the others stood by waiting for her. Driving the car for the past few hours had been a learning experience, but she had mastered it. She now felt thankful she had watched Sherm driving when she rode with him.

*****

"That was a good supper, Mama," Charlie said. "I was really hungry."

"Glad you liked it, Charlie. Time to clean up now and get some rest," Ellen answered. The family all walked toward the central shower.

Dirty clothes were left behind at the shower with Ellen. Bertie dried off each of the children, put on their nightshirts and got them inside the cabin. "I want the top bunk bed, Maw," Neet said. Ellen stayed behind to rinse the children's clothing.

"No, I get it," Charlie said.

"Neither one of you can sleep up there. I don't want you falling down on somebody below you," Bertie answered.

Bertie had finally gotten them in the double bed in the room when Ellen returned. The cleaned clothing now hung on a line outside the cabin. The warm night air and slight breeze would soon dry everything. Ellen picked up a book to read them a story before they slept. "It's my turn to shower. I'll be back in a little bit," Bertie called as she left the room. After her shower, she got into her night shirt, then washed her underclothing and her dress, and hung them next to Ellen's laundry and went inside. They were all asleep. She smiled and shut out the light.

*****

Morning came quickly. Ellen awakened first. The warm night air had dried all their clothing. Helen brought them in, dressed herself, then awakened the others. Together, she and Bertie got the children dressed and ready to go.

Breakfast in the restaurant was a combination of things. There were pancakes, eggs, and bacon for everyone with milk for the kids and coffee for the ladies. Blueberry muffins were served after the breakfast. "I want a muppin," Neet called to anyone who would listen.

Ellen grinned. "You'll have a muppin if that's what you want, little one."

"Where you all headed?" the waitress asked as she poured coffee at the table.

"We'll be headin' for Lexington. Should be there before evening, if all goes well," Ellen answered, then rolled her eyes, and grinned at her mother.

"Yes, ma'am, you should be I believe. It's a pretty nice town I hear, though I've never been there." She sat a plate of muffins on the table.

"We hope so. We're anxious to get there," Bertie answered.

"Good luck to you all," the waitress answered.

Getting up from the chair, Ellen motioned for the children to follow her. While Bertie paid for breakfast, she walked with the children to the outside, toward the outhouse. She looked at the dilapidated building, hesitated for a minute, looked all around, as though hoping for something better. Then with a look of resignation, she took the children inside the outhouse for the last time before heading to the car.

Bertie pulled the car out onto the road, and headed for Lexington. "Where we goin' Mama?" Charlie asked.

"To home and a future," Bertie answered.

"Where's that?"

"Lexington, Kentucky," Ellen responded. "Remember we told you that yesterday. Now you just sit back and talk to your sister. We'll be there today some time. You kids are just gonna' have to be patient until we get there. It's a long ride, but we'll make it."

"It's a place called home, kids," Bertie added. "It's a town with real streets, lights on the streets, stores, and all the things we never had before. You'll like it, just you wait and see."

"What about Daddy, Mama?" Neet asked.

Ellen thought for a moment, then replied. "Well, honey, Daddy had things he had to go do, so we'll just let him finish those things. Some day maybe when he finishes, we'll know where he is. Just wait and see. He's fine I'm sure, so just try not to think about it." Her heart ached for her children, but she trusted that in time they would forget him. The love she herself once had for Sherm had slowly turned from love to hurt, to anger, and finally, to pity. Today she felt no love at all, just a nagging and constant worry. Sherm had snuffed out the lives of two men yesterday – he would have to pay dearly for this, she knew. The men he shot had no doubt left families to mourn their deaths. Who were they, she wondered – did they have wives, children? There was no way to know, but whoever they left behind mourned their deaths today, of that she was sure. The thought made her nearly sick to her stomach. Even though two lives had just ended, hers was just beginning again. This made her feel both guilty and grief stricken. The hurt the families of the dead agents were aching today and Ellen felt free at last. Broke she was except for the money they had found, but she didn't yet know how much was there nor how much a place to live would cost. There was still a long road to go, but with a beginning, she had hope. Sherm's actions were out of her control. In time, hopefully, she could face it without pain. She would tell the children one day when the time was right. Her future lay at the top of a hill, but the climb would be worth the end. When she reached the top, she would be stronger, having survived and surpassed where she had been. She prayed for strength to get her there.

Tabors Creek

Suddenly, as quickly as a streak of lightening, Ellen felt free, free to think, free to feel, and free to live again. Turning to Bertie, she smiled, then burst into laughter. "Child, what has come over you?" Bertie asked.

"Mama, I'm free, I'm free, don't you see? I don't know where I'm goin', but I'm free."

"Yes, honey, you're free. I'm gonna' help you to get where you're goin' until you're able to make it on your own, and you will. You just wait and see, you will."

"I know I will, Mama. I know I will."

The laughter soon became contagious. Awakened from their nap by the laughter, Charlie looked at Neet, at his mother, then back to Neet. He began to chuckle, which soon turned into hard laughter. Neet followed, then Bertie joined them. When they quieted down some, Bertie began to sing, "If you knew Susie, like I know Susie, oh, oh, what a girl. There's none so classy as this fair lassie." Ellen followed, and before long the children were trying to sing along with them, catching words they knew here and there.

III

1929

Sheriff Workman walked into his office in Tabors Creek. The look he wore on his face told his story. Deputy Sheriff Bell raised his head and looked as the door opened. "The son-of-a-bitch got away," Sheriff Workman related, shaking his head in disgust and disappointment.

Standing quickly, Sheriff Bell asked, "Where'd he go? Can we get some more men out there? I'm sure we could get some volunteers. Lots of people round here would like to see Sherm Peck behind bars, me included."

"No, no. He's gotten too far and we don't know which way he went," said Sheriff Workman. "It's getting' dark out there too. We'll try again tomorrow, early in the morning. He's gotta come back to get his car. He'll lay low, but we'll watch for him. We'll catch him. Where's the car?"

"The car's gone."

"Gone? What are you talking about, gone? Where the hell is it?"

"Bertie Potter, Sherm's wife, Ellen, and the kids – they all got in it and drove off. We got the agents' car out back. We found the other agent dead back behind Sherm's house. He fell right where Sherm shot him at the operation in his back yard.

"Jesus Christ! What kind of animal would do that?" Sheriff Workman asked. "Them women alone?" Sheriff Workman continued, talking to himself, but didn't expect nor wait for an answer. Concerned about the women driving, believing they didn't know how to drive, he continued, "God, they can't drive that car and they aren't safe alone out there either. I tried to get Ellen to leave him a long time ago, but she wouldn't hear to it. I was planning to marry her, don't you know?"

"Well, they did it. They drove right outta here," Sheriff Bell answered.

"Where'd they go?"

"They didn't say – just drove outta town. They said they didn't want to be here if Sherm came back. Can't blame 'em, Gordon."

"Where would you guess Sherm mighta gone, John?" Sheriff Bell asked.

"No idea. He could try to cross the mountain over into Marysville, or as I said, he may come back, hopin' to find his car. He's crazy enough to do that."

"I've contacted the Feds in Frankfort," Bell continued. "They're sending a hearse tomorrow for the bodies. Those poor bastards – even they didn't deserve that. I've wired the Kentucky, W.Va., and Virginia State Police to be on the lookout. Think I'll also notify Ohio and Tennessee. Don't think he can get much further than that, if that. He has no money with him probably. He just might try to rob a bank. If so, we'll find him then."

"Wonder what she'll do now?" Sheriff Workman asked.

"Who?"

"Ellen, that's who."

"You gotta put that behind you Gordon. You know that," Bell said. "She's a smart lady. She knows how to survive as long as she's not with that bastard. Also, she's got her mother with her. They'll do okay."

"Yeah, I know, but it's not easy, John, not easy," Sheriff Workman said, shaking his head in regret. "I loved that woman long before he did. Wish I'd been smarter."

Sheriff Bell walked to his desk, took a seat and with a concerned look added, "It wasn't supposed to be, that's all, Gordon. She fell for Sherm and he promised her anything he thought she wanted. She believed him. She didn't know you were sincere, I'd guess. You should have jumped right in there. It wasn't that you weren't smart, just not fast enough, I guess. Just wait now and see what happens. You never know."

"Yeah, I'm sure you're right. Thanks, John."

*****

It was dusk as Sherm found his hiding place. He was certain they had been hunting him, but he felt sure he'd managed to throw them off. He left tracks he knew they'd follow down to the river, but once there, he'd walked along the riverbank, in the water, for what seemed like miles before he got out. Walking out of the water on rocks, he'd left no tracks leading from the water. He walked on dead leaves and fronds from the trees in order to hide his footsteps. He found an area on the side of the hill that had thick, heavy clumps of low willow brush. He crawled through the brush into the center, cursing the heavy, strong branches as they slapped at him, scratching and tearing his skin. However, they provided him with shade and a place he needed to hide while he rested. The perils from hell played games in his mind for what seemed like hours, racing back and forth, over and over. Half asleep, he drifted in and out of places where he feared, the worst being when they were hanging him. Finally, exhaustion overcame all and he slept.

Hours later Sherm jumped to his feet from a sound sleep, when he had been dreaming that he'd seen a dead man lying in front of him. Coming to his feet, he had tried to get away from the body, then realized it was only half dreaming. There really was a dead man. He had just killed him. No, them – he had killed two men! The reality of his situation began to slowly move over him like a low, heavy cloud cover and he began to tremble uncontrollably. His life from this point forward would never be the same again. He began to cry, not for the men whose lives he had taken, but for his own predicament in which he had placed himself. There had been many fits of temper in the past, but never before had he killed a man. Once by accident a man survived what should have been his life, which Sherm intended, but nevertheless, he'd lived. It happened in downtown Huntington, W.Va. He shot at a man who surprised him in the filling station he was attempting to rob, but the bullet had missed him. Claiming it was an accident, Sherm got off with just six months in jail for attempted robbery. Luck was with him that time. Not this time, however. *The sons-of-bitches had no business in my yard. What did they think – they could just go in there and break up my still. I had spent days and weeks of work to build that place and hours and hours running it. They got what they deserved – the sons-of-bitches.* No, he wasn't sorry he shot them, but sorry he was in this mess now.

What the hell would Bertie do now? She would have to get her fat ass out and get a job – no more mooching off of him. "Ellen was your responsibility long before she was mine, Bertie, you bitch," Sherm said aloud. "You can damn well still take care of her too." *She had kids to feed too, Bertie. How you gonna take care of them?* He didn't consider them his responsibility any more. Oh well, that was their problem now, not his. He had to get back into town and get his car. They would probably be holding it at the jail. Maggie would help him. She could find out where it was and he would get it at night when no one was around. He felt pretty confident they wouldn't think to look under the seat where he had put his money. Damn, he should have grabbed that before he took off running, but there was no time to think. He had run for his life.

Somewhat rested, Sherm left his hiding place and headed for Maggie's. It was now at least a couple of hours shy of daybreak. He could get to her house before it got light. No one knew of his and Maggie's affair, so they wouldn't look for him there. That god damned Bertie thought she knew, but she was only guessing. What the hell did she know? If only the Sheriff didn't talk to her. The bitch would tell him in a minute if she thought they could catch him. But he realized she didn't know where he was any more than the Sheriff knew. She probably was still stuck at the house with no way to get into town. She'd never ride in his car again, the proud bitch. Yeah, he decided, Maggie was his best means of escape.

The full moon provided Sherm with enough light to see where he was going. He walked some, ran some, resting when he had to. The thick brush fought him as he pushed his way through, tearing at him like they had arms that had come to life. At the point he felt he was getting close to Maggie's, he quickly came down the mountain side to find he still was at least a mile from where he wanted to be. "Goddamn it," he yelled. "What the hell did I come down here for?" The flat ground made it easier to travel and so he began to run. There was still only enough moonlight to let him see where he was going, yet not enough for someone to see him unless they were pretty close. That wasn't likely. Out of breath and panting, he stopped and looked periodically for as far as he could see in all directions, then continued running till he came to an open field where he could see Maggie's house. It was just before daybreak and he still had a lot of area to cover before the sun came up. His chest hurt and breathing got harder with each step. The pain he had felt in his legs had stopped. Instead, his legs had gone numb. There was no time to think about the pain, the breathing. He had to keep moving. Through the field he ran as fast as his legs would carry him. A dog barked in the distance. When he looked in the direction of the sound, he stepped into a hole and fell. "Son-of-a-bitch," he cursed. "God damned dogs, to hell anyway." Still, he picked himself up and continued to run desperately, never looking back. He could feel his heart pounding against his shirt. Being out in the open field, he knew he was exposed to anyone out at that time. However, he counted on being out of that open field before the sun came up to expose him.

The night air had cooled, but he was on fire - perspiration soaked his clothing, not just from physical exertion, but fear – fear that the next step could be the last one if someone saw him. He thought for a second he could hear the sound of a rifle going off. Still, he was alert enough to realize his mind was playing tricks on him, so he kept running. Winded, his burning chest was beginning to feel unbearable and his out-of-shape legs ached. The pain from his head to his feet was all-consuming. With every step he took, it seemed a branding iron seared his feet – first his left foot, then the right one – back and forth with every step. He couldn't last much longer.

Blood began to ooze down the side of his face from a cut he'd suffered in the fall. Wiping it onto his shirt, he kept running. *Running scared like a rabbit is what I am, but I gotta keep goin.*

Maggie's horses were in their stables in the barn, as he expected they would be. Maggie would hardly be gone anywhere at this early hour. *Damn, no light on in the house.* But, he had made it. He hugged the barn door, thankful to be there. Sherm took one final look to assure himself no one was around, then sped to the back door. It was just breaking daylight when he knocked.

"Open the door, Maggie. Open the door," Sherm cried, leaning on the door for support, not certain he could stand alone.

Maggie jumped from her bed. Opening her door, she cried, "Sherm, oh my God. What are you doing? Where have you been? You're bleeding. What's going on? Oh my God!"

"Just let me in, Maggie." Sherm pushed the door open, went inside, and as soon as he was close enough, slinked into a chair at the table.

"Oh dear, let me get a rag and some water," Maggie said. She scurried to get a wash pan of water. "I'll clean you up, but tell me what happened to you," she pleaded.

Sherm sat leaning forward, holding his head in his hand while he tried to catch his breath. "I'm in trouble, Maggie. I need your help."

"Well, of course I'll help you, Sherm. What kind of trouble are you in?" Maggie asked.

"You ain't been to town?" Sherm asked her.

"Not since you left, Sherm. Didn't have no need to yet, so I've just been waitin for you to come by."

"I have to find my car," Sherm answered.

"Where is your car?"

"That's what I need you to find out."

"What'd you do, Sherm? What is going on? Tell me the whole story."

"I need you to go into town, Maggie. They're gonna tell you I killed a man. Well, two men. You gotta act like you don't know anything about it. It was – I hadda kill them, else they was gonna kill me."

"Sherm, what are you saying? You killed someone? I can't believe that. Are you sure?" Maggie said excitedly. "You gotta tell me."

"What the hell do you mean? Of course I'm sure. They were Feds, Maggie, they were Feds. They came and wrecked my operation. All that work I'd done – all my jugs, all my everything, just like they owned it. The sons-of-bitches just came in and took over. It's all gone."

"But Sherm, what are they gonna do to you?" Maggie asked.

"If you help me, we'll get my car and take off. They'll never find us, Maggie.
Come with me."

Maggie continued to wipe Sherm's face and arms as she spoke with him. "Sherm, I'll go to town and see what I can find out. You just get some rest after you finish cleanin' up and get some clean clothes on. Good thing you left some clothes here, you know. I'm glad you're back though, Sherm." She ran her hand over his chest as she continued, "I been needin' you real bad."

"I been needin' you too, Maggie, but not now. We gotta figure out how to get us outta here."

"Where do you think I should go to in town? Maggie asked."

"Go to the General Store and talk to Tom. Don't tell him you saw me. Don't even mention my name. Just wait till he tells you or asks you something," Sherm instructed her. "Let him bring it up and see what you find out."

*****

Maggie walked into the General Store and looked around. From behind the counter, Tom addressed her. "Hi there, Maggie. How are you doin?"

"I'm fine, Tom. I was right in the middle of bakin' and ran out of flour, so just come on in now to get some," Maggie answered as she walked toward the flour on the shelf.

"Guess you heard about all the fuss here, huh?" Tom asked.

"What fuss? I ain't heard nothin'. Out where I am you know, ain't much goin' on. What happened?" she asked, attempting to sound unknowing.

"Them Feds was here in town. They wrecked George Ellis's operation out there by Tarpon Station. They got Bart's supply over at the tavern. Someone musta told them about Sherm's operation. When they left here, they went out and I hear they wrecked Sherm's operation. Then they went out and wrecked Sherm Peck's operation. Sherm got in a fight with them, while they were out at his house, it looks like. He must have shot one of them out behind the house, then the other one tried to get away," Tom explained excitedly.

"Oh, my God," Maggie exclaimed. "Did the other one get away?"

"Nope," Tom explained, "He got in his car and headed for town with Sherm in hot pursuit right behind him in his car. Sherm shot him at the crossroad there as you come into town from out that road where Sherm's house is – and yours too I guess. The guy was drivin' like hell to beat Sherm into town I guess, but that wasn't fast enough for him. I don't know where he was headed, probably to the Sheriff's office, but he never made it. Poor devil. He got as far as that intersection, then he had to stop to let a carriage go across or else he'd have hit it. Sherm pulled up behind him, got out of his car and ran up and shot him."

"Well, where is Sherm now?" Maggie asked.

"Don't know where he is, but he ain't around here. The sheriff chased him up the hill right there beside the car, but he lost him somewhere. I doubt that he'll ever come back here. Wouldn't be too wise," and with that Tom roared his buffoon-like, loud, bellow.

Ignoring his laughter, Maggie asked, "Did Sherm take his car?"

"Nope, he'll never get that."

"I guess not if he ain't comin' back." Maggie said.

"Well, it ain't just that - them women came to town, Sherm's wife Ellen, and her mother, Bertie, with the two kids and they got in that car and took off. Nobody's seen them since."

"Where'd they go?"

"Nobody knows where they went, just got in the car and headed outta here," Tom answered. "Like I said, I don't think Sherm will come back here, but then if he thinks he can get that car, he just might try it, I don't know."

"You're probably right, Tom. He'd be pretty foolish to show his face again around here."

Maggie paid for her items and hurried out of the store to her horse and wagon. "Thank you, Tom," she called as she walked out the door. She turned her wagon around in the middle of the street as Tom watched her from the door.

"She was sure in a hurry," Tom spoke out loud to no one.

*****

It was about 4:00 in the afternoon when Bertie drove the car into Lexington. Charlie and Neet were asleep in the back seat. Ellen sat looking out the window. Turning to her mother, she said, "Can't hardly believe we made it Mama, can you?"

"No, honey, I can't, but we did. Now we need to find a place to live," Bertie answered.

"Let's us find a place to eat first, don't you think? We can go in and talk to the people in there and see if they can give us some idea of where to go," suggested Ellen.

"That'd be a start, wouldn't it?" a smiling Bertie answered.

The two of them sat silently, the only sound came from the engine of the car. They passed several places until they reached one that seemed most appropriate. "That looks good there, Mama," Ellen said, pointing to a roadside restaurant that had ample parking and again some small cabins where they might spend the night. A sign reading, "Vacancy" hung in the restaurant window. Bertie pulled in and parked the car.

*****

On an early August morning in Louisville, Kentucky, Joshua Gibbons stood leaning on the fence surrounding the racetrack, watching the new colt, Freedom. Freedom had just arrived at Holiday Farms the evening before and was getting his first exercise run. He was a thoroughbred, not quite a two-year-old, sired by Vigil, winner of the 1923 Preakness, and Pay Station, mother of two former Kentucky Derby entrants. From what he could see now, Joshua was certain he would do justice to his heritage, and with some luck, surpass them. Winning the coveted Run for the Roses, the Kentucky Derby, was Josh Gibbons' dream with each new race horse purchased by his father and Holiday Farms. He had come close with Thomasina.

The day was going to be another scorcher, but for now a cool breeze blew lightly across the fields of grain and corn beyond the oval track, creating varied, beautiful shades of gold and green. The beginning colors of fall covered the distant hills, which stood like a guard at attention, protecting the precious fields of labor. Two unassuming cats lay sleeping on the fence ignoring the running colt. A cardinal sang loudly from the top of a tall oak tree next to the track. He seemed to be singing, "Come here, come here." In the distance, a matching song could be heard – his mate, Josh assumed. The mate sent back what sounded like an echo. "Hey fellow, she said, 'yes,'" Josh laughingly called to the red-plumed male cardinal high above his head. The cardinal flew away in the direction of his mate, as if he understood Josh's remark.

Trainer Brock Fegan gently trotted Freedom around the track, waving at Joshua as he passed. During the third lap he began to increase his speed and by the sixth lap, let him choose his own pace. Josh stood with his mouth agape as he raced past him. It had been a long time since he'd seen that kind of speed at Holiday Farms. Brock brought him back to a trot and then to a walk during the last lap.

With Joshua applauding, Brock rode over to the fence where he stood. "Good morning, Josh. He's sure a beauty – don't you think?" he asked.

"He is that, for sure. I think he's got what it takes, don't you?"

Brock dismounted the horse and shook hands with Joshua. "Good morning, Brock," Josh said. "I agree. He's got what it takes. He is a beauty. Believe he loves to run. Hope he loves the Derby as much as he does here!"

"Yeah, he does love it," Brock said, gently rubbing the young horse's neck. "Good boy, Freedom," he assured him. "I had to work at holding him back there at first. He wanted to hit it hard on the first lap. I wanted to ease him in till he gets the feel of it. But that's not all bad. The first thing a winner has to have is that drive, as you know – that drive that says, go for the roses. If they got that, then a good rider can work with it and adjust it when and where he needs to. Yep, I think we can expect to see some great things from this one. Course, I usually do think that of most of them." He chuckled aloud.

"Welcome to Holiday Farms, Freedom," Josh said as he stroked the horse's head. "Make us proud."

"He comes from some pretty good stock. Guess your dad told you," said Brock.

"Actually, I haven't had a chance yet today to talk to Dad about him. I was just headed into the house, but I knew all about him weeks ago. Dad and I had discussed him coming here for training. He's been doin' great I hear."

"Yep, he has. It's going to be a hot one again today; hope that's a good thing for him," Brock said. "Humidity is about as high as the temperature. It'll come fast if I don't get moving here. I'll get him back to the stable and get out with another trainee."

"Let me have him. I'll take him for a short ride and I'll put him back," Josh said.

Brock looked with approval. "That'll save me some time. Thanks. He's yours." He handed the reins to Josh. "I need to get the other horses out before it gets too hot to run them. Take care and I'll see you later on today, I'm sure."

Josh mounted the sleek-looking, brown colt. He noticed on Freedom's head, just above his nose, and below his eyes, there was a white, diamond-shaped patch. "Hey, big boy. That's a good sign. Every good horse has an identification mark. Separates the winners from the runners, you know." Josh leaned over to take a better look at the white patch as he spoke. When he did, Freedom flipped his head around, as if to say, "Keep up the bragging – I love it."

"Wow, you are a proud one, aren't you?" Josh laughed and headed toward the field. "See you, Brock."

*****

Inside the house, Joshua spoke to his father. "Hi Dad."

"Hi Josh. I saw you headed out to the track. Did you take a look at the newcomer?" Josh's father, Hal, asked.

"I did. He's a beauty, dad. One to keep our eyes on I think," Josh replied. "I took him out in the field for a short run. He's good."

"Well, you have a good eye," Hal said. "I picked up Freedom to help fill that big hole Thomasina left us with. And, I think he'll do good business for us." Josh shook his head in agreement. It had been pretty solemn around the estate since Thomasina was no longer with them. "He's been hard to replace. I've been looking for months now. When I saw what Jim Rowe could do with Freedom, I was pretty impressed. That's over at Challot Farms," Hal continued. "Who knows, maybe I just found us a winner. How many years has it been that we've tried to take the Derby?" Hal looked down, shaking his head.

"I think you might be right. I liked what I saw of him so far," Joshua answered. "I watched Brock run him. He's fast and he's got a lot of heart. He was running for the joy of running, you could just tell. As I mentioned, I took him out in the field for a short ride. There'll never be another Thomasina, but maybe there is an equal, who knows?"

"Good. Glad you liked him. You could train him yourself if you want, or train him with Brock, or even let Brock do it alone too. Do whatever you like."

"Thanks, Dad." Josh answered as he patted his dad on the back. "I'll work with Brock on it. I doubt that he needs me, but I'll be there watching."

Josh closed his eyes, remembering the pain of losing Thomasina on that day. He had just barely broken loose from the pack after leaving the starting gate at the Preakness when he stumbled and fell. The following horse and rider following closely behind and unable to avoid her, had also fallen, seriously injuring both. Thomasina's jockey, Eddie Ellis, had fortunately managed to escape with scratches and bruises. Both horses, however, had to be put down. The owner of the other horse, Dave Thompson, had filed a lawsuit against Hal and Holiday Farms soon after, claiming Thomasina's jockey had deliberately tried to knock his horse, Ready-Maid, out of the running. Eddie claimed it was Ready-Maid's jockey who had intentionally bumped him, but no one listened. As crowded as they were at the starting gate, no one had been able to see just what had happened.

"How well do you know Dave Thompson, Dad?" Josh asked.

"Do you mean other than the lawsuit?"

"Yeah."

"I know him very well," Hal said. "We go way back." Hal turned his head and stared blankly into space for a few seconds.

"How's that?" Josh asked.

"Oh, it's a long story that I haven't time to go into right now. One of these days when we have nothing to do, I'll tell you all about it, okay?" He grinned and gave a gentle slap on Josh's back and left the room.

Josh was aware there was still a pending lawsuit, which Thompson had filed. More than two years had passed since then, with no change in the situation. Bitter feelings between the two families still existed.

*****

Sherm paced the floor waiting for Maggie to return. What could be taking her so long? He'd already had time to clean up and change clothes since she left. He walked hurriedly to the window. His rough, battered hands shook as he held the curtain back to peer down the road. No sign of her. He began to plan how he would get away if she had screwed up and let the bastards know he was there. If so, the law could be tailing her. He could run out the back door and hide in the stable till she got rid of them. On the other hand, that wouldn't work – they'd probably see him run out. If they didn't, the first place they'd look was the barn. Perhaps, he'd go to the wood room off the kitchen, maybe hide under the pile of wood. That probably would work. Jail was not for him. They might even want to hang him. *That'd be an awful way to die*, he thought. Trying to calm himself, he sat at the table for a few minutes rubbing his hands through his hair and repeated an old phrase he used to hear his mother say. "You don't begin to worry until you see you have to, and even then, you don't worry, you fix it." He'd 'fix it.' He'd shoot the bastards if he had to, but that would be more running and he was tired, real tired. Nothing he could do yet except be ready to move.

He walked to the galvanized water bucket sitting on the table by the door. He picked up the ladle and took a drink. When a tin cup fell from the table, making a loud noise, he jumped and grabbed for his gun. Terrified, he returned to the window to see if he could see her coming yet. With a view of road dust rising in the distance, he assumed it was her. He watched to be sure that no one was following her until she turned into the lane leading to the front of the house. She was alone as she pulled the wagon into the stable. Seeing no more dust on the road, and no one following her, Sherm felt the weight coming from his shoulders and he relaxed slightly. Another panic faced and buried.

With her purchases in her arms Maggie ran into the house. "Sherm, my God, what have you done? They're gonna kill you, Sherm!"

"Did you find my car?" he asked.

"You car's gone."

"Gone! Gone, where?" Sherm yelled.

"Tom said Bertie, Ellen, and the kids drove it out of town," Maggie exclaimed.

"Out of town. To where?"

"He didn't know," Maggie cried.

"Jesus Christ! I'll kill her. I'll kill her." Sherm hissed under his breath. His eyes glowed with hate and his face reddened with anger, as he slowly drew his fingers in a position as though he had his hands around someone's neck. Ellen's neck, Maggie assumed. In his mind, he was obviously shaking that person by the neck as he held his hands in the air and rocked back and forth on his feet, in a quiet rage, calling, "My money, my money."

Maggie stood back, terrified. She had never seen him this angry before. She eased toward the door, took hold of the door handle. Instead of running, she first tried talking to him. "Sherm," she called, "what money?"

He didn't answer. Maggie gently opened the door. The sound of the opening door suddenly brought Sherm to his senses. He quickly turned toward the door, grabbed Maggie by the arm with his left hand and slammed the door shut with his right hand. "Sit down," he yelled, pushing her into the chair with a force that sent her and the chair reeling to the floor.

*****

Sheriff Workman sat at his desk rolling a pencil between his hands and staring out the window, obviously in deep thought. A steaming cup of coffee sat to his left and an empty tablet lay in front of him. Sherm Peck had been gone two weeks now with no sight of him since he took off. Where he might be was anyone's guess and there were no good guesses. The case was being handled by the Federal Agents, but Sheriff Workman wanted to find him for personal reasons. If Sherm had been back to Tabors Creek looking for his car, he'd know by now that the car was gone. If he had a contact in Tabors Creek, then he knew Bertie and Ellen had left in the car. No one knew where they went, but in time he could possibly find out. He'd kill Ellen if he found her, the Sheriff was sure. No, he couldn't sit here any longer and wait for Sherm. He had to find Ellen. He had to find her before Sherm did. If he found Sherm first, that would be even better. He'd be locked up for life, or even hung, but first they had to find him.

Assistant Sheriff Bell walked into the office. Seeing the Sheriff deep in thought, Bell asked, "What's on your mind there, Gordon? You're heavy into somethin' or other."

"Yeah, you're right, I am, John. I'm just thinking. Actually, I'm tryin' to think like Sherm Peck would think and that's pretty hard to do. He doesn't think like most human beings. Where is he, is what I want to know? Where in the hell would he run to? As a killer, with his profile out there, he can't have too many options, so you'd think I could figure it out."

"Well, he didn't come back here," Bell answered.

"We don't know that for sure, do we? He may have a contact here – somebody who'd help him. Somebody who needs money - they get paid, so they help. Who knows?"

"You might be right, but my good guess is that he'll keep running just as far as he can run. Guess we'll see some day. For right now though, we gotta just keep our eyes open and watch for him," Assistant Sheriff Bell warned. "Let the U.S. Marshall do his job."

"I can't sit any more, John. I'm going to take some time and go looking for Ellen. If that bastard ever finds her, he'll kill her. You know that. I'll let you in charge for a couple of weeks while I go and see if I can track her and her family down," Sheriff Workman replied.

"Gordon, I know you want to find him. I understand that, but you know that the Federal Agents are on his tail, along with the U.S. Marshall. You don't need to take on that job. In fact, you can't take on that job. It's bigger than you can handle," Bell said. "Let it alone. When they need your help, they'll ask you for it. As for Ellen, you're looking for a needle in a haystack. We don't even know what city she went to. We know nothing."

"I can just picture Sherm out there finding her first and what he'd do if he did. This is not official duty either. It's personal." He walked to the window and looked up at the sky. The dark clouds were coming lower and lower. His could feel his heart beating against his chest, the rhythm of each beat seemed to keep time with the rain falling softly outside. It represented a shower of sorrow for the sheriff - sorrow for what he had missed, sorrow for what Ellen was suffering through now, and for what lay ahead. He was filled with emptiness – not alone, but yet alone. The bitter memories of losing her years ago were still suffocating. He had to find her, had to put out the fire that burned inside his soul. Sometimes when he felt low, he pictured them married and living in their new home, with a couple of kids, and loving each other. Just maybe there would be another chance, if only he could find her.

Holding a map of Kentucky and West Virginia in his hand, the Sheriff walked to stand by the window where there was good light. He had an innate gift of mind reading. If ever he needed it to work, he desperately wanted it to work now. He needed help to trace Ellen and her family, as well as Sherm. Which way did they go and where were they now? Perhaps Sherm traveled the same path as Ellen, if in fact he was out there looking for her. If not, he soon would be. The Sheriff had a gut feeling that he already was. He clung to the hope that he'd find him first. It would save a lot of trouble. Would he shoot him on sight? He spoke out loud to himself: "no, I'd first ask him why he did what he did?" He knew the answer wouldn't be satisfactory, but it just might help. John looked at Gordon, wondering what he had said. Shaking his head, he went back to work.

"You know when those women left here, they traveled west. We both know that. That's got to be Kentucky since there's nothing west until you get into Kentucky. Bertie didn't know her way I'm sure, so she'd probably just go straight into Kentucky as far as she could get away from here. They never would have turned around and come back through here to go to West Virginia, so we know pretty darn well they're in Kentucky somewhere," the Sheriff said.

"I'd say you're right about that. I'd also guess they wouldn't stay long in any small towns or villages along the way. They'd be too obvious there."

"I'm sure. It's about 100 miles down to Winchester from here. From there they could have headed to Richmond or Lexington, would be my best guess."

"I'd agree with your guess," Bell answered.

"Just for the hell of it, I'm going to drive in that direction. I'll stop along the way and ask questions. Maybe someone would remember if they'd seen two ladies with two children driving alone. That wouldn't be a common sight."

"So when are you heading out, Gordon?" he asked.

Sheriff Workman stood up, folded his map, tucked it under his arm and walked towards the door. He didn't reply until he had his hand on the door. "I'm on my way, John. I'll be checking in every day."

With nothing more to say, Sheriff Workman opened the door, turned and waved as he left the building.

*****

Ellen and Bertie had driven around Lexington streets for several hours looking for signs advertising places to rent. They had gone inside three of them, but found none that were suitable. Most were in complete disrepair and others too small for what would soon be a family of five people, after the baby arrived. "I'm not sure we'll find anything this late in the day, Mama," Ellen said. "We may have to take a room for at least one night. We can get up early in the morning and start looking."

"I think you're right, Ellen. It's getting late. I'm hungry, you're hungry, and I'm sure the kids are too."

"I'm hungry, Mama," Charlie called."

"Me too," Neet chimed in.

"Well let's see if we can find a place where there might be a restaurant next to a room or maybe a cabin or something." Driving through town Bertie spotted a house with a sign in the yard. She stopped, pulled in front of a blue, white-shuttered, older-looking, two story, Victorian style house with steps leading up to a large front porch. Two white rocking chairs sat on the porch. In the front yard stood a "FOR RENT" sign. Ellen, Bertie and the children walked up the front path. "Can I knock on the door, Mama?" Neet asked. She leaned on the door and raised her small hand to knock. Just as she did, the door opened and Neet fell into the front entryway.

"Oh, I'm so sorry. Let me help you," a gentle, soft-spoken lady holding the door offered, as she extended her hand to Neet. Embarrassed, Neet jumped to her feet. "Are you alright?" Sally Crossen asked. A somber faced Neet hid behind her mother's skirt.

"She's fine, ma'am, just a little embarrassed I think," Ellen said, placing her arms around her daughter.

"Well, come in, all of you," Mrs. Crossen said. "I'm Sally Crossen."

"My name is Ellen Potter and this is my mother, Bertie Potter. You met my daughter Neet already." Ellen smiled and rolled her eyes. Pointing to Charlie, she continued. "This is my son, Charlie. We saw the For Rent sign in the yard and we stopped to see what you had. We're looking for a place for the five of us."

"Are you new in town?"

"Yes, ma'am, we are."

Mrs. Crossen took the family for a tour of the downstairs of the house at 356 E. Salem Street. "I live in the upstairs," Mrs.

Crossen said. "You can let me know whether or not you're interested."

"We're interested, aren't we, Mama?"

"I think it's perfect for us," Bertie answered. "When can we move in?"

"Whenever you want."

"We're needing a place today, Mrs. Crossen. We were just going to see if we could find a room somewhere," Ellen said.

"You'll do no such thing. There isn't a lot of furniture here, but there are beds. You just bring your things in and get those children taken care of."

"Thank you so much. We're so grateful to you," Bertie said. She turned to Charlie and said, "Charlie, why don't you help me to get some things out of the car and into the house."

*****

As a horse trainer, Brock Fegan had taken his share of bruises and bumps in the racing business. His biggest hurt, however, had come two years ago when he was let go from Chinook Farms by owner, Dave Thompson, where he'd been for ten years, and where he had a full barn of well-bred runners. Though he had a heavy work schedule at Chinook he had taken on one more horse to train, Thomasina, at Holiday Farms as a favor to Hal Gibbons, a long-time friend. Brock's days were filled to capacity, but he had seen the promise of his friend's horse, Thomasina, just as Hal could see the promise of what Brock's expertise could do with her. Brock was at the track the day of Thomasina's fatal race and watched as she fell. He had loved that horse and had cried at the sight of her being put down. Dave Thompson watched as Brock stood grieving, but when they looked at each other, Dave had mysteriously walked away without saying anything. Later in the day, Dave Thompson confronted him. "What's with you and that horse of Gibbons'?" he asked.

"I'm not sure what you mean," Brock answered. "She was one hell of a good horse. I trained her. Sad as hell to see her go down. Is that what you're asking me?"

"You trained her?" Thompson yelled.

"Yeah, I trained her. Why are asking me? What's the problem? I'm not sure I understand."

"You work for me, not Gibbons. Me. Do you understand?" Thompson's face was filled with fury.

"I work for you, that's right, but I also trained Thomasina," Brock said. "Is there a problem with that?"

"Yeah, I have a problem with that. You don't work for me anymore," Thompson had yelled and walked away, leaving Brock standing there, not understanding.

When he learned of the lawsuit against Hal and Holiday Farms, he understood. It wasn't like Brock had messed up – in fact he had guided Dave's Chinook Farms through six banner seasons that netted a racing purse of six figures each year. Later, Brock had tried, but there was no reasoning with Dave.

Just a year earlier, Brock's own horse, Talent Scout, died of colic after placing in a stake race in Louisville. He had needed that Chinook job. He and his wife, Kathy, had just moved into a new home and she had been expecting their first child the following November. He knew he had a career to rebuild with no time to waste.

After a couple of weeks Brock had paid a visit to Hal Gibbons. Hal had known Brock for many years. Before Chinook, Brock had worked part time at Holiday Farms for a couple of years, but when the full time job had opened at Chinook, he had left Holiday and taken the prestigious job at Chinook. Hal still liked and trusted him implicitly, even though long ago Hal had given up trying to be on speaking terms with Dave Thompson.

"It will take me a long time to build things back to where they were for me at Chinook," Brock related to Hal. "It's been tough, real tough, pretty disheartening at times," he added. "But I wouldn't consider leaving Kentucky or the racetrack. It's my life. I need work - take me back on and I'll do you a good job. You know that."

Hal had three other thoroughbreds of his own and a constant turnover of yearlings and two-year-olds in training from across the east coast, particularly from Virginia. His method of breaking yearlings, unheard of until Holiday Farms, was rapidly growing popular and his number of clientele had doubled in just two years. Hal knew another trainer was now a necessity. He counted his blessings that Brock had shown up at Holiday looking for work.

"I know what you can do, my friend. I've seen it. If you want a job, you're hired." That was two years ago. Hal had never stopped being thankful for his good luck, although he was sure Dave Thompson was madder still. In fact, months after Brock began at Holiday, Dave had apologized to him and attempted to rehire him. It didn't work. Now he longed to see Dave Thompson's face the day one of Holiday's horses took the Derby, or perhaps even the Triple Crown.

"We break our horses to a cart," Hal had informed the news media during an interview. "We ground-drive them first and then get them to jog with the cart. This gets them partly fit and gets them broken without putting any weight on them. When we're done, they're really broke." That advertisement and word-of-mouth had almost instant results. There were calls from owners far and wide. Proven results of his method of cart-training had already spread far and wide and would no doubt continue for years to come.

"I'm sure our success is due for the most part because of you, Brock," Hal said.

"Thanks, Hal. I do my best."

*****

Tabors Creek

Holiday Farms was 124 acres of forest-green, rolling hills with manicured landscaping completely encompassed by white rail fencing. The largest of Holiday's barns housed five standing stallions belonging to Gibson and also served the dual function of a breeding and training barn. It contained 50 stalls, each 10' x 24'.

Along side the breeding and training barn sat the main barn, which contained 30 slightly smaller stalls and two administrative offices under the same roof. It housed foaling mares in the winter and yearlings for sales preparation in summer. This barn also housed an Aquaciser, used primarily for the preparation of yearlings destined for the sales ring, but also for the rejuvenation of lay-ups from the racetrack.

The three-quarter mile training track with a starting gate was located to the north, in front of the two barns. At the east side of the track was another, smaller barn with 20 stalls used only for lay-ups. Six one-acre grass paddocks and six additional half-acre grass enclosures were south of the barns.

A white graveled parking area separated the barns on the west side from the large, gray, stone Gibbons' family home. A one-fourth mile long lane lined by white rail fencing led from the main road to the farm.

A four-bedroom guest house located near the entrance to Holiday Farms housed resident veterinarian, Henry Kokos, and trainers, Phil Johnston and Wes Etter. Each one, as well as Brock Fegan, had the responsibility of planning and overseeing training schedules tailored to the needs of each horse under his care and worked as a team. Josh Gibbons assisted Brock in training when he could, but his duties as manager in charge of foaling and sales preparations took up the bigger portion of his workdays. As the owner, Hal Gibbons was overseer and the farm's stallion manager.

Numerous top competitors received their initial training at Holiday. It was a hub of activity, busy, profitable, and exciting.

*****

Maggie Sellers drove the wagon out of the lane that led to and from her house. She looked carefully up and down the dirt road. Assured there was no one else around, she cracked the whip and the two horses pulled the wagon onto the road and headed towards Tabors Creek. Sherm lay hidden on the bottom of a wooden tool box, placed at the head of the wagon to help alleviate the pounding his body would take from the ruts and holes, which the wagon was destined to hit. And too, there would be less attention drawn there than in the center or back of the wagon. Sherm had nailed the box in place to hold it fast. On top of him, Maggie had placed a lightweight sheet and straw on top of the sheet just in the event someone looked inside. That wasn't likely to happen, but she did as Sherm ordered and took the precaution. She placed his gun by his side, as he had ordered. *Stay calm*, she told herself. *Don't give him a reason to use it.* She was frightened for what she was doing, but just as frightened to refuse to haul him.

They reached the edge of town well before noon. Fear began to choke her as they passed the spot where the second Federal Agent had died. Blood stains still lay at the side of the road. That, she assumed, came when they took him from the car where he had been shot. She wanted to run, but how could she? She knew Sherm was desperate enough now to shoot her too. She thought she loved him before, but now, how could she love him after what had happened? She didn't know. All she knew for sure was that right now, this very day, she had to do whatever he wanted. Perhaps circumstances would provide answers to the questions she now was asking herself.

She crossed the intersection keeping her eyes focused straight ahead then continued on to the front of the General Store. She tied the horses to the post and began to talk aloud to herself. "Be calm. It's okay. Don't be nervous. Walk slowly." She walked up the steps and entered the store holding her head high.

"Hi there, Maggie. How are you?" Tom asked.

"Why I'm just fine, Tom, thank you for askin'. I just needed a couple of things. Thought I'd come and get them before it gets too hot out there."

"It's gonna be another scorcher, I do believe. It's already hotter'n I like it. I'd say you're bein' pretty smart there, Maggie," Tom said. "You just go ahead and get what you need."

"Thanks, Tom," Maggie said, trying with her heart and soul to look happy and act nonchalant. She glanced ominously out the window at the wagon and hurriedly did her shopping. They really didn't need much since they planned to go only as far as Ashland, Kentucky, but a stop here now might save a lot of trouble later. Besides, stopping had been Sherm's idea, so she had no choice. He wanted to know what Tom knew and this was the only way to find out, he said. Maggie picked up several apples, some saltine crackers, and a few pieces of candy. She placed them on the counter.

"Anything new on Sherm Peck, do you know?" she asked.

"Not a thing. Can't even guess where he might be. Sheriff Workman went out looking for him though, and they got his name out in other stations. I hear they even found a picture of him, so that's a good thing. Don't expect the Sheriff'll be back for a couple of weeks. Sherm better hope he don't catch him cause he's out for his hide, that's for sure."

"I think you're right, Tom. The sheriff ain't too nice when he's mad, is he?" Maggie smiled.

"He's kinda like a bear with a turd crossways, you know what I mean?" Tom bellowed with laughter sounding somewhat like a laughing hyena with a bass voice.

"Okay, Tom," Maggie said, handing him 50 cents. "I'll be going. I have to stop at the tack shop yet."

Tom handed her the 30 cents change and continued guffawing as she hurried out the door.

Purposely not looking at the tool box for fear of being watched, Maggie climbed into the wagon seat and headed toward

Ashland, her hands shaking as she held the reins. Stopping several times along the way, she chose wooded areas and a time when no one else was around to allow Sherm to stretch his legs and take a break. He was soaked with perspiration and full of dust that had seeped into the box through the slats. Between stops while cramped and bent in a fetal position in the box, time seemed to have had allowed his temper to wane slightly. Maggie relaxed somewhat, no longer fearful for her life. Perhaps there was a side of Sherm that she hadn't seen before. Without reason it seemed, he had emerged into a new guy.

They reached Ashland late in the evening. Maggie pulled the wagon into an inconspicuous spot along a side street off the main street leading into Ashland. Sherm jumped out of the box as fast as he could. "Goddamn it's hot in there," he said.

"I did the best I could, Sherm. I knew you was hot, but I couldn't do nothin' since I was afraid for you."

"Just move over. I'll drive now," Sherm answered, ignoring Maggie's conversation. Sherm hadn't shaved since he left Tabors Creek. He now had about three inches of new beard growth and combed his hair differently. "Give me your comb. I don't want to look like the picture they got of me – if they have one," Sherm said.

"Tom said at the grocery store that they had a picture of you and that the Sheriff was lookin' for you," Maggie answered.

"Let 'em look, I don't care. I can walk lookin' like this and they'll never know. The bastards. Besides, I don't know nobody in Ashland anyway."

*****

Ellen was tired, very tired. It was the end of the day. She and Bertie had spent most of the day cleaning the new house. Ellen had scrubbed the kitchen, beginning with windows, then cabinets and counter, and had just finished scrubbing the floor on her hands and knees while Bertie washed the floors and windows in the other rooms. Rubbing her aching back, she stood up and leaned against the counter. A stabbing, sharp pain ran across her back and into her side causing her to double over briefly. *Probably from sleeping on that hard floor last night*, she thought. The stack of blankets Sally had loaned her to make temporary beds on the floor had been sufficient, although not comfortable. She had put the kids in one of the beds Sally had given them and Bertie in the other. One more night on the floor and tomorrow they planned to go shopping for some used furniture and other household necessary items - and start living again. Ellen walked to the window and looked outside, her hands resting on her back, remembering the excitement of finding the money in the car. Where they would have gone had it not been for that money was only a guess. Their choices would have been much more limited. *This must be divine intervention,* Ellen decided. Still, the fear she felt was so real; his anger was real – his reaction to frustration was too great for her not to be worried. She thought of Sherm's retaliation when and if he found them. What would he do? *Did he know yet they we're gone? Was he plotting his revenge?* Their absence alone wouldn't be cause for Sherm to hunt them, but in her heart Ellen knew taking his car was cause to make Sherm furious. Worse yet, finding and keeping his money would make him insanely angry. Yes, she knew he would hunt them. As she stood there, Bertie came in to check on her. "Hi honey," Bertie said. "How are you doing?"

"I'm fine, Mama. Had a few pains though, so I thought I'd better just take a break for a little bit."

"You go sit down for a little. I'll get some things done."

"I will, Mama. You know I was just thinking about Sherm. He's gonna be in a wild rage when he realizes we have taken not just the car, but the money too."

"Let him rage. Who cares?" Bertie asked. "That eight-thousand dollars can last us for a long time if we're careful and I take in some ironins. It might even get you all the way through nurse's training. You'd have been there years ago and finished by now if it hadn't been for him interferin'."

"I know, Mama, but that's behind us – way behind us. No use lookin' back."

"That's right, honey. Sorry I brought it up. I just get so angry every time I think of how he's messed up your life and mine. The light is startin' to shine through now and you'll go and get your trainin' and then you can go to work. But, first, the baby, then trainin'."

"It's so exciting. I'll do it too, Mama. I'll do it. I really do like this place. Dreams can come true, if you believe, and I do. Some day we won't have to be worrying about where Sherm is, I hope."

"Sooner or later, Ellen, he'll get his ass in such a jam where he can't get it out. When that day comes, we're free."

"Just think too, Mama, each of us are gonna' have our own bedroom, a real bathroom, and kitchen. It's hard to believe." Grateful tears filled her eyes.

Bertie put her arms around her. "Go sit down for a bit, honey. The more tired you get, the more you worry. Go sit."

"Alright, Mama, I agree. This is not the time for tears or worry." *Don't look back, she reminded herself. It's all over now. Look ahead. Work toward the dreams and pray that Sherm never finds us.*

She yelled aloud when the next pain came, this time centered in her lower stomach. She recognized it this time as a contraction. "Oh, God, no," she cried. "Mama, Mama," she called as Bertie came running back into the room.

"What's the matter, honey?"

Ellen lay on the floor, a pool of water under her feet. "Mama, get the doctor, get the doctor. My baby – it's trying to come. Oh, please God, not now," she cried. "It's too soon."

Sally Crossen, hearing the commotion, came running down the outside stairs. Seeing Ellen lying on the floor, she knew what was happening. "Stay right there," she urged her. "I'll run for Doc. Bert. He's only two blocks away." Bertie placed a pillow under her head.

*****

Sheriff Workman had spent the last half of the day yesterday driving west through Kentucky, stopping several times along the way where he guessed Ellen and her family might have gotten gas or spent the night, or both. No one had seen or remembered them. When he arrived in the small community of Winchester, he pulled into a gas station. He spoke to the attendant who had come to wait on him. "Hi, there. I'm Gordon Workman." Workman extended his hand as he introduced himself. "I'm the sheriff in Tabors Creek. I'm trying to locate an old friend. I'm wondering if she might have stopped here."

"Yes, sir. I'll help you if I can. By the way, my name is Tom Wolf. I run this place, and who was it you're looking for?"

"If she did stop here, I think you'd probably remember her. She's a very pretty and very pregnant lady. She'd have been with her mother and two small children. They were driving a fairly new Ford."

Fortunately, the attendant did remember waiting on them. "Yes, I do remember them. They stopped here about two weeks ago, got gas, had dinner, and spent the night in one of the cabins. If I remember right, they stayed in Cabin 2, over there," as he pointed toward the cabin. "The next mornin' they had breakfast, then left. Said they were headin' to Lexington, I believe. Those were some cute kids," he said. "The younger lady was a real pretty lady, but she sure did look tired, I noticed. I wondered what she and the other woman was doin' out here travelin' alone with no man along to help. Her bein' pregnant and all."

Sheriff Workman learned that Bertie was headed for Lexington. He drove in the direction of Lexington for the next hour. Knowing she had made it this far assured him that she must have made it to Lexington. He began to think more rationally the further he drove. Providing he did drive on to Lexington, how would he find her in a city that heavily populated? He slowly rationalized the futility in driving there. There was no way he could find her. Not this way. It wasn't even a sure thing she went to Lexington. Perhaps she might contact him in Tabors Creek, so it would be wisest, he believed, to turn around and go back and wait, be there if she came in or called. He'd get in touch with the police department in Lexington and let them find her for him, if they could. It appeared to be the wisest thing to do. Maybe he'd be lucky enough to find Sherm. If so, at least Ellen would be safe from him. With that in mind, he turned his car around at the next lane and headed back to Tabors Creek, defeated, but anxious with hope. What he didn't know was the Lexington police would never find Ellen Peck. She was now Ellen Potter.

*****

Ellen lay quietly in her hospital bed staring at the ceiling above. Although her body ached from the rigors of child delivery, her heart hurt more for the loss of the child she had carried. Bertie sat beside her on the bed holding her hand. "He was so little, Mama," Ellen said. She sobbed quietly.

"I know, honey. He was little, and he wasn't healthy on this earth. He's in Heaven now. There's no more pain for him. God has chosen to have him close by to care for him, as only He can," Bertie answered. "You must think about how happy he is, where he is."

"Just one more month and he probably would have made it." She paused and looked at Bertie, desperate for some words that would ease her bleeding heart.

"You got to hold him for just a couple of minutes. I know that's not good enough, but it's all we were given. Keep that memory forever."

"Why, God, oh why?" Ellen begged for an answer as her body trembled with wracking sobs.

"It's not ours to question, honey. Some day we'll see the reason, but for now, faith is all we got," Bertie said. Her heart too was aching, as much for her daughter as for the little grandson she'd lost. "Try and think about where he is now. Maybe that will help. The only other thing is time, and time is a blessing, even if it doesn't look like it right now."

"I'll never forget him, Mama. I asked them to name him Sammy on his death certificate."

"No, you shouldn't forget him, and neither will I. Now sleep, honey. You've been through a lot today. You've lost a lot of blood and you must rest if you hope to get better." Bertie said no more. She ran her hands through Ellen's hair, rubbed her arm, and waited till she went to sleep before she left.

*****

When Ellen returned home from the hospital three days later, Bertie, with help from the landlady, Mrs. Crossen, had the house warm and inviting. Everything was organized nicely and the smell of fresh bread filled the house. Ellen was thrilled when she walked in the door, seeing furniture in the living room. Even a picture hung on the wall. The sound of the children was the crowning jewel. "Mama, mama," Neet cried. "Where were you?"

"Hi sweetheart. Where was I? Well, I was away trying to get better, but I'm all fixed up now, and I'm home." Not able to lift Neet, Ellen placed her arms around her and pulled her close.

"What's the matter, Mama?" Charlie asked.

"Oh, it's all okay now, Charlie. Mommy just had a couple of days being sick, that's all. I have been sleeping and sleeping. Don't you worry about me. I'm okay."

Charlie and Neet, satisfied with Ellen's answer, were off to play.

Bertie and Ellen walked around looking at their place. "Mama, it's beautiful, isn't it? I don't see how you got all this done though in just three days."

"Well, I probably wouldn't have by myself," Bertie said. Sally Crossen helped a lot. She either took me shopping or stayed with the kids while I was shopping. Then she helped me to arrange everything."

There were three bedrooms, one for Ellen, one for Bertie and one the children would share. Looking in her room, Ellen was ecstatic. Bertie had found a used maple bed and dresser. Ellen's bed was covered with a pink chenille bedspread and a small lamp with a pink shade sat on the table beside the bed. Her belongings had been placed on the bed. "This is so pretty, Mama. I love it."

"Good. I'm glad you like it. I put your things there on your bed. You can put them where you want them. I wanted it to be as cheerful as possible for you."

In the kitchen there was a table and four chairs. A plate of sandwiches and a pitcher of lemonade sat on the table. On the counter was a plate of chocolate cookies. "I did the sandwiches," Bertie said. Pointing to the cookies, she continued, "Sally did the cookies."

"Just look at this kitchen. It really is pretty with the furniture in it. I love the table and chairs. This is nice, Mama. Thank you." She hugged her mother. "I really am hungry too."

*****

Sherm didn't lose any time in setting up an operation at the small house he and Maggie bought. Located on a rugged hill in remote Melody Mountain, it was an ideal spot, far removed from most of the traffic with no other homes in the vicinity. In addition, the location near the Ohio River opened the door for exporting whiskey down the river to several cities, should he choose to do so.

Tabors Creek

He had used Maggie's savings to buy the house and equipment to begin his still operation. In a log-built, two-room shed separate from the house Sherm had placed two 80-gallon barrels and an ample supply of pots and kettles for brewing. There were also utensils for stirring, buckets for carrying supplies, cups for measuring, sugar, grains and other ingredients. The yeast he used for brewing was kept fresh in an icebox, which sat along the wall next to the barrels. A wood-burning stove, placed in one corner on the opposite side of the room, across from the barrels, served as a cook stove as well as a source of heat for the room during the winter. He'd purchased enough corn and rye, which he hoped would last until next year.

Calling to Maggie from upstairs, Sherm said, "Maggie, did you pick up some of those empty jugs and some of the sugar we need?"

"I did Sherm," Maggie called back. "I'm down in the kitchen right now, but coming upstairs shortly. I put everything up there." The open, second floor he'd used for storage of grain, the corn, and other supplies. He would be able to depend on local farmers for future products. In the ground near the shed, Sherm dug out an area to build a root cellar. In there he would preserve his supplies of apples and other fruit stockpile. He worked feverishly to get everything set up and in operation before the first freeze or snowfall.

Outside, on the steep hillside behind the house, he built a steamer still. The front of the house was hidden from view by the sloping land, as well as numerous trees and shrubbery bushes, providing him with the necessary privacy. The thickly populated area of oak, ash, and locust trees behind the house served as a protective cloak around his activities while also furnishing him with an ample supply of wood for fuel.

Sherm spent days cutting down ash and hickory trees, which he used for heating the boiler that would make the steam to distill the mash. While the city slept at night, and smoke went unnoticed under stars and the moonlight, Sherm built his first fire using fast burning hickory. The hot fire had the boiler heated and making steam in no time. Just before sunrise, he switched to slow-burning ash - the slower the fire burned during the day, the less chance smoke would alert townsfolk or the local authorities. Placing one end of an ash tree into the open fire and continually pushing it forward as it burned away worked well and eliminated chopping wood into logs. One ash tree would usually last for as long as two days. When nothing remained but hot embers, a new tree was pushed into the fire while a temperature of near 180 degrees was the target aimed for. Sherm started his operation into full motion when he brewed his first pot of mash and set it aside to ferment.

He had promised Maggie a home just the way she wanted it, if she'd work now while he got his "business" going good. "If you go to work, I'll buy you the biggest house in the city, Maggie," he bragged. "You'll have a well, indoor water, a bathtub, and I'll even get you your own wringer washer. It'll only be for as long as it takes me to get my first sale." Hearing what she wanted to hear, she had eagerly agreed.

"Oh, Sherm. I can't believe you'd even ask. Of course, you know I'll get a job." With those words, he got what he wanted - all of the money she had in savings, money her late husband had left her. He was confident that she would stay as long as he needed her.

*****

Maggie found work at the local newspaper, the Weekly Tidings. She worked from early in the afternoon until late in the evening, standing on her feet during most of the shift. As the metal print plates came off the press following the printing, they were placed in tubs of cleaning liquid where Maggie and two other employees scrubbed them with brushes, then placed them back in the stack for reuse. This continued until the paper was completed for the day. At that time, the presses themselves had to be cleaned and readied for printing the following day. It was a tiring and generally boring cycle. At the end of the day, Maggie was dirty from the ink and her body ached with each step she took. When she grew weary and tired of trying, she convinced herself that one day she and Sherm would have a nice home of their own and this would all be behind her. On one particularly exhausting evening, she confronted Sherm. "Sherm, I'm tired, really tired. My feet hurt and my back aches most of the time. How long will it be before I can just be at home? Are we ever gonna' buy a new house?"

"It takes time to make contacts, Maggie. Jesus, lay off me, will you. I'm tryin' hard as hell to make money. Don't you know how to be patient?"

"I'm sorry," she said submissively, afraid his irritation might turn to aggression.

Sherm took the money as she earned it. He allowed her a small amount for spending, and managed the rest himself.

*****

Maggie looked outside. The rain was falling pretty hard now. She picked up her umbrella and purse then walked to where Sherm sat eating. "Bye, honey. I gotta go to work. It's a long walk and I'm slow when it's rainin'."

"No reason to be slow, is there," Sherm replied, only for the sake of conversation.

"What are you gonna do tonight?" she asked.

"I have some things to do outside and then I'll listen to the radio. Don't worry about what I'm gonna do. You just get yourself goin'." Sherm stood wringing his hands while staring at Maggie, anxious for her to leave. Maggie could feel the tension and turned, knowing she should hurry before an argument ensued.

Sherm watched her from the window as she walked down the road. As soon as she was out of sight, he quickly checked his still, pushed in another ash tree, and headed out for the evening, as he often did. This time he was on a mission – to a bar named "Duke's," which he had seen on an earlier trip into town. 'Dixieland Music – 8:00 p.m. to Midnight' the sign on the easel had read. It was 8:00 o'clock as Sherm walked in the door. He headed straight for the bar. The six-piece band was moving into their spots on the bandstand. "I'll have a ginger ale," Sherm said to the bartender.

The band began to play some Dixieland jazz and Sherm turned to watch and listen as he waited for his drink. Though he'd never before heard Dixieland music, he liked what he heard and listened intently. Seated at the bar, he was keeping time to the music with both feet when the bartender delivered his ginger ale. "Since that's the best you can do, I'll take it." Sherm said.

"Not sure I know what you mean," the bartender replied.

"Well, I don't guess you have any good stuff," Sherm said.

"What else did you have in mind?"

"I always like something with a bite to it." Sherm guffawed loudly.

"A bite?"

"Yeah, a bite, you know, a kick to it." He looked to see what the bartender's reaction would be.

"Hadn't you heard, that's illegal?" asked the bartender. "It'll get you tossed in the clink if you get caught – that's makin' or sellin' it."

"Oh, you gotta know how," Sherm boasted.

The bartender, Haley Jones, brought the manager, a large, muscular man with a ruddy complexion, to the bar. Looking at Sherm, he inquired, "I hear you'd like something with a bite."

"You gotta' admit, it would beat the hell outta' ginger ale. Of course, if you ain't got it, you ain't got it."

"What makes you think we have it?"

"No, wait just a minute - I ain't sayin' you have it," Sherm paused and grinned, then looked the manager in the eye.

"But you could have, if you don't. That was all I was sayin'."

"And how do you figure that?"

"Cause I figure I can make you the best." Sherm bragged, with a wide grin of confidence.

"Come talk to me," manager Hiram Pauls requested, motioning to a room behind the bar. Sherm followed. In the room Pauls poured and handed Sherm a drink and asked, "Can you match this?"

Sherm sipped, dramatically swished the liquid back and forth in his mouth and swallowed it, "I can do better'n that. I can also keep my mouth shut." After a short discussion, the two shook hands and Sherm had his first customer.

The band was playing "Somebody Stole My Gal" when Sherm returned to the bar. The trumpet player appeared to be in friendly competition with the clarinet player to see who could hit the highest note and the piano player was keeping an intensified rhythm as he rose on and off the piano stool without missing a beat. With the effect of the alcohol taking place and the electrifying sound of the music, Sherm's innate desire for thrills grew stronger. His eyes strayed to a female who smiled at him from the other end of the bar. Her long red hair hung down over her shoulders, partially covering her spaghetti-strapped, emerald green, satiny dress. Her face was attractive, but bore lines of cigarette and alcohol abuse. "Somebody stole my gal, somebody took her away," the singer's words rang out. When their eyes met, the lady in green ambled toward Sherm.

"Did somebody steal your gal, honey? You look so sad." She ran her hands through his hair.

"Right now, who cares? Purty as you are," Sherm answered.

"I can fix whatever it is that's bothering you," she purred.

Sherm went when she beckoned him to follow her. Manager Pauls winked as Sherm left the bar to follow the lady. Sherm returned the gesture with a nod and a smile.

*****

When he reached home, Maggie was already there.

"Where have you been, Sherm?"

"Doin' business deals, that's all. Why?"

"Just wonderin'," she answered, although the lipstick on the side of his face told a different story. I didn't know you did business deals this late at night."

"You don't know anything about my business, so don't ask questions when you don't know what you're talkin' about."

Maggie could tell he'd been drinking and the look he gave her was one she knew well. Another word from her would only mean he would follow with a slap or a fist. She said nothing as he headed to the door.

Outside, Sherm walked through the operation to check the fire and the equipment. "Atta baby," he spoke, gently patting the condenser. He was pretty proud to see it was doing its job, changing the hot vapors back into distilled liquor. Unable to find a new or used one, he had spent many hours building his own. He kept ice packed around it as much as he could, though it melted fast during the daylight hours. The ice helped to speed up the operation. Copper pipes carrying the distilled liquor from the distiller into the 80-gallon kegs inside the storage house were in good order as well.

The fire being slightly low, Sherm pushed the log in a bit further and sat down beside it, watching the burning log and contemplating his future. How high could he rise? He wasn't sure, but he was going to try like hell and aim for the top. Tomorrow, when he would make his first delivery – to Duke's. His first production line had yielded him 40 gallons. The next production would be closer to 80 and this was only the beginning. His greed for big money, the hatred he felt toward Ellen, Bertie and the Feds were the fuel that drove him. Each time he thought about the money that had been in his car, he got so angry he nearly cried. Money would get him out of the area where they'd never find him. Before he left though, he would find Ellen and

Tabors Creek

Bertie. He'd go nowhere until he did. He'd have enough money now if they hadn't taken his car and his money. "I'll kill you both when I find you," he mumbled to himself.

IV

1930

It was now several months past Ellen's hospital stay. Recovery was painfully slow, often appearing hopeless, but once again she felt strong and her spirits were high. In the newly furnished house, filled with warmth and comfort, she found that the love of family and newly-made friends were the medicine she needed to heal. Charlie and Neet were happy in their new home and found delight in making new friends in the neighborhood. Bertie's sense of optimism was never ending and a great source of strength for her.

"No more sleepless nights, Mama," Ellen had told Bertie. "I don't have to lay awake waiting for Sherm to come home, wondering where he was, who he was with and wonderin' what they were doin'. It feels so good." It had been devastating wondering whether or not he was in another woman's arms or her bed, or both?

"I know, Ellen. It was hard for me to see you worrying over a man that wasn't worth two cents or the powder to blow him to Hell," Bertie had answered.

Many were the times Ellen had gotten out of bed, walked the floor, or stared out the window watching the road for car headlights wishing he'd come home, only to have him curse her for waiting up. That burden, that hurt had been washed away, never to return. He had killed any love she had ever felt. She had tried to tell him so. "Sherm, you know you're killin' everything I ever felt for you."

It hadn't helped at all. "Go to Hell Ellen. I ain't never gonna' change, you know that."

Sitting on the side of her bed, she could hear Neet's voice calling, "Charlie, I'm hided. Come find me."

"Where are you?" he called.

"I'm here in the closet, in my bedroom."

Bertie laughed out loud in the kitchen where she had been doing some ironing. Ellen walked to the kitchen laughing. "Who taught her how to play hide and seek, I wonder."

"It sounds like Charlie did," Bertie said, laughing aloud.

"Have you noticed how happy the kids are now? That they don't mention their no good daddy any more?" Bertie asked.

"Yes, I have noticed and I'm really thankful. It feels so good to see them laughing and playing without fear. I think they've even forgotten how they were so afraid of him – afraid he'd slap them. That's your doings, you know, Mama. You're the reason for it."

"Well, not just me, honey. It's a combined effort, you know that. I had hoped they would forget him in time, and I think too they have. Some day, when the time is right, years down the road, of course you'll have to tell them the truth. But they'll be old enough they'll understand."

"I will, don't worry. When they're old enough to understand. That time isn't near yet." Ellen rolled her eyes and frowned.

*****

The rain fell hard today as Ellen walked the street from her house to the University Library. She suddenly had the strongest urge to dance her way there. Waving her umbrella back and forth, she started skipping and humming, until she reminded herself that she was an adult, and resumed walking. Today her heart and soul had opened up to sights and sounds she had not seen for years. Birds singing sounded sweeter than she ever remembered as she walked along the tree-lined street. "Rain, rain, go away. Come again some other day, little Neet and Charlie want to play." she sang. A dog barking in the distance sounded friendly, begging to be petted, she imagined, and in a yard she saw one small girl run after another. The one being pursued giggled so hard she couldn't run any more and fell to the grass, while the one chasing fell beside her laughing. She passed Rogers Restaurant on Main Street, then the Fayette Meat Market next door where two butchers taking a break stood outside, under the awning, watching the light rainfall. "Good morning, ma'am," they both said in unison as she walked past them. It felt so good to be noticed and greeted, all new and heart-warming to her. Others she passed along the way also offered their smiles and greetings. Today, it was a wonderful world. "Please God, let it last," she murmured.

Reaching the University grounds, staring at the beautiful, massive buildings, not paying attention to where she stepped, she tripped and nearly fell head first into some bushes. She closed her mouth when she realized she had been staring, with her mouth hanging open. She was suddenly reminded of what her father used to say to her. "Ellen, I could never take you to the city, you'd sunburn the roof of your mouth staring up at the buildings." She smiled at the thought of him. Even though she walked this street frequently, she still was in awe of the beautiful structures. The red brick University Memorial Hall, with its towering steeple that housed a built-in Roman numeral faced clock was awesome.

She loved the two-story, white columns that appeared to hold up the balcony on the second floor. It was a beautiful place. Lexington felt like home now and the people had accepted her and made her feel welcome. One day she could give back to the city something – caring for the people as a registered nurse. She vowed to be the best. Until she left for nurses training, she would take advantage of being able to visit the library where she had access to books, papers, and other information related to her future training.

Stepping inside the library, Ellen stopped to talk with the Librarian. "Where might I find information about Nursing? I'm planning to go to nursing training and want to read up on some things I know I'll be studying.

The librarian smiled, and replied, "you'll find everything you need right over there," she said, pointing to the Medical Section. There were several shelves with nursing information. She stood and gazed at the two murals in the browsing room, depicting rural life in the State. An idyllic scene of a farm with a house and barn, cows and horses in a field of green grass, surrounded by a white fence nearly filled the wall. It looked so peaceful, this country scene. She was reminded of the hellacious country scene she left. *This artist never saw Tabors Creek*, she thought. Visions of their house in Tabors Creek abruptly invaded her thoughts – the *leaking tin roof, the chamber bucket that sat in the middle of the sleeping area leaving an odor throughout, the hanging sheets in the room dividing sleeping areas. Oh God*, she thought.

She had traipsed many times outside in rain, thick mud, and even snow to empty the bucket and other garbage down over the bank next to the house. *That scene, that house – wish the artist could see it. That's rural,* she thought. *That's the real picture an artist ought to paint.*

"That's pretty good art, isn't it?" came from a voice Ellen thought she recognized.

Startled, she jumped, her arms flew in the air, and her books dropped to the floor. Before she looked behind her, she quietly called, "Sherm?" There was no answer. For a second she stood frozen, certain he was behind her. She flinched downwardly, expecting to be hit. When no one assaulted her from behind, she waited a second expecting he must be going to grab her arm, take her outside before he beat her, or worse. Finally, she turned to look behind her only to see a pleasant looking gentleman she didn't recognize wearing a serious look of wonderment on his face. Holding her stomach, hoping she didn't vomit out of fear right where she stood, she began to cry. "Oh, hello, sir. I'm sorry. I thought you were someone else."

Picking up her books and laughing aloud, he said, "Well, I'm afraid to ask who you thought I was."

She wiped her eyes as she answered. "Oh, no one in particular. Yes, I think too the painting is nice. It reminded me of a place I once knew." After hesitating, Ellen continued, "Or once saw, I mean."

"Well, seeing you appreciate this piece of art, I can see you have good taste. I'm assuming those were tears of appreciation. At least I hope they were." He pointed to the picture. "This artist was a former student here whom I knew. His paintings depict some of his early years, and I think he does a great job." He smiled then and handed her the spilled books. "My name is Adam Hawthorne. I'm an instructor in the Art Department. Are you a student here?"

"No, sir, I'm not, but it's nice to meet you. I just like to come in here and read. I'll be a nursing student in Logan starting next month, so I stop in here every chance I get, to learn as much as I can on nursing."

"Oh, I see. Well I'm sorry I scared you" He turned to walk away. Looking back he continued, "Hope you don't see anyone else as scary as me."

"Thank you. I'm sorry. I'll be fine."

Ellen stood in the hall waiting to regain her composure and for her trembling knees to stop shaking before she continued to the library. Once there she found herself a table and sat still for a few minutes before she began some research.

It was so difficult to forget that Sherm was out there somewhere, perhaps walking behind her. On good days the fear disappeared, but days like today brought her back to reality, a place she didn't want to be. Seated, she tried to concentrate on reading, but finding it difficult to keep her thoughts focused on subject material, she closed the book and walked home.

Stepping inside her front door, the sound of laughter brought her out of the depths of sorrow to a world where she felt warmth and comfort, a place she longed to stay. "Mama, Mama, you're home," Neet cried.

"Hi, honey," she said. Taking Neet into her arms, she hugged her as tears of joy rolled down her face. "You feel so good and I love you so much." *Funny*, she thought, *how their laughter can make me cry, just as easily as their tears can do the same.*

"Oh, hi, honey," Bertie said, seeing Ellen holding Neet. "I was just about to read to them a story about Peter Rabbit. Maybe you'd like to do it while I get some soup on to cook for supper tonight."

"Tonight, I'd love to, Mama. Where's Charlie?"

"Oh, he's here somewheres. Can't be too far."

Hearing his mother's voice, Charlie came running to the living room from the bedroom. He ran to mother and wrapped his arms around her.

With their little hands in hers she led them to the couch. "Wait a minute, Mama. I'll go get the book to read." Charlie hurried to the stack of books on the floor.

*****

Sheriff Workman settled back into his routine of being the peace-keeper in the small rural town of Tabors Creek. The biggest excitement was often no more than perhaps a drunk who walked into the wrong house or was kicked out of the bar after a fight. Then there was an occasional theft of tools, or other pieces of equipment. Last week a goat had been taken from the yard at Tom Drew's place. Most often, however, it remained calm and quiet. The Feds' trip to town had been the unexpected and unusual. Sheriff Workman felt somewhat responsible for the death of the Federal Agents. Perhaps he could have avoided the shootings if only he'd taken the initiative to investigate what he knew was occurring. "If I'd only taken the time to go check out the rumors of stills around here, maybe those Feds would never have been shot, you know that, John?"

"We've been over this before, Gordon. You can't let that blame fall on you, now can you? Sherm Peck would have put up that still of his anyplace he wanted. If you'd tried to stop him, he'd have killed you instead of the agents. I didn't want nobody killed, but sure as hell not you," Deputy Sheriff John Bell answered.

"Thanks, John. You're right. Sherm Peck was, and still is, I guess, unpredictable, that's for sure. Guess I'll never know what might have happened, but I'll always wonder."

He sat there looking out the window. When John Bell could stand it no longer he stood up and paced back and forth in front of Sheriff Workman's desk until the Sheriff turned to look at him. "Okay, I see you John. What's up with you? I know you got somethin' more to say, so go ahead and say it."

"Okay I will!" Sheriff Bell said emphatically. "I want you to know before I say this though, that I like Ellen Peck. I have a lot of respect and admiration for her. And, I might add, I feel sorry for her. She should have left that bastard years ago. I also think you're probably the best damned sheriff in this part of the country and you have a lot to be proud of. But I don't like to see the way you're sittin in here worryin' about somethin' you shouldn't be worryin' about."

"Like what?"

"You know what I mean. I just don't want to see you get your hopes up over this lady and then watch you fall down again. I seen you do that before, you know. You deserve better'n that."

Sheriff Workman stared at Bell for a minute before he spoke. "I appreciate your concerns, John. You know, years back I thought there was not enough of my heart left to break any more. That was after she married Sherm. Now, I'm annoyed with myself that there is, and it's obviously happening again. I also know that I need to realize there may not be a perfect ending here. I'll accept whatever happens. I'll find her one day, of that I'm sure, and I'll need you to remind me of this conversation when I do. If nothing else comes from this, at least she's away from Sherm Peck. That's a good thing."

"I agree with that. And I promise you, I will remind you of this conversation sometime down the road," Bell said, pointing his finger at the Sheriff. "Have you talked with Lexington Police yet to see what they've done in lookin' for her there?"

"I have, yes, and without success, so far. I'm sure after I do find her, then I'll know what my next move will be. Until then, just ignore me as I get through this. Okay?"

"Okay, as you wish. Just be careful, that's all I can say."

With that Sheriff Workman dug into some folders, ignored Bell staring at him, and tried to work off his frustrations.

Bell put his hat on his head, walked out the door saying, "I'll see you after lunch."

There was no acknowledgement.

******

The truck and trailer pulled into the white graveled lane of Holiday Farms. The sun shined brightly, although the nip in the air was a sure sign fall was here. The wind created a moving shadow as it bristled through the sweet gum trees, which lined both sides of the lane, their leaves beginning to turn gold and wine colors. Driver, Brad Jackson, and his truck moved slowly toward the Gibbons home on the left on his way to the stable area ahead on the right. He waved to Marsha Gibbons who stood on the front porch of the large two-story stone home, framed by baskets of blooming red geraniums on each side of the steps leading to the white front porch. A white swing hung from the rafter on one side of the porch and a white rocking chair sat on the other. She smiled, "hi Brad," she called, waving to him, and wondered what the special occasion might be. She had seen many trucks come and go at Holiday, but this one must be special since both her husband and son were waiting for the truck to arrive. She walked to the swing and took a seat to rest a bit while she viewed what was happening. Soon the porch would be in full sun and the heat would drive her inside.

Josh and Hal Gibbons stood waiting at the side of their house as the driver pulled near the whitewashed stable where he parked. The two men reached the truck and trailer as the driver stepped out.

"Good morning, Brad," Hal Gibbons said as he shook Jackson's hand. Brad Jackson had made periodic deliveries and pick-ups in the past, so was well known to both Hal and Josh, as well as Marsha Gibbons.

"Good morning, Mr. Gibbons. Good to see you again."

Josh shook his hand as well, "Good morning, how are you?"

"I'm doin' fine, thanks. Brought you the new filly. Think you probably already know all about her."

"Yeah, we know all about her – been expecting her," Hal laughingly spoke slowly and methodically as if to make light of Brad's statement. They certainly had been aware of Doc Weide's new purchase. She was the biggest sale in all of Kentucky in the last ten years or so, having cost Doc Weide $30,000. Brad opened the doors of the trailer.

"Doc Weide is on his way. He made a stop back there somewhere for lunch," Brad said.

"Good," said Hal. "It'll be good to see him again."

Hal and Doc Weide had spoken at the horse auction at Triple R Ranch the previous month. Hal had just purchased Freedom and Doc Weide was in the process of bidding on Brandywine when they met. After the bidding was complete and Doc had the final bid, he strolled over to where Hal stood. Doc liked the way Hal broke in the young two-year olds and this one needed some breaking. "She's a stubborn one, Hal. Do you think you can break her?" Doc asked.

"Of course, I can," Hal said, expressing pride in his voice and a smile of confidence on his face.

"Well, they've been trying here at Triple R for the past month and no one has stayed on her yet. I figured if anyone could break her, you could. I've heard stories about you," his wide grin exposed his yellowed, tobacco-chewing teeth.

"Oh you have, huh? Do you believe everything you hear?" He chuckled out loud.

"Guess I believe what I want to," Doc answered.

"Like I said, I can break her and when she's finished, she won't know what happened to her," Hal said, laughing as he shook Doc's hand. He liked Doc Weide, of Ashland, Kentucky, and knew his reputation as an outstanding general practitioner.

Now Brandywine had arrived at Holiday and Doc would be stopping in shortly to check her in. Hal and Josh stood watching as Brandywine walked the plank out of the trailer. "God, what a beauty she is, huh?" said Josh, shaking his head back and forth.

"She sure enough is, Josh," Hal replied. "Wouldn't mind keeping her."

Brandywine stopped and looked at them, her black, silk-like hair glistening in the sunlight. She was all black with the exception of one white, round patch on her breast and another diamond-shaped patch in the middle of her forehead. She stood still and erect as if modeling in a fashion show. She gracefully swung her head up and to the left, seemingly proud of her mane, another swing to the right, then strutted off her runway, the plank.

Brad Jackson handed the reins to Josh as he walked to the back of the trailer and closed and latched the door.

"Our biggest job right now is breaking her. Doc says she has tossed everyone off who's been on her so far," Hal lamented.

"Watching her right now though, she acts like she's just itching to race," Josh said.

"Looks like to me she's darin' us to try and ride her." Hal smirked ominously.

"Guess we got lots of work to do, huh? We'll find out what she's so proud of," Josh answered. "Let's get her into a bath before we stable her. The cool water on her legs will probably feel pretty good today. She's been standing and bouncing around inside that hot trailer for the past five hours I'd guess."

"Yeah, that's about how long it took us, I do believe," replied Brad Jackson. "That was just from Triple R. I've got to get back to Ashland, so guess I'd best be on my way now. It was nice to see you again, both of you."

"You bet, Brad" Hal answered. "You're welcome to join us for supper before you leave if you like."

"Thanks, but I need to get on the road. I'd like to get this trailer back before it gets dark if possible. Thanks for asking." Jackson turned and headed to the truck.

*****

Bertie stood near the open window where the slight breeze was of some comfort on this sweltering, sultry day. Hot steam swirled into her face from the iron she pushed over the curtains. She wiped the perspiration from her face, barely catching it before it fell onto her ironing board. Just one more piece to iron, she noted, looking at the basket that had been full of dampened, rolled up clothes. She was nearly finished with Mrs. Adams' ironing. Hers were always the worst with all the starched, white shirts, and this time she even had extra curtains. The pay was good and the more pieces ironed, the more she earned.

Just then, the door opened and Ellen walked in.

Charlie called running to greet her at the door. "Hi, Mommy." He held her tight around her legs for a minute then released his arms as she bent to kiss him.

"Hi honey," she said. "Looks like you've been eating something red, like maybe strawberries or cherries, haven't you?"

"How did you know?" His large, brown eyes stared at her in surprise. His lips were bright red and he wore a red cherry-stained, white shirt.

"Oh, I just know these things," she snickered.

Awakened by the voices, Neet jumped up from her nap and hurried to the

door. "Hi, Mommy," she sleepily whispered.

"Hello, sleepy head," Ellen answered, then stooped to pick her up.

"Hi Mama," Ellen called to her mother in the kitchen. "You are still ironing!" she continued in a scolding voice. "You were doing that when I left this morning, weren't you," making a statement, rather than asking a question.

With Neet in her arms, Ellen walked to the living room and sat down in the rocking chair. Charlie followed and stood holding the arm of her chair. "You could look at your book, honey," she spoke to Charlie. "Let me rock your sister for a minute."

Instead, Charlie began to play with a yoyo lying nearby. "I could read pictures to you, if you want me to," he answered, looking to Ellen in anticipation of an 'okay'.

Ellen laughed aloud. "Yes, honey, I would like that, but just a little later, okay? Wait till little sister wakes up a bit. Then you can read your pictures to both of us."

"I got one more piece to iron and then I'll fix us somethin' to eat," Bertie said. She carefully laid the newly ironed curtain over a chair back.

"No, you rest awhile. I'll fix supper as soon as you're finished there."

"Well, that would be nice. I am a little tired."

"You work so hard, Mama," Ellen sighed.

"I know, but it brings in money. Don't you worry about me. I'm fine. It ain't like it's forever, now is it? You go get your nurse training and let me worry about what I'm doing here at home. You can go ahead and start supper. I'll be finished in a couple of minutes."

"It's just that I hate to see you get so tired. Don't you think we have enough money to make do without you having to take in ironings?"

When Bertie didn't reply, Ellen stood Neet on the floor and headed to the kitchen

"Okay little one, I've work to do if we're going to eat supper tonight. And Charlie, we'll just have to wait until after we eat and then we'll read. Okay?"

"That's okay, Mama," Charlie answered. "I'm hungry."

While she peeled potatoes at the sink, the children played in the living room with a puzzle. Bertie finished the last of her ironing, sat down at the kitchen table and sipped on a large glass of cold ice water. "Glad that job's done."

"So am I." Ellen shook her head in dismay.

"It's gonna' be so hard to leave next week, Mama. You know I won't even get home for vacations, except maybe a little bit in the summer, but that's all. I'm not sure if I can even come home then. It's so expensive to take the train. Christmas will be the hardest. I think we get two weeks off but I guess I'll just stay there."

"Honey, it ain't gonna be easy, that's for sure. It's just gonna be two years you have to give up doin' what you want and just do what you have to do. That's the only way you can do it if you ever want to be a nurse, that's all there is to it. We'll just have to wait and see about Christmas."

"I know, but you and the kids will be here alone. I'll miss you so much."

"You'll probably be so busy, you won't have time to think about us. I'll take care of the kids, don't you worry about them. You just take care of yourself and get your trainin'. That two years'll go pretty fast, you'll see."

Bertie stood up, folded her wooden ironing board and set it against the wall of the kitchen. She stopped for a minute to rub her aching back, then took dishes from the cupboard and began to set the table.

*****

Despite a nagging pain in his stomach, Sherm had to keep moving. His business had grown almost faster than he could get his product distilled and delivered. With the new still, he had doubled his assembly line process and thereby doubled the amount he could produce. His arrangements with Duke's Bar was followed closely by Windham's Lounge after the two owners had talked. Supplying Duke's and Sam Rivets at Windham took everything as fast as he could produce it. The pain in his stomach would have to wait until he had time to deal with it.

Sherm reached in his shirt pocket and took out a pack of cigarette-making papers, tore one out and replaced the pack in his pocket. He rolled the empty paper around his finger. Next, he pulled a can of tobacco from his pants pocket, opened it and poured enough tobacco into the paper to roll a cigarette. Holding the open paper with tobacco in his left hand, he closed the lid of the tobacco can with his right hand and placed it back in his pocket. With both hands he rolled the paper around the tobacco into a cigarette shape, licking the paper to seal it. From his pocket, he got a large wooden match, struck it on a rock and held it to the cigarette end. "God that smells and tastes good too!" he said. "Been an hour or so I ain't had a cigarette."

With Maggie gone to work for the evening, Sherm was free to pull out his money once again and count it, a ritual he practiced almost daily. He slid the big and heavy empty pot off of the thin sheet of tin on the ground. From under the tin sheet, he lifted out the metal box hidden in a hole. With a big smile of satisfaction, he sat on a stone and counted and recounted. While staring at his money, he continued to smile as if imagining what he could do with it one of these days. After a few drags on the rolled and crooked cigarette, and realizing he still had lots of work to do before he left for the evening, he returned the money into the box and placed it back in the ground.

As he walked toward the fire pit, another sharp pain grabbed his stomach causing him to stop where he was and wait until it subsided. "Damn," he said softly after the pain eased up some. "Not now. I don't have time, goddamn it."

There was no time to be too sick to work and no time to see a doctor. He couldn't be away from the operation for long, not yet. Not until he found at least one and maybe two helpers whom he could trust to help him run the operation. There were now two stills running and as business picked up, he'd need to set up another. With extra help, he'd have someone to do the hard labor of cutting wood, carrying water, and watching the fires while he was away.

Next Sherm carried twelve gallon buckets of water to a 100-gallon tub, which he had placed outdoors over a wood fire. When the water began to boil he added a large handful of hops and a half bushel of corn-meal.

It was hot tonight and the flies, the damned flies. He swatted one on his arm. "God damned flies to hell," he said. "They're a bigger pest and cause more trouble than the heat! With a large whittled stick he had made for this purpose, he stirred the pot well, then he poured in another twelve gallons of boiling water, which he had heated over a separate fire in the yard. The buckets were heavy and he hated it all, but money was a pretty powerful driving tool for Sherm.

Next, Sherm added half a bushel of meal and stirred out all the lumps. With this done, he pulled the burning tree from under the tub in order to put the fire out. He allowed the tub to sit until the mixture was cool enough that he could place his hand in it without burning himself.

In the meantime, he readied some trees he had cut down earlier, cutting off the branches in order for the logs to slide under the bedrock platform and into the fire pit. He stacked the branches for kindling. He cleaned new jugs and stacked them, cleaned the pots he'd used and then it was time to do paperwork. This was the chore he liked best. The more money he made, the more he liked it. Paperwork with customer names and records of orders and sales had to be handled in Maggie's absence. He kept those hidden out of sight in the metal box with the money where she would never see them nor know how much money he earned or spent. For all Maggie knew, he only had one client. She knew he was supplying Duke's, but she didn't need to know he had the Windham and several smaller bars. He stashed away the bigger portion of his intake. He went back to where he had his money, moved the heavy pot again and took out the paperwork.

In the kitchen, Sherm walked to the cupboard and took out a tin can of baking soda. In a partially filled glass of water, he added a large spoonful of the baking soda and stirred. He leaned over clutching his aching stomach, in obvious pain. The sweat dripped from his brow onto the floor as he stood bent at the waist and waited for the pain to subside. At that point, he quickly downed the liquid.

When the outside mixture had cooled some, Sherm added a half gallon of malt and four gallons of rye meal, stirred it periodically until it had totally cooled. When he had finished this, he filled the tub with cool water and added half a gallon of yeast. Tomorrow he would stir it and put it in the distiller. Tonight, however, he was anxious to get started, deliver his goods, get his money, and have a little fun.

He pushed in a faster-burning hickory log under the bedrock platform and under the still to boost the fire for the evening until he returned. It would soon be dark enough outside and the extra smoke would go undetected. Before morning, he'd pull out what was left of it and replace it with a slower-burning ash log for the day.

After Sherm had loaded the wagon with the jugs to take to the Windham, he gathered up his paperwork from inside, walked to the yard, replaced the paperwork under the pot, and headed to town.

*****

The town clock was striking 8:00 when Sherm pulled the wagon in behind the Windham Lounge. Sam Rivets had been pacing the floor waiting for him. The bar supply was low on this busy Friday night and too, he was anxious to talk over his proposition with Sherm. Rain was falling hard and dripped from Sherm's hat onto his arms as he tied the horses to the hitching post. "You bring me the juice?" Sam Rivets asked, standing in the back doorway and out of the rain.

Sherm turned. "Brought it all," he answered.

"I'll get you some help to carry it in. Looks like you need to get inside and get dry." Pointing to Sherm's pants, he chortled as he continued, "Look at you. You're one hell of a mess."

"Yeah, guess I am. I wasn't expectin' a downpour."

Sam motioned to two of his employees, and Sherm showed them where the jugs were hidden, in the wooden box he himself had traveled in once. "You sure you want all of them?" he asked Sam

"I'll take all you got."

While the two helpers carried in the jugs, Sherm followed Sam into his office, where he would get paid with cash. Once seated in his stuffed chair behind the desk, confidence beamed through the smirk on Sam's face. "I have a proposition for you, if you're interested."

"A proposition?"

Certain that Sherm would buy his ideas, Sam replied, "Yep. One I think you'll like."

"Guess there can't be no harm in listenin'."

Pointing to a chair in front of his desk, Sam invited Sherm to sit. "Have a seat." Sherm took the seat and as Sam talked, Sherm rolled a cigarette.

"Well, the subject, as you might have guessed, is alcohol and more alcohol. You produce, I deliver, and we both make money."

"When I hear the word money, I listen," Sherm answered with a smirk stretched wide across his face.

"What we need though is brandy, some real Southern brandy. I don't mean the over-sugared stuff. I'm talking about the real stuff." Sam knew pure brandy didn't need much, if any, sugar. Sugar was often added to rush the process, but the product wasn't as pure and the taste not the same. "I've got a run for it, a great run," Sam continued.

"And where would that be?" Sherm asked.

"Well, here's the story," Sam began, as he shoved his chair back from the desk and took a drag on his cigarette. "There's some big business going on down in Hollywood, Florida."

"Florida?" Sherm look surprised.

"That's right. Florida. Hollywood, Florida. There's a man by the name of Young, a Mr. Joe Young, well known in the southeastern part of the country, but particularly in Florida. He has built a city there – a real smart fellow – built the entire city."

"And how has he done that?" Sherm asked.

"It began in about 1921 when he purchased a lot of land down there. Then he laid out a city on paper and made it happen. He took undeveloped land and built a city by using salesmen to entice people to live a 'life of leisure', so he called it, in Florida. The salesmen would come north, generally during the wintertime, when folks were fed up with the hardships of northern cold weather and the illnesses that often goes with it. He herded potential customers down there on bus and rail, lured by the free transportation and food, more so than to look at land."

"You mean people would go all the way down there just for a free ride?"

"Sure. It was more than just a free ride. They got out of the cold weather for a week, free of charge, plus all their meals for free. Most of them didn't go to buy anything. They believed they'd just spend a leisurely week in the sun. Wouldn't you take advantage of that offer?"

"Yeah, I suppose I probably would," Sherm conceded.

"On the way there, these people heard speeches by the sales staff about the great weather, the opportunity for success, and the wonders of not having snow and ice to deal with. By the time many of them got there, they were ready to buy even before they'd seen the land. After they took a walk in the warm water of the ocean, they were looking for mortgage papers to sign. He's built an entire city this way and it only took him about five or six years. And still, it just keeps on growin' and growin'. Most of the growth now is people telling other people, or those down there bringin' in their relatives. Not as many of those sales trips anymore, but they're still runnin' some of them."

"Sounds pretty good for them, but what's that got to do with us?" Sherm questioned. "It's a long way to Florida."

"These salesmen come in here and they talk of course. They been telling me about the bars and the clubs and the speakeasies that have opened up. They're getting a lot of hootch from the Bahamas where it's legal to produce it, but they're paying plenty for it too. I think we can do better. They think so too."

"Hmm. Still say it's a long way down there," Sherm said, shaking his head.

"I took a trip down there with them to see for myself. I needed to know what was there and how it was running before I talked with you," Sam said.

"Yeah, and what did you find out?" Sherm asked.

"I found bars and private clubs with alcohol, but very expensive alcohol. They pay lots for it and charge the customer lots. If we undercut their current wholesale price, they cut their cost to the customer and increase their number of customers. We make them happy - they make us happy."

Sam watched the grin on Sherm's face widen as he considered the proposition. It looked like this was going to work.

"I can tell you this, I got the best damned brandy there is. Right now I been making only enough for me and I don't drink that much of it. It gets pretty expensive to make and takes longer than the other juice. However, my big question is not answered yet. How do you plan to get it down to Florida? There's the river, but the Ohio only runs so far, so there'd be too many transfers."

"I'll get it there. You just have to worry about getting it to me. I'll take care of getting it to Florida."

"Well, if all I have to do is make it, and if he can wait till I can get it ready, I think we could get something going."

"As I mentioned before, Sherm," Sam said, "They know the good stuff. That's what they been getting, so you can't fool them. No need to even try that. They already had that stuff and can still get it. There's plenty of cheap alcohol and it's easy for them to get hold of it. That's not what they're lookin' for. You understand?"

"I got the good stuff. That won't be no problem. It takes some time though to get that first run, so you can't be in too big a hurry for it," Sherm said. "I think I'd prefer the cheaper stuff, personally. That good stuff tastes mighty good, but it can sneak up on you pretty quick. You drink too much of it too fast and in no time you might be layin' down, wantin' to move and can't." Sherm smiled. "I only drink it just now and again, times when I don't plan to go anywhere but home."

"Well, we'll let them worry about that. Our job is just to get it to them. How much time you talking?" Sam asked.

Sherm thought about it for a couple of minutes. He would start with peaches. He already knew where to get plenty of them. They'd take a week to ten days to rot. With the malt and a little bit of sugar, he'd need 72 hours or so before they'd be ready for the distiller. That'd give him time though to start the next batch, and the next.

"I'm thinkin' probably about four to six weeks for the first batch and then I'll have the others comin' right behind the first. Fermentin' the better stuff takes a little bit longer. I'm needin' some help though, specially with this project. Maybe you'd have some ideas there – some good men you know of – some you can trust to work hard and keep their mouth shut."

"I might. I have a couple of guys I know that I can talk to, and if this deal is as big as I think it is, you're gonna' need more than one helper. I'll get back with you on that, after I do some checking."

"Looks like I got lots to do, if the price is right." Sherm stated.

"How about $30 a gallon?"

Stunned, it took Sherm a minute to regain his composure. Thirty dollars - that was almost more than he made last week. He hadn't dreamed he could make that much money at one time. "It's a deal. I'll have it to you as soon as it's ready to bottle – as I said, four to six weeks. I'll be making peach and apple brandy first. These fruits are the best right now. When they're available, I'll do some berries."

"We can probably bring back the berries from Florida, after the plane is emptied of the drink," Sam said.

"Plane – you plan to fly this stuff down?"

"We'll see. It's a thought." Sam was careful not to share too much with Sherm, although he had already made flight arrangements.

"That's a deal. Bring me all the berries you can find. Otherwise, it'll be summer till I can get them."

Sam rose from his chair. Sherm stood as well and walked around the desk to where Sam stood and shook his hand.

"How about a drink on a sealed deal?" Sam asked, as he walked to his private, office bar. "We're in for some good times." He couldn't have been more pleased. His take of $50 a gallon set him up pretty good. He could tell by the look on Sherm's face, he too was just as satisfied.

V

1930

Mixed feelings of excitement and trepidation filled Ellen as she stepped off the train in Logan, W. Va. She was thrilled to be coming to Hatfield-Logan Hospital where she was finally going to realize her dream of becoming a Registered Nurse. She nervously took a quick glance around. The House Mother, Miss Withers, had written that she'd be here to pick her up, but how would she know her. She hadn't said what she'd be wearing or what she looked like. Where was she? What if she didn't show up? What then would she do? Ellen wanted to be brave, but she wasn't feeling brave right now. She had confidence in herself, and quickly reminded herself of that. That couldn't erase the loneliness she felt at this minute, however. She'd be gone for a long time from her babies and that made her heart seem to weigh a ton. They would be alright, she knew that, but oh, she'd miss them, no matter how busy she was. She wouldn't even be able to talk to anyone about them. It was against rules to be married and have children. It made her feel guilty to leave them, but in time it would benefit all of them if she could earn a good salary. She didn't like to be deceiving, but there was no other way if she was going to be a nurse. She kept remembering what Mama had told her. 'Keep your chin up and your head high. Just remember that and you'll be okay.' Right now though, it wasn't helping much.

Mona Papoutsis

The rain falling on this warm September day wasn't helping her spirits either.

She looked around. This place looked so different than Lexington and there would be no one here she knew. Nobody cared about her here. For just an instant, she doubted her decision to leave her family and come here. She wanted to cry, to turn around and go back home, but she wouldn't. Just as quickly, she focused on why she was here. "God, please help me. I feel so lost and afraid. Tell me what to do," she said softly to herself.

The platform looked bare except for one group of women standing at one end. Carrying her bag, she walked toward them. Perhaps they could tell her where to find a telephone or maybe give her a ride to the hospital. Her stomach felt weak with worry, as she silently prayed again for some help from somewhere above. From some very loud speakers an announcement of the train arrival was made. Just then a young girl broke from the group of women where she was headed and ran towards her. "You must be Ellen," she said, obviously excited to see her.

"Yes, yes. Oh, I was afraid I had been forgotten. I didn't see anyone."

"No, no. I'm sorry. Your train was a little bit early. We didn't realize you were here until the announcement. We all came together to pick you up," pointing back to the other two ladies walking towards them. "My name is Martha. Martha Pickard. I'll be your roommate."

"Hi Martha. I'm so glad to meet you," Ellen said, nearly singing her answer as she shook Martha's hand.

Turning to the others, Martha introduced them. "This is our House Mother, Miss Withers."

"Hello, Miss Withers. I'm glad to meet you," Ellen said as she shook her hand.

"I'm glad you're here, Ellen. And next to me," as Miss Withers turned and touched the girl on her left, "This is another young student you'll be working and studying with, Rita Burkett."

"Hello, Ellen," Rita said. "We were anxious for you to get here."

"Oh, it's so nice to meet you, Rita. I'm really glad to be here. Have you been waiting very long?"

"No, we just arrived a few minutes ago. I'm glad we were early though. Your train wasn't due in for another twenty minutes or so."

"I'm glad too. I was a little nervous when I looked around and wasn't sure who I was looking for." They all laughed.

"Okay," Miss Withers said. "Let us get on back to the hospital. I'm sure Ellen is tired, and we have a big day starting tomorrow."

Rita picked up one of Ellen's bags and she got the other. The four ladies walked to the car parked near the edge of the platform. With the weight of worry suddenly lifted from her shoulders, Ellen felt lighter on her feet as she hurried to keep up with the girls.

*****

The Nurses' Home was a separate large, gray and tan stone building situated on a lot outside hospital grounds. Once a privately owned home, it had been purchased by the hospital and converted to living quarters for the student nurses. The front of the building faced the front of the hospital on a Hospital Avenue, a tree-lined street near the end of Blackburn Avenue, the main street through the town of Logan.

Ellen was delighted to see curtains hanging on the entryway windows as she entered her new residence, giving her a sense of feeling at home. The entry room served as a living room for the girls with bedrooms off of the hall leading from there. In one corner stood a large brick-front fireplace that featured a dark wood mantle across the top with matching side pieces. Two large, dark green davenports sat corner to corner, forming an L-shape in front of the fireplace. Along the wall was a table with a vase of plastic flowers in the center, a Queen Anne style chair on each side. The hardwood floor was covered with a multi-colored large rug, fringed at each end.

"Oh, this is beautiful," she said, looking around the room from floor to ceiling. She began to feel like she was coming home and felt herself relaxing a bit.

"You can follow me," Martha said. "Our room is just down the hall."

"Martha, you and Rita can let Ellen know the house rules, find her a snack in the kitchen if she wants, and then be in your rooms and bed before 8:00," Miss Withers said, firmly, but kindly. "That'll give you about an hour."

"Yes, ma'am," all three girls answered.

"And, remember too that all of you are to be in the dining room for breakfast no later than 7:00 o'clock. Your lecture starts in the hospital lecture room, promptly at eight."

"We'll be there, Miss Withers," Rita called.

"Goodnight, girls."

"Goodnight," they all replied.

*****

Hatfield-Logan Hospital consisted of forty-five beds divided into four and eight-bed wards, with several private or semi-private rooms. In addition, there were the standard medical treatment rooms, a dining room, a kitchen, a supply room and various other utility and storage areas that make up a large hospital.

Martha and Ellen, excited to begin their first day of training, awakened early. "It's hard to believe I'm really here, Martha," Ellen said. She stood looking in the mirror brushing her hair.

"Me too. My mother started preaching to me about going to school to be a nurse when I was probably only six years old. How about your mom?"

"My mama was probably as excited as me when I left to come here," Ellen answered.

"Do you have brothers and sisters," Martha asked.

Ellen reminded herself to be careful how she answered. She could tell no one she had been married and had children. "No, I'm the only child my mother had. My father died when I was very young. My mother never got remarried."

Ellen reached for a hanky, which she put in her pocket. "I'm ready to go. How about you?"

"I'm ready. Let's go. We'll be early, but that's probably good. I know Mrs. Ramson doesn't like anyone late. She's pretty strict the other girls said. You and I are the only first year students. All the others are either in their second or third year."

Rain fell softly as the girls sped from their house to the Lecture Hall. They held their umbrellas close to their face as the wind tried to pull them from their hands. Inside, they shook them off and propped them in the corner of entrance.

Mrs. Ramson was standing on the raised platform in front of the class when they entered the room. Of the sixty-five student nurses, about half were already there. Ellen observed all of the girls already there and those just arriving. She wondered how many of them had secrets besides herself. She guessed none of them because they were all smiling and seemed so carefree. She wished hard that she didn't have to be here deceiving everyone. She wanted to tell everyone how proud she was of her two children, but that would have to wait.

Soon, all the girls were seated and Mrs. Ramson began her lecture. "Welcome to each of you. It's nice to have you here. I hope each of you are anxious to get started and learn the art of nursing. It's not an easy job, as you'll find out. I'm aware that some of you are newcomers and others have been here a year or two in some cases. To be a good nurse, you have to want to be here. However, it's probably one of the most rewarding fields you'll ever work in.

"You will be meeting in this lecture room all day, Monday through Friday, for the first month. After that you will alternate your time between here and the wards or areas which you will be assigned. Each designated area will be a three-month scheduled period of time. Before each new assignment, you'll meet in this room for lectures from either the head nurse on the ward or one of the doctors on staff where you'll be working. Occasionally, there will also be other lectures here, which you'll be required to attend. Your rotation through the hospital will include all of the wards, as well as the kitchen, where you'll learn to plan meals according to doctors' orders, as well as prepare and serve them. All of you will be working 12 hour shifts, which could be extended if you get caught in the middle of a procedure or an emergency at the time your shift is supposed to end."

She looked sternly around the room, causing the students to sit up straight and look directly at her. "I don't think I have your attention – not all of you anyway. I need to know that each of you are listening and heeding my advice. Hear me when I tell you, it's easier to send you home than it is to teach you, so I want each of you to look at me and let me know you're listening when I'm talking to you. I don't want to waste my time on anyone who doesn't want to be here."

When satisfied that each student was giving her their undivided attention, Mrs. Ramson continued. "Shifts begin either at 7:00 a.m. or 7:00 p.m. with each student rotating between the two, one month on each. The House Mother will make bed checks each evening at 9:00. If you're not at work, you must be in bed at that time and no excuses will be accepted for absences, outside of work. No visitors are allowed in the Nurses Home. Any student caught breaking rules will be expelled for misconduct. Students with an inability to keep up with classes, inefficiency, or neglect of duty will also be expelled. What we don't want is to waste our time teaching you if you aren't learning or out breaking rules and getting yourself pregnant. This is no place to be if you have kids to raise."

Tabors Creek

Ellen could feel her face turning crimson. *Does Mrs. Ramson know my secret? Can she see it in my face?* She wanted to be a nurse for her own sake, but for the children too. She prayed Mrs. Ramson couldn't read her thoughts or ask her any questions right now, for she'd never be able to talk.

"Make sure your shoes are white, and your pinafores spotless," she warned, as she looked down her nose through rimless glasses. Her bright red hair was piled high on her head, while her stiffly starched white hat hung on for dear life. The pin holding the hat appeared to be sticking in her head and not her hair. The comic relief made Ellen smile. "You'll be sent back to your room to make it right if you show up for training any other way. That wouldn't look good on your record."

Mrs. Ruth Ramson was a moderately sized lady with much of her excess weight gathered in her bosom and around her waist. Her legs were small and pencil-shaped. Intimidated by her overall appearance and the strictness of her voice, Ellen lowered her head, filled with anxiety.

"We'll help each other," Martha leaned over and whispered.

Ellen felt somewhat relieved. "Thanks," she said. "You must have read my mind."

"Your time in the wards will be spent accompanying the doctors who will teach you how to be good nurses. At the end of your rotation through all of the departments, you should be qualified to take your state license test. With no unforeseen illnesses that would cause you to get behind, all of you first year students should be able to graduate at the same time. That's what we aim for. We hope to see no failures. Good luck to all of you." With that, Ellen began her training.

*****

"Dear Mama," Ellen wrote after her first month of classes, "I am still spending every day, me and the other students, studying all the things we need to know before we begin working in the hospital with patients. We have to meet in the lecture room at 8:00 o'clock every morning, starting on Monday and ending on Friday evening. This is supposed to happen for the first year we're here. Saturdays we do our laundry and ironing. Sunday we go to church, which is just a little ways away from our house. We have a lot of reading and writing to do, so we spend our evenings in our rooms doing that. I really like my roommate. Her name is Martha Pickard and we are good friends. I talk to her about you, but I don't say anything about Neet and Charlie. I can't take a chance on that. I am so afraid someone will find out, even if I don't tell anyone. I wish I could tell her how much I miss them, and I do miss them so much. I want to sit and read to them and hold them in my lap. I've only been here one month and I do get really homesick, but some of the other girls do too, and that helps me. Two years is going to be a long time. I will have three weeks off for the summer, but it would be too expensive to take the train home I think. You know the money I will make when I work in the hospital all goes to pay for my room, so I can't save any."

Lectures on Physiology, Anatomy, Hygiene, Fevers and Contagions, Surgical Nursing and Sepsis, Urinalysis, Toxicology, Skin Diseases, and lots of other medical words of advice and patient care continued for three months. Superintendent Ramson interviewed each student nurse at the end of the classroom training after they had attended for two weeks. As one girl came out, another knocked at the door and waited for her approval to enter the Superintendent's office. Ellen knocked on the door and entered when called. "Good morning nurse, what is your name?" Mrs. Ramson asked.

"Good morning," Ellen answered, her voice quivering in anticipation of her interview with Mrs. Ramson, who was seated in a small armchair behind a desk. A sheet of paper lay on the desk in front of her. "I am Ellen Potter."

Looking down at the sheet of paper, Mrs. Ramson made a check, obviously next to Ellen's name. "Have a seat, Ellen."

Ellen sat in a chair in front of the desk, her legs trembling as she sat. She placed her hands on her knees to steady them. Ellen attempted to sit perfectly still, but with each question Mrs. Ramson asked, her knees began to shake even more.

As Mrs. Ramson looked at the sheet in front of her, Ellen stared at the table in the corner with pictures of two young children, a boy and girl who appeared about the same age as her own children. Mrs. Ramson, noticing her attention to the pictures, said, "Oh, those are my sister's children. They're like my own though."

"They're very cute," Ellen replied, then looked away, wondering what her own children were doing at this moment.

Glancing again at the sheet in front of her, Mrs. Ramson said, "I see you've done quite well in your classroom studies, Ellen. That's very good."

"Thank you."

"Well, I hope that you'll continue to do well when you receive your first assignment. You may think you've worked hard up until now, but you haven't seen anything yet. Working on the wards will be a challenge, even for the strongest of you. The hours are long and they're hard. You begin your days at 7:00 in the morning or 7:00 at night, as you were told in your lecture, and last for 12 hours. This is where we usually lose those students who aren't cut out to be nurses. Do you understand?"

"Yes, ma'am, I understand."

"I expect you to be on time every day and ready to start when you arrive there. Are you ready for the challenge?"

"Oh, yes, ma'am, I'm ready. I know it will be hard, but I'm excited," Ellen answered.

"Good. I don't like to see any of our student nurses fail for any reason whatsoever. I've had some failures in the past and often with the same excuse, 'I didn't know that.' I don't like that excuse and I don't want to hear it. So if you have any questions, please ask them now while you can."

"I have no questions," Ellen said, trying her best to look confident, when deep inside she was weak with a mixture of both fright and excitement, together like rain and a rainbow. She wondered then what she would do if she did have questions. She wasn't courageous enough to ask them. She was somewhat comforted by believing that perhaps the children in the picture on the table were truly Mrs. Ramson's own children, not her sister's, and she was hiding it just like Ellen was. She hoped so with all her might. It lightened the burden of guilt just slightly.

"As you know, you'll rotate through the entire hospital, even the kitchen, where you'll work with the dietician."

"Yes ma'am. I do know that."

"Do you have a preference of where to start?"

"No ma'am. I'll go wherever you send me; however, I do love the children, especially the babies."

*****

VI

1931

Sherm's agreement with Sam Rivets at The Windham Lounge was working just as he wanted. He spent the winter pushing his three stills to produce all the brandy possible, and Sam was buying it as fast as he could deliver it. His apple brandy was his highest yield. The Hog Sweet apples made the best brandy, and fortunately, they were the most plentiful. There had been an ample supply of peaches also with no one particular peach better than the other. To avoid suspicion, he bought from various farmers, careful to avoid telling what he was doing with the fruit and where he was taking it. "My kids love apple juice," he said to one pleasant farm hand. "They drink lots of it. Most of the peaches - they eat them pretty good too." He had a different story for each fruit farm he visited.

At Sam's recommendation, Sherm hired Elwood Maynard to help out. "He got into a shootin' match a couple of years ago down in Johnson County I think it was and so he's layin' low for a while," Sam said. "All he needs is steady pay and a place to sleep. He won't talk to nobody, so you'd have nothing to worry about and have you some good help. You just treat him right and you'll have him for as long as you need him."

Sam had been right. Elwood needed Sherm as badly as Sherm needed his help. Sherm didn't know what he was hiding from, but he didn't care, so long as he could work hard and keep his mouth shut. Sam wouldn't talk either, Sherm knew that; there was too much at stake for each one of them.

Today Sherm was out to buy more supplies and take care of business. He entered the General Store first. He spoke to the young man behind the counter. "Let me pay you for ten of them bags of sugar. Then I'll load 'em on my wagon."

"Doin' some jelly makin' are you," the young man asked with a smile.

"Yeah, my wife is stockin' up on sugar so she'll have it when the berries are in and the peaches and apples start comin'."

"Don't know what we'd do without them ladies, huh?"

"Guess so," Sherm answered. He handed him the money and picked up a bag of sugar and headed to the wagon.

"Dumb son of a bitch," Sherm said softly as he loaded the first bag of sugar.

From there he drove to another store on the other side of town and picked up more sugar. Next week he'd send Elwood in to both places to avoid suspicion.

Next Sherm headed for the bank. "Have you got a box I could use to put some jewelry and valuables in?" he asked the teller.

"We sure do. How big a box do you need? We have small ones, medium sized ones and some are big enough to walk in," he grinned, hoping he'd made a joke. Sherm didn't react.

"All I want is a box to put some of my important papers in. My wife's wantin' me to be protectin' things," Sherm said, trying to sound like the responsible husband.

"I think probably you'd need one of them there on the left." He pointed to the wall of boxes. "Take number six. It's empty." He handed a key to Sherm.

With the key, Sherm walked into a room with various sized boxes. Finding his number, he opened the box, took his money from his satchel, kissed it, and with a smile placed it inside the box and locked it. Feeling quite proud of himself, he strode from the bank exuding with confidence.

If he chose to, he could now get the car he had seen and liked and still have a nice amount left over. It was a new Pontiac

Big Six and sold for seven hundred, forty-five dollars. He wasn't quite ready for that just yet though. When the time came to buy a car, he wanted it to be closer to the time he was leaving this place and he wanted a lot more money than he had just yet before he went anywhere. There were other matters to settle too. First, there was Ellen. She had earned a visit from him and that would be almost as satisfactory as a substantial amount of money. "The bitch. She'll wish she never had run away with my car and my money when I find her." After a short pause, as if he'd forgotten. "Bertie, I'll kill you too, you son-of-a-bitch." He talked aloud to himself; hearing it said, even if in his own voice, seemed to assure him he would find them.

One thing Sherm knew for certain, he would need cash to run when the time came. His name would hit the news when they discovered Sherm Peck had lived right here in Ashland. That time was certain to come when he found Ellen and Bertie. That meant he'd have to give a phony name when he bought the car so they wouldn't know what he was driving when they started to hunt him. By the time they had it figured out, he'd probably be on the West coast, or wherever. As for Maggie, he'd leave the wagon and horses with her and anything else that he didn't want or wouldn't fit in the car. She'd never know where he went. He guessed she'd just pack up and go back to her house in Tabors Creek, not that it mattered to him.

*****

In her room, Ellen stood looking at herself in the mirror. First she put on her petticoat, and then her white blouse. She loved the new uniform she was now wearing. She buttoned up the white blouse then pulled the blue striped pinafore over her head. As she buttoned the side, she smiled at her reflection. She dreamed of the day she would be wearing the all-white uniform with the white starched hat with the navy blue stripe, but for now this one looked very good. She wished Mama could see her wearing it.

And Sherm, what would Sherm say if he could see her, she wondered. The thought of him no longer had the effect it once had. She remembered how it was when his smile could make her heart race with love she felt for him. She would have done anything for him, if only he had loved her as she had loved him. Now, there were no feelings left. He had slowly killed all of that. With each act of deceit, each lie, every derogatory remark and ridicule, a little bit had died until there was nothing left. Then the shootings were indescribable and unforgivable. No, there were no feelings left. Except fear. She still couldn't shake that off. Today though, she would put him out of her thoughts. She liked what she saw in the mirror. She felt proud and thankful to be where she was.

"What are you thinking about?" a voice came from the opened door.

Ellen turned to see her roommate enter. "Oh, hi, Martha. I was just looking in the mirror to be sure my uniform has no spots, no wrinkles and anything that would get me sent back to my room," she chuckled.

"You were looking deep into a place somewhere outside of here when I walked in," Martha said.

"Oh, was I? Hmm, I'm not sure where I was then."

The girls snickered. Martha continued, "I got off of my shift a few minutes early today. We were so busy all night, and all of us were really tired. So when Aileen came in a little early, Doctor Powell told me to go ahead and leave, 'get some rest,' he said."

"What was happening last night?" Ellen asked.

"Well, in one case, we had three people come in from a bad car accident. One of the ladies had been in the back seat and when their car hit a tree, she was knocked to the floor. Her husband who was seated in front of her – his seat went forward, then came back down on her, with him in it, of course. She had bitten her tongue really bad and her arm was broken. He was a pretty big guy. He's a patient too, but not hurt as bad as she was."

"Oh my, poor thing. I guess they'll keep her for a while."

"I'm sure," Martha replied.

"It's about time now for me to get goin'. We had three ladies in labor last night when I left. I spent a lot of time taking blood pressures, giving them drinks of water, and trying to be helpful as their labor progressed. I hope for their sakes, they've delivered by now."

"Hope so too. Well, have a good day. I'm going to eat a bite of breakfast and go to sleep. Seven o'clock this evening will come pretty quick again, you know."

Ellen waved to Martha as she walked out the door. "Sleep well."

*****

Ellen watched the outstretched hands of Doctor Walter Brewer as he waited for the unborn baby to leave the comfort of mother's womb and enter into this new world that anxiously awaited him or her. The expectant mother had been with contractions for nearly 24 hours now. She was exhausted and growing weary. "Give it just a couple more good pushes and we'll have a new little prince or princess here," Doctor Brewer said. "I know you're tired, but in just a few minutes you can take a nice long rest." He was a kind man and the patients as well as the nurses loved being part of anything he was doing.

"My husband, is he here yet?" the patient asked.

"Have you seen him, Ellen?" Doctor Brewer asked.

"I didn't see anyone waiting before I came in, doctor, but he may be here, I'm not sure."

"As soon as we have a baby, I'll do some checking and let you know," Dr. Brewer said. The expectant mother had been a patient since the previous day without a sign of her husband or other family members, so he guessed no one would be coming. He shook his head in disgust and sympathy as he looked at Ellen.

Ellen stood at the patient's head, which was wet with perspiration. She dipped a face cloth in a wash pan of clean, cool water then wrung it out. Wiping the patient's face, she could nearly feel the pain she read in her expressions. "Are you wanting a boy or a girl?"

The expectant mother answered, "It doesn't matter. I just want a healthy baby. I also want this to be over with." She smiled and squeezed Ellen's hand tightly as the pain worsened with the next contraction.

As soon as the new baby popped into his hands, Doctor Brewer cleared the baby's breathing passage and smacked her lightly on the bottom. He placed her on a sterile bath towel near at hand. "Here," he said to Ellen, placing the child in her arms, "You know what to do now."

Ellen knew, but this was the first time she'd done it by herself. She quickly bathed the baby's eyes with sterile water, while the doctor placed a clamp on the mother's end of the umbilical cord and another to the baby's end and the cord was cut.

"Welcome to this world, little one," Ellen cooed to the baby while she extracted excess mucus from its lungs. "I'll get you all cleaned up and you can have your very first bed of your own. You see that little crib over there – it's just waiting for you. It's nice and warm." The new baby continued to wail during the process. "You sure have a great set of lungs, I see. That's a good thing, you understand, so you just keep on yellin."

As she worked with the newborn baby, from across the room Ellen could see the doctor kneading the mother's stomach after the placenta had been expelled, trying to stimulate the contraction of the womb. When finished, he turned to Ellen, "You get to deliver the next one," he said. "I'll get to watch."

Tabors Creek

Ellen grinned. "I'll be proud to do it." Working with Dr. Brewer had given Ellen a sense of self-confidence she had never known.

*****

Snow had fallen lightly all morning in Tabors Creek, and the outside temperature had dropped drastically since noon. Sheriff Workman was distracted from his reading with the sudden realization that the inside temperature had cooled down too and he was feeling chilly. He walked to the corner stove, opened the door, and threw in another two logs. At the small sink in the other corner, he hand pumped water into the percolator, rinsed it out, added more water, and made a fresh pot of coffee, which he placed on top of the stove. He was alone for awhile this afternoon, which allowed him the pleasure of toying around with his thoughts. He was good at setting scenarios in his mind, a big asset in his job and often helped him outsmart a criminal mind.

It had been more than eight months since Ellen and Bertie had driven out of Tabors Creek. He wondered where and how she was. He wondered too where Sherm was and whether or not he'd ever be caught. There had been no leads since he shot and killed the federal agents and left town, and no signs he'd been back to the area. Would he try to come back in the winter to check on Ellen, the Sheriff wondered. Sherm had no way of knowing she wasn't here, as far as he knew. The Sheriff had never gone back to the house and site of the killing. After they removed the agent's body from the hillside behind the house, there had been no reason to go back. However, maybe a ride out there wouldn't be a bad idea – he could check to see if anyone had been there. Now seemed like a good time for a drive. The weather could get nastier today if the snow kept up, or started to fall heavier. In years past, March had brought some pretty bad storms.

Wondering about the weather, he walked over to look out the window when Deputy Sheriff Bell opened the door and came inside.

"Hi, John. What's it like out there."

"Cold as hell, that's what it is."

"What about the roads?"

"Oh, they're not so bad, not yet anyway," Bell answered.

"I been sittin' here thinkin' about Sherm Peck and just wonderin' if maybe he's ever come back here or not."

"What makes you think he'd come back?" Bell asked.

"He's pretty sly, like a fox, you know. If he thought Ellen was back here, you know damned well he'd try to sneak back."

"Think I'll take a ride out there just to have a look myself, settle my curiosity," Sheriff Workman said. "I would rest a lot easier at night if we had that murderer in the State prison."

"I think we all could," Bell answered. "You would think the Feds would have gone out there, wouldn't you?"

"Maybe they have. If so, they never came by here, so don't know."

Sheriff Workman could tell by Bell's manner that he thought riding to the house was a waste of time, although he didn't say so out of respect for the Sheriff. The Sheriff's reasons were two-fold, and only he knew the depth of his feelings. There was no need to try to explain. He placed his hat on his head, picked up his gloves and walked to the door. "Don't forget to bank the fire when you leave, John," he called from the opened door. "That temp is going down in the teens tonight."

"I'll get it, don't worry."

*****

Driving toward the Peck house, Sheriff Workman passed Maggie's homestead. "Hmm, isn't that strange," he noted aloud to himself, as he saw no sign of activity or life there. "You'd think nobody lived there." There were no recent wagon tracks in the lane, and the horses, often in the field nearest to the road, were not there and no sign they'd been there recently – no tracks in the snow. He made a mental note to stop in there soon to be sure all was okay. He realized he hadn't seen her in town for some time. In the past she sometimes walked by the office on her way to or from the General Store. He'd seen her at the train station once or twice before as well, but nowhere lately.

As the Sheriff continued on to the Peck house, he began to question his decision to do what he was doing. Perhaps he had been foolish to come out here alone. What if Sherm was in the house. He knew Sherm would shoot him if he saw him. If he was in that house, he'd have a good aim at him as he walked up the hill toward the house. Sherm could stand in the door or the window and pick him off before he got half way up the hill. The more he pondered the possibilities, the more frightened and nervous he became. Maybe he'd just turn around and forget the idea. He could come back tomorrow or another day with John; that seemed to be a better idea.

Aware that he was already pretty near the house, he slowed his speed some as he tried to decide what to do. Before he could make up his mind to turn around, he reached the house and stopped the car at the bottom of the hill. Eyeing the surrounding area he noted there were no footprints in the snow leading to the house and no car or wagon tracks in the road. There was no smoke coming from the chimney, which meant there was no heat inside the house. He began to relax a little bit. No heat or footprints indicated there had been no one there since it began to snow early this morning. He wouldn't have spent the night there without heat - not hardly. Not in this severe cold weather.

Finally making a decision, the Sheriff turned the car around and parked it facing town, just in case he wanted to leave in a hurry. He climbed out of the car and started walking up the hill. Still apprehensive, he stopped and looked toward the house. If he saw movement, he planned to lie down and roll as fast as hell down that hill. He felt a little secure, deciding it was doubtful Sherm could hit a moving target from the angle he'd have to shoot from. Seeing no movement at all, he continued walking toward the house, while keeping his eyes focused on the front window and door.

Reaching the house, the Sheriff stood to the side of the front door, his pistol in his hand, pushed it hard until it opened, then waited. Hearing no sounds, he looked in. There was just one room and it was bare; he knew Sherm couldn't be hiding. He stepped inside and walked around. The house reeked of an indescribable foul odor. A partially filled spittoon sat beside the mattress on the floor. A frozen mouse lay on top of the mattress. In the corner stood a chamber bucket. A blanket was tossed in the corner. The ladies had obviously left in a hurry. There were no signs anyone had been here since that fateful day.

As he walked toward the door, the Sheriff spotted a picture frame partially hidden by the mattress. He reached for it and stood staring at a picture of Ellen and her first child, Charlie. Tears filled his eyes. He took the picture from the frame and placed it inside his leather billfold, tied it shut and placed it in his inside jacket pocket. He headed for the door. He thanked God Ellen was out of this pig sty. He wanted to do so much for her. She deserved whatever he could do. One thing he was certain of, Sherm had not been here.

*****

Doc Weide's horse, Brandywine, had now been at Holiday for two weeks. Brock allowed each new horse-in-training a two-week period to adjust to their new surroundings and to feel calm around the staff. The adjustment period consisted of a walk around the premises in the early mornings, intentionally done by different handlers. In the stable, Brock walked to where Brandywine stood. She pranced around in a circle when she saw him. "So, you recognize me, do you?" he asked. "Good job, girl.

Let's go to the track and practice a little." She nuzzled him on his arm, as if anxious to go somewhere. He opened the gate to her stall, and led her to the track.

Josh was readying the cart on the track when Brock arrived. "Good morning, Brock, how you doing?"

"Great, thanks. I think this lady is as anxious to get on the track as I am to get her there."

"That's good. What's your plan?" asked Josh.

"First, I just want to walk her around the track a couple of times pulling the cart. Then I'll get in the cart and hope she lets me stay there."

"Guess we'll find out pretty soon," said Brock. Both men looked at her and laughed as Brandywine snorted and pranced around. She appeared to be as regal as the King of England. "Let's get this cart hooked up. She's anxious I do believe." Together the two men attached the cart to the side rails. They then hooked the rails to a bar which led from a metal frame Brandywine wore on her back.

"She's okay with the track now, I think. She's walked it without the cart every day," Brock said. "She should be ready for this."

Jockey, Eddie Ellis, walked to the place where the men stood. "Hi Eddie," Josh said.

"Good morning," he answered. Brock nodded his head and turned back to his job of anchoring the cart. "Okay, she's hooked up. Let's give it a try." He took the reins in hand and began to walk Brandywine around the track as Josh and Eddie stood watching. Neither spoke.

By the time they reached the backstretch, Brock was comfortable with Brandywine's reaction to the cart. At that point, he got in the cart to test how she would react. Surprisingly, the ride went smoothly enough and Brock stayed in the cart for three laps around the track. He headed to the gate area where Eddie and Josh waited. Eddie placed the blanket on her back. "I want to try a blanket rather than a saddle to break her in," Eddie said, attempting to erase the concerned looks he was getting from Brock. "Stop your worrying. Look at her, she's anxious to get going." Brandywine appeared to be dancing as he talked, her graceful front legs raised high as she pranced in place.

"I wasn't questioning the blanket. I just think you should ride in the cart with her for a couple of laps before you saddle up," Brock said.

"Nah, no need for that. If she'll pull you, she'll haul me. She's ready, I'm tellin' you," Eddie said emphatically.

"Alright. Well, you get on and I'll loosen the cart just before you take off," Brock said, speaking in a questionable tone.

"We're listening," Josh chuckled. "Now remember, I want to see her run, not dance."

"Well, we'll see," Brock said to Josh. "As usual, Eddie isn't listening to my advice." Looking at Eddie, he continued. "You're pretty sure of yourself, there Eddie, aren't you?"

"You worry too much, Brock. Just relax." Standing beside Brandywine he patted the horse on the hip, readjusted the blanket, and moved closer to the stirrup. Brock moved in place to release the cart. Brandywine turned to look at Brock then at Eddie, perhaps as a warning no one saw, or maybe just ignored. Eddie put his foot in the stirrup, and placed himself on her back. It took no more than two seconds until Brandywine threw her head in the air, reared on her two back legs and promptly tossed Eddie to the ground.

Although his pride was somewhat tarnished, he sat unhurt and laughing on the ground as Brandywine continued by herself around the track, pulling the empty cart. Brock was thrown to the ground by the force of the cart.

Realizing they weren't hurt, Josh joined in on the laughter. As Brandywine neared them at her starting position, she came to a stop, shook her head and stared at them.

"I think she just smiled at us," Brock said laughing out loud, "just like she was telling us what fools we are."

"I think she's had enough of you guys, is what I think," Josh said with a smile.

"Maybe next time you'll listen to me," Brock chided Eddie.

"Oh, probably not. In fact, I'm ready to try again. How about you?" asked Eddie, rubbing his shoulder.

"Are you brave enough to try again, right now? You could wait a while," replied Brock, dusting himself off, patting both hands over his shirt and pants. He took the hat from his head and knocked it against his pants leg to shake off the dust.

"Let's go ahead and try it and see what happens. If I fall on my ass, then I fall on my ass."

Eddie got up in Brandywine's face and spoke. "Hey pretty lady. I don't know about you, but I didn't like that. Why don't we do it again, the right way this time. That would be my way, okay?" Brandywine raised her head up and down as though nodding an okay-by-me answer.

"You guys are nuts," Josh called from the fence.

After the cart was removed, Brock stood in front of her, holding the reins, not allowing her to go forward, nor rear up, while Eddie slowly climbed on her back. "She's a beauty," Eddie said. "Hold her there a little bit. Let's just give her some time and she ought to be okay."

"Want a cushion to put in your pants?" Brock joked.

"Oh, you of little faith, just watch this. She likes me! She just wanted me to know she's in charge – not me."

After several minutes of talking to Brandywine and rubbing her back and head, Brock handed the reins to Eddie and stepped out of the way. Eddie rode slowly on the back of a broken and calm Brandywine around the track once, trotted her slowly on the second round and by the third, she wanted to run, which she did. On the fourth three-quarter mile run, Brock timed her. He stood with a look of disbelief when he realized the speed she'd shown on her very first run.

"My Christ," he cried to Eddie, "We've got a streak of lightening here. Doc Weide is gonna be mighty pleased when he hears this."

*****

Brandywine had her chance to show what she could do at the Whitney Handicap, a race in Lexington. Doc Weide was there to watch her as she got out in front and stayed there, winning by two lengths.

After the race, Doc Weide turned to Hal and shook his hand. "Thanks, Hal. You've done a great job, you and the others. I owe you a lot."

"Just doin' our job, Doc. Even so, she was a pleasure to train. She's a real beauty. Maybe we've trained her too well," he joked. "Hate to see her against our Freedom."

"Well, that's both good and bad," Doc agreed. "When that happens, may the best win, and hope it's mine." Both men laughed aloud. "I'll get her back home now and let her work with our guys for the rest of the year."

He offered an envelope to Hal, then shook his hand. "Here's full payment for your services. I hope to have another horse or two one of these days – that is, when the right one shows up. Let me know if you get a good one in training that'll be goin' up for sale."

"Thanks, Doc. I'll be glad to take 'em. Anytime. I'll keep my eyes open for a winner."

Doc waved as he walked toward the truck where Brandywine was being loaded on board. "So long, Doc," Hal called.

VII

1931

Doc Weide was minutes away from closing his doors. Fifteen patients had come and gone from his office today, a few of them pretty sick. He was tired, but felt comfortable with himself knowing he'd done all he could to help ease their pain. He walked to the door to lock it just as it opened and a couple walked in. "Can I help you?" he asked the disheveled looking pair standing in the waiting room.

"Are you Doctor Weide?" Sherm asked.

"I am. What can I do for you? I was just about to close the office."

"I've got a terrible pain in my stomach, doc."

Doc Weide locked the door behind Sherm and Maggie. "Have a seat ma'am, and you," pointing to Sherm, "follow me into the exam room."

Maggie sat nervously wringing her hands while waiting for Sherm. She was tired and feeling somewhat defeated today. Sherm hadn't been in any condition to get himself to the doctor, so she had to take him. That meant going in to work late and for that, she would pay dearly. The boss would be livid with her and would yell obscenities at her just like he did at anyone who came in late or missed a day. It didn't matter what reason they offered, it was never good enough.

She and Sherm had been in Ashland for more than a year already and still she had no money except for what Sherm handed her, hardly enough to buy groceries with and nothing for herself. She looked at her shoes with the sole coming loose on one of them. Sherm had reattached the other by pounding in a couple of tacks. She was wearing one of the three cotton dresses she owned, each of which now had multiple ink stains from the press, in spite of the aprons she wore. Her arms and legs ached today and every day. Sherm was seldom home when she returned at night and she was tired of coming home to an empty house. She had tried to stay awake for him, but when exhaustion overtook her, she slept. With her head in her hand and her elbow resting on the chair arm, she fell asleep in the doctor's office, waiting for Sherm.

"Let's go, Maggie," Sherm said, knocking her hand out from under her chin.

Startled from a sound sleep, Maggie jumped to her feet. "Oh, sorry. I didn't hear you come out."

Outside Sherm headed to the wagon. "We gotta git you home so you can get back to work."

"I'm so tired today. I'd like to stay at home and rest."

"I ain't hearin' talk like that, Maggie. You'll be okay after you get movin'," Sherm answered.

"What'd Dr. Weide say about you?" she asked.

"Maybe got me an ulcer, he thinks. I have to come back again if it don't get any better."

"What are you supposed to do for it?"

"Don't worry about it. I'll take care of it."

The truth was, Doctor Weide had insisted Sherm stop drinking any alcohol, drink lots of milk and follow a strict diet, which he had written down for him. He had also recommended he stop smoking.

"You better listen to 'eem, Sherm."

"Don't bother me, Maggie. I'll take care of myself."
Maggie said no more during the ride home.

*****

Snow had fallen earlier in the day, but then had turned to rain. The roads were wet and slushy, but the sky was clear now and the stars out bright. Sam had his regular run to make regardless of road conditions or how tired he was. Even though the drive to the Huntington Airport was a short one, some days seemed longer than others. Waiting until after dark was more trying on those long days, but there was no changing that. During the day was not the time to be loading alcohol.

His friend, George, was there waiting for him. "Thanks for being on time. I'm beat tonight," Sam said.

"I got out a little early, so I got here a little early," George said.

"That's good. Gets to be a long day. I guess the same for you, huh?"

"Sure enough. I was on my feet all day today except for a half hour lunch." Then dismissing the formalities, he continued. "You have enough for a full load do you?"

"I've got a full load. Hope you can fit it all in."

"I'll fit it in, don't you worry. Better get goin' with it before anyone comes lookin'. We got a full moon tonight. Wolves howl on nights like this, don't they?" Both men smiled, tired or not.

"Some people are just as bad."

They carried the jugs, two at a time, from the car to the plane, a Ford 5AT, for the flight to Florida. Designed to carry 13 passengers, they had altered the inside of the plane, replacing the seats with wooden boxes anchored to the floor. The jugs were carefully stacked into the boxes, the lid closed and tied in order to keep the jugs secure when George encountered turbulent weather.

"The weather looks like it'll hold tonight. That turbulence gets to you in the stomach sometimes when the weather's bad. I hope one day they make these planes so they can fly higher than 6,000 feet so we can fly above that stuff," George said.

"You can rest assured - one day they will too, but wouldn't do me any good, even when they do. I'm not much of a flyer," Sam said.

When Sam handed the last of the jugs to George, he shook George's hand. "Thanks again."

George counted out the money, placed it in an envelope and handed it to Sam. "I'll be takin' two of them jugs, so here's money for them," pointing to the jugs. See you same time, same place, next week?" he asked, a question rather than a statement.

"I'll be here," Sam replied. He stepped into his car and headed back to Ashland.

Sam knew George would take a profit on delivery of the brandy, although he didn't suspect the price doubled when it left him. Even so, Sam knew this job for George was more about his love of flying than how much money he made. He didn't need the money, and this weekly flight to Florida was an escape from the daily boring routine of Monday through Friday. Still, the delivery paid for the trip, plus it gave him a day or two in the Florida sun, depending on the weather.

Close to being jealous, Sam turned and walked back to his automobile.

*****

At the age of 29, Eddie Ellis was one of the best jockeys riding in the upcoming Kentucky Derby. He was here at Holiday Farms today to continue training Freedom, not just on-the-track training, but to familiarize him with other areas of the ranch, off the track. It was a frequent occurrence lately as he tried to condition him to sights and sounds other than racing. Not only did Freedom and the other young colts have to learn to accept a rider on their back, they had to be familiar with hot-walkers, pony horses, and trailers – and anything else they might be exposed to at a racetrack. "Come on boy, let's go look around," he called to Freedom as he raised himself into the saddle.

Eddie slowly rode astride Freedom all around the farm, intentionally stopping to see various things. Once he stopped for a moving tractor pulling a wagon. Another time he walked him past Josh as Josh drove up the driveway in his Model T. Josh stopped his car.

"Out for a morning stroll, are you?" Josh asked.

"I guess you could call it that. We're doing our exposing. I don't want him to see anything at the race track that he hasn't seen before."

Eddie knew there would be many more cars, people and other distractions at Churchill Downs than Freedom had seen before at the smaller tracks.

"Good job," Josh said as he drove away, then parked his car and watched as Eddie and Freedom headed to the five-eighth mile training track, which included a chute and banked turns. Brock spoke to Eddie as he approached the gates. "You're set for a run, I see."

"Hi Brock. I have to be. Freedom here is getting antsy to get goin'. I believe he's tired of walking around. Guess he thinks we're wasting his time," he said smiling.

"Well, he isn't one to parade around and show off, you know, unless he's running."

"That's true. So guess we gotta run, huh?"

"Let's do it," Brock said sitting astraddle of another colt-in-training. He guided the young colt over to a gate, two away from Freedom. When inside the chute, an assistant standing at the side, on a signal from Brock, opened the gates. Brock's colt-in-training led the pair out of the gates, but Freedom faltered some, seemingly having trouble coming out of the gate. Eddie made a mental note to return Freedom to the starting gate later and repeatedly run him through there until he grew comfortable with it. However, after Freedom was out of the gate, Eddie held him back as best as he could, not allowing him to rush the race until he rounded the first turn. At that point, he let him settle into stride. Freedom, a natural stretch runner, was two lengths ahead of the other colt by the time they had made one lap of the track. He never slowed down and in fact, picked up speed during the second lap, winning by more than four lengths.

Brock shook his head and grinned as he looked at Eddie. "He's got lots of energy, doesn't he?"

"You probably couldn't see how he started. He wouldn't let me hold him back. He wanted to get out there and stay out there, so that's the way we'll have to run him. He did the same thing last time we ran."

"Looks like he's just coming into his own, doesn't it," Brock said. "That's what this training is all about, you know – you find out what they like the best and then work with it. They get to know you too and what you'll let them get away with."

Eddie returned Freedom to the Paddock and together with Brock continued to run all twenty of the other stabled horses, two at a time, through the gates and onto the track. After running, they were returned to the paddock. When they had finished, they repeated the process so that each horse made two morning runs.

By noon the sun was out bright, and the skies resembled a beautiful cerulean blue piece of satin. Large puffs of white clouds decorated the sky like candy cotton balls. Grass was turning green now and the yellow daffodils that lined the lane from the main road to the ranch house were all in bloom. In the fields on either sides of the lane, large cherry and apple trees hung heavy with white blossoms that seemed to mimic the lace of a wedding dress. Marsha Gibbons stood on the porch of her home admiring the beauty of her surroundings, as she often did. She could see the horses out in the paddock and knew the routine enough to know they had been racing. She knew the crew would soon be hungry, and she was ready for them.

She walked back into the house, out the back door and toward the stable where she ran into Josh. "Josh, are you guys hungry yet?" she asked.

"Are we hungry? Now, Mom, you already know the answer to that. When is lunch ready?"

"It's on the table, just waiting for all of you," she said softly.

Josh put two fingers in his mouth, whistled as loudly as he could while Marsha held her hands over her ears. "My lands, son. You'll hurt my ears."

"It works though," he said with a grin.

"This is the best part of my day," Brock joked, catching up with Josh and Mrs. Gibbons. They headed toward the house.

"Mrs. Gibbons is the best cook this side of the Mississippi River." Brock hurried to be the first one in line to prove it.

Eddie Ellis called to the others working in the paddock. He joined them and headed to the house, close behind the others.

On the table in front of them sat sliced smoked ham, cheese and homemade bread for sandwiches. Noting the tureen filled with hot, creamed potato and bacon soup, Brock called to Josh, "You can just give me the whole tureen, I'll eat out of that; those guys don't need any."

"And I'll take the hot apple dumplings," Josh answered. "He doesn't need any dessert. He's big enough."

"That leaves the pecan pie for me," someone called.

In the mayhem, everyone laughed out loud.

The men had a choice of fresh lemonade or water to drink.

Just as the group sat down at the table, Hal Gibbons entered the back door. "Well, looks like my timing was just right," Hal said.

"I doubt that was by accident," Marsha Gibbons joked to Hal.

"You're too late, Dad," Josh called. "Everything is spoken for. We'll call you if there's anything left."

"Well, we'll see about that."

With smiles on their faces, everyone talked and mingled as they filled their plates.

*****

Doc Weide and Hal Gibbons watched as the two-year-olds rode up to the starting gates at the new racetrack in Lexington. Freedom, with Eddie Ellis in the saddle, trotted down the track toward the chute, seemingly oblivious to the rain falling softly on this April afternoon. Rain had been falling slowly, but steadily since yesterday and the track was muddy and appeared slippery. Brandywine took her place shortly after on the far side away from where Freedom was gated. Both Doc and Hal were pleased with the spots they drew.

"Well, it's been awhile since these two were in the same race," Hal said.

"Yeah, it has been. It's gonna be an interesting one, for sure," Doc answered. "We have a couple of great horses, but there are two or three others in here that have been turning heads too."

"Funny isn't it, how every owner feels that his horse might be a champion," Hal said.

"That's right. You have to think that way. It goes with this business, as you know." Doc answered. A short man, with a balding head, his thin, gray hair, wet from the rain, lay lacquered in strips across his head. A love of good food was evident by his pear-shaped waistline, which shook when he laughed heartily.

"How well I know! You have a pretty good idea of what you have within a year – whether you've a good horse or a great one. It doesn't take long for you to figure out if you've invested your money wisely," Hal said with a smile. "We gave your Brandywine a good start I think."

"Hell yes, you did," Doc replied. "She's had some good training since then too with her jockey, but this'll be her first time racing in the mud. I tell you though, she's a feisty thing. She still doesn't really like anyone on her back. I finally found a kid who wasn't afraid of her. The first day he tried to ride her, she tried to shake him off and she couldn't. That discouraged her I guess because she gave in after a while and now runs hard for him." Doc paused, and with a look of confidence, smiled and said, "Of course I hired him. He's doin' a great job. I expect next year he'll be riding her in the big races. That is if she does well the rest of this year."

"She ran for Eddie, but only after she threw him off once," Hal smiled and shook his head, remembering that day.

"Oh, I remember hearing about that," Doc chuckled. "She's gone a long way since then, and I hope she's got it all together today. If she wins this race, I'll be mighty proud. If she doesn't, then I'll reluctantly but gracefully, accept second to your Freedom."

"The same goes to you, Doc. If we lose, I hope it's to you."

All eyes were on the starting gates as the gun sounded and the gates flew open. "Come on girl, get out there," Doc yelled. "Don't go wide, don't go wide. Get over there."

Hal's eyes were on Freedom who seemed to falter slightly as he bound out of the starting gate. Just as quickly, he recovered his stance and didn't seem to let it slow him down. Eddie kept him to the right of the rail running in fourth place at the first turn and held him there at the turn onto the backstretch. On the turn, Paceforth caught up and into the backstretch the two of them took the lead, with Paceforth on the rail and Freedom on his left.

"I'm counting on you buddy. Stay out there, don't let up," Hal called. "Get him on the rail."

On the backstretch Freedom held his own, running neck-to-neck with Paceforth, who was still hugging the rail. Eddie knew he had to get Freedom on the rail if he was to win this race. Halfway down the backstretch, Eddie decided there was only one way to get there and it wasn't going to be easy. There was no way he could get on the other side of Paceforth except to go around him. It was risky. If he didn't make it back to the rail before the turn, chances were good he wouldn't get in at all. With all the force he had, he pushed Freedom to his limit. Like a streak of lightening, Freedom took off and came around Paceforth and moved in next to the rail.

Paceforth, was charging him, but there was no catching Freedom. He was two lengths ahead moving out of the turn. He kept the pace right up to the finish line. The crowd was buzzing loudly as Freedom passed the grandstand, realizing they were witnessing the run of a great horse. They cheered loudly as they would for a champion, and surely, Freedom was a champion today. As a long-shot, he made a lot of fans happy with his big payoff, but a big disappointment for those who had overlooked his capabilities. As he crossed the finish line in this mile and a quarter race, Freedom was three lengths ahead, setting a record of 2 minutes, 30 seconds. Brandywine finished third.

*****

Ellen remembered the lecture on how tough it would be working on the wards. She could still hear Mrs. Ramson's ominous voice. "When you're on the wards, you must be aware that it's going to be very, very tiring. Each one of you will be on your feet for twelve hours with just time out for bathroom breaks and your half hour of lunch or supper, depending on what you want to call it. It's hard to know what to call meal time when you're eating in the middle of the night shift. It'll often be frustrating as well. Be sure you eat well, don't skip any meals, and get all the sleep you can get. You'll need it. To be able to tend to sick people, you have to keep yourself healthy."

Of course she had been right. At the end of each long shift of standing and tending to patients, Ellen returned to her room with a tired back and aching feet. Still, it was part of caring for the sick, and the satisfaction of helping patients made it all worthwhile. For those patients who would recover, she tried hard to ease their healing periods and make them as comfortable as she could. Her co-worker, Nicole Bradford, looked as exhausted as Ellen felt this night. "Are you okay, Nicky," Ellen asked. "You look exhausted."

"I am, Ellen, in fact, I'm not feeling too good this evening."

"We can't afford to leave, you know, even if we feel bad."

"I know. I'll get through this, like it or not."

For those patients who weren't likely to survive, both young ladies helped to ease their pain, doing whatever they had the ability and strength to do. They consoled the families of sick and dying patients, feeling the pain of each and every one. As they cared for and assisted each patient, they learned. Each ill patient taught each girl something new. There were new diseases and illnesses and each patient was different in their diagnoses and healing. They welcomed it all and enveloped it like a gift of love. They listened eagerly to the doctor's diagnoses and treatment, which they knew would aid in caring for the patient. Some patients proved more challenging than others, for various reasons. One of the most difficult problems for Ellen so far was controlling her empathy for battered women, whom she could so closely identify with. It brought the memories of Sherm and Tabors Creek to mind.

On Ellen's first day in the Women's Ward, she entered the room of Lorene Witten who was the victim of an angry, drunken husband. Ellen learned that Lorene had been admitted two days earlier with a broken arm and ribs, along with wide spread bruising.

"How are you feeling today, honey?" Ellen asked, stroking Lorene's hair and moving it from her face.

"I guess I'm okay."

"Are you having much pain right now?

"Yes, a lot, through here." Her face grimaced in pain as she pointed to the area of her breast and ribs.

"Well, it'll take some time to heal. You were hit pretty hard."

"That's what they tell me. I can't say as I remember it though."

"In a few days you should be able to sit up and walk around some, but it's gonna hurt some still. You'll come through this though, I know."

"I hope so. I've got kids, you know."

"You just concentrate on getting better now and you'll be able to take care of your kids in time, don't worry. I just came in to give you a bath and get you into a clean gown. After that, we'll get you some clean sheets. You'll feel like a new person."

"That would be nice," Lorene answered.

Ellen continued to talk while she bathed Mrs. Witten. "What will you do when you leave here? Do you have a plan?" Ellen secretly hoped Mrs. Witten would be going anywhere except where her husband was.

"No. I 'spect I'll just have to go back to him. I've got two small youngins that I need to care for."

Ellen wanted to cry and to shout, *Run. Get your children and run wherever you can. Go anywhere, but don't go home.* Of course, giving any advice other than medical to a patient was forbidden. She gazed sadly at Mrs. Witten, hoping the lady could read her thoughts. The hell that went with living in fear of a man whose anger was unpredictable and uncontrollable was surely hell on earth. "Well, honey," she said, "Pray for some answers. They do come in time."

*****

Discipline was severe when rules were broken. Ellen knew she had to be cautious every minute of the day to avoid bringing any unwelcome attention to herself. She lived in fear that her personal life might be discovered, and give reason for expelling her from training. Her future as a registered nurse rested in her ability to adhere to all the rules and do whatever was right. She desperately wanted the career that was not only personally satisfying to her, but would open the door to a good job with an income to raise her family. And there was Bertie; she deserved so much more than she was getting. *I promise you, Mama, I'll make it here*, she thought.

Only yesterday Ellen's friend, Rita, had been called in by Mrs. Ramson and reprimanded for what was she interpreted as flirting with a man. Ellen had found Rita sitting at the small table in the Nurses Home dining room wiping her eyes.

"Rita, what's wrong?" she asked.

Rita raised her head and looked at Ellen. "Oh, Ellen, it was awful. All I did was stop and talk with the young man who brings our mail to the house," Rita had explained.

"Our house?"

"Yes, our place, our house."

"And what happened?" Ellen asked, showing her concern.

"Mrs. Ramson found out somehow and I got called to her office this morning just before I got off of work."

"Oh, no, I'm really sorry," Ellen said expressing her sympathy. "Who would have told her that, I wonder?"

"I don't know, but I was so frightened, my knees were weak. I thought I was going to faint when she started telling me why I was there."

"But she didn't expel you, did she?"

"No."

"Well, I'm glad to hear that. Are you alright now?"

"I'm okay, thanks," she said standing up. "I'm just thankful I'm not going to be sent home, and I'll not do it again. I just didn't know I couldn't talk to him," dabbing her eyes with a handkerchief. "I learned a lesson."

"No, I didn't know that either, and I'm sorry you were the one to find it out. Come on, let's have some breakfast, then you go to the house, get some rest, and I'll get off to work."

Ellen had learned something for which she was glad. She herself had on occasion stopped to chat when she saw the mailman. She already knew that undue familiarity with ward patients could bring a reprimand or even dismissal, but she hadn't given any thought to men like the mail man. However, she had been very careful to keep her patient contact as impersonal as possible, yet caring and friendly. Her thoughts strayed to Sherm. If ever he learned her whereabouts, she was certain he would either harm or kill her. If she survived him, it would be the end of her career. Like a dog trailing a fox in a hunt, he would always be looking for her, she was certain. Nearly two years had passed since she last saw him. One more year before she could stop worrying about him finding her at the hospital. *Dear God, what would I do if he found me*, she wondered. If only he could be found and put in jail, she could stop worrying. There would never be rest for her until he was either dead or behind bars. When she finished training, she would move the family to a new state, far away from where Sherm was. Her bedtime prayer tonight would be the same as always – to get her diploma and move away before Sherm found her.

*****

Summer was nearly over and Bertie was glad. Each day that passed drew her and the children closer to the time Ellen would return home. She had finished one year of her training in July. Now August of 1931 was here and the beginning of Ellen's second and last year before graduation. Bertie knew Ellen had spent many lonely days at school and her heart ached for her. Christmas and New Years had been the worst, but the summer break was somewhat harder with most of the other students gone to see their families. Ellen had volunteered at the hospital during those times too, which made the days go faster and allowed for additional training.

Tabors Creek

Bertie and the children were managing very well, but they all missed Ellen. The loneliness was made somewhat easier by faithful letter writing back and forth. In each letter Bertie reminded Ellen to destroy her mail after she finished reading. "Don't forget to burn this when you finish. No need to take a chance someone will read it," Bertie wrote time and again.

*****

Charlie had finished his first year in school and was about to begin second grade. Neet stayed at home during the day with Bertie, although she anxiously awaited the time when she too could go to school. On Sundays, Bertie and the children leisurely walked to church in the morning. At home in the afternoon Bertie cooked the children's favorite meal – fried chicken and mashed potatoes, with a vegetable, usually corn.

Today the heat was stifling , made worse by the dampness in the air. Rain had been sporadically falling for the past two days and didn't appear to show any signs of stopping yet. Bertie stood ironing for one of her "ladies," as she referred to her clientele. Ironing filled four or five of her days each week.

"Maw, I'm hot," Neet called, walking toward Bertie. Bertie turned to look at her then began to laugh aloud. Neet had stripped down to her underpants.

"You get your clothes on girl. Do you want somebody to see you like that?"

"There ain't nobody here, maw, just you and me."

"Well, what if someone comes to the door, child. Whacha' gonna' do then?"

"But, Maw."

"Do as I tell you child, right now," Bertie spoke in a tone of voice that Neet recognized as firm. She had learned not to push at this point. She quickly turned and headed to her room. Bertie stood laughing to herself. It was very hot, she knew, and she felt bad for the children. Fall couldn't come too soon for her.

A tap on the door leading from the kitchen to the upstairs startled her for a second. That door was never used since it led to the landlady, Mrs. Crossen's, place, and Bertie kept it locked so the kids didn't bother her. The stairs had been essential when it was a one-family home, but that was before it had been converted to a lower floor rental. She took the key from the nail on the wall above the door and unlocked it.

"Well, hi, Sally. How are you?" Bertie asked. Mrs. Crossen stood smiling.

"I'm pretty good. How about you?"

"Well, a little bit surprised – wasn't expecting anyone at that door. I guess I could always be better. Right now I'm a little tired and hot. Come on in."

"Oh, it is a stickler out there today, I'll tell you. And you a ironin'," Sally said, walking toward the kitchen table.

"Yeah, seems like all I do is iron. What brings you downstairs, and using the inside door? First time I think you've ever come this way."

"Well, I just wanted to ask you a favor."

"Sure, what is it?"

"I've been havin' a little trouble – not feelin' so good actually. Nothin' serious, but just thought maybe if you'd leave that door unlocked, just in case I'm needin' some assistance, you know," Sally Crossen explained.

"You know I will. What trouble you havin'?"

"Doctor says my heart's been workin' too hard for my own good. Beats so hard sometimes it scares me, 'specially at night."

"You just call me when you need me," Bertie assured her, taking note that Sally looked pale and her eyes carried heavy bags beneath them. "You've done me many favors keepin' the kids now and then. I always appreciate it, so it's good I can do somethin' for you."

"Thank you, Bertie. Now, how's Ellen doin'?"

"She's pretty lonesome, of course, but she's doin' okay. One year finished and one more to go and she'll be home. I'm countin' the months now. Be countin' the days before too many more months."

"She's got a lot of courage to do what she's doin', Bertie. I seen her with the kids many times and I'm sure she's a missin' them somethin' fierce."

"She is that, for sure."

Bertie walked to the table and moved a chair out from the table. "I need a little break. Have a seat, Sally."

"Think I will, Bertie."

Seated at the table, Bertie said, "You're the only one knows where Ellen is, Sally. You know that, don't you?"

"Yeah, I know. Don't you worry. I told you I won't tell a soul. We've talked about this before."

"I know we have, but it's always a worry. I'll sure be glad when she's finished. After she gets her trainin', they's nothin' they can do about it then, you know."

"Well, as I said, I sure do admire that girl. That's hard work and bein' away from you and the kids gotta be hard too."

"It'll all be worth it one day, you'll see."

I'm sure it will. I don't have any doubts. By the way, Bertie, what ever happened to Ellen's husband? I'm a guessin' she had a husband."

Bertie didn't answer, but looked at Sally.

Noticing the look of concern on Bertie's face, Sally quickly continued, "Maybe I shouldn't be guessin' that, huh?" she chuckled.

"Well, it's a long story, Sally. Yes, she did have a husband, but I'm gonna' have to wait awhile before I tell you the whole story. Wait'll Ellen's finished with her trainin', then I'll tell you."

"Oh, sure. I wasn't meanin' to be nosey, course."

Before Bertie could say more, Charlie came running inside. "Maw, I'm so hungry, I could eat a goat."

Bertie and Sally laughed out loud. "A goat?" Bertie asked. "With hair on it and maybe horns, and all that?"

"Maw, don't say that. I just mean I'm hungry," Charlie said, fidgeting with frustration.

"Well, then guess I won't fix a goat. How about some soup beans I got cookin'? Think you'd like that?"

"Ma, I didn't really mean a goat! You knowed that! Charlie said frustratingly. "I love beans though."

"I know, honey. Maw's just funnin' with you."

"Are you fixin' cornbread too?" he asked.

"You bet, cornbread too. Maybe Mrs. Crossen will eat with us."

"You don't need to feed me, Bertie."

"I know that, Sally, but we'd like your company, wouldn't we, Charlie?"

"Yes, ma'am," Charlie answered.

"Well, thank you. I'd love to, Bertie. Let me go up and feed my cat and I'll be right back down."

"Might as well take the inside stairs again." They both laughed aloud.

"Might as well I guess."

"I have two more pieces to iron," Bertie stated. "Then I'll get the cornbread in the oven, so no need to hurry."

*****

Perspiration poured from Ellen's brow. She wiped her forehead on her apron and continued peeling potatoes for the evening meal. This fall seemed much hotter than last year, but of course she wasn't working in the kitchen last year at this time. She tried to take her mind off the heat by thinking about Charlie and Neet. "I wonder what they're doing right now," she said aloud with a wide smile on her face.

"What is who doing?" the dietitian, Mrs. Phillips asked.

"Oh, I'm sorry. I was thinking about my little sister and brother and wondering about them. I didn't realize I was even talking out loud." She winced with fear inside, hoping Mrs. Phillips wasn't good at mind-reading. Better yet, she hoped her white lie was told with conviction.

"That's okay, but don't slow down on the potatoes. We've got 50 patients to feed tonight and a staff of almost that many. Any left-over potatoes will be used for breakfast, so they won't go to waste."

"I promise," she smiled.

"Okay. As soon as you finish that, you can get them on to cook and while they're on the stove, you can get a start on washing some of those pans over there," pointing to a sink full of pots and pans.

"Yes, ma'am," Ellen agreed.

Mrs. Phillips walked to the girls washing and preparing the vegetables. Ellen could see she was instructing them on how to do their jobs on this hot afternoon as well.

*****

Ellen's shift finished at 7:00 p.m. She hurried from the kitchen, hoping to escape from the dreadful heat inside. Her back and legs ached from standing on the hard floor for most of her shift. Outside the hospital, she headed alone to the Nurses' Home, walking slowly and enjoying the slight breeze that blew through her hair. The sun had set for the day and the sky was dark, although clear. She looked forward to sitting down for a few minutes, writing a letter home, taking her bath, and going to bed. She began to hum an old song her mother used to sing to her, *The Things A Little Girl Should Do*. As she sang aloud, she was unmindful of being afraid in the dark, as she so often was. "Pick up the dolly, pick up the books, fold up the blanket, and be my sweet, by golly."

Suddenly, Ellen's happy song was interrupted by a sound she heard coming from the area beside her house. She could hear the rustle of leaves and breaking of twigs underfoot. It took her pure willpower to keep from screaming. A feeling of dread filled her body – a flash of fire starting from the top of her head to her knees. She stopped, frozen. Her heart was pounding and felt like it would surely burst. She clutched her chest with both hands and quietly cried, "Sherm, oh my God, no, please." She waited for whatever it was to come from the shadows.

In only a second later, a small shadow began to appear from the direction of the noise. A young boy came around the corner house in her direction. "Oh, you scared me," Ellen cried.

"I'm sorry ma'am. I've been out lookin' for my dog that ran away in this direction. Have you seen a big, black dog?"

"No, I'm sorry, I haven't." Shaking, Ellen hurried inside.

In her room, she sat at the desk, her head in her hands and cried. She was sitting there when her roommate, Martha, walked in, having just finished her shift on the Men's Ward. "Oh, my gosh, honey. What's wrong?" She placed her arm around Ellen's shoulder. "Why, you're shakin' like a leaf, Ellen. What in the world happened?"

"Oh nothing, I'm sorry. I'll be okay. I just got scared when I saw a shadow beside the building."

"What was it?"

"Oh, it was just a young boy looking for his dog, but I didn't know what it was at first."

"Well, what did you think it was? Are you afraid of something, or just everything?" Martha looked puzzled but smiled regardless.

"No, no, nothing. I was just being foolish." Ellen's hair was wet with perspiration and her apron was filled with grime and dirt of the day. She looked a mess.

"It's a wonder you didn't scare the poor boy looking like you do." They both snickered as Martha pointed to Ellen's apron.

"Well, thanks a lot. You just wait; your turn to work in the kitchen is coming."

"I can hardly wait," Martha said, facetiously, rolling her eyes.

Ellen had learned to love Martha and wished she could tell her about her family. It might give her some needed strength. She thought she could probably trust her, but it would be taking a risk she couldn't afford to take.

"I'll fix us some tea," Martha offered. "Then I'll get my bath while you write your letter home. I'm sure your Mom loves hearing from you all the time."

"Thanks Martha. Yes, Mama loves to get letters and I love getting hers too." She had to leave out that part that said how much she needed to hear about the children. "Some day you'll get to meet my Mom. I hope she comes to graduation, but she probably won't be able to. It's pretty expensive, you know."

"It is really expensive, I know. I don't think my Mom will make it either," Martha said as she headed toward the bathroom.

*****

"I'll beat you this afternoon," Hal Gibbons said, half joking, to Doc Weide. The two men were running their favorites, Brandywine and Freedom, against each other in a match race at the Lexington racetrack later on in the afternoon.

"Just a matter of opinion," answered Hal. "What's your bet?"

"I'll take about $1,000. Can you match it?"

"Sure can. Wouldn't miss a chance to take your money. You're forgetting who trained her!" With both smiling, they shook hands, confirming their bet.

Seated at the grandstand table, waiting to order lunch, the men raised their glasses to toast the bet. "She's made about $45,000 already this year, in spite of losing the Derby," Doc said. "Adding your $1,000 with today's $10,000 purse, that would make it about $56,000." The two horses had finished seventh and eighth in the May Derby, disappointing both owners.

"Don't count your money too soon there, my friend," Hal joked. "They were pretty darned close in the Derby, even if they didn't win it. As for Freedom's income so far, I'd guess he's got about the same amount of winnings to his credit as Brandywine has. Have to ask Josh to know for sure. That's his job – he's the bookkeeper. He's got an eye for the best horses at the best prices too, as you know, I'm sure. He's a big asset to the business."

Doc nodded his head, soaking in what Hal had said.

"In case you didn't know already, your Brandywine would have been ours if you hadn't gotten there first. Josh had his eye on her too."

"So that's why you agreed to train her, huh? Wanted to see what you missed, did you?" Doc Weide asked. Both men smirked and Doc threw his hands in the air.

"You mentioned that Josh was good at choosing a good horse – I've heard that before, like you said, and that's something I wanted to talk to both of you about. There's a horse for sale at Johnson's Ranch over in Logan." Doc turned to see the waitress that walked up to their table. "Just bring me the waffles with chicken gravy, please."

"Yes, sir." She looked at Hal Gibbons, awaiting his order.

"That sounds good to me too," Hal said.

"Thank you. I'll be right back with your orders." Both men's eyes followed the attractive waitress as she walked away with their order.

"Anyway, as I was saying, there's a horse I'm interested in at Johnson's Ranch in Logan. I have two questions to ask you," Doc paused, looked around as if he didn't want anyone to hear what he was about to say. "First, if I get him, can you train him? He's just barely a two-year old so could run in the Derby next year if he's as good as I think he is. He's done well in a few short races, but I think he can do better. If anybody can get him going, it's your bunch. I'd like two in the race next year."

"Sure, we'll take him," Hal said. "What's your second question?"

"I'd like Josh to take a look at him, before I buy him, see what he thinks. Since he's a good judge, I'd go along with his opinion. If he thinks he's got what I think he does, I'll buy him." Doc Weide rested both arms on the rail in front of him and stared at the ground. He seemed lost in anticipation of something great.

"Sounds like you already have your mind made up," Hal joked.

"No, not necessarily, but I have a good feeling. If Josh could come down to Johnson's Ranch with me, say maybe next week, then if I buy the horse, he could just bring him straight back to Holiday with him."

"Sounds good to me. Josh will be here in a little bit. See what we can work out, but I think he can probably do that. See what he's got on his schedule."

*****

Josh watched as the horses entered into the starting gate. Brandywine had drawn position number three. Freedom was in chute number six. Breakaway, owned by Dave Thompson, was in Eddie Ellis' favorite number two chute. Because Thompson was still actively pushing the lawsuit against Holiday, Josh tried to avoid seeing him. He was glad Breakaway and Freedom weren't next to each other. Hopefully, Eddie could get Freedom next to the rail and out front early. He didn't trust Dave Thompson and hadn't known he'd entered this race until today. Luck wasn't with him right now, he guessed, especially since Breakaway had not only drawn the better chute, he was also the favorite. He hoped Freedom could hold his own in that crowded number six chute.

Knowing his slow out-of-the-gate pattern, Eddie knew that could put him too far behind the leading horses to find room to move out in front. It was a known fact among the owners and trainers - almost always, the horse on the inside stood a good chance of winning, if he or she kept the pace and stayed on the rail. Any horse that races all the way around on the outside of a one-mile track covers about an additional 64 feet, and a horse loses about one length (six to nine feet) for every path away from the rail, on a turn. A path was generally figured to be about three to four feet.

Eddie was the best jockey around, and he knew it. He knew his horse too. When Freedom got out of the gate, he had to get out of that middle and to the rail as soon as he could. If the other jockeys were as smart as Eddie, they wouldn't allow a hole to open up in front of Freedom. Still, that $3,000 Holiday had paid to enter was beginning to look like money wasted. Nothing he could do about it but pray right now.

*****

In the grandstand, Hal and Doc Weide had just finished lunch when they saw the horses being led to the starting gate. Jockey Eddie Ellis, riding Freedom, waved to the grandstand, knowing Hal Gibbons was seated there. "God damn it," Hal said. "I didn't want to see that number on him."

"Guess I lucked out a little bit, didn't I?" pointing to Brandywine wearing number three.

"Hell yes, you did, that is if Brandywine can move out and get near the railing before she hits the turn. A good chance she can." Standing up, they watched until each horse had taken their respective chutes.

"Well, good luck. If we don't take it, I'll be rooting for you," Doc said. They shook hands again.

"Good luck to you too."

As the last horse moved into the shoot, Josh arrived at the table. "Good luck to each of us," Josh announced.

"Oh, hi, Josh," Doc Weide said, turning to his side where Josh stood. Shaking his hand, "Good to see you again."

"Nice to see you too, Doc."

The grandstand was filled now and ladies in their bright colored fall dresses, many with matching hats, along with their decked out husbands, exuded the air with wealth. The scent of cigar smoke filled the area, along with the smell of barbequing beef. All of the tables were filled with both mixed drinks and glasses of wine. Mint juleps also dressed many tables, leftover habits of the Kentucky Derby.

With the sound of the starting gun, the horses were out of the chutes. As expected, Freedom fell slightly behind coming out of the gate and Breakaway was out in front. Right behind Breakaway, Singing Susan quickly moved up from the number one chute and the two were in a head-and-head duel for the early lead. "Get on out there Freedom," Josh yelled while Doc Weide yelled for Brandywine. Hal quietly watched with a concerned look on his face, wanting something exciting to happen before he began yelling.

Behind Breakaway and Singing Susan, Weekender quickly moved up and on the turn drew away to a one length lead. Only one other, Flying Fantasy, with jockey, Tom Papous possessed enough speed to be a threat to either Freedom or Brandywine. He was pretty certain he could take this race. "Come on Fantasy, let's do this damned thing. You got the speed and the drive. Let's do it." Tom stood and yelled as loudly as he could.

At the end of the turn, Brandywine, moved to the outside edge, and with incredible speed, took third position behind Weekender and Singing Susan. Breakaway took fourth position. Down the stretch, Eddie Ellis pushed Freedom, where he knew he could excel, and he did. Freedom pushed through the hole created by Weekender, and took his place beside Brandywine. Out in front, Weekender was now two lengths ahead of the pack and kept her lead through the stretch.

Into the beginning of the next turn, Eddie pushed Freedom to the rail, nudging Weekender for the coveted spot, but

Weekender's jockey held her tightly to the rail. By the end of the turn, Freedom, hugging his position behind Weekender moved to the outside with Eddie Ellis giving him the whip. "You can do this boy, get out there, get out there."

In the stretch, Eddie moved up tight on Freedom, and with constant pushing, moved into first place. "Come on guy, you can win this," he shouted. "Push it, push it," as he came down with the whip.

At the beginning of the final turn, Freedom was two lengths out in front, Weekender was in second place, Singing Susan was in third place and Breakaway a close fourth. But Brandywine was slowing down. Suddenly all eyes were on her. She began rapidly dropping behind the others. By the end of the race, it was Freedom by two and a half lengths and Brandywine was limping several lengths behind the others. It was evident something was very wrong. "Oh Christ," Doc Weide said.

*****

Maggie looked out the window and watched Sherm go about his still. She had come inside to get ready for work. When he had awakened her in the morning, she hurried through a bite of breakfast then helped him wash and ready his pots, pans, utensils, and any other items that had to be cleaned. There wasn't much time for sleep. Sherm had tired of taking her to work, so had bought her a bicycle, which she rode to and from work. When she finished her shift around midnight, the two mile ride home took her at least half an hour, depending on the weather. Before long, Maggie tired of the condescending treatment she was receiving. "Sherm," she said, "why are you doing this? Are you treating me like you do so that I'll leave? Is that it?"

"What the hell are you talking about Maggie? You know damn well that's not true. What would I do without you? I'd have no one to help, no one I could trust with anything and who would be doin' the cookin'?"

When winter came, Sherm would have to give Maggie a ride to work; not a pleasant thought. She knew he was producing a lot of his "juice" now, but she had no idea what quantity, nor the amount of money he was making. Where he kept it and how much he had saved was a mystery she hoped to solve one day. She knew better than to ask him. As she watched, he carefully lifted each glass-filled jug and replaced it with an empty one. He had spent most of the day on the hill chopping wood, replacing jars, carrying empty ones back to the work house for Maggie to clean, along with other daily chores. While she washed jugs and utensils, he would alternate his cooking and stirring the mixtures with collecting juice that was ready.

Sherm kept his two hired helpers busy all day, six days a week. Maggie watched as the two workers loaded the wagon full of jugs, covering them carefully with blankets, overlaid with planks of wood to disguise what was underneath. It was now August 1931 - a year since he began the operation here in Ashland.

After Sherm pushed a log further into the fire, he grabbed an empty, dirty pot off the ground and headed toward the house. Maggie turned to the sink and continued washing dishes, lest he catch her looking at him. "I need this pot washed," he called to her.

"I have to go to work, Sherm. It's already 2:00 o'clock and you know I have to be there no later than 3:00."

"You got time to do this one. I need it now." He spoke in a demanding tone of voice.

Maggie began to scrub the pot. When she finished, she turned to where he stood stirring. "Alright, here it is. I'm leaving now."

Sherm didn't respond, but picked up the pot and headed to the back yard.

Maggie watched as he broke into a coughing spell and had to hold onto a tree until he could compose himself. His face reddened and his eyes watered as he gasped for breath, but she knew in minutes he would light another cigarette. In disgust, she looked away, realizing for the first time she felt a bit of hatred. Sympathy she once had for Sherm was fading fast.

*****

Shortly after Maggie left, Sherm dismissed the hired help. When he was sure they were gone, he went to the back yard and took the tin box from under the ground, pulled out the money and papers, then went inside the house. At the table, he counted the money then wrote the amount on a piece of paper. "Damn, not bad," he said aloud. To that amount he then added what he expected to get this evening on his delivery to Sam at Windham. "It's time I buy me a car, by God. I've earned it," he said aloud to himself. He had enough now without taking any from what he'd placed in the box at the bank. Tomorrow he'd get the hired help busy with their jobs then he'd take off. He returned the money and papers to their place of safekeeping.

Back in the house, Sherm filled a wash pan with warm water, took it to the washstand and gave himself a rag bath. After that he shaved and changed clothes, then headed to town on the horse drawn wagon.

As soon as the wagon pulled into the back of the lounge, Sam was there to meet him. Darkness had set in, lessening the chances of being seen. Together with help from the lounge staff, Sherm unloaded the wagon as quickly as possible.

Inside Sam's office, Sherm took a seat on the other side of the desk. Sam pulled out a bundle of money from the desk drawer, and counted out fifty twenty-dollar bills. Sherm recounted the money then placed it in the inside pocket of the vest he wore. "I have a question, Sam," he said.

"Okay, ask it," Sam replied.

"How are you gettin' this "juice" down to Florida?"

"Oh, I got my ways – gotta' friend who flies it down. Why do you ask?"

"Just wonderin' that's all. Thought maybe if we deleted the middle man, we'd have a little more for ourselves."

"Can't do that, Sherm. It's a bit risky for one thing – and for two, it's a long way down there. We have no way to get it there."

"Well, why couldn't we get it there the same way your friend does?"

"Would be too risky, as I mentioned, and a variety of other reasons. I don't fly. You don't fly. Too far to drive. There's just no way. Don't go rockin' the boat now, Sherm," Sam warned. "I started this with this friend and I aim to stay with the friend." He paused, smiled facetiously at Sherm, "I'll keep running things." After waiting for a minute, he continued, "my way, I might add."

"Okay, I hear you, loud and clear. Just thought I'd ask. Guess it was a bad idea."

"No harm in askin'. Care for a drink?" Sam asked.

"Sure do, thanks."

Sam poured them each a drink and headed from the office to the bar. Sherm followed, his curiosity unsolved. Perhaps when he left this town, he'd drive to Florida, set up his own brandy-making operation right there. He'd cut them all out, Sam included. That wasn't too far in the future either, he decided.

At the bar, Sherm returned a smile to a curvy, red-headed and freckle-faced female seated next to him. "Haven't seen you here before," he said. He placed his hand around her shoulder.

"Waiting for you, honey," she purred.

*****

Josh was anxious to get moving – it was going to be a long and tiring day. He planned to drive to Doc's place in Ashland where he would spend the night. He and Doc would drive to Logan the following day. It was more than 100 miles to

Ashland and another 80 miles or more to Logan, so Hal had told him. Hal had made that trip many times in the past. Pulling the horse trailer behind him would of course make it slower than normal.

Doc had invited him to spend the night in Ashland, which was good. "Thanks, Doc." Josh said. "I'd really appreciate staying the night. I'll get a good night's rest that way before I start the drive to Logan."

On the return trip, he'd spend the night again at Doc's. It would be good to give the horse a rest too, providing Doc bought it. With Brandywine's injury, he felt certain he would. Even though it would be a long trip, Doc would pay him well for his time and for training the new mare.

"Come give me a hand with this trailer, Brock," Josh called to the horse trainer.

"Sure thing." Brock Fegan was a big man, stronger than Josh by half a man. "Think you'll be bringin' back a new one, huh?"

"Oh, I'd bet on it," Josh replied. "Thanks. Gotta get goin.'"

"Still think you oughta be takin' someone else along with you."

"Na, I'll be fine."

Good luck," Brock called. "Be anxious to see the new mare."

"What makes you think it's a mare?" Josh offered with a large grin.

"You said her name was Princess Angie, damned well better be a mare."

Both men began laughing at the same time until Josh answered. "Guess you're right."

Josh opened the car door, and sat down as Marsha Gibbons came rushing from the house to the car. "Here is some lunch, some water and snacks. Drive carefully," she warned as she offered the basket to Josh.

"Thanks, Mom. I'll be fine. Don't worry. See you in a few days." He waved as he pulled from the front of the barn, heading down the lane to the highway.

VIII

1931

Sherm rose early. Today he would buy a car and never again would he have to do the horse and wagon thing, not if he could help it. He didn't like the damned horses and hated having to feed them every day. Maggie could do that from now on, unless she wanted to let them starve. *I'll just tell her she has to do it*, he thought. They could stand out there till they rotted, so long as he didn't have to feed them. And that God damned Ellen – he'd still have a car if it weren't for her and her God damned mother. He hoped to kill them both some day. He also hoped that Ellen worried every minute of every day about the day he would find her. She'd wish to hell she'd never met him when he did find her.

Outside, he gathered all of his full jugs once again and replaced them with empties. He took all of the dirty pots and utensils, the empty jugs and rags inside the work house for Maggie to clean before she went to work.

Back outside, he looked for Elwood Maynard, one of his helpers, "Make sure you keep these fires goin' while I'm gone, you hear?" he instructed him.

"I understand."

"Just push the log into the fire as it burns down and it'll stay goin' alright."

Inside the house Sherm called to Maggie, "Get up. I gotta get goin' into town and you'll have to bring the horse and wagon back home."

"Where you goin' Sherm? I didn't get to bed until really late."

"I don't care what time you got to bed. I gotta' go, so get up."

"Why you goin' so early?"

"You ask too damned many question, woman. I'm buyin' a car today, that's where I'm goin'."

Maggie sat up quickly. "A car. You got the money for a car?" A look of both concern and surprise filled her face.

"Don't worry about what I got. Just get dressed and take me in town."

Maggie hurried to get ready.

*****

In town as soon as Sherm jumped off, Maggie turned the wagon around and headed home. There had been no conversation on the way into town about anything except when he reminded her to wash all the dirty items in the work house before she went to work. Maggie, realizing she was being used like a slave, she wandered how easy it might be to shoot him just like he had shot the agents. Sherm had disappointed her and hurt her feelings numerous times since she left Tabors Creek with him, but now she was angry. He'd have his new car, she thought, and she would still be either walking or riding a bicycle to work. It didn't seem fair, especially since she had given him all of her savings so that he could set himself up in this wretched business. "I'm fed up!" she said aloud. "I don't have to take this anymore and I won't." The more she thought about it, the more upset she became. By the time she had reached home, she was furious and crying.

After parking the wagon and putting the two horses in the barn, she tossed them some food and fresh water and went inside. "Where could he have his money hidden?" she said aloud. "It has to be here someplace."

She walked around the house until she had looked everywhere that she could guess he might have hidden it. The last time she checked the box under the bed, there was nothing in it that suggested money. She would look again anyway, even though he had warned her to leave it alone, telling her, "It's mine and mine alone." She hurried to the bed, kneeled and yanked the box out from under the bed. Her hands trembled with anger and trepidation as she lifted the lid. Inside the box lay a stack of notes and a small notebook, along with some pictures – one of his mother and others of ladies she didn't recognize. "Who the hell are these women?" she asked herself. Also in the box was a deck of playing cards with various pictures of sex scenes on one side and regular printing on the other. There was no money. Her hopes deflated, she started to put the box back, then picked it up again. She read aloud from one note. "Call me." A phone number was written below the message and signed by Eunice. Another note was similar and signed by another female. Inside the book were names of other females she didn't recognize, but knew they weren't names she'd heard in Tabors Creek. No, in fact, these were new since she had last looked. She felt defeated and used. She already knew she was a fool, but this doubly confirmed it. She hung her head and cried. Tears trickled down her cheeks, "Oh God, please help me; tell me I don't deserve this," she begged. On her knees, she lowered her head in her hands and began to cry with sobs that wracked her body. After a few minutes, she put the lid back on the box and placed it under the bed. She needed to walk.

Outside, she slowly strolled through the still operation in the back yard. Sherm had sent the helpers up in the woods to chop and stack wood. She could hear them sawing and faintly talking. She stopped after a few minutes, stared into the woods, and listened to the peaceful sounds of chirping birds. What to do, she wondered. There was no way to run, to go and hide where he couldn't find her. She couldn't go home to her parents, could she? He'd surely follow and kill her if she did. Alone and feeling desperate, she cried harder, sobbing aloud. "My God, what have I done?" She had no money left, and couldn't save any here. It all went to Sherm. As she stood begging for answers, she took notice that the one pot that she had placed on a grill over a fire pit this morning was now moved to the ground. She lifted it up wondering why he had moved it. Underneath she saw a sheet of tin. Curious to know what was underneath, she lifted it. There sat a metal box inside. She pulled it out and opened the lid. Inside the box, there were papers and only a small stack of one-dollar bills. She had found Sherm's hiding place, but there had to be more money than that. A key lay beside the cash, on top of some papers. She picked it up and looked at it, but not knowing what it was for, she laid it back down. Opening a piece of folded paper, she saw a receipt for a box at the bank. "A box," she said aloud. "What could that be for?" *The bank has boxes*? Suddenly, she realized. That's where he was hiding the money. He was putting it in the bank. *How clever of him*, she thought. She quickly folded the receipt and placed it back where it had been.

Maggie stood there wondering what to do next. *Wait*, she thought. *Wait and make a move when he isn't expecting it. Then take the money and run.* There wasn't much in there. Perhaps he had taken all he had put in there with him to buy the car. She closed the lid on the box and hurried into the house, leaving everything as she had found it. He would never know, not now. She had to plan carefully. An inner calm flooded her body for she finally had a plan. She began to sing as she got ready for work.

*****

Today was Ellen's first day in her newly assigned area, the Men's Ward. She had just completed a month of training with the dietitian in the hospital kitchen. Mrs. Ramson entered the kitchen shortly after Ellen's day had finished. "How did it go Ellen?" she asked.

"Pretty good, thank you Mrs. Ramson. It was important I know to learn how the kitchen operates, but I'm thankful I've completed that portion. I'm anxious to get back to caring for patients." Although she appreciated learning how patients' food was prepared and why certain foods were given to patients with various illnesses, she truly was thankful to be out of the kitchen. It was all very interesting and necessary to know, but long hours preparing the food had been exhausting. Standing at the sink, washing pots and pans was sometimes nearly unbearable. Worse than anything was the heat. This August had been nearly unbearable, especially in a hot kitchen. She did, however, get immense satisfaction when delivering food to the appreciative patients. Nevertheless, she was anxious to be back to what she loved, helping patients.

Mrs. Ramson was waiting for Ellen and three other student nurses when they arrived on the war for their first day. "Good morning girls. I'm glad to see you're all on time. I hope that continues. I'm sure you already know we don't tolerate tardiness. Of course, that's not only true for today, but every day you're here, on this ward or any other where you're working."

She stepped away and looked behind the girls as though she were expecting others.

Standing amid the other girls, Martha looked at Ellen, both of them nervous and excited in their new assignment. "I'm so glad we'll get to work together finally," Martha said.

"So am I. No oversleeping so that means no staying up late."

Mrs. Ramson continued. "There must be nurses covering the ward at all times. That means the nurses on duty during the previous shift must stay until you arrive before they're off duty; you should know that from working on your previous assignments. It's the same here - if you're late, they're going to be very unhappy with you." She paused for a second, then continued very ominously, "and so will I."

The nursing students followed Mrs. Ramson to the nurses' station, where she stopped and introduced each girl to the head nurse, Mrs. Deanna Warrell, seated at the desk. "Mrs. Warrell will be your guide and instructor. I'll leave you with her now. Remember, you'll learn a lot from her and from the physicians on the ward. Listening and paying attention will be your best friends." With that, she turned and walked away.

"Good morning, girls," Mrs. Warrell said. "It's nice to see your shiny, smiling faces. I can tell you're excited to learn, and I'm sure you'll all do a fine job. Each of you will be assisting the doctors on their rounds. They'll be teaching you how to treat wounds, cuts, incisions, help with the relief of suffering and the compassionate care of all the patients. Working on the ward is often the same routine over and over, but if you like people and nursing, your reward will be your patients' comfort. When the doctors are not on the ward, there is still a lot of work to do, much of it following the orders the doctor has left. You'll be bathing the patients, walking with some of them, freshening their individual water containers, and many other assigned duties. You'll get your instructions here at the nurse's station. Do you have any questions?"

Martha raised her hand. When Mrs. Warrell acknowledged her, she asked, "Is there an assignment waiting when we arrive in the ward or do we wait and speak with you?"

"Good question, Martha. It's always better to ask when you don't know, rather than go ahead and make errors. In nursing, there just isn't room for errors. Now, the answer to your question. You always get your instructions here at the desk. If I'm not here, another nurse-in-charge will be here and she'll have your assignments. When you finish a particular job, you come back here and get your next assignment. That way you know what to do and we know just where you are."

"Thank you," Martha answered.

"Another important factor you should know, if you don't already. You must always be professional, on duty or off. You are all young, attractive girls, and young men like young, attractive girls. You are on the men's ward and you're here to tend to them, nothing more. Sometimes a very sick patient may become too appreciative of his care and may confuse his gratefulness for infatuation – he might see you as the one who made him well again. There will be no fraternization with the male patients, none at all. This you must take very seriously.

"It might be tempting to react to young men who find you attractive, and they will, rest assured. You will always be polite, but in those instances, your response should never be more than a 'thank you.' Boundaries will be pushed but there is absolutely no dating while you're here. I know you already know that, but I'm reminding you again. You must stay professional and keep your conversations on a professional level. Do you understand this?"

Each girl replied "Yes, ma'am," in unison.

"Ellen, I didn't hear you. Do you understand?"

"Oh, yes, ma'am. I'm sorry." She put her hand to her throat. "Maybe I'm just a little hoarse this mornin'."

Actually, hoarse wasn't how she felt. Panicky would have better explained her feelings. The last thing she was interested in right now was dating. Getting through nurses training before her identity was discovered was her goal. The desire to be a good nurse was compelling her every move.

*****

On her first day in the men's ward, Ellen assisted Nurse Warrell in bathing several patients, changed their sheets, and took an exercise walk with one patient. When Doctor Olson arrived on the ward, Ellen accompanied him and the head nurse and two other student nurses in making his rounds. She watched as he changed a dressing on a patient who was recovering from an appendectomy, listened to him counseling a diabetic patient about diet, and assisted him in cleaning an open wound on this patient.

"Diabetics," he said to the patient, "have to be extra cautious not only in their diet, but also need to be extra careful not to injure themselves. An open wound on a diabetic patient is much more serious than on a non-diabetic." The patient, Timothy Corwell, had burned his foot severely when he dropped a hot branding iron on it as he took it off of the fire. "Do each of you understand this?"

Ellen replied with "yes, doctor, I understand. I know now."

To the patient, the doctor instructed, "the nurse will be back a little later with a soaking solution. I want you to soak your foot in that for about fifteen minutes. Then I want you to repeat that every two hours for the next couple of days, or until your foot begins to look better than it does now. We don't want you to lose your foot."

"Yes, sir. I will. I don't want to lose my foot either," he answered.

When the doctor left, Ellen followed his instructions, bringing Mr. Corwell a pan of treated water. When she had finished, she went from room to room with Martha as the two of them changed beds and helped patients throughout the ward. Ellen felt a great sense of accomplishment at the end of the shift, feeling as though she'd learned a lot today. Something she'd heard from Mrs. Ramson kept coming into her thoughts making her more sensitive to her patients' feelings. Mrs. Ramson had said, "Always keep in mind as you meet patients that any ill person, about to enter as a patient is frightened. The word 'patient' often carries the gloomy foreboding of a sentence, if not to death then to lengthy and depressing confinement. This dread is what often keeps sick people away from hospitals and doctors' offices until they're too sick to keep going. Some are very sick by the time they finally reach the hospital. This is one of the reasons we have varying degrees of patients' illnesses, on this and other wards. They depend on your actions and words to help them heal, physically and mentally." Ellen took to heart those words and knew they would be her guidance for years to come.

Walking back to their home, Ellen turned to Martha and asked, "How can you be sure when a patient is really hurting or just wanting attention?"

"I don't know for certain, but I'd guess that in time we'll know the difference. In the meantime, we just assume it's real. If it isn't, I'm sure the head nurse will know what to do. Anyway, we don't have to worry about that right now, do we?"

"No, you're right, Martha. You're always right," she said with a smile.

"Well, not always, but you know we were taught at the lectures that understanding our patients is a tribute to our intelligence and adaptability. Those are qualities a good nurse must have. You either have it or you don't, they said. If you do, you'll be able to read your patients. If you don't, you won't make it through the training. I have a feeling we have it, don't you think?"

They both laughed. "Of course we do. I'm hungry again. How about you?"

The girls entered their home and headed to the kitchen for a snack before they retired for the night.

*****

The sun was just beginning to set as Josh pulled into the drive that led to Doc Weide's house. Fortunately, the weather had been accommodating. No rain had fallen to cause pot holes and the truck had no breakdowns, for which he was grateful. He was glad to be finished driving. A nagging pain in his side had made him uncomfortable for at least half of the drive. He had stopped along the way to rest for a little bit and ate the lunch his mother had sent with him, hoping he would feel better after getting back on the road. That hadn't happened. In fact, he was feeling worse now than before.

Doc Weide's house sat at the top of a hill at the end of a long lane with acres of woods behind and a barn with stable in the back. Across from the stable, Doc had built a track where his jockey could run the horses. Josh liked this house; it reminded him of their home in Lexington. "Wow, nice," he said. Regal looking, it was a three-story brick home with three gables on the second floor, upstairs bedrooms on the front side of the house. In the center, on the third floor, just below the roof line, a fourth gable stood alone, obviously the attic. Chimneys rose like bookends at each side of the house, appearing to be holding up the structure. Doc heated with the fireplaces; Josh cherished the memories of times here with Hal and Doc's many other friends gathered around the fireplaces. Most interesting to Josh were the many kinds of wildlife that lived and roamed around the property. Doc was an avid photographer and loved taking and showing pictures, particularly those of the deer and turkeys.

Standing at the kitchen sink, Doc spotted Josh driving into the lane, pulling the horse trailer. He quickly dried his hands and left to greet him. "How you doin'?" he asked Josh, as he stepped out of the truck.

"Doin' just fine, but glad to get here. That's a long damn drive."

"How was the trip?"

"It was good, no truck problems, and as you can see, no rain. It's nice to be back here again," Josh said.

"Glad to have you back, Josh. It's been nearly a year, I guess."

Josh stood holding his side as he talked to Doc.

"What's the matter there?" Doc asked, pointing to Josh's side.

"Oh, nothing much. Just got a little ache in my side."

"Well, let's go in and have some supper. I'll bet you're starving. Maybe that'll fix you up. The missus has fixed a meal to die for, just cause you were comin.' I'm glad you're here finally. I'm starvin' too and she wouldn't let me eat until you got here."

"Golly, you didn't have to wait for me."

"It was her, I tell you. I wasn't so loyal. I wanted to eat an hour ago." Both men roared.

Inside the house Mrs. Weide greeted Josh. "It's good to see you again, Josh."

"I'm glad to be here Mrs. Weide. This is great country around here."

"I'll have supper up in about ten minutes now that you're here. Gives you time to go wash up before we eat."

"Thanks. I think I will," Josh answered and headed to the washroom.

*****

Josh went to bed early, but didn't sleep well. He awakened several times and paced the floor unable to sleep for the pain in his side. He decided to wait until after they had taken a look at the horse for sale before he told Doc how badly he was hurting. The wonderful aroma coming from the kitchen made him wish he felt better. When he had finished getting ready, he headed downstairs. Doc and Mrs. Weide were sitting at the table having a cup of coffee, obviously waiting for Josh.

"Good morning," Josh tried to sound enthusiastic.

"Good morning, Josh. How are you feeling?" Doc asked.

"Not too bad, but still a little tired from the drive. I'll be alright though. Sure smells good in here."

*****

At the Johnson Ranch, Josh and Doc headed to the paddock where Princess Angie was out for exercise. "That's her over there," Doc said.

Josh saw the mare standing very regal on the other side of the paddock from where they stood. "What a beauty," Josh said, watching as Princess Angie raised her head high and quickly headed to where they stood, stopping in front of them.

"Think she knows what we're here for?" Doc asked.

"You'd think so, wouldn't you?" They both laughed out loud. "It's uncanny the way she pranced right up to us. What's her history?"

"She was trained by Sam Booker at Booker Farms, but she was sired by a little known stud," Doc said. "She belongs to Omar Henderson, and I don't think he realizes what he has. Because she's not sired by a famous stud, he thinks she's not capable. He made it known to a friend that he just wants his money out of her while he can get it. I personally think she's a sleeper."

'What makes you think that?"

"My jockey, Jack Ellis, says she's the greatest sprinting mare he has ever seen. Omar raced her only once. In that race, the jockey, Tommy Burdem, lost his whip at the top of the stretch and gave this as the reason for her defeat. Omar mistakenly, I think, scoffed at that, saying that was just an excuse. He fired the jockey and put Princess Angie up for sale."

"What was her time, do you know?"

"Going in at 110 in a six furlong route, she came in second at 1:09 3/5. Just think what she'd have done if the jockey hadn't lost his whip."

"I think you've figured this out as well as I could have, Doc. I'd say buy her if you want. If you don't, however, I will."

"That's all I needed to hear, Josh. She's gonna' be mine. I'd have bought her even if Brandywine were still in there racing. I'm planning to use Brandywine for breeding, and I need another good runner. Who knows, one of these days I may stand Princess Angie for breeding too. Hell, I might even go into the business."

Josh grinned. "Probably not a bad idea. Sure sorry to hear Brandywine won't be racing again. That's really too bad," Josh said.

"That's the chance you take, you know."

"Yes, I do know. You remember Thumbalina."

"All too well, I remember, Josh. Such a pity. She was a great horse."

"She was more than great. She was a winner all the way."

"Still, you got a prize winner with Freedom, I'd say, wouldn't you?" Doc asked.

"Absolutely. Next year I'm planning on winning the big races with him. You sure you want to run anything against him?" he joked.

"Did you ever hear of a dead heat?"

"You think so, huh? Well, all joking aside, Doc. We'll train her to be the best, you know that?

"Of course, I know that. I wouldn't be standing here with you if I didn't. Besides, you'll be running Freedom next year. I'll be looking at the following year. She'll be just barely a two-year old in May without enough experience. She probably couldn't qualify that quickly anyway."

"That's true. She wouldn't, I'm sure," Josh answered.

"Wait here, Josh if you will," Doc said. "I want to go in the office and put in my offer. See when I can pick her up," Doc said.

As Doc Weide headed to the office, Josh took a seat on a bench under a nearby tree. The pain in his right side encompassed his entire stomach. In fact, he wasn't quite sure where the pain was coming from anymore. He knew one thing for certain - he'd have to tell Doc as soon as he could.

*****

Inside, Doc filled out the paperwork for intent to buy. "I'll plan on picking her up tomorrow morning, if that suits. Okay?"

"Yes, sir Doc, that's fine. We'll have everything ready for you," the accountant at the counter answered. "About what time do you think you'll be here?"

Hearing some commotion, the accountant glanced out the window before Doc could answer. "Looks like somebody needs you out there, Doc. Some guy looks pretty sick," he spoke as he moved closer to the window to have a look.

Doc turned toward the window and saw Josh doubled over in a fetal position on the ground. He rushed out the door, as he placed the paper he carried in his shirt pocket. "My God, what's the matter, Josh?" he asked.

"Something in my stomach's got me, Doc."

Kneeling down beside him, Doc felt for Josh's pulse, felt his head for fever and looked in his eyes. "You're hotter than a firecracker, son. We're just minutes away from the hospital though. Can you hang in there till I get my car and get you to the hospital?"

"Okay," Josh answered, grimacing in pain.

A gentleman standing nearby turned to Doc. "You know him?"

"I do. He's with me. I'm a doctor. Stay with him until I get my car and I'll take him to the hospital. Looks like a bad appendix." Doc ran to where his car was parked.

Tabors Creek

*****

At Logan Hospital, Josh was rushed into surgery with Doc Weide assisting the resident surgeon. He lay on the operating table waiting for the surgery to begin with Doc standing beside him. Through a window in the background Josh could see the surgeon in a green, two-piece surgery outfit scrubbing his hands and arms. Although he felt some apprehension, the pain was so great, he was anxious for the doctor to help him, even if it meant surgery.

"Looks like you got a bad appendix, Josh," Doc said. "Gotta get it outta there before it bursts and makes a mess for us."

"That's what I hear. Don't know what spot hurts the most; it hurts all over." Josh looked at Doc Weide for some sign of encouragement. "Tell me it'll go away soon, Doc, okay?"

"We'll get some ether to you in a second and you can sleep for a little bit, give us a chance to do our job, and you can get some relief," Doc assured him.

"Sure hope so. Never had anything quite like this before."

"No doubt about it, son. Don't worry though, you'll be up and about in no time at all. You're in good hands." Doc patted him lightly on the arm. The surgeon nodded to the anesthetist to place the mask on Josh's face.

The last thing Josh remembered was the sound of the ether being turned on.

*****

Hours following the surgery, Josh opened his eyes to find he was lying on his back in bed, in a strange room. It took a minute or two to realize where he was. "Oh God, I hurt," he said aloud.

Nurse Warrell was standing at the head of his bed with the student nurses at her side. "You're in Logan Hospital, Mr.

Gibbons. Your appendix had ruptured and you've been a pretty sick guy."

"I hurt," Josh repeated.

"I'm sure you do. Your appendix had ruptured. Too bad you didn't get some help sooner than you did. However, it could have been a lot worse than it was. I'm sure that's not any consolation right now though, is it?"

"Not much," Josh answered.

"Each day you'll feel better than the day before. In a week or so, you should be just fine. In the meantime, I promise you we'll take good care of you."

Josh looked up at Mrs. Warrell and the student nurses standing behind her. He tried to smile, but there wasn't one in him. He was comforted somewhat by the ladies' smiling faces.

"Now that you're awake, I'll give you something for pain. That's what your doctor ordered – as soon as you awakened," she said. "I imagine you'd like that now, wouldn't you?"

"I sure would."

The young student nurses laughed aloud.

Six white, metal beds filled the room, three at each side. Lined up foot to foot and headboards against the wall, there was a narrow path down the center between the feet of the beds. Their half-moon shaped headboards, made of metal tubing, backed against the wall, created a fan-like pattern, a subtle reminder of the inescapable heat of the day. Each bed was divided by a two-panel, folding screen covered with white gauze-like material gathered on curtain rods in the center of each one. A stand with empty pitchers stood at the end of the room. Josh was in one of the end beds nearest the door. The other beds were presently empty.

Mrs. Warrell turned to the nurses and motioned for them to come forward toward the bed. "Ladies," she said, pointing to the chart, "Note here, the doctor has ordered a shot of pain medication for Mr. Gibbons." The student nurses struggled as they attempted to read and decipher the poorly written chart notes.

"I know, I know. Sometimes the doctors' writing is atrocious, but in time you'll become excellent at deciphering their notes. Never did understand how doctors can be so smart and yet not be able to write." She smiled at the girls trying to read what was written.

"Ellen, you're standing closest to the foot of the bed. Please unfold that blanket there," she said, pointing to a white blanket folded and laying across the foot of the bed. "Pull it up part way over Mr. Gibbons. It's going to get warm today, but slightly cool in here right now."

Ellen opened the blanket and pulled it up till it covered about half the bed. She couldn't help but notice that Josh was a handsome young man with dark, curly hair. He looked ruggedly strong and tall. His eyes were closed, as she began to pull the blanket up. He looked to see who she was and she could feel her face flush as she met his gaze. Embarrassed and feeling uneasy, she quickly moved away and forced herself to stare at Mrs. Warrell. "That's fine," Mrs. Warrell said. "If you get too warm, let us know and we'll take it off. Okay, Mr. Gibbons?"

"Yes, ma'am." Josh said.

"Seems like there are a lot of nurses in here," Josh said quietly, glancing slowly to his side.

"Just enough to take care of you, Mr. Gibbons. I'll be your nurse during the day shift and these student nurses will be assisting. Right now they're going to watch me give you something for your pain." The students watched as Nurse Warrell gave the shot to Josh. She then placed a pillow under his head. "Now get some rest and we'll be back later. You can push the buzzer if you need anything before we return."

"Thank you," Ellen heard him say as they exited his room. She was thankful to move to the next room. She was irritated with herself, knowing the rules of nursing didn't allow for personal feelings. Tomorrow she wouldn't look at him at all, she vowed. She didn't dare.

*****

With his pocket full of money, Sherm walked into the car dealer office, ready to purchase a car. He knew exactly which one he wanted. He had seen it parked in the garage next to the office. "How much you want for that Pontiac you got out there?" he asked, pointing to the garage.

"Let's walk out and have a look." Sherm followed the salesman to the garage.

"I like the looks of that one," Sherm said, pointing to the Pontiac Big Six sedan with red spoked wheels.

"Just got that one in last week, brand new out of Pontiac, Michigan," the salesman replied. "Has a powerful engine created by Lovejoy, hydraulic shock absorbers, easy to steer, and gears that shift smoothly and quietly. It's the Pontiac Big Six. This one is a sedan with lots of room if you have a big family."

"I got no family, just me, but I need lots of room," Sherm replied with a grin, thinking how much easier it would be to deliver his goods in this car than in the wagon. "How much?"

"Well, it was $850, but we've got it marked down today to $745," the salesman offered.

"Yeah, marked down, my ass," Sherm mumbled quietly.

"Pardon me, I didn't hear you."

"I said, I like this car and I'll take it."

*****

Sherm's already powerful ego was doubled with the purchase of his new car. He drove around the small town going up and down the few streets, waving to anyone he saw on the street. From there he drove to the Windham Lounge. Inside, he talked with Sam at the bar. "Hey, Sherm. What brings you out so early in the day?"

"Just got me a car – no more damned horses and wagon."

"Oh, good deal! What kind? I suppose it's a Ford."

"Nope. Got me a Pontiac Six, sedan, lots of room."

"Great. How about a drink to celebrate?"

"A good idea. One drink then I'll head home – got some things to deliver this evenin'."

Sam looked around to insure no one was listening. "I'll be here all evening. How many you got?"

"Well, I got some fine jugs of brandy this time. Got ten of them and I should have that many more tomorrow."

"Just what I need. They're chompin' at the bit for it," Sam replied.

Sam walked to assist another customer at the bar. In the meantime, Sherm emptied his glass, stood up and walked toward the door, waving to Sam as he exited. With tonight's delivery, he was one step closer to where he wanted to be, but there were still some bridges to cross before he could leave this town. He needed more money and he desperately wanted to find Ellen and Bertie. That would always be his number two priority, right after making money. He might even be able to get back some of the money they stole. He'd get the car too if they still had it. Sell it and keep the money. "You son-of-a-bitchin' Bertie, I'll get you, you'll see."

*****

Two weeks passed after surgery before Josh was up and walking, though very slowly. On the arm of student nurse, Martha Pickard, and holding a small pillow in front of his stomach, he made his way from the bed to the nurses' station, then headed back to his room. "Where are you running off to?" Doc asked, as he came walking toward them.

"Hi, Doc," Josh said, raising his head to see Doc coming down the hall. "I'm not off to anyplace very far, just getting a little exercise. Nice to see you."

"Good to see you, Josh. Glad you're able to be up walking around. That's a good sign." He stood back and took a picture of Josh and Martha, just as Ellen was walking out of a room in front of the other student nurses. "Great. I got a picture of all of you. Your mother asked me to get a couple for her since she can't be here."

"Well, Mom knows you're quite the photographer, but today wasn't a good day for pictures," Josh said. "I know I look like hell because that's how I feel. You just might have broken your camera." Josh held the pillow in front of his stomach and tried not to laugh.

Doc just grinned. "You did that to yourself. I didn't."

Josh walked slowly back to bed. In the hall Mrs. Warrell gave instructions to the two student nurses, sending them in different directions. She sent Ellen to fold towels in the linen room. Ellen was glad to be away from Josh's room. Earlier in the day she had gone in to collect dirty linen and replace towels. Fortunately, he had been sleeping. She had hurried out of the room as fast as she could. She would be glad when he left. If she couldn't see him, she could get him out of her thoughts. Just a week ago, he was a complete stranger and today he occupied a place where he couldn't belong.

When she finished with folding towels, she was given mail to distribute to patients. She paused for a second before she entered Josh's room with a piece of mail attempting to mask her feelings. "Here you are, Mr. Gibbons," she said, handing him an envelope. Quickly, she turned and walked out without glancing at Josh.

"Thank you Miss." Josh paused. "I don't even know your name, even though I've seen you every day for the past four days."

Ellen stopped and glanced toward Josh. "You are welcome, Mr. Gibbons. My name is Miss Potter." She turned toward the door, hoping he didn't reply.

"May I call you by your first name?"

"You can just call me Miss Potter, if you will please." She quickly exited the door without looking back at him. He could never know how her heart raced at the sight of him, nor that she wanted to know everything about him. It would be her secret and she would have to keep her distance at all costs.

*****

Back in her room at the end of the evening, Ellen relaxed in the chair with a cup of tea. Her roommate, Martha, entered the room carrying a cup of tea and a plate of cookies from the kitchen. She offered Ellen a cookie, then took a seat in another chair next to the radio. Guy Lombardo and His Royal Canadians were playing *You're Driving Me Crazy, What Did I Do To You?* "That's pretty appropriate, don't you think?" Martha asked.

"I don't know what you mean. Why do you say that?" Ellen asked, looking very serious.

"Oh, I was just thinking about our patient Mr. Gibbons. Have you noticed what you're doing to him?"

"What I'm doing? I haven't done anything to him."

"Ellen, wake up. He can't keep his eyes off of you, it's so obvious. Like the song says, I think you're driving him crazy." She rolled her eyes and looked away.

"Oh, Martha, that's silly. I don't think so. You've got to be wrong. Besides, you know the rules. We're not allowed to let that happen. It just can't." With her hands shaking and her heart racing, Ellen picked up her cup of tea and took a drink.

"I know. I know, but we can't control what he thinks, now can we? And look at you shaking," Martha joked. "He is really handsome though, don't you think?"

"I don't know. I haven't noticed."

Martha smiled. "Ellen, I'm your friend, remember. You can be honest with me. You know I don't believe you for a minute."

"Even if I want to think he is, I can't. He's our patient and it has to stay that way. You know that, Martha."

"Yes, I know, so what are you going to do?"

"Do? About what? Right now I'm going to get my bath and go to bed. That's enough of this conversation." Ellen stood up from her chair and headed out of the room. "Goodnight Martha." She looked back at her and smiled as she headed toward the common bathroom. "We'll not have any more conversations like this until after graduation next May."

*****

It was now the fall of 1931 and the town of Tabors Creek had nearly forgotten the shooting of the Federal Agents. Two years had passed with no sign of Sherm Peck. He seemed to have disappeared completely. The town had settled back to the normal routine of a small farming and mining community. Times were hard, money was scarce, and folks focused on raising families. Summers were for growing food, canning or curing meats and vegetables for the long winter months ahead. Entertainment, for the most part, wasn't much more than a ride into town on Saturday with the family, shopping at the General Store, or the occasional town meeting. The town bar was open, but there was no sign of alcohol. Rumor had it that alcohol was available, but no one talked about it. It was hidden out of sight and only locals that could be trusted were served. Moonshine stills were working too, but that was another subject never mentioned. Sitting at his desk, Sheriff Workman called across the room to John Bell. "John, you know it's been two years now – where do you suppose Sherm got to?"

"You know I can't even guess. He could be most anywhere I suppose. He'll never show up here though. You can be sure of that!"

Sheriff Workman suspected there might be a couple of illegal stills operating in the area, but he played ignorant of them. He would continue to unless forced by a complaint or a bust. He stayed busy with the usual – the family feuds, thefts that occurred when folks got bored or hungry, and other cases, some serious, some trivial. Then there was Ellen; he still longed to find her. He knew if Sherm found her first, he wouldn't hesitate to shoot her. Therefore, finding Sherm was just as crucial now as it was two years ago. Ellen had been the Sheriff's first love and the longing for her had never left him. "Hang in there Ellen; I'll find the bastard and you'll never have to worry again." If only he had pursued her harder before she met Sherm, he might have her today, but she had tired of the long evenings alone while he worked all day and many evenings. She hadn't believed he'd ever marry her. He didn't see it coming until it was too late. With Sherm out of the way now, dead or alive, there could still be a chance. Where to look though was a mystery. Lexington was a big city.

"I'm headed out to Maggie Sellers' place, Jon," Sheriff Workman said to his deputy as he walked toward the door.

"What's out there?"

"Well, I'm not sure. I just want to have a look. I haven't been out that way for more than a year, and the last time I was out there, the place was quiet, looked deserted to me. You remember Maggie Sellers used to live out there?"

"Yeah, I do," Deputy Sheriff John Bell answered.

"I just thought I'd run by that place. It's been ages since I last saw her. She used to come into town now and again."

"I don't get it. What are you thinking? Why do you care?"

"Like I said, I'm not sure. I just have a suspicion about her. I've had it for some time now – should have done something sooner."

"About what – I'm still not following you."

"Her and Sherm Peck," Sheriff Workman said.

"What? Sherm Peck!" Bell practically yelled. "Good God. Do you really think so?"

"I don't know. I'm just thinking now, understand? Never see her any more. It's been over a year since I've seen her in town. I was by there once if you remember, a while back. I asked Tom at the store the other day if he'd seen her and he said she hadn't been there in ages. Anyway, it's worth havin' a look at. If she's not there and if it looks like she's not been there, then I'm gonna be real suspicious."

"Well, what made you put them two together?"

"Oh, I don't know. Just two and two, I guess. She's a widow and I've seen her talkin' to him in the store and over at the bar too a few times. He's on the run and she's the only one I can think of that I've not seen about town. I think she liked him alright – just might have wanted to help him. He hadda go somewhere for help – why not her, huh? Know what I mean?"

"I guess so. How long's it been since you were out there?"

"I went out to Sherm's place back about March of last year, I think it was. I remember it was cold and there was snow on the ground. In fact, it was snowin' the day I went there. And, it had snowed pretty heavy the week before. When I passed Maggie's place, I noticed there wasn't any tracks in the snow down the lane, so nobody had come out of there – or gone in, obviously. And strangely enough, there wasn't any horses out in the field – just no sign of anyone. At the time I made a mental note to check that out at some point, but I just never did. I was thinking about it today and since I haven't seen her, I think it's a good idea to go have a look."

"I think you're right. Jesus! I can't imagine she'd be tied up with him, but strange things happen every day. Never thought Sherm would kill a man in cold blood either, but he did – two of them."

*****

Sheriff Workman headed up the lane to Maggie's house. He noted, like before, there were no horses around. He knew she had horses – they were her only transportation. The hot summer sun had scorched the grass to a burnt umber color. The long, thin blades leaned on their side, too burned, heavy, and tired to stand up any longer. Obviously, it hadn't been cut all summer. An old, rusted plough sat in the field at the entrance to the narrow, dirt lane. Sheriff Workman recalled it had been in that same spot over a year ago. The tin roofed, two-story frame house, once painted white, sat in disrepair with bare wooden spots and flakes of paint hanging loosely from the front and sides of the house; it had been like that for as long as he could remember. "Damn, that house needs somebody's attention before it falls down," he said to no one, since there was no one to listen.

The barn behind the house was closed up, even on this hot fall day. The Sheriff assumed there would be nothing alive in there today even if there had been.

He rode his horse up to the house and tied it to a railing. He looked around the front yard and across the covered porch, which ran the length of the front of the narrow house. It had been some time before anyone had swept anything. Burnt, brown, and dried leaves had blown onto the porch and filled the front doorway. A swing hanging by a single chain, one end in the air, the other touching the floor, was partially filled with leaves as well. Sheriff Workman knocked on the door and waited. When no one answered, he tried the front door, which surprisingly was unlocked. He stuck his head inside and called, but as he suspected, no one answered. He walked inside and called again. "Anybody home? Hello! Maggie – are you here," he called. It was obvious no one was there nor had been there for some time.

Dust filled the kitchen table. On the counter lay an oily rag tied to the end of a long, thin stick resembling a flag of surrender, and a partial pack of cigarette papers. He had never seen Maggie smoking and suspected they might be Sherm's. He presumed the rag had been used to clean and oil a gun barrel. He walked to the bedroom where he found a pair of men's pants laying across the bed. Holding them up, he could see there were rips and snags in them. They had to be Sherm's, most likely torn when he was escaping through the woods. Sheriff felt certain now – Sherm had gotten a change of clothes here, cleaned up his wounds and he and Maggie had left town. *Why the hell didn't I check this out before*? he thought.

Back in the office, Sheriff Workman put out a wire to the federal investigators and to all police stations in the surrounding states notifying them of his findings. It might be easier to look for Maggie rather than Sherm.

*****

Josh had mixed emotions about going home today. His incision had healed completely and although still a bit weak, he felt pretty good. For this he was thankful. He was anxious to get home and back to work and begin the slow process of rebuilding his strength. However, the thought of leaving the hospital reminded him that he was also leaving his chances of getting to know Ellen better. Her presence in his room each day was like awakening to sunlight coming through a window. She was beautiful in her white collared blouse and blue and white striped uniform, her brown curls glistening around her face. There was something electrical that happened the first time he saw her. *How beautiful she is*, he thought. He thought of lightening striking when he remembered her walking into his room. She was so graceful; almost as if she were floating in and out. Soon that would end for Doc would be here within the hour to pick him up.

Mrs. Warrell, accompanied by Ellen, and Martha, entered Josh's room with last minute instructions for him. "I'm so happy to see you feeling better, Mr. Gibbons," Mrs. Warrell said. "I'm sure we'll miss seeing your smiling face here, but we're still glad you're well."

"Thank you, Mrs. Warrell. I'll miss this group too," he said, glancing at Ellen, hoping he might find an unspoken response in her gaze. When his eyes met hers, she was staring at him. He hoped he read what he wanted to hear in her stare. He wanted to know she was feeling what he was - like he had just leaped from the top of a mountain into a soft, spongy cloud, even if there wasn't such a thing.

"Well, we'll leave you now and wish you the very best, Mr. Gibbons. Although we would all like to see you again, we'd rather see you stay healthy," Mrs. Warrell said. "Miss Potter will get you some fresh water one more time before you leave us." She pointed to the pitcher on the bedside stand and nodded to Ellen. She and Martha went in one direction while Ellen picked up the pitcher and went in the other direction to fill it. Josh knew he had to tell her something – anything he could think of – it was either now or not at all. The idea that she could rebuff him gave him an ominous feeling, but he had to do it.

When Ellen returned to the room, Josh asked, "When do you finish your training, Miss Potter?"

"I graduate next May."

"Then what will you do?"

"I'll go back to Lexington." The sound of her own voice seemed to be coming from someone else. She was making every attempt to hold a short, professional conversation without emotion, even though her heart was pounding against her chest and her face felt on fire. She hoped he couldn't see on the outside what she was feeling inside.

"I didn't know you were from Lexington. That's where I live too."

"It's a very nice place." She turned to look at Josh, her heart still racing. His eyes were on her – he was staring straight at her. Although not teasing, they were nevertheless unnerving to her already crumpling frame. Could he see the way her blouse was moving with the beat of her heart? *Be calm. Be reserved. He isn't special. Stop being childish.* She needed to be polite and yet quickly get out of the room before she said the wrong thing. "It's been nice knowing you, Mr. Gibbons. I hope you continue to feel better," she said.

"Please don't go yet. I want to ask you something."

Oh no, please don't ask me something I can't answer, she thought. Ellen waited for just a couple of seconds that seemed like hours before he continued. "Can I see you again?" he asked.

"Mr. Gibbons, I am here to go to school, nothing more. Student nurses are not allowed to have dates nor have conversations such as this one."

"I'm sorry," Josh continued. "I just find you fascinating and want to get to know you. May I write to you?"

She never answered. There was nothing she could say. *No* wasn't the answer, not to this man she didn't want to resist, but one she had to stay away from. For so many reasons, she had to ignore him, but yet be polite. There was nothing more to say. She turned and left the room before she could answer.

*****

Maggie had already left for work when Sherm arrived home in his new Pontiac. He parked behind the house. No need to chance anyone seeing it. The car and the neighborhood didn't match, much like salt and sugar. No need to bring attention to himself and his operation. Not that there were many residents in the area, but it could only take one. He stepped outside the car, strutted around it, front to back on both sides, smiling broadly.

Satisfied that he'd done a good thing, he headed inside to check his brew. Stirring a pot of syrup and still smiling, he spoke to himself. "God, I can't wait to get in my car and get outta this place. It's comin'. It's a comin'. If I make it through the winter, it's a comin. Gotta work harder this winter on finding the bitches though."

The searing pain in his belly caused Sherm to mix up a little baking soda and some water. With one hand on his stomach and the other holding the glass, he drank it in one guzzle. "Goddamn this gut." He leaned forward for a minute allowing time for the mixture to settle, then headed up to the wooded area where his two helpers were cutting and stripping trees to make fire logs. As he walked through the woods to where they worked, he noted the leaves had begun to change colors to golds, yellows and some orange hues. "Christ, already," he mumbled. "Gonna' get colder 'n hell pretty soon."

Reaching the men, Sherm said, "How's it going?"

"Okay," Elwood Maynard said. "This damned wood is hard, but that new saw you got works pretty good."

"We need that soft wood more'n anything else. We need some of the hard wood too, but the softer wood burns faster and we use more. Then when you get the logs down to the work area, I want them stacked like always – the hard wood on one pile and the soft on another. Make about half of them short, about half the size of the others. The long ones should be about half the size of the tree, depending on how tall the tree is."

"No problem. We'll bring them down tomorrow, using the horse to pull them."

Pointing to the standing trees, Sherm asked, "You see these damned trees, don't you?"

The men looked up, obviously confused.

"Look at the leaves on them. They're turning color already. Give 'em a couple more weeks and they'll be no more green. You know how damned hard it'll be to cut and haul trees after it gets cold? Even worse when the snow starts to fall – colder than hell then."

"Yeah, you're right, Sherm," Elwood said.

"Okay then, let's get goin' here and get as many as we can during the next two weeks."

"You bet," he answered. Sherm turned to go inside the house.

Inside, he busied himself with readying jugs in which to put his apple brandy. Peach brandy had nearly finished running and much of it had been bottled and sold. He still had a lot to bottle, cap, and deliver tonight. The stills had been started with some of the apple mixture. Apple pomace had been made weeks before. Sherm and his helpers had beaten the apples, mostly Golden Delicious, after which they ground them to make the pomace. They had scalded them, left the mixture to ferment or turn sour, which had taken much of a week. To each 55-gallon barrel Sherm had added 25 pounds of sugar and one peck of rye meal. When he used the more sour apples, extra sugar, up to 50 pounds, was used. Each morning after that he had stirred the mixture and allowed it to sit until it stopped foaming and cleared up. That's when he began to run it through the still. For every 55-gallon barrel, he would get 10 to 11 gallons of brandy.

Tomorrow he should be able to start bottling some of the apple brandy. This evening while there was still some daylight hours remaining, he hurried outside to bottle and cap the peach brandy and start more of the apple mixture. He had a delivery to make. When he had loaded the jugs into his car, he covered them carefully and went to the still area. There he walked around the yard and pushed logs under the stills, all of them now running his apple brandy, and returned to the inside.

*****

Sherm washed his face and hands, changed shirts, and combed his hair. In his new car, he headed to see Sam Rivets at the Windham. After arriving, he parked the car behind the bar and began to walk to the front when Sam came out the back door. "Hey, Sherm," he said. "I saw your car, thought that was you. Pretty good lookin' car that is."

"Thanks. I like it. Got somebody to help me with some juice?"

Sam sent out a couple of helpers who quickly unloaded the car. Sherm went to the bar.

Sam placed a drink in front of him, and quietly laid an envelope beside him. "Here you are, Sherm. Best apple juice in town," he said.

"You're damn right it is." He placed the envelope of money in his pocket.

A well-known face at the bar, Ida Mae Larson, had watched Sherm enter the bar and take a seat. Looking for some excitement, she walked up behind him, brushing against him as she passed by. "Hello, honey, how are you?"

Sherm turned to look. The tall, attractive blond with crimson lips, caused Sherm to sit upright, look her up and down from head to toe, while his body twitched with desire for the leggy female. "Sit down, right here," he said, pointing to the seat beside him. "I'll get you a drink."

"Don't mind if I do. I see you in here quite regular. You from around here?"

"I am now."

"What kind of job you got?"

"Well, I work for a company that makes juice."

"Juice," Ida Mae said. She looked at Sherm and rolled her eyes. "What kind of juice?"

"Oh, they're just fruit juices."

Sherm kept Ida Mae beside him by buying her another drink. In a short time, her hands wandered across his shoulders and she cozied up to him as closely as she could.

"Let's take off from here," he said.

"You have a car, huh?"

"Why don't we go look?"

Sam watched as the two of them moved toward the front door. "Get too warm in here Sherm?" he asked. Both men laughed, each aware of Sherm's motive. Sherm waved as he left the Windham.

Later in the car with Ida Mae, Sherm drove to a hidden area where he parked the car. "What do you say we break in the back seat?" He ran his hands under the blouse she wore and across her breasts.

She quickly opened the car door and moved to the back seat. With the temperature dropping, they quickly finished what they were there for before it got too chilly. "You're good, Sherm," Ida Mae said. "The best I've seen; we need to do this more often."

"I'm a plannin' on bein' here again tomorrow evenin', how about you."

"Of course, wouldn't miss it."

*****

Before fall had officially ended, cold weather had arrived. Worse yet, if predictions were correct, it was going to be one of the harshest winters in many years. Josh threw a log on the fire in the office fireplace, in a building next to the stable, and sat down at his desk. He tried to concentrate on the present, but his mind kept drifting away. He realized he had read the same thing three times or more. He stood and walked back to the fireplace. *Where was she today,* he wondered. *Would she be waiting for me to write? Was there another man in her life? What to do? I'm going to write to her.* Looking out the window, he watched as the snow fell. "It's cold as Hell in here," he said aloud.

Reaching no decisions, he returned to his desk. He read the last three months' trial times for their Kentucky Derby hopeful, Freedom. Freedom had accomplished everything Josh had hoped for, and more. He had won all of his races but two over the past year and those losses were explainable. On the last loss, Jockey Eddie Ellis had held him back in Frankfort for two reasons. Dave Thompson was running their biggest rival, Black 'N Blue, in the race with Freedom. Neither Hal nor Eddie wanted Thompson to see what power Freedom had, what he was capable of, nor his style of running. Thompson still carried a grudge against Hal Gibbons and Holiday Farms and they didn't trust him, on or off the track. Even though he had settled the lawsuit out of court, deep down, Hal knew the fight would never really be over. Earlier in the day Hal spoke to Eddie, "you know Eddie, even though the lawsuit was settled with Thompson, I still don't trust the son of a bitch. So if you can hold Freedom back, do it. I don't want him to see what Freedom has." .He had also told the same thing to Josh and warned them to beware. Eddie had suggested intentionally running Freedom on the outside track where he knew Freedom would slow down. Hal agreed and Eddie ran him there, knowing he'd lose the race. He also knew that's where Thompson would tip his jockey to look for him in the Derby, on the outside.

Freedom's other loss had been near the beginning of his racing and was a learning experience for Eddie Ellis. He had tried, based on Freedom's remarkable speed, running him from the middle of the pack to the outside and then push for the front, which proved to be a bad move. Freedom seemed to have lost his confidence on the outside and slowed down. In the next race, he kept him to the inside where he found his niche. He followed the same procedure in his succeeding runs. "Having that railing to his left is like a baby with a pacifier. He seems to want it for himself, like a security blanket," he told Hal. "I think maybe he thinks he owns it."

"Good job, Eddie. Keep him there. You know him
better'n anybody else. I trust
your call." They shook hands.

"Thanks, Hal. I'll do my best."

Josh walked from his office to the heated stable where Freedom stood. Standing next to him, he ran his hand over the side of Freedom's face. "You're the best, no doubt about it, big buddy. You're gonna' make us all proud, I can feel it."

Freedom seemed to sense Josh's approval. He lay his head on Josh's shoulder, his eyes focused on Josh's face.

"So what are you saying there, huh?" Josh asked. Freedom nuzzled closer to Josh's face. Josh hugged him. "For that, you get a treat," he smiled. "How about a hot bath?"

He knew he should be ecstatic – Freedom had a good chance of winning the Derby in May. The truth was, he couldn't keep his thoughts focused on today, nor yesterday for that matter. His mind kept wandering back to his hospital stay, and Ellen. Three months had passed since he left the hospital. He had tortured himself since then with thoughts of her. Today, perhaps because of the cold weather and the thought of more to come, his mood was in a downward spiral.

He daydreamed of having her beside him, of holding her in his arms, of kissing her, of riding horseback through the fields with her. He dreamed of them stopping to rest under one of the big chestnut trees and holding one another, hungry for each other's lips. They would end the ride with a picnic lunch on a blanket under a shade tree in a secluded spot, then he would make love to her if she was willing.

Thinking then of the hopelessness of it, Josh felt defeated, like he'd been punched in the stomach. With his hands holding his head, he looked out across the field, trying desperately to figure a way to either see her or get it out of his head.

"Hey, son, what are you doing out here?" Hal Gibbons walked up to Josh.

"Oh, hi Dad, nothing, nothing. I just came out to check up on Freedom. I needed to walk a little bit – been sitting at the desk too long."

"What are you thinking about?" Hal asked.

"Oh, not much, I was going over the training runs – looking at Freedom's results. They're pretty damned good, don't you think?"

"Hell, yes. I think they're even better than we expected. That's not my concern right now though. I want to know what the hell is wrong with you. You've been moping around since you got home from the hospital. That's at least three months now. Are you sure you feel okay?"

"I feel fine, Dad."

"Then what the hell is it? Tell me."

"It's pretty ridiculous, Dad. I don't think you would understand," Josh answered.

"Try me. I can tell it's personal and you know, I was your age once too."

"Okay. Well, here's how it is. When I was in Logan at the hospital, I met a student nurse who came into my room nearly every day. She was beautiful, Dad."

"Nothing wrong with that, son."

"No, but I tried talking with her and she wasn't allowed to talk to patients, except about their pain, or get their water, make their bed, or whatever."

"Did you try to see her later?" Hal asked.

"I talked just briefly, but she wasn't allowed to discuss anything. She just said that she wasn't allowed to date while she was a student."

"Did you ask her when she finished training?"

"I did. She finishes in May. I found out it's the week after the Derby. She couldn't talk about it though."

"How about writing to her?"

"I asked her on the morning I was leaving if I could write to her and she didn't answer me," Josh said.

"Well hell, you don't need permission to write – so write her and get it out of your system. That way you'll know. Don't ask questions. Tell her what you're thinking. See what happens,"

Hal advised. "You know that old saying, 'Nothing beats a trial but a failure.' I heard that years ago from my mother."

Josh was all smiles, obviously pleased that his Dad had understood.

"One more thing, Josh," Hal continued. "Let me tell you a story. It's something your mother and I have kept to ourselves, but we were planning to tell you when the time was right. I think it's time. It might help you make up your mind."

"Oh, yeah?" Josh said, grinning at his father.

"You know that your mother and I originally lived in Frankfort – that was before you came along."

"Yes, I knew that," Josh said.

"Well, we moved here for several reasons, but the main reason was to get away from the people of Frankfort who knew us and knew about us. Your mother and I met when we were in grade school. I think I had a school-kid crush on her from the first time I saw her. After high school, she went away to college. I never forgot her, but she didn't know me very well when she left."

"I never knew that," Josh said.

"No, I know you didn't. Let me finish. When she came home, after she graduated, I was working at a nearby horse ranch. She came there to inquire about riding lessons. I did various jobs at the ranch, but most of the time I was a riding instructor. Fortunately for me, she enrolled in my class. Well, we fell in love and became the classic case of the poor boy who falls in love with the rich girl and the parents want it to end. They never thought I was good enough for her."

"Why have I never heard this story before?" Josh asked. "My grandparents never told me either."

"No, they wouldn't I'm sure. They had a reason for not telling you. We didn't tell you out of respect for them." Hal nervously rubbed his hands together, careful to choose the correct words he wanted to say.

"Anyway, when they realized we were seeing a lot of each other, they insisted your mother stay away from me. She tried, and we didn't see each other for months. In the meantime, she began to date a man her family had chosen for her. He was a wealthy man from a very wealthy family and she was beautiful, as she still is. He knew she didn't love him and he could see her slipping away from him. In order to keep her, he forced himself on her and she became pregnant."

"Oh, my God," Josh said. "What happened to that child?"

"Just a minute and I'll tell you," Hal said. "It's not a nice story, but I think it's probably easier on your mother if I tell you, rather than her."

"When she learned she was pregnant, she came to me crying. She didn't want to marry him. I told her we could run away and get married, but it would mean giving up her inheritance. She didn't want any inheritance. She only wanted what I did – for us to be together. We left the next day, came here to Lexington, got married at the Court House where no one knew either one of us. It didn't matter to me that she was pregnant. I would have loved the child as if it were my own. She had left a note for her parents telling them that she was leaving and would be in touch in a couple of days. She did reach them, but when she did, it was too late for them to annul our wedding."

"Good Heavens, Dad. That must have been awful."

"It was sad for us both, but it was also the happiest day of our lives when we said, 'I do.' I still feel the same way, son. It wasn't a mistake. My mistake would have been if I had let her go."

Josh walked to Hal and hugged him. "Thanks, Dad. What about the baby?"

"She lost it a month later. It just wasn't meant to be, that's all."

"What ever happened to the other guy?" Josh asked.

"It was Dave Thompson."

"What?" Josh yelled. "Oh my God."

*****

Leaving work, Ellen once again headed back to the Nurses' Home, her shift over for the day. *Christmas Eve*, she thought, *and I'm here and they're back home.* With her eyes focused on the path in front of her, she pretended she was walking toward her front door at home in Lexington. Neet and Charlie would greet her at the door. "Mommy! Mommy!" Charlie would say, while Neet would just be there to greet her with both arms outstretched, a face full of smile, anxious to be hugged. How wonderful that would be! If only she were doing just that. Her heart ached to be home with her mother and children this Christmas, but the cost of taking the train home was an expense she couldn't afford. She wasn't totally alone, however. She kept repeating that to herself to help kill the loneliness. There were several student nurses who stayed for the same reason. They would get together and comfort each other, she supposed. Walking up the steps to her home, she hoped none of them were there just now. Her feet ached and she wanted some time alone. Later, she could decorate the Christmas tree in the living room of the Nurses' Home and make it feel somewhat like Christmas.

Inside her room, Ellen sat down to rest for a few minutes. Looking down at her clothing, she ran her hand over the edge of her striped pinafore; the plainness of it reflected the emptiness she felt at this moment. She both loved and hated it at the same time. If only she could run her hands through her little Charlie's hair and hold him close. She longed to listen to Neet struggle so hard to read to her, tell her she missed her. The tears began to fall onto her lap as she stared down at nothing. Bertie had written to her offering to send her the money, but Ellen had declined. It was an expense they could do without. Even if she went home, leaving again would be too hard on her and the children. Only five months to go and she would go home forever, a small price to pay in order to give her children a better life. And Bertie, who asked for nothing, had earned and deserved so much more than what she was getting. "Give me a little time, Mama," she had written. "I promise to make it all up to you just as soon as I get home. I owe you the moon and stars for all you've done for me." However, for now she would make the best of it, just as she had so many times in the past. She would be diligent in her drive to make their lives better.

There were many mistakes she'd made that she regretted, but that was in the past now. The world was full of mistakes, which she used as justification for the past and as a building block of prevention for the future. Even as lonesome as it was, there had been worse times.

Ellen knew she had to shake off this feeling before she spiraled downward too far. *It's Christmas,* she thought. *Be happy! It could be so much worse.* She remembered the Christmas from hell some years ago - a night when Charlie was a baby and before Neet was born. Sherm had come home drunk just after she had finished decorating the Christmas tree. He had knocked the stovepipe off of the stove and black soot had filled the room, ruining the tree. Fortunately, there had been no fire in the potbellied stove at the time. She was heating their small house with a portable gas-fired stove because she had run out of wood. He later passed out in the bed and slept while she took the decorations off of the tree, washed those she could salvage, and threw the tree outside into the backyard. But that was over! She didn't want to think about him, not now, not ever, if only she could make it stop.

Ellen's thoughts drifted off to Josh. She fantasized that they met at the end of the day. He was anxious to see her. She opened a Christmas gift he had bought for her. It was wrapped in beautiful red and white striped paper, with a matching red bow tied at the center. She pictured him standing in the jewelry store agonizing over which bracelet she would like, the gold or the silver one. He had chosen the silver one telling the clerk, "This is for the girl I love." Even better yet, she saw a beautiful diamond ring that he was putting on her finger.

Realizing how juvenile she was acting, she spoke aloud, "Stop it, silly." She stood up and got out the last letter she had received from Bertie. Seeing the children's scribbles and pictures they drew on a page cheered her for the moment. *Ridiculous anyway*, she thought, *daydreaming over something that couldn't and wouldn't happen.* She was what she was. In her own eyes, she felt as a frail, skinny young woman, with pallid skin, eyes that were too large for her face, hair that was too curly, and lips that were strangely shaped. They reminded her of the arched shape of butterfly wings, too high and too narrow. She laughed out loud as she thought of that.

She continued to read the letter she held in her hands. "Your divorce is finally settled now," Bertie wrote. That was good news. Even though she was sure she would remain single, at least for as long as it took to raise her children, and probably forever, it felt good knowing he was legally out of her life. She had the love of her children and her mother, and that would suffice.

Ellen was thankful Martha wasn't in the room. She was good at reading her thoughts, which had to remain unspoken, even with her best friend.

In the kitchen, Ellen found a student nurse, Mary, stirring a pot of vegetable soup on the stove. "Oh, that smells wonderful," Ellen said.

"Well, I figured since we have to be here for the holidays, we might as well eat something good, don't you think?"

"I sure do," Ellen answered.

"Are you hungry?" Mary asked.

"I am starving. I ate at noontime, but I never got supper. We were really busy this afternoon and I never got a break.

We're really short-handed, as you know. I'm thankful to be busy though."

"I made enough for all of us," Mary said. "Mrs. Ramson gave me permission to get vegetables and a small piece of beef from the kitchen. I think she probably felt sorry for us having to stay here while everyone else went home. I think there are five girls who stayed."

"Yeah, I believe you're right," Ellen said.

Mary pulled several bowls from the cabinet. "Wait for about half an hour and we'll have soup,"

"Thank you. I'd love some. While it's cooking, I think I'll pull out those Christmas decorations from the closet and maybe start to decorate some."

"That's a great idea. I'll help you."

The two girls pulled out a box they found in the closet, which was marked, XMAS. First they took out some garland, which they draped over the fireplace mantle. They placed some small figurines of Santa and his elves in front of the garland. There were three hooks in the stone wall behind the mantle. The girls laughed aloud when they found three stockings in the box. "Looks like the hooks were left up for a reason," Ellen said.

"For three reasons," Mary said, holding the three stockings. They both grinned.

When they finished, they stood back and admired their work. "It isn't much, but it'll do just fine for this year," Mary said.

"It's beautiful. Thanks, Mary."

"Oh, you're welcome." she said. "Come on. Let's eat." She touched Ellen on the shoulder.

*****

The pot of soup stayed on the stove for the girls as they came in to eat. Mary and Ellen cleaned up the kitchen and when they finished Mary announced she was tired and sleepy. She headed for the hall and her bedroom. "I'll see you tomorrow," she said.

"Yes, tomorrow," Ellen answered. "We five stragglers are all working the day shift so we'll be there with the patients who don't want to be here any more than we do. Maybe we'll be good for each other."

"I'm sure we will. Merry Christmas, Ellen, and thank you for the nice evening. It helped a lot."

"Merry Christmas, Mary."

The other girls ate and went directly to their rooms. Ellen was left alone. She reached for the switch to turn out the light when she remembered she hadn't checked her mailbox. She walked to the entry where a shelf, which consisted of numerous slots, hung on the wall. Each nurse had an assigned slot and her name was taped to the bottom of her particular mailbox. She found her own and was pleasantly surprised to find two letters waiting for her. One was from Bertie and the other had no return address on it. Although she was curious, she decided to open it later. She placed the mail on her nightstand and headed for her bath.

Back in her room, and ready for bed in her flannel nightgown and socks on her feet, Ellen sat down in the rocking chair in front of the fireplace. The warm fire felt wonderful on this cold evening. Although very tired, she was excited and anxious to read both of her letters before she crawled in bed. She read Bertie's letter first. Just as she expected and hoped, everything was going well. Neet was reading much better with each passing day. Both she and Charlie asked about her often.

"I read aloud the most recent letter from you to them, once in the morning and again in the evening before they go to sleep until a new letter arrives. I start all over then with the new letter until the next one comes," Bertie wrote. The children, she said, had begun to check the mail themselves in the evening to see if there was a new letter from her. "They are counting the days, honey, until you come home, so please know they miss and love you," Bertie wrote.

Ellen folded the letter and returned it to the envelope. Her lithe body filled with tenderness for her loved ones, which flooded the depression that was fighting to emerge. She smiled, reached for a pillow from her bed and held it close. She closed her eyes and rocked, all the while pretending that she was rocking her son to sleep. She began to sing a lullaby that she had sung to him many times. "Rock-a-Bye Baby, on the Tree Top, When the wind blows, The cradle will rock....."

*****

At 1:00 a.m. Ellen awakened from a dream to find herself still in the rocking chair. The fireplace had cooled to a few red embers and her arms were chilled. For just a minute she sat trying to recall her dream, but most of it was gone, except that she had been at home with her family. Bertie was baking cookies and the house smelled wonderful. A gentleman sat at the table and applauded each time a tray came from the oven, someone special, but she couldn't remember whom. When she stood up, he walked toward her, arms outstretched, just as she awakened. Perhaps when she went back to bed, she could bring back the dream until she was finished. *Doubtfully*, she decided, but worth a try.

Rising from her chair, Ellen realized, "Oh, it's Christmas morning." Crossing her arms, she rubbed them with her hands in a wasted effort to warm herself. Out of habit, she walked to the window and looked outside. Snowflakes appearing as large as quarters fell heavily under the lamplight at the end of the pathway leading to their home. "Oh how beautiful," she cried aloud. She stayed there admiring and enjoying the beauty of the falling snow while wondering if it was snowing at home as well. The kids would be up in a few hours and anxious to see what Santa had brought. She longed to be there. Bertie had made a Christmas for them, "nothing elaborate," she had written, but they would be happy.

Glancing at the clock, she shook her head, knowing how foolish she'd been to sit in the chair and fall asleep. It was now 1:15 a.m. and she was wide awake. Tomorrow would be a busy day and she needed to get her rest. Still, time spent looking at the beautiful scene out the window was worth the loss of sleep, *just this once*, she told herself. *After all, it's Christmas.* After second thoughts, she scolded herself, "Get to bed, get to bed." Pushing away from the window she headed to her bed.

With her left hand pulling back the covers and her right knee on the bed, she reached to shut off the lamp, when she saw the envelope laying on the stand. "Oh, I almost forgot," she said aloud. She opened it quickly, anxious to see who it was from. She pulled the letter from the envelope. In a hand-written note, it began, "Dear Ellen," and she gave a sudden gasp of delight, for what reason, she didn't know. Perhaps it was a subconscious wish for a Christmas gift - a surprise for herself. Or *it could be from Josh*, but no, he wouldn't be writing to her. He surely hadn't remembered. Whatever it was, it was excitingly addressed to her personally. She quickly looked at the end of the letter on the second page to see who had written it. It was signed, "Lovingly, Josh Gibbons."

"Josh Gibbons, oh my gosh," she cried, completely surprised.

With the letter in her trembling hand, she stepped back on the floor and moved to the rocking chair. "Dear Ellen, I'm sure you'll be surprised to hear from me," he wrote. Her heart stood still, she was certain. She couldn't believe she had just read his name on a letter addressed to her. She checked the signature again to be sure. It truly was from him. She poured over the rest of the letter slowly, wanting to savor every line of it, hoping he wrote what she wanted to hear, what she had day-dreamed about. "It seems so long since I last saw you, but I have thought so much about you since that time. I scarcely know where to begin or what to write, but I will do my best." By the time she reached the second page, tears were streaming down her face. In spite of everything, it was going to be a Merry Christmas for her too. She read and re-read the last paragraph. "I am hoping that you will understand me and know that I am sincere in my thoughts of you. I will continue to write to you, knowing that you probably are not able to do the same. However, I can wait. All I ask of you is that if you choose not to receive my letters, send just one short note and tell me so, if you are able to do that. Otherwise, I will be there to meet you on your graduation day. I pray that we can get to know each other better then. Until that time, you will remain in my thoughts and prayers for you." He had added his address at the bottom of the page. Suddenly, she was thankful Martha was working the night shift. How could she have explained this?

Could this be happening to her? She wiped the tears from her face on her sleeve. Was it too much to hope for? So much of her life had felt so sad. Now to think that the one person who made her heart sing, the one who made her tremble to think about, just might feel the same way about her was hard to believe. He was a horse trainer on a ranch, he had written. *A horse trainer wasn't a rich man, was he?* she asked herself. She had so little. No wealthy man would find a girl like her attractive. She hugged the letter to her chest, picturing him next to her. Maybe, just maybe, there could be a chance. An indescribable thrill filled her being. *How will I ever sleep tonight? I can't think straight*, she thought. Perhaps the answers would come later. For now, she didn't need to do anything, couldn't do anything. She just needed to try and sleep.

Sitting in the window again, watching the snow, she read the letter over again and again before she finally went to bed. Lying in bed she made the decision to say nothing to him. She would wait to see if he came to her graduation. Perhaps he wouldn't. If he didn't, there would be no problems, just disappointment, which she had learned to accept. If he came, she would have to tell him her background. That would be very difficult, but necessary. In the meantime, this fantasy would help carry her through lonely times. It would make the next five months bearable. She heard the clock on the mantle strike 3:00 o'clock before she finally went to sleep.

IX

1932

Christmas came and went. Sherm ignored it as just another day. Wind and cold weather ushered in January of 1932. Snow drifts were piled as high as the windows in Sherm's back yard. "This god damned weather isn't for shit," Sherm said to no one. He had spent the morning shoveling a path to his car and around the stills. Even wearing heavy coat and gloves, he was still cold. His work was outside though, like it or not. He shook his hands in a wasted effort, partly just a subconscious move and partly disgust at the cold air. The wind blew viciously as he moved from one fire pit to another, where he changed the logs from the soft wood to the hard hickory for the daylight hours.

It had snowed all night long and the roads were impossible to drive on. His two helpers hadn't showed up, nor did he expect they could. If they got the damned roads cleared, maybe they'd make it yet today. Sometimes he wished he just made room for them in the small shed out back, but that arrangement would take away his private time; he needed that too. He picked up the shovel and began again to clear pathways around the stills. He had three running now and Sam was taking brandy and "juice" as fast as he could produce it. For this he was very happy, as his savings were accumulating even faster than he'd dreamed. In fact, at this rate, there would be no reason he'd have to stay after summer arrived. Feds would be this way looking one of these days. They were sure to find his operation some time or other, but he planned to be gone by then. *Let them find the God damned empty bastards,* he thought. *Maggie can take the heat if she hangs around.* Then there'd be no more of this God damned weather, not where he'd go.

Sherm walked inside to where Maggie stood washing some of the returned jugs he brought home to refill. That too was one of his hated chores, so he gave Maggie that job. "You ain't got them finished yet?" Sherm asked.

"I just started them, Sherm. It's only 9:00 o'clock in the mornin'. Remember I worked until midnight. I have to get some rest, you know. I had a hell of a time getting home in that snow. She looked at him with a look of disgust.

"You can rest when I get these things delivered. I can't drive in this weather so I have to take the God damned horse and wagon."

"How am I supposed to get to work, Sherm?"

"You can't even ride bicycle in this shit. I'll deliver early and come back home and you can have it then, I reckon. No way in hell I'm comin' to pick you up at midnight. Guess I'll have to stay home this evenin'."

"I would think you have plenty to do here anyway, don't you?" Maggie asked sarcastically.

"I don't think that's any of your god damned business, do you?"

"Sherm, how would you like me to talk to you like that?"

Maggie was looking down into the tub where she washed the pans when the back of Sherm's hand came crashing against the side of her head.

"How would you like me to send you to hell back to Tabors Creek?" Sherm yelled.

Maggie never answered. Sherm walked back outside.

Tabors Creek

*****

Tears of fright and despair rolled down Maggie's face. Her head stung from the slap. She dried her hands on her apron and rubbed her head. She guessed nothing was broken. She ran her tongue over her teeth, but didn't feel any cracks. He could have killed her had he used his fist or a board. This was the last time he would ever hit her, she vowed. There was a better life and she would find it. She would leave him. Where could she go? What could she do? There had to be a way. She had to figure out how and when. First, she needed money. She had none – he had taken everything she had with the promise to return it. There was money in the bank, she was certain, but how could she get it? Did she have the nerve to take the key and go to the bank? She had to plan her escape out of here very carefully. In the meantime, she would stay out of his way while she decided a plan, as perfectly as she could.

*****

The sun had melted most of the snow on the road, making travel possible again. Sherm was anxious to work on his new cherry based juice, which he referred to as Cherry Brandy, and get it delivered. During late summer he had found a place on his mountain where giant black heart cherries grew in abundance. Two of his workers picked them during the day while Sherm worked the yard. Who they belonged to didn't matter, so long as no one was around. He had instructed the workers to listen and watch for anyone. Within a week they had managed to strip many of the trees without detection.

Sherm had worked the cherries as fast as they brought them in. To one gallon of his clear corn whiskey, he added two quarts of water and five or six quarts of the large cherries. He filled numerous gallon jugs with this mixture, put a cork stopper in each jug and let them sit for three months. That had been last October. Now on this cold January morning he decided to work inside to complete the process. With one and one-half pounds of white sugar to one pint of water, he made a thick simple-syrup. He strained each of the jugs, and to the juice added syrup to taste. When finished, he bottled and corked the jugs. He considered it easy money – all he had to do was let it sit for three more months. As he stacked the brandy, he spoke aloud, *"Wish to hell I'd done this before – easier than that other stuff."*

*****

Three weeks had passed since Josh mailed the letter to Ellen. She hadn't answered, yet, which he took as a good sign. If she was going to say 'don't write,' she probably would have written by now. At least he hoped so. This thought put him in a great mood. It wasn't much, but something to hold on to.

There was work to be done today, and being in a good frame of mind made work seem easier. In spite of the frigid weather, maintaining a regular riding schedule, even if modified, was a must for all of the horses in training. That included Freedom. Jockeys Eddie Ellis and Phil Hazelepp and trainers ensured that each horse got at least two hours of running two or three days a week during the winter months. It was also good work ethic for the horses, particularly in the young horses. Josh and Eddie had waited until the sun was up before they began today's runs. The warm sun was inviting to both the men and the animals.

Inside the stable, Josh ran a brush down Freedom's back. Like the others, Freedom had to be groomed before going out of the cool stable to "wake up" the muscles. "There you are my friend. You're looking mighty handsome this morning," Josh said. He patted Freedom on the back. "Wish I could find you a girlfriend, but that's way down the road. I'm afraid you'll have to earn that. Your lady friends will want a winner."

Freedom nuzzled Josh on the neck, then with a swing of his head, knocked the brush from his hand. "Hey guy, what the heck did you do that for. You understood me, huh? Well, just take it easy – don't get your hooves in a huff. I'll find her – in fact, lots of hers." Josh hugged him around the neck. "I love you, but you need to behave yourself."

Eddie Ellis walked into the stable carrying a blanket and saddle. "He givin' you a rough time, is he? I heard you scolding him."

"No, he's just feeling his oats." Josh laughed aloud.

"Good one, Josh."

"Let me ride him this morning, Eddie. I haven't been on him in a while," Josh asked.

"You sure you're feelin' up to it?

"Oh, yeah. I'm fine. I'll go easy. How cold is it out there?

"We're okay. It's about at the freezing mark, around 32 or 33 degrees. We're fine if it's above 20. Fortunately, there's no wind. I warmed up several bits and saddles, including this one – took them from the tack shop into the stable in front of the stove.

"That's good. Freedom and I both will appreciate that."

"I was expecting I'd be riding him, that was the real reason," he joked.

"Thanks a lot," Josh answered. "I'll remember that."

*****

Although the track was clear, the snow was beginning to fall lightly as Josh entered the three-quarter mile training track. Freedom was anxious to run, but Josh knew he would have to warm him up before running hard. He allowed him to slowly trot around once, increasing his speed with each succeeding lap.

Eventually, they were running at maximum speed for a couple of laps, followed with slower trotting. This pattern they continued for about forty-five minutes. When finished, Josh dismounted and led Freedom by the reins. "We don't have a wind blowing today, so you get to walk this last lap – help you cool off before you go inside," Josh said. Light snow continued to fall, but became water as it touched the sweating chestnut brown horse. Looking back at him, he said, "You did good out there, as usual. Think you're pretty hot stuff, don't you, fellow?" After Josh turned his face away, Freedom nudged him in the small of his back causing Josh to laugh out loud. "You are something for the books, I'll tell you," Josh exclaimed. "You're still a beauty though – the young mares will be standing in line." As if he understood, Freedom nudged him again.

Inside the barn, Josh loosened Freedom's girth, although he left the saddle in place allowing circulation to return gradually. Sudden cold air he knew could cause cramping. He lifted the horse's feet to check for pieces of ice and snow. From the spigot, he drew a bucket of fresh water and placed it in front of Freedom. "How about a brushing while you drink, huh?" Freedom drank from the bucket as soon as it was placed in front of him. Josh brushed the matted areas on Freedom's coat, one side then the other. "I'll let you stay here for a bit while you cool off and dry. I'll be back. It's a little warmer here than in the stable." He patted him on the back and headed to the track.

Eddie was just walking the last lap with one of the resident horses in training. Josh waited until he came in. "I'll take him into the barn if you want to head out with the next one," Josh said.

"Good. Save us some time. How'd Freedom do?"

"Just like always – great. You know he's almost human. I swear that horse knows what I say to him."

Eddie grinned. "Sure he does," as he rolled his eyes in gest.

214

"You know, he's got what it takes to win in May," Josh said.

"No doubt about it!" Eddie exclaimed. "You know a horse has three characteristics that make him a great race horse. That horse has them all."

"And what would those things be?" Josh asked.

"Most important of course is the way he actually runs. You know right off the bat Freedom has that down pretty good, now don't you?"

"The other two are?"

"Second is how much time he loses on the turns. We know when Freedom gets near the inside rail, he doesn't lose any time. That's his place, and that's where he has got to stay to win. It's my job to keep him there."

"You're right of course. And, third?"

"The general impression he conveys."

"That's funny, actually. Freedom is about the cockiest horse I've ever been around. He is one proud pony!" Josh said.

They both laughed out loud, remembering the first day he came into the yard from the trailer. He had stood still for a few seconds as he stepped from the trailer to the exit ramp, looked around as if surveying to see if it was good enough for him. Pleased, it seemed, he flung his head throwing his mane in the air and pranced off, his head held high.

"Do you remember the day." Josh started to ask.

"I know what you're thinking and yes, it's a day I'll never forget," Eddie said.

*****

Late in the afternoon Eddie Ellis finished running his last horse, Princess Angie, Doc Weide's horse. Josh had exercised two horses and Eddie, with the help of the trainers, had done the rest. As with the others, he walked Princess Angie the last lap to cool her off before stopping.

Josh busily placed feed in each of the stable stalls for the horses and led them in as they were dried off. He was patiently waiting in the barn for the last one when Eddie entered with Princess Angie. "This it for today?" Josh asked.

"She's the last one."

"How'd she do?" Josh asked.

"She did great, like she always does, but she's not Freedom. Still, she's good. Damned good as a matter of fact."

"Doc Weide was supposed to come in today to take a look at her, but haven't seen him yet. He had some business to do in town, don't know what it was, but he said he'd be here after he finished that," Josh said. "Hope he didn't get into any trouble on the roads."

"It doesn't look too bad out there, actually," Eddie said. "It's just snowing lightly, like before, and not sticking much. Temperatures I think are still sitting about 33, so it shouldn't be freezing."

"Well, I hope he gets in before dark, before it starts to freeze."

"Be a good idea."

Josh left the barn and headed to the stable to toss a shovel full of coal into the corner coal stove, which sat at the back wall behind the stalls. The stove kept the stable reasonably warm, even though a window was left open at each end at the front of the building for fresh air. The stalls were within eyesight of the house. Hal had laid an electric fence around the front of the stable, which triggered an alarm inside the house should someone try to enter. The back doors were kept locked at night.

As Josh walked toward the stove, he smelled smoke. It took just a second to register that something was on fire. "Oh my God," he yelled. His heart raced as fast as his legs moved. "The stove." The sound of his feet hitting the floor told him his rubber legs were moving, though he couldn't feel them. Surely his chest was going to explode before he could get there. Flames were shooting in the air lighting up the room. "Oh, God, no, no." *The horses*! *The horses*! "Eddie, Eddie, come quick." *What the Hell has happened?* "Dad, where are you? Are you here?" *Oh, no, no, no. The horses! Gotta get 'em out. My face is burning up! Oh shit! My legs are numb. I can't breathe. Where is everybody?* "Help, help."

Then somehow he was there, in front of the stove. The door was open and hot coals had fallen to the floor starting a fire. He ran for a bucket of water and pulled on the large bell at the top of a post to summon for help!

Within minutes Hal Gibbons was out of the house. From the door he could see the flames shooting up toward the ceiling. He turned back and called to Marsha, "Call for a fire truck, quick." Marsha ran inside.

Having heard the bell ring, Eddie and employees from the bunkhouse, along with others from scattered areas of the farm, ran to the scene. Everyone worked together, first to get the horses out of the stable and into the paddock behind the house. They grabbed buckets of water and tossed them on the flames. They ran back and filled their buckets over and again trying uselessly to put out the fire, which was raging out of control by the time the fire truck arrived.

The elegant, gold pin-striped, red Seagrave pumper, containing a deck-mounted gun and hose reel and a booster tank of water, instead of chemicals for the first time, arrived on scene soon after they received the call. The right side of the fire truck carried bright yellow ladders. Realizing the ladders weren't usable on the burning structure, the firemen jumped to the deck and unwound the hose from the reel. "Move that truck as close as you can get it," a supervising fireman yelled at the driver. They bravely fought the fire until they exhausted their booster tank of water. By then the fire was burning itself out. The firemen joined the group in a bucket brigade to fight the remaining flames of the simmering catastrophe.

Doc Weide turned into the lane just as the flames were beginning to die. He sped up the lane, parked the car down near the front of the house and ran to the stable. Josh met him in the parking area. "The horses are fine, don't worry." Josh said.

"Thank God," Doc answered. "Nobody hurt is there?" A look of terror filled his face.

"No, nobody's hurt. It's bad, but thank God for this bunch of people. The Lexington fire truck was here, but they couldn't save the stable, but kept it from spreading to any other buildings. We got all the horses out, fortunately. They're all over in the paddock."

*****

Late in the evening the crew led the last horse from the paddock into the barn where they had created a temporary stable.

"Let's just be thankful no one was hurt – the animals are all safe and the barn and the house are fine," Hal said.

"You're right, Dad. We can rebuild the stable," Josh answered.

"I'll go inside and see if Marsha's got food for us all. I'm sure she does." Hal headed into the house, limping as he walked, a tired, but thankful man.

"You will be spending the night, right Doc?" Josh asked.

"If you got the patience for me," he joked.

"We have patience to spare! Wouldn't have it any other way."

"It's probably not so important now, after all that's happened here tonight, but I brought you the picture you wanted – taken of the staff at the hospital," Doc said. "How's that going anyway?"

"I don't know, Doc, don't know."

"She's sure a pretty girl."

"That I do know," Josh grinned as he spoke.

*****

Tabors Creek

The end of another day of training and Ellen was very tired as she headed from the Nurses Home to the hospital, daydreaming as she walked. She was now working the late evening-to-morning hours, which she preferred. *A good thing* she thought, *for the next and last two months.* Soon May would be here and she would be finished. Evenings were the loneliest time of day for her, but when working, the hours went fast.

She had anxiously awaited the daily mail for days, hoping to hear from Josh. He had promised to write her again, even knowing she couldn't respond. Yet, there had been no word from him. *Has he forgotten me?* she wondered. How could she blame him? She should have known. *It's been nice to have these dreams anyway*, she told herself. Even though not hearing from him was disappointing, the excitement of her graduation in two months was still utmost in her thoughts. Soon she would see her babies again, as well as her mother. Nothing could ever make her leave them again. She could barely stand to wait. She knew she needed to forget Josh, just as soon as she got home, but for now, the excitement of daydreaming about him and what might have been would help carry her through.

Ellen was reminded of a time long ago when she thought Sheriff Gordon Workman was for her, but that hadn't happened either. She waited many months for him, but he was always working. She assumed at the time he didn't really want her. When he did, it was too late. She would never know if it could work for them because she would never go back to Tabors Creek. When Sherm came into her life, she thought she loved him, but he had killed that love and left her with some indelible fears and scars.

She wasn't sure if she could ever trust again, but time would tell. Presently, her children were her first concern. After she received her registered nurse license in May, Ellen would be qualified to find work she loved to do and provide for her family. She couldn't want for more. In a letter to Bertie, she had written, "Mama, can you believe I have only two more months left after this one and I will graduate!! I am so excited and anxious to come home. I want to see the kids and you so badly." Visions of moving thousands of miles away just as soon as graduation was over – someplace where he'd never find her, became the seed of a future plan. She would do that and be rid of this fear she carried with her now wherever she went. Bertie would go. They could start all over again - somewhere else. She could barely contain the excitement she felt when imagining herself wearing the uniform of a Registered Nurse. "Just imagine!"

"Who are you talking to?"

Startled, Ellen looked behind her to see her friend and fellow nursing student, Alice Wetherly, walking behind her. "Oh, hi, Alice."

"Who are you talking to?" Alice asked.

"Oh, I guess I was talking to myself."

"Do you get any answers?"

"Well, sometimes I do. If I need to know something right away, then I give myself my own answer." They both laughed out loud. "I was just thinking how exciting it is when I imagine myself wearing a registered nurse's uniform."

"I know. I feel the same way. It's getting very close you know. Too bad about Rita Beckett."

"What about Rita? Nothing bad, I hope. I saw her just yesterday morning."

"Oh, I guess you hadn't heard," Alice said. "Last evening when we were working, Mrs. Ramson called her into the office and this morning she left."

"What happened? Was something wrong at home?"

"It's just a rumor right now, but I heard she had a husband, which you know isn't allowed."

Ellen could feel color drain from her face. "I wonder how they found out," she said.

Alice continued, "Her husband got angry because she hadn't written him, so he called and told them everything. Poor thing. If she had just made it two more months, they'd never have known."

"Oh, no," she cried. "That's terrible." She knew how deflated and disappointed Rita must be. If Sherm learned she was here, it would be worse than that. He'd surely come after her. He'd hurt her, maybe kill her, and anyone else if he had to. She began to stammer and falter, "er, uh, uh." Her stomach churned and she was certain she was about to pass out. She placed her hand at the side of her face and placed her head in her lap.

Alice glanced at her as she faltered. "My gosh, Ellen. Are you alright?" she asked.

"I'm sorry. I'm fine, just a little lightheaded. It's a bad time of the month – just started today."

"Oh, God. I do hate that, don't you?"

Ellen had regained her composure by the time she reached her floor to begin her shift. She had calmed herself by repeating over and over, *You're safe. Sherm doesn't have any idea you're here*. She would be a nurse, or else!

For the next two months she would be working once again in the Women's Ward, for which she was thankful. She felt relieved to be out of the Men's Ward, where Josh came to mind each time she walked past the room where he had been a patient. Of all the places she'd trained, the Women's Ward was her first choice.

Today was going to be another busy one. All the beds were filled when she left at the end of her shift this morning. Busy was good though.

*****

She heard the crying woman as she came on the floor. She stopped at the nurses' desk to get her instructions and as she stood there, the crying continued to come from down the hall. "Come with me," the floor supervisor, Mrs. Masney said, motioning for Ellen to follow her. Ellen did as she was told. The crying became louder as they walked. When they reached the room of the crying woman, Mrs. Masney entered with Ellen behind her.

Seeing the battered woman lying in the bed, Ellen was filled with pity. She quieted the cry that tried to escape from her throat by placing her hand over her mouth. The lady was unrecognizable to anyone who knew her before. Her bruised, black and blue eyelids appeared to be swollen shut. Black stitches on both cheeks held together the bruised and swollen tissue, once white but now a deep blue blended with a darker black. *"Oh my God! What happened to her?"* she wondered. Her right arm was in a cast up to her armpit and her left leg was in a cast, held up by a sling attached to an overhead rail. Nurse Masney brought a shot of pain medication with her, as the patient's doctor had ordered. "She just came in after lunch time and went straight to surgery. She was in there for nearly three hours. They brought her here just about an hour ago. It's time now for more pain medication. In her chart, which I should have showed you, her doctor ordered a shot for pain every four hours until he lets us know differently."

Ellen assisted by holding the patient's gown aside and allowing the patient to hold her hand with the fingers of her uncasted arm. "You'll be okay, Mrs. Witten, just hang in there, honey," Mrs. Masney said. "I'm giving you something for pain."

"Mrs. Witten, did you say?" Ellen asked.

"Yes, do you know who she is?"

"She was a patient here when I was here last fall, if it's the same lady," Ellen said.

"That's right, she was. I didn't remember that you were here then."

"I didn't recognize her this time, but I remember her. Of course I didn't see her this time either."

"She would be hardly recognizable," Mrs. Masney said, "not in her condition."

"Oh, I'm so sorry for her," Ellen said.

"Well, she's been beaten on once too many times, I'd say. How about it Mrs. Witten?" Mrs. Masney spoke in a voice loud enough for Mrs. Witten to hear her.

The crying stopped some, eased by the comfort of knowing someone who cared was in the room with her. "I understand he's in jail, Mrs. Witten. So don't you worry about him hurtin' you any more. I hope they throw away the key this time," Mrs. Masney said. "Life is going to get better, you just wait and see."

To Ellen, she added, "She needs constant watch for the next couple of hours, so I'd like you to just stay here and report any change. Check her blood pressure and pulse every half hour, and don't give her anything to drink yet. We don't want her to get sick on top of everything else."

*****

Ellen had been sitting with Mrs. Witten for the past hour and nothing very eventful had occurred. Her blood pressure was slightly high at the first reading and normal the second half hour and her pulse had been normal both times. The patient awakened twice from a sound sleep crying for help. Ellen tried soothing her nerves by holding her hand and talking to her. "I'm here with you Mrs. Witten. You're okay. I'll stay with you. Try to rest." She gently rubbed the patient's free arm. "You're going to be fine." Both times Rosalynn had gone back to sleep.

The longer Ellen sat with Mrs. Witten, the angrier she grew. *"How dare this man, this husband of hers, worse than any animal, probably twice the size of the diminutive Mrs. Witten, beat on her, someone unable to defend herself. What gave him the right to touch her?"* Much like Ellen herself, Mrs. Witten probably had loved her husband at one time, never imagining he could be so horrific. By the time she saw him in a clearer light, she had children. Ellen knew how that felt too. She knew too how hard getting away from him and on her own could be. It felt good to be just two months away from being free.

To keep herself occupied while Mrs. Witten slept, Ellen tidied the room and walked the floor. She saw the small hospital bag of personal items belonging to Mrs. Witten. In the bag she saw the dress she'd been wearing – blood stained and torn. Perhaps she'd get visitors tomorrow who could bring her clean and unstained, better clothing. She made a mental note to check to be sure Rosalyn had someone from home taking care of her needs.

When she could find nothing else to do, Ellen sat down on a chair at the side of the bed, fighting sleep herself. She walked intermittently to stay awake. When she checked Rosalyn's blood pressure at midnight, it had dropped dramatically. She quickly checked her pulse and it too was falling rapidly. Hurrying to the desk, she called Mrs. Masney.

The physician was called and while they waited for him, the nurses valiantly tried to do everything they could to save her, but Mrs. Witten continued to spiral downhill until she finally lost her battle to recover.

As soon as she was alone, Ellen began to cry. She had tended to some very sick people in her training, but this was the first patient she had seen die. She cried as if her heart would break. The tears were for Mrs. Witten, but they were also for all of the women, herself included, who suffered at the hands of a monster husband. They were for her own heartache, of the past, and the present. They were for what she could perhaps foresee for herself one day. She knew she was supposed to be strong, unaffected, and keep a professional distance from the patient. But they were taught to be caring, too. *"How could you be caring and not be affected?"* The line between the two seemed too fine to define this night. She tried not to let Mrs. Masney see her, but Mrs. Masney had walked into the room as she was sobbing. With training nearly complete, she couldn't afford to be disciplined now – not now. Mrs. Masney glanced at Ellen as the orderly came and wheeled the body to the morgue. Ellen feared the worst as the head nurse walked toward her. She knew she had not showed professionalism tonight and she feared the consequences. What would happen now? She felt sick with worry and with pain. When Mrs. Masney reached her, she stood silent for a minute, then placed her hand on Ellen's shoulder. "We all have at least one time like this, Ellen, somewhere along the line. Let this be your one time. Now go to the bathroom and get yourself together. It's over. We're nurses, damned good nurses, but we're also human."

*****

April 1931 - Sheriff Workman had been far too busy during the past two weeks to spend much time trying to find Ellen. The normally quiet Tabors Creek had seen numerous acts of vandalism, thefts, and fights. He and Deputy Sheriff Bell had spent hours tracking down the troublemakers, locking up some, fining some, and warning others. Each one entailed hours of follow-ups with interviews, notification of family, and the ever-annoying paperwork. He had found time to send a wire out the previous week to police stations in Lexington requesting them to check the 1931 census and see if Ellen or Bertie could possibly be listed. He also had them check for Maggie and Sherm. There was no luck with any of them. A police sergeant in Lexington called Sheriff Waterman, "I'm sorry Gordon, but I don't find any of the names you gave me on any list, residential or legal." He guessed Maggie and Sherm were using other names, if in fact Maggie was with him. Perhaps Ellen and Bertie would do the same. He decided if no leads had been reached by May, he would drive to Lexington and personally go through the census records himself. While he was there, he'd visit the local police station. In the meantime, he would stay in Tabors Creek and hope for some kind of lead or tip. After two years, the trail was getting much too cold. He feared it would soon be too cold to follow.

"I'm headed out to Maggie Sellers' place, John," Sheriff Workman said, then slammed the door on his way out. He wasn't in any mood to hear his deputy John Bell question him about anything. The first question he would ask was "*Why?*" He didn't have time to waste either. The road was muddy, prompting the Sheriff to ride horseback, which was easier than by car. He needed to just have one more look to see if Maggie might have returned.

Riding up the lane, nothing looked like it had been changed, as he had guessed. At the front door of the house, he noted the same mess on the porch as when he was there last. He knocked, but as expected, no one answered. He pushed the door open and walked inside. It was obvious no one had been inside since he was there in the fall.

*****

Nearly two months had passed since the fire at Holiday Farms. All of the employees of Holiday, as well as neighbors from nearby farms, had gathered together and worked as a team from morning until late evening to rebuild the stable. Some worked one day a week while others worked three or four days, giving whatever time they could afford away from their own farms. Even the trainers acted as construction workers when they weren't running, feeding and tending to the horses. Marsha Gibbons and a young helper, Angela, daughter of a trainer, spent each day in the kitchen preparing and providing food for them all. On occasion, other ladies came by and spent the day helping her.

Josh began his days at 6:00 each morning. After breakfast, he headed to the stable where he hammered and nailed along with the rest, with breaks for lunch and supper his only stops. "Dad," Josh called. When darkness curtailed the work day, he took a bath and collapsed into bed, exhausted. "Mom, I'm headed to bed. Been a long day. Tomorrow we'll get the horses all in the right stables finally though."

Mrs. Gibbons smiled as she replied, "Have a good night's sleep, Josh. I know you're tired."

One day followed the next until finally, here they were at completion. There had been no time to write to Ellen, although she was in his thoughts each day as he worked.

Now today, the final chore of placing the other animals back into the stable was about to take place. Freedom was first. With pomp and rein, Josh led him from the barn to his designated spot in the new stable, the stall nearest the house. "Okay fellows, each of you get one of the horses and move him to his new spot," Josh called to the crew. "Each stall is marked with a number, same as the number on the temporary stalls they're in now. Then, we're finished."

With huge elation, the crowd of helpers, ten or so, yelled, "Yea! Hurrah!"

Hal Gibbons watched as the last of the horses was led into the stall. He rang a bell to get the attention of the group. When it grew quiet, he spoke. "I just want to thank each and every one of you for all the help you each have given us here. We were desperate. We were hanging and you rescued us. We'll never be able to thank you enough, but when we can help any of you in the future, please know that we'll be there. Now, the next thing," he paused for a second while the crowd, which had once again gotten noisy, quieted down some, then continued. "I want to invite each and every one of you to a hoedown or whatever you want to call it, tomorrow evening out in the barn. We got a pretty lively square dance band comin'. There'll be plenty of food and drinks for everybody, so come on out. We'll be ready to start any time after 6:00. Be sure to bring your best girl, or your wife, with you, if you plan to kick up your heels," Hal Gibbons laughed as he announced the affair.

Once again the crowd shouted, "Yea." One voice could be heard over the others announcing, "I'll bring the corn likker." Those that heard him roared with laughter.

"I heard that," Hal smirked. "You know we're in the prohibition times, so if there's any 'likker' as you called it, I don't know about it. That'll be something I'll leave up to you. I just won't be furnishin' it. I can get myself into enough trouble without the Feds helpin' me. Understand?"

The crowd agreed unanimously, cheering as they chatted among themselves.

Hal held up his arm to get their attention once more. "This afternoon we'll get busy and get this barn in shape for a party. If any of you want to hang around for that, you're invited there too," he smiled. He was sure they would.

*****

In the grassy lawn beside the house, tables sat end-to-end, filled with food and drink. Marsha Gibbons and her helpers had prepared many dishes, keeping in mind this was a hearty and hungry group of men for the most part. They served fried chicken, baked ham, pork ribs, and sliced beef. There were cooked and uncooked fresh vegetables from Marsha's garden including white mashed potatoes with gravy and yams, which had been cooked, mashed, then baked in a casserole with brown sugar, butter, cream, and pecans. Many of the ladies brought cookies for dessert to go with the homemade ice cream the men would churn during the evening. "Hey, Mom, you have enough food here to feed the whole city of Lexington," Josh cried.

"I rather doubt that, Josh, but there'll be plenty, I hope."

"Plenty!" he exclaimed. "That's an understatement. We were going to dance this evening, but after these people finish eating all this, they'll not be able to get up, let alone dance. With all this food, I invited the band to eat too."

"Oh, Josh. Stop teasing now," Marsha snickered.

"Teasing! Who's teasing?" he joked.

Seeing the band members getting out of the car, Josh headed to where they were. "I'll get them set up and bring them back to eat."

"Okay, son, that's fine," Marsha said.

On the table Marsha had placed plates and napkins, along with condiments, dishes of pickles, beets, onions, and tomatoes. For utensils she brought out old silverware she had been saving for informal social events. On the fire pit near the table, Hal busily placed more ribs on the grill, while some people were just arriving and others gathered in groups eating and chatting. Three galvanized tubs held blocks of ice and chipped ice filled with Cokes and other pop.

When the band began to play, some folks gathered around waiting to see who would go dance first. After a while, the wife of the square dance caller began to ease couples to the floor and demonstrated steps for those that didn't know them. She soon had enough couples on the floor to start the promenade. *I'm rollin' in my sweet baby's arms,* sang the band as the dancers went round and round.

Josh watched as the crowd partied and danced. Music filled the air. He turned to pick up a soda pop from the tub, when he saw the pretty girl walking towards him. "Come dance with me," she said.

"Fraid I don't know how to do that."

"Well then, just come and learn how."

Josh followed her and was soon trying to dance as best he could. "You're doing great, Josh."

"Thank you," he said. "I think you're just being kind."

"Oh, no. I meant that. My name is Hedda. Of course, I already know yours."

"And how did you know?"

"I asked. I'm here with my dad. He's the band leader. I just came along to help get things set up and get people dancing. My mom and me."

Josh spent much of the evening dancing with Hedda. She was a beautiful girl, he assumed to be about his age. Her long, blonde hair hung in one large curl down her back, held together by a pink bow that matched the pink and white dress she wore. He couldn't help but notice her wide, dark brown eyes with beautiful, long eyelashes and full lips. Although it felt good to relax and have fun, away from the work of the past weeks, a pretty girl at his side, still his thoughts kept returning to Ellen. When the evening came to an end, Hedda kissed Josh goodnight. "Please call me," she said.

Inside the house, Josh sat down at his desk and wrote to Ellen.

*****

Ellen's hand shook as she opened the letter. The handwriting was Josh's. It had been a long time. *This is probably a letter sending apologies for not being able to attend my graduation. Well, at least he was polite enough to write.* She felt like her dream was over before it began, but it was what she had expected. Wasn't he too good to be true? Alone in her room, she read, "Dear Ellen, please accept my apologies for not writing for the past couple of months. However, we have all been frantically busy rebuilding our only horse stable, which burned to the ground not long after I wrote to you in January. I have been working from daylight till dark and going to bed exhausted, leaving me no time to write."

"Oh, I'm so sorry," she cried to no one. The rest of the letter she didn't remember until she went back and re-read it later. She had hurried to the line that said, "I'll be there for your graduation." She was dancing around the room holding the letter close to her and grinning when her roommate entered the room.

"What are you so happy about?" Martha asked.

"Oh, hi, Martha. Oh, I'm just happy. It's graduation next week, remember?" Ellen said.

"Sure I remember, but what's the letter you're hugging? Who's it from? I've never seen you so happy."

"It's just a letter from my mother. She's anxious for me to come home. I'm sure she needs my help. And also, she's just glad that I'm graduating," Ellen answered.

"I don't know, but I'll bet you're not telling me everything, Ellen Potter, and I'm your friend. The excitement I see in you right now isn't because of your mother, I would bet."

"Martha!" Ellen said loudly, "I promise you nothing has happened yet that I haven't told you. When it does, you'll be the first one I'll tell. Okay?"

Martha placed her hands on her hips, smiled and turned her head sideways, giving Ellen a look of skepticism. "Alright," she said. "I guess that'll have to do since that's all I think I'm going to get."

"I'm sorry, Martha. Don't be mad at me."

"I'm not mad. I wouldn't get mad at you. I'm just curious, maybe even a little nosey." She grinned. "Looks like I might as well go get my bath." She turned and walked from the room.

After Martha left to get her bath, Ellen hid the letter in the bottom of her suitcase.

*****

Ellen was filled with excitement. She could hardly believe tomorrow was graduation day. She had just finished her last shift. Her work here was done. No more wearing the striped pinafore; now she would wear the stiffly starched, white uniform with the equally starched white hat – she liked to think of it as a crown. She was as proud as she had been the day she gave birth to her first baby.

In her room, she held the gown she would wear for the ceremony up to her body as she looked in the mirror. "Oh, I wish Mama could be here. She'd be so happy! I can't believe I made it, Martha, I made it," she cried. She danced around in a circle holding the gown in front of her.

"Did you ever doubt you wouldn't?" Martha asked, with a smirk.

"Oh, Martha. So many things have happened. There are so many things to talk about. We'll be on the same train tomorrow night going home. We'll have a couple of hours to talk before you get off I think. Where in Kentucky is your home?"

"I live in Paintsville. It's probably a two hours ride from here. Then you're going on to Lexington, right?"

"Yes, Lexington is home, I can hardly wait to get there," Ellen said wistfully.

"Two years, Ellen," Martha said. "Just think - we've been together two years. I'm going to miss you so much."

"I'll miss you too, Martha," Ellen answered. "But we can write to each other and who knows, maybe we'll end up working together one day. You never know. I'm not sure where Paintsville is. I am going to try and find out though, and then I'll know how close you are to me."

"I'm not sure, but I think we're just about fifty miles apart. That's just a guess though. But whatever it is, it's only a train ride away."

"I'll write to you and by the time I do, I'll probably know how far it is," Ellen said. "You must promise me though that you'll answer me when I write. I don't want you to forget me after you get a job and a boyfriend - or maybe a husband."

"I won't forget you, Ellen. You know that," Martha said. "And I won't be getting a husband soon. Don't worry about that. You'll be sending me a wedding invitation long before I send you one, I'm sure."

"Don't be so sure, Martha. That's not for me. I need to find a job now."

Martha had been packing some items in her suitcase while talking. She stopped and faced Ellen, wearing just half a smile – a look that said much more. Had it been interpreted, she said, *I don't believe you.* "You're not telling me everything, Miss Ellen! I want to know if you're going to forget about that handsome patient you had?"

"What handsome patient?" Ellen asked.

"You know what handsome patient I'm talking about." Martha said.

Ellen knew, but she had to pretend, even if she didn't want to. She wanted to shout how excited she was to have gotten two letters from him and, *he's coming tomorrow, he says.* However, graduation was too close; she couldn't take a chance, not even with her friend, Martha.

"Well, I'm not sure who you're talking about, but if it's who I think you mean, then the answer is 'nothing.' You know we were just patient and nurse," Ellen said. "That's all it was and all it could be, you know that."

"Well, I know that's what it's supposed to be. Nevertheless, I saw the way he looked at you, the way he watched you, and even asked about you," Martha said.

"All I want is my diploma, Martha. Nothing must interfere with that."

"I know. I know. I just thought maybe he might write to you even if it's after you leave here."

"I am sure he won't so don't worry your pretty self about it. Besides, he doesn't have my address. He has no idea where I live." Ellen gave her a conjured, but friendly, look of disgust.

"Well, you'll have to let me know in the letter you plan to write! Come on now. Let's go out to the living room and see if the others are out there," Martha said. "This evening was everyone's last shift, you know."

"Let's go." Ellen said, with a grin. She hung her gown on a hook on the wall and headed out the door behind Martha.

*****

Most of the student nurses had gathered in the living room with their address books, exchanging addresses with each other. Two girls sat on the sofa, each writing a note in the other's notebook. Another student nurse, Mabel Waterman, stood behind them crying softly. Ellen spotted her as she came into the room and walked straight to her. She placed her arm around the crying girl. "You're supposed to be laughing, not crying," Ellen said.

"Oh, I know. I'm just sorry to leave all my friends here."

"It's hard, I know, but I'm so excited to go home so that's all I'm thinking about," Ellen said. "I do want to keep in touch though so I want to get addresses tonight. I'll start with yours if you'll give it to me."

"Oh, yes, please give me yours too." Mabel said.

Ellen had been told that Mabel hinted in conversations that she had an abusive father. She hoped the girl would be able to get a job and move out of her parents' home. "Alright then, smile now and think about how great it'll be to be at home and going to work in your spiffy new uniform. You can start earning money and do whatever you want from now on."

"You're right, Ellen. I'm just being rather silly, I know." She wiped her eyes and hugged Ellen, then exchanged books with her.

As the girls chatted and wrote in their notebooks, Mrs. Ramson entered the room. She looked around the room until she spotted Ellen. "Oh, Ellen, may I see you for a minute."

Ellen froze. *Please, dear God. Don't let anything happen now. Please allow me to get my diploma. What was wrong? Had someone found out?* Was she about to be sent home without graduating? Her heart was breaking slowly as she walked toward Mrs. Ramson. *Has Sherm found me?* She followed her into the hall to hear the news. Her legs felt like blocks of wood carrying her along. When she saw the look on Mrs. Ramson's face, she imagined the worst. *Sherm had called. One of the children was ill.* Something terrible had happened and now she wouldn't graduate. *I've wasted two years – two years of hell without my babies. This can't be happening.* In the hall, Mrs. Ramson turned to face her. "I received a phone call."

Ellen felt lightheaded and about to faint. She leaned against the wall and took hold of the edge of the wainscoting. "Are you alright?" Mrs. Ramson asked.

"Oh, please, please. Nothing can go wrong now," she pleaded. Her eyes began to fill with tears.

"Oh my dear girl, what do you mean, 'go wrong. It isn't that bad. Listen now. Your mother has fallen and broken her arm. She's at home, but she called to let you know that she's okay. She had planned to surprise you and be here for your graduation, but she won't be able to make it."

Ellen hung her head in her hands and openly sobbed. It was a mixture of sorrow for her mother, but relief from her worst fears at the same time. After a brief cry, she raised her head, "I'm sorry, Mrs. Ramson. I'm very sorry."

"Don't be sorry my dear. I understand. It's been very difficult for you I'm sure. Two years away from home is a long time. I assume you're planning to go straight home tomorrow, aren't you?"

"Yes, ma'am, I will be on the 7:00 p.m. train," Ellen answered. "Thank you very much for telling me."

"You are welcome." Mrs. Ramson turned and left the building.

*****

Ellen was up early. She had slept very little. The excitement was too much. She went to the kitchen to have a cup of coffee hoping it might help to calm her nerves. At days end today, the fear she carried now would lessen when she held her diploma in her hands. The diploma was her ticket to freedom. Next, they would find a new state, a new city, and a new job where the family could live in peace. Never should any of them have to worry about Sherm again. No more would her children have to be secrets from anyone. But for today, she had several more hours to worry.

An afternoon meal was planned for the newly graduated nurses following the ceremony. Later in the evening she planned to be on the train, headed home. Her mind was racing from one thing to another. After Sherm, it was followed with, *Was Bertie okay? How had she fallen? Did she hit her head? Were the kids excited and anxious to see her? Was Josh coming to graduation?* "Stop," she said aloud. "It doesn't matter if he does or not." With her coffee in hand, she walked back to the room. Martha was still sleeping. From under her bed, Ellen pulled out her suitcase and placed it on top of the bed. She began to fold clothes and put them in the suitcase when Martha awakened.

"Good morning, Miss Sunshine," Martha said. She sat on the side of the bed rubbing her eyes.

"Good morning. Thought you'd never get up," Ellen joked.

"We are headed into the working world after today," Martha said, sleepily. "We should take great advantage of this last day of our lives as we know it now."

"Oh, I suppose so, but I've too much on my mind."

"Like what?"

"Just things. I'm really anxious, that's all," Ellen said.

"If you say so," Martha said sheepishly. She rose from the bed and began to dress.

*****

At 12:00, the girls headed to the hospital wearing their long, black graduation robes. Their heads were left bare. "We're having the ceremony in the auditorium, you know," Martha said.

"Yes, I know. I'll be glad when we're finished," Ellen answered.

"Look at you, your hands are shaking. What is wrong?" Martha worriedly asked.

"I told you before. I'm just nervous. I'm okay, don't worry."

Walking in the front door, they noticed a sign directing visitors to the upper entrance of the room and graduating students to the lower. The auditorium was where students had met for training classes and briefings, but today it was the location of the graduation ceremony. There was a small stage in front of the room and seating was pie-shaped with each row growing wider and higher moving away from the stage.

"I wish my parents could have been here," Martha said. "But I'm the oldest of seven kids and Mom is pretty busy with the others."

"I thought you said she was coming," Ellen said.

"Well, she tried, but she couldn't get away, and dad is too busy with the farm, he'd never be able to leave for more than a couple of hours."

"Oh well," Ellen said. "It'll be over soon and we'll be home. My mother was planning to be here, as you know. I'm glad she didn't try to travel with a broken arm though."

They took a seat in the front row. Ellen couldn't get Josh out of her thoughts, but she chose not to turn around and look to see if he had come. If he was here and she knew it, she would feel very self-conscious. The disappointment of knowing he wasn't here was something she wanted to avoid as well.

When everyone had taken their seats, the ceremony began. Ellen sat rigidly, unconsciously squeezing the arms of her chair tightly, stopping only when her fingers began to grow numb. She listened as Mrs. Ramson spoke from the stage. "Welcome to all of the graduating students, and to the staff and visitors gathered here today. We are about to usher twenty young girls into the world of Registered Nurses. These young ladies began their training here two years ago and have managed to learn the duties of a Registered Nurse, while adhering to the strict rules of discipline that accompanied their training. Unfortunately, seven of the original class either withdrew at their request or were asked to withdraw. Those of you here today to graduate have come a long way. You entered your training among unknown people, worked at getting to know and getting along with everyone, accepted your responsibilities, and worked hard to learn what a good nurse must know. It is a tribute to your intelligence and adaptability, and to your understanding of people. These are qualities all good nurses must possess in order to be successful."

Ellen kept her eyes on Mrs. Ramson, soaking up all of what she had to say. Yes, she would be a good nurse. All she needed was the chance.

Mrs. Ramson's speech was interrupted by a deafening sound that Ellen interpreted as gunfire. She sat frozen, feeling as if ice water was running through her veins. For a second she couldn't move. *Was it Sherm? Was he here? The nightmare was going to happen after all.* Martha, seated beside Ellen, turned behind her to look. Ellen could see the smile on Martha's face. Instantly, she felt relief. She herself then glanced behind her only to see a volunteer standing nearby, clasping his mouth with his hand, shocked by what he had done. He leaned to pick up the metal chair he had just dropped. Ellen could feel the color and feeling return to her body like the sand in an hourglass. Frowning, Mrs. Ramson continued. "I apologize for the person who created that interruption. As I was saying, all of you remaining here are deserving of what you are receiving today – your license to be employed as a registered nurse." Ellen tried to listen to everything that Mrs. Ramson was saying, but her thoughts were much too busy to stay still. There were the children, her mother, graduation, and Josh. So much excitement and so much to think about. Then she heard Mrs. Ramson reach the end of her speech with, "I'd like each one of you to come forward as your name is called."

The girls took the stage one at a time. Mrs. Ramson pinned the crown of a Registered Nurse, a white hat, on the head of each student, handed each one a diploma, and the girls exited the stage. As Ellen walked from the stage, tears of joy rolled down her face. Headed to her seat, she looked to the back of the room. Seated in the last row was Josh Gibbons. Her mouth fell open.

*****

Following the ceremony, Josh headed down the steps toward Ellen. Ellen could see that Martha was watching him with a wide grin on her face. She looked at Ellen. "You have some answers to my questions that I can't wait to hear."

"I have my own questions, thank you," Ellen said.

Josh reached for Ellen's hand. "Congratulations," he said. "I hope I'm welcome here." He looked at her for an approving smile and an answer.

"I'm very happy you're here, Josh, although I really didn't think you'd come all this distance." Her racing heart felt like a drum beating within her chest. Her face felt flushed and the thrill of seeing him was affecting her thoughts and self-consciousness to that point where she was sure the next thing out of her mouth was going to be something totally inappropriate, something most embarrassing.

"I told you I'd be here."

"I know, it's just that, that," she stammered. *Slowly*, she thought, *don't say the wrong thing. Take your time.*

"Say no more. If you don't mind that I'm here, I'd love to have some time to talk with you now that you're no longer a student," Josh said with a smile. When he smiled, Ellen felt captivated.

"I'd like that."

"I had hoped you wouldn't write and tell me not to come. Of course, I'd probably have come anyway." He smiled as he gazed at her.

Ellen wanted to pinch herself. This scene didn't seem to be hers. It was one from a book, not her life. It couldn't be. It was a bubble about to burst.

Martha had politely walked away as Josh came toward them, and now she stood watching from the side of the room where some of the graduates had gathered. Ellen was sure Martha was filling them in on who he was and anything else she had imagined she had seen between them. Each of those in Martha's group had taken turns looking at Ellen as Martha talked. They reminded Ellen of a bunch of bees.

"Let me talk with my roommate, Martha, for a minute. There's a reception planned now for all of us. I'm sure she's going there with the group I see her with over there." She pointed toward the side of the room where they stood. "I don't feel very much like having anything to eat right now. We could go for a walk before I leave for the train station."

"I'll wait right here for you," he said. "I don't want to take you from your lunch though."

"That's fine. I'm not hungry. I'll be right back." Ellen walked to where the girls were standing.

Martha was the first to talk. "Was I right, huh, was I right, or what?"

"Well, you knew something I didn't, I guess," Ellen said. "And what are you telling all of these girls?"

"Never mind. What's next?" Martha wanted to know.

"I have just met him. What do you mean, 'what's next?' Nothing is next. I just want some time to talk with him, that's all. You go ahead to the reception. We're going to take a walk. I'll see you back in the room."

"I want a full report, do you hear?" Martha said with an impish smile.

"Go on," Ellen laughed as she gave her a slight push toward the reception room then returned to where Josh waited.

Noticing them standing together, Mrs. Ramson walked toward where they stood. Ellen saw her coming and waited there for   her.

"Well, Ellen, congratulations on your graduation." She

240

looked at Josh with a questionable look. "You look familiar, but I'm not sure why."

"This is Josh Gibbons, Mrs. Ramson," Ellen said. "He may look familiar because he was a former patient."

"A patient, huh? Well, that leads to questions I have, to which the answers would be immaterial at this point, wouldn't they?"

"He was just a patient, Mrs. Ramson," Ellen said. "That's all. Nothing more."

"Well, as I said, it's no longer a point of discussion. I wish you the best of luck, Ellen." She turned and walked in the direction of the reception.

"Well, that was easier than I thought it was going to be," Ellen said. "Looking at Josh, she asked, "Shall we go?"

"That's all, and nothing more, huh?" he asked.

"Isn't that correct?"

"I guess you'll have to speak for yourself. Actually, I guess you're right," he said. "You wouldn't talk to me."

"My goodness," she joked. "Listen to you. I just met you and you're picking on me."

*****

Ellen felt like she was walking on a cloud as they headed down the sidewalk in front of the hospital. "Which way shall we go?" Josh asked.

"I've actually had no time to wander around the area, so your guess would probably be as good as mine."

They stood looking in both directions. To the left was a path leading down a hill and toward a park area where benches sat under several large oak trees. Among them stood a huge magnolia tree dressed in a full bloom of pink blossoms. Fallen petals of pink had covered the ground underneath the tree, creating what appeared to be a round, pink carpet decorating the ground.

In the right direction, there was a sidewalk that led past a small limestone building and beyond that, a creek that ran behind the hospital. Ducks were floating in the stream. Lavender in partial bloom grew intermittently along both sides of the sidewalk intermixed with white daisies. Along the bank of the creek were poppies in vivid colors of orange, red, and yellow.

"I vote for the creek, what do you think?" Josh asked.

"I think we should do both. Let's go see the creek, then we'll still have time to walk down to the park area."

Walking to the creek, Josh asked, "What time do you have to leave?"

"Our train leaves at 7:00 and our ride will take us there about 6:30. I have my suitcase already packed except for a few last minute things, like my diploma." She held it up to show him.

"Congratulations again. I know you've worked hard for that."

"Thanks. Yes, it's been very hard, very hard without my family. Speaking of family, there is so much about me that you don't know – so much to tell you."

"I'm sure it's all interesting."

"No, it isn't all as it seems, Josh. You must hear more about me before you go any further. I feel bad that you came all this distance and you don't really know me."

"I trust you want me to be here?"

"I really hoped you would be, but I knew too that it was wrong for you. In that sense, I almost hoped you wouldn't come," she answered.

"I can't think of any reason I wouldn't want to be here or why it would be wrong for me. You have fascinated me since the first time I saw you, even when I was too sick to want to notice you."

"I felt the same way, but I couldn't want you for a number of reasons. I attempted to stop it. Even though I tried to ignore the way I felt, it wouldn't go away."

"So tell me what I should know about you," Josh said.

"Well, to start with, you know we're required to be single to be students here, no boyfriends, husbands, or children. I have children, Josh. I have two children. I was married. So, I've been living a lie for the past two years. My only excuse is that I needed a career in order to take care of my family and this was the field I've always wanted to be a part of."

"You were married. Are you still married?" Josh expressed a look of disappointment that Ellen found hard to face. She could see a wistful desire that seemed to be dieing with that news. He would now realize he had made a mistake coming here, she was certain. Regardless, she had to answer the questions and keep the conversation going until he walked away.

"No, I'm not still married, but I still have two children and always will have. I've had to keep that hidden from everyone, or I'd never have been allowed to go to school here. I wanted to tell you, but I couldn't talk about anything while you were a patient and I couldn't write to you. Even if I had talked with you, I wouldn't have mentioned that I had been married. I have told no one until now." She hesitated for a minute watching for his reaction, knowing it would hurt. "So now that you know, you can get this whole silly idea out of your head." The reality of the hopelessness of her situation crept through her like cold air coming through a draft. She wanted to run and hide, somewhere alone, to cry in her own space. She dropped her head and waited for the end to come.

"Do you think it's a silly idea?" she heard him say.

Her voice dropped and she nervously ran her fingers through her hair. Had she said the wrong thing? Had he lost interest in her? He was too good to be true, she knew all along, but couldn't stop hoping. But she wanted so badly for it to be real. If she kept talking, would he even hear her? "I really like you Josh. I have from the first time I saw you, but it's silly for me to think that you can be infatuated with a lady who has been married and has children. My children are my whole life and they'll always be my first priority. I don't expect you to accept that, even if it's just dating. You can go now before you get involved and no one gets hurt." Now it was said. She looked for his reaction, sure that he would excuse himself and leave. Maybe he'd say 'goodbye', but maybe he'd just turn and walk away. That would be the easiest for both of them. She could imagine he'd just say, *well, it was a nice thought anyway, Ellen. Too bad we couldn't make it work for us.* Yes, that's what he would do. He was too polite to leave without saying anything.

She felt Josh's arm around her shoulder. "Why don't you let me decide that?"

She turned to face him, trying her best not to cry. It had been so long since anyone had truly cared for her. Could he really accept her with her background? He put his arms around her and drew her close. His arms felt secure and honest, a place of peace. She was ecstatic. The pain of the past drained from her soul like melting ice into water. Standing beside the lake, he brushed a tear from her face and kissed her. She fell into his arms, soft, like butter on a warm day. It felt so right. For this moment anyway, nothing else in the world mattered.

*****

Ellen was grateful for the long train ride back to Lexington. She wanted the time to reflect on what had just happened. Josh had taken another train heading to Ashland to visit with Doc Weide. She and Martha boarded the train at 6:30 and were on their way home at 7:00. "Okay, when are you seeing him again?" Martha asked as soon as they sat down on the train.

"You don't waste any time, do you?" Ellen joked.

"No, we don't have that much time. What do we have? Maybe two hours I'd guess and you have a lot to tell me between now and when we get into Paintsville."

"First of all, to settle your curiosity, he's coming to my place on Wednesday evening when he gets back into town. Okay? That gives me four days to get home and see my family and get settled back into my old life."

"Well, that's a start. How much do you like him? And how long has this been going on, right under my nose?" Martha asked. "I had suspicions of course, but I thought that's all they were."

"You had suspicions, I know, but there was nothing going on – not really. I couldn't say anything to him while he was a patient and I wasn't allowed to write. He wrote to me, however. He said he'd be at graduation, but I really didn't think he would. I like him much more than I should, I know."

"Don't be silly, Ellen. You can care as much as you want about him now."

"There's so much in my life that has gone on and still going on. He may tire of that, I don't know."

"Like what? You've heard that love conquers all, haven't you?"

"In stories, that's true."

"It's true, period. Trust me. I don't know what is so bad in your life as you say, but if he cares, and you care, it will work out, believe me."

"There was an instant flame as big as a forest fire when I first saw him, I have to admit," Ellen said. "It has burned bright since that time, even though I tried desperately to put it out. It all seemed so hopeless."

"And to think you kept telling me there was 'nothing.'"

"I had to, you know that," Ellen said.

"What else is it that you're hiding? I don't understand what is so bad."

"Since I have my diploma in hand, I can tell you now. I had been married and I have two children."

"You do? I can't believe that. Where are they?"

"My mother has kept them for me so that I could go to school."

"What about their father?" Martha asked.

"We're divorced." Ellen couldn't chance telling even Martha that Sherm was a wanted killer. Some day perhaps when he was behind bars, she could feel safe enough to talk about it, but not until then. When Josh had asked about him, she couldn't lie. She told him Sherm was on the run without going into great detail. Eventually she would explain everything.

*****

Ellen looked up and down the platform when the train stopped. It didn't take but a minute to spot the kids. Charlie was waving his arms and jumping up and down, a bouquet of slightly wilted wildflowers in one hand. Neet was holding on to Charlie's shirt as he jumped. Bertie stood behind them, one arm in a sling and the other waving. With her suitcase in hand, Ellen ran towards them. "Mommy, mommy," Charlie yelled. Ellen threw her arms around him and hugged him tightly.

Neet hung back, standing behind Bertie, reluctantly looking at Ellen. Although she knew this was Mommy, she wasn't quite sure how to react. She was slightly bashful, and more reserved than her outgoing brother. Bertie had tried hard to keep a picture of Ellen fresh in the minds of the children by frequently showing them a picture of her, one Ellen had mailed home. Each letter that arrived from Ellen, Bertie had read to the children. Ellen reached down next and picked up Neet and hugged her. "I love you, Neet." She paused for a minute giving her daughter time to feel her arms around her. "Please remember me, honey. I've missed you so much." Slowly, her little arms went around her mother's neck. Holding her in one arm, Ellen reached for her mother with the other. "Mama, it's so good to see you. I owe you so much."

"You've paid me already just by finishing your training and coming home. That's all I wanted," Bertie answered. "I'm so glad you're home, honey. It's so good to see you. I've missed you."

"I've missed you too, Mama, and Neet and Charlie." She sat Neet down and took her hand. Charlie took her other hand while Bertie carried the suitcase with her good arm. Looking at Bertie, Ellen said, "It feels so good to be here. Can you believe I'm all finished? I still am having a hard time believing I'm a registered nurse now."

"You've worked hard, I know, "Bertie said. "But I knew you could do it."

"Mommy, are you staying here now?" Neet asked.

"I sure am, honey. I'm never leaving you again." She squeezed their little hands in hers as they headed for the car. "Tell me how you fell, Mama, and what the doctor says about it."

"Just one of those crazy things is all. I walked outside to sweep the porch because there was a lot of dust and leaves from a windstorm we'd had. I guess I wasn't payin' attention when I was sweepin' off the steps. I thought there was three steps and there was actually four. Then I lost my footing when I thought I was off the steps and I wasn't. The next thing I knew, I was laying on my arm, in pain, I might add."

"I am so sorry."

"I'm fine now. It's just a nuisance, that's all, wearing this cast and sling. It's just a lucky thing I didn't break my ankle or my hip. The biggest problem I have now is my ironins. I've got several to do and can't do 'em."

"Guess I came home at the right time, didn't I?" Ellen said.

"You need a job as a nurse, not one ironin' clothes."

"I'll get a job, but I'll do what I have to do at home until you're feeling better. Besides, Mama, I've been giving it a lot of thought, you know - where I'd like to work – and where it'd be best for all of us to live."

"And what did you come up with?" Bertie asked, smugly, but with a smile.

"I just think if we were further away, maybe Illinois or even down south further, it'd be a lot safer, for now, don't you think?"

"You're probably right honey. Better wait till I get this arm healed though before we think too much about that. I wouldn't be much help right now. It's hard enough to drive. Good thing it's not my gear-shiftin' arm in a cast. I only go where I have to."

"I'm gonna have to learn to drive too, I think."

"I think that'd be a good idea," Bertie said.

"There's something else too, Mama."

"Let's get in the car and you can tell me on the way home," Bertie said.

*****

In the car, Ellen continued. "Mama, it's so good to be here."

"I know it is. We've missed you too, you know. It was harder for you though. What was it you were going to tell me in the car?"

"Well, while I was working in the hospital, I met a very nice man – a patient."

"Oh, you did, huh? Hmmmm, now ain't that nice? What did your leaders think about that?" She turned to look at Ellen with a wide smile.

"They didn't know how I felt and I didn't do anything that would have gotten me in trouble either."

"So tell me more," Bertie said.

"He's actually from Lexington, but he had gone to Ashland, over in Kentucky, to visit a friend of his. He and his friend came to Logan for a day and while he was there, he got appendicitis, so they brought him to our hospital. His appendix had ruptured, so he was a pretty sick guy. He was our patient for a couple of weeks. Even though I only talked to him about things that had to do with him getting better, he wrote to me twice at the hospital after he went home. I didn't write back to him because I couldn't. It was against the rules. Also, with my situation, I don't think I'd have written anyway, even though I really did want to."

"Yes," Bertie said, smiling. "What about this man?"

"He showed up at my graduation. He had written in his letter saying he was coming, but I didn't really think he would, but he did! I couldn't believe it. We spent the rest of the day together, after graduation, walking around the grounds of the hospital. I had never seen much outside of my room or the ward I was working in since we were so busy all the time. I either rested or wrote letters to you when I had some spare time. The grounds were so pretty. We had a really nice time. I have invited him here for supper one day. He had something planned – a big race, he said, for Saturday, so next week one evening I've invited him for supper, if that suits you. That gives me a couple of days to get settled and catch up on what needs to be done at home."

"Well, that's pretty fast, honey, but only you know how you feel about him. I just want you to be careful. You've already had enough fear and trauma to last forever," Bertie said.

"Yes, I know. I think of that and I think of Sherm still bein' loose out there, not knowin' where he is or when he'll show up. It's scary."

"What is this man's name and where does he work? Also, have you told him anything?" Bertie asked.

"I've told him everything that I thought I should at the time. All of the most important things he knows." Ellen carefully selected her words so as not to frighten the children.

"How about the federal agents? Does he know about them?"

"No, I didn't figure I knew him well enough to go into too much detail at the time. I did tell him that I had been married and divorced, and that I had two children. I let him know that Sherm was wanted, but without ugly details."

"Good," Bertie answered.

"I'll tell him the entire story when the time is right. His name is Josh Gibbons," Ellen continued. "He works at a place called Holiday Farms. Guess he trains horses. He isn't home right now, but should be by tomorrow or the next day. Just before I left, he took another train to Ashland to visit his friend before he came back to Lexington."

"I'm glad you told him about the kids and about Sherm," Bertie said. "I think it would have been wrong to bring him here not knowing that."

*****

At home, Ellen stepped from the car and looked at the house. She felt like kissing the ground. "Home, I'm home, finally! It's the best day of my life," she said. The children carried the small items to the house, while Ellen carried the rest.

In honor of the occasion of homecoming, neighbor, Mrs. Crossen, had brought sandwiches and soup for everyone. "It's good to have you home, Miss Ellen," she said.

"I'm loving being here, Mrs. Crossen. Thank you so much for helping my mother so often."

"It was my pleasure, dear. You enjoy your supper and your family. I'll excuse myself for now and let you folks be alone."

Being home at last was a dream come true. Ellen had waited so long for this day. She walked around the house just looking and touching. Bertie watched her with a face full of pride. She had sacrificed the ultimate, being away from her children so that she could provide a better life for them, and fortunately, in a field she loved.

Following supper, Ellen sat with the children and Bertie. "Mommy, come here and see my new books," Neet said.

"I'd love to honey. Come Charlie." She held out her hand to him. They walked to the couch.

"Want me to read to you?" Charlie asked.

"I want to read," Neet cried.

"You don't know how to read yet, Neet," Charlie scolded.

"Well, why don't we let her try and both of you can read, okay?" Ellen asked.

"Okay," Charlie answered.

Neet pretended to read while Ellen listened intently. Charlie sat next to his mother, watching her longingly, wanting to know her better. Ellen was thrilled. "That was beautiful, Neet. Wasn't it, Charlie?" He smiled and snuggled up close to her. The children sat still for as long as their attention span would last, then went to their coloring books.

Exhausted from riding the train most of the night, Ellen's eyes began to flutter up and down like butterfly wings and her arms grew too heavy to lift. The more Bertie talked, the sleepier Ellen became until her head nodded and she suddenly caught herself from falling sideways. "Okay, enough talking for tonight. I know you're tired. Let's get to bed," Bertie said.

*****

Months had passed since Maggie had found Sherm's hiding spot for his paperwork, the small amount of money, and the key to his bank box. She periodically had checked the box in the yard, counting the money each time. She noted the amount was up and down, so she knew he was moving it, most likely to the bank. There was enough money here to get her out of Ashland, but if she had the chance to get to the lock box, she would take that as well. After all, she had earned it. He had borrowed all she had, which she knew he never planned to return. There was the abuse she had taken from him; that was worth whatever she could get from him. She planned to take the key with her just in case she could get in the box, and just in case the money was there. Depending on the circumstances, she would go there on her way out of town, that was providing all went well getting away from home.

The time, she believed, was right to get away from Sherm. She was bruised and sore from slaps. Her body was exhausted from the long hours at work and at home. She couldn't take it any longer. The weather was finally warm and roads were clear enough for travel. The next evening that she was supposed to go to work, she would leave home and instead, head to Tabors Creek. He wouldn't realize she was missing until the next morning after she left and he awakened. He would be furious, she knew, so she had to be far enough ahead of him and at a place where he wouldn't expect to find her. She would take the two horses and the wagon, a lot slower than the car he drove. However, if she had a good head-start, she could be in Tabors Creek before he knew she was gone. He couldn't come there.

She washed the last of the jugs that Sherm had stacked for her to clean, then picked up the first of several pots to be scrubbed. As she moved toward the wash tub, Sherm opened the door and came in bent over forward and holding his stomach. "I'm sick, Maggie. I need to go see Dr. Weide."

Maggie turned around to see Sherm in complete distress and in obvious pain. "What's the matter, Sherm?" she asked.

"My stomach – it's on fire."

Without sympathy, but with a sense of duty, Maggie quickly got the horses connected to the wagon and helped Sherm into a seat. She drove the team to Doc Weide's. Sherm held on to her arm as he hobbled up the steps and into the doctor's office.

*****

Sherm felt somewhat better as he sat waiting in Dr. Weide's office. He looked around the room, taking note of some pictures on the wall as Doc sat at his desk writing notes in his medical record. "Looks to me like you got the makings of an ulcer, Sherm. I told you before you had to stop drinking. Have you?"

"Don't drink much anymore," Sherm lied.

"I didn't advise you to drink less; I said you should stop drinking, no alcohol, period. Remember?"

"Yes, I remember."

"Well, now you've got first hand knowledge on what happens when you drink alcohol, eat the wrong foods, and don't follow instructions. If you insist on drinking alcohol before this is healed, you'll kill yourself, and that's a fact. If you want to drink, then drink milk. The more milk you drink, the better. Understand?"

"I hear you, doctor."

"I'm going to write out a list of things I want you to eat for the next month, and I want you to follow it very closely. If you do, you should get better. If you don't, I won't be able to help you. Nobody will." He turned back to his desk and began writing out a list.

Sherm continued to look around the room, while the doctor wrote, paying particular interest to a picture on the wall of Doc with a horse. The horse had the same unusual markings as one of Maggie's horses. There was a diamond shaped patch of white in the center of its forehead, which was fairly common, but the unusual marking was another round patch of white on her breast. That horse has the same marks as the horse we got, Doctor," Sherm said. "It has a diamond patch on its forehead and another on its chest. I never seen that before, 'cept the one we have."

"That kind of marking is actually pretty common, but it's a favorite of mine. Yep, that's a pretty special horse. Her name is Brandywine. She had a great future, but messed up her leg, so she's just standing as a breeding mare now. You like horses, do you?"

Although Sherm didn't like horses, unless he had to depend on them to get him someplace, he let Doc believe he did. "Yeah, I do. Always wanted one."

Doc picked up a stack of pictures and handed them to Sherm to look at. "Here's a couple of shots of my other hopeful. Her name is Princess Angie. I just bought her not so long ago. She's over in Lexington right now getting some training. She's gonna be a great one too I think. These aren't the best pictures, but I'm still learning how to develop my own."

"Sounds like a good hobby," Sherm said.

"Well, next to horses, photography is fast becoming my favorite pastime."

Leafing through the pictures, Sherm stopped and stared at the picture he held, his mouth wide open, and for a second he was speechless. He held a picture of a woman who looked like Ellen, standing in a group of other women all wearing the same thing. *Could it be,* he wondered. This lady was wearing a striped uniform that looked like a nurse's outfit. Ellen wasn't a nurse, or at least she wasn't the last time he knew. She had talked about always wishing she were, but that was long ago. *No, it couldn't be her, or could it?* As calmly as he could pretend to be, he asked, "Who is this lady?" as he pointed to Ellen.

"Oh, I forgot those pictures were in there. Sorry. That's a student nurse. I have a friend who was in the hospital and this was a young nursing student there at the hospital at the time. He thought she was very attractive and asked me to get a picture of her," Doc answered. "I just haven't gotten it to him yet."

The more Sherm looked at the picture, the more he was convinced it was Ellen. Even though the rage inside him was building like a wind-driven forest fire, he made every effort to remain as calm as he could. He needed more information from Doc. "What hospital was that?"

"Oh, that's down in Logan, Kentucky, not around here."

"I see. This was just taken not so long ago then, I guess?" Sherm asked.

"Well, not too long ago, back last winter, before Christmas, I guess, why do you ask?"

"Just wondered," Sherm said. "I had a sister who wanted to go into nursing. This might be a place she'd be interested in." This was the only reply Sherm could think of for a quick response.

*****

Maggie sat in the waiting area while Sherm was being seen by the doctor. When finished, he came storming out into the waiting room, passed by her and headed for the exit. She could tell he was enraged as soon as she saw him. He slammed the door and went outside ahead of her. She quickly followed him to the wagon. Afraid of him when he was in a fit of anger, she sat quietly on the ride back to the house. He didn't speak until they reached home. Once inside, he began shouting. "That bitch. She's been having a good time on my money," pointing to himself, he pounded on his chest. "My god damned money!" He threw his jacket to the floor and paced back and forth. "I'll kill her. As soon as I find her, I'll kill her."

"Who are you talking about, Sherm?" Maggie asked.

"You know who the hell I'm talking about. Ellen, that's who." He stormed through the house, went into the bedroom and came back to the kitchen carrying his revolver. He opened a box of shells. Assured there were plenty in the box, he closed it.

"Where is she?" Maggie asked.

"She's been learnin' to be a nurse down in Logan, that's where she is. She's at the hospital there and I'm gonna' find out where the hell it is and I'll go after her. I'll kill her and her god damned mother. I'll kill both of them."

"You don't know what hospital she's in, do you?" Maggie asked.

"Quit asking me so God damned many questions," Sherm said. "The town ain't that big. Can't be more'n one hospital.

I'm goin' in town and make a couple of telephone calls. I'll find out where she is." He placed the gun in a holster that fit around his back and under his arm, then slipped into a concealing hunting vest.

"Sherm, you can't do that. You'll get caught and when you do, you'll go straight to prison. You know that."

Ignoring her, Sherm went out the door and brought in some empty jugs, and called to Maggie. "I want these washed before you go to work. Do you hear?"

"I hear you," she answered. After he went back outside, she watched him for a while from the kitchen window, then slowly walked to the tub to wash the jugs. She needed to do anything he asked her to do in order to keep from giving him a reason to strike her. Her time was coming, perhaps this afternoon or tomorrow, when she would be gone, but for now, fear dictated her every move. Circumstances would be her guide.

Sherm walked to the still and began capping jugs that were ready and placed them in the car. When he had finished, he came inside to see what Maggie was doing. "When I get home from delivering these, I'm headed to wherever she is, wherever I find the bitch, understand?"

"I do," Maggie said quietly.

"Is that all the hell you can say?" he asked.

"No, Sherm. I just didn't know what else to say."

"That's the damned trouble. You talk, but you never say anything. Get in the God damned bedroom." Looking at her, he pointed toward the bedroom.

Afraid, Maggie dried her hands on her apron and walked to the bedroom.

"Get your clothes off and lay down on the bed," Sherm ordered.

Standing, Maggie began to do as he asked, afraid to say anything. First she placed her shoes under the bed. She took off her apron. Sherm laid his gun on the chair, took off his pants and underwear, while Maggie was slowly getting undressed, fearing what was coming. She had seen him take off his gun. Was he going to shoot her, she wondered, or was it just sex he was after.

Angered by her slow movement, Sherm grabbed her from the back, by the collar of her dress, pulling as tightly as he could. Choking, she turned and he let go. She fell backwards onto the bed. "Get movin'. I ain't got all day," he yelled. She sat up and lifted the dress over her head. As she did, he slapped her hard on her left leg with his open hand. Maggie grabbed hold of her leg, and let out a scream as the pain seared through her body. Just a second later, his right fist slammed into the side of her right butt cheek. "Oh, God, Sherm, please don't," she begged.

"You're nothing but a slut. Open your legs," he yelled.

Maggie couldn't fight the inevitable. With all the force he could use, Sherm took her. When he finished, he quickly got dressed. She sat up on the side of the bed, holding her dress in front of her, subconsciously hoping he wouldn't see her. She feared what was coming next, so she said nothing. He tightened his belt and walked toward the kitchen.

"Get those jugs finished," he yelled as he walked out the door.

*****

There was no time for crying or for limping even though every step on either foot sent waves of pain up the side of her thigh. Maggie knew she had to get out of here now. There could be no waiting for tomorrow. Maybe the next time, he would kill her. She hurriedly threw her clothes on, ran to the window and watched as Sherm pulled out. She then went outside and fed the horses. While they ate, she rushed to the place where Sherm's money was hidden. She uncovered the can, looking all around her to be sure she was alone. She reached inside and carefully took the wrapped money. She then took the key to open the bank lock box and put the can back inside the ground, as she had found it. Inside, Maggie quickly got together the few things she had, placed them in a pillow slip, and put the clean jugs where Sherm would find them. She checked to make sure everything was in order, just as it would be if she were coming home after work, as she normally did. Hopefully, by the time he discovered she wasn't coming home, it would be too late. She would be well on her way. In the yard, she hooked the wagon to the horses and quickly pulled out onto the road.

In town, she looked up and down the street, and assured Sherm's car was nowhere near the Main Street, she headed to the bank. Noting his car was not at the bank, she went inside. Nervously, she looked around, hoping she didn't appear to be conspicuous. "Good morning," the clerk spoke.

"Good morning," Maggie answered. Although sophistication was foreign to her, she knew she had to be somebody different in here. She had watched the strong women at the newspaper office as they paraded through the offices. Always envious of their confidence, she wondered if their lives at home were as peaceful as they appeared at work Although shabbily dressed in a faded, plaid colored, long dress, Maggie was an attractive woman. Her long black hair was pulled up into a chignon, making her look presentable. She did her best to imitate the walk of the ladies she'd studied at work as she headed to the row of bank boxes. Her shaky hand finally got the key into the slot and the box opened. There was money lying right on top – a stack of it in a money bag, which she recognized as her own, the one she had given Sherm with her money in it. *Ironic*, she thought. *My money coming back to me in my own bag.* She retrieved the bag, placed it in her own purse and slowly sauntered, as best she could, across the floor toward the door. When she reached the door, she hurried down the steps and into the wagon. Again, noting his car was nowhere in sight, she pulled out and headed for Tabors Creek.

*****

Sherm parked his car behind the Windham. As usual, Sam met him there and helped him unload the jugs in through the back door. Sherm followed him into the office, where he was paid. "I have a favor to ask," Sherm said.

"What's that?" Sam asked.

"I need to make a couple of phone calls, down to Logan. If I could use your phone, I'll pay you for the calls. Don't have a phone at home."

"Sure. That's fine," Sam said. "Go ahead and make your calls and when I get the bill, I'll just take it off the next load of juice payment. How does that sound?"

"That sounds good to me. Fine."

"Come with me. I'll show you where the phone is." Sam led Sherm to a small room with a desk and phone. He pointed into the room, motioning for Sherm to go inside. "There you are," he said.

"Thanks," Sherm said, anxious for Sam to leave.

Sherm called the telephone company information first. He would find out if she was in Logan before he did anything more. "I need to reach the hospital in Logan, W.Va.," he said to the operator.

X

1932

"Holy Christ," Maggie yelled as she felt the thump of the wagon hit the roadway. "Whoa," she called to the horses dragging the broken sled. She jumped from her wagon seat and raced to the tilted, right side of the wagon, half afraid to look at the damage. When she did, it was obvious she wasn't going anywhere soon – not until she got some help. "What in hell's acre am I going to do," she moaned looking at the broken wheel lying in a large rut behind the wagon. "I made it maybe one mile out of town."

Defeated, she waited in the heat, mentally and physically exhausted, for nearly two hours until help came. She saw the car coming her direction in the distance and held her breath. If it was Sherm, someone would find her shot and laying along side the road some time. She'd be buried and no one would know or even care who she was. There was no place to hide. *What to do?* Nothing she could do, but stand there and pray. Maybe he'd hit her with a hammer. At least that would be quick. Or, maybe he'd choke her to death. She wondered what kind of death that would be. It sounded awful. The car stopped behind the broken wagon wheel. A tall, thin man stepped out. Her prayers were answered: It wasn't Sherm. "Howdy, ma'am. Got a problem, I see."

"Yes, I sure do, and I don't know what to do about it."

Tabors Creek

He looked at the broken wheel. Finally, he stood up and announced. "It's too far gone to fix here. I'll take the wheel back into town and get it fixed for you."

"Thank you so much, Mr., er. I'm sorry, I don't' even know your name."

"Not important, but it's Emory, Emory Baling. Just helpin' out where I can."

*****

It was late in the evening before Maggie got on the road again. When it grew too dark to see where she was going, she finally had to pull over along the side of the road and rest. Temperatures had dropped during the night and she grew chilly after a while. She reached in the box on the bed of the wagon and pulled out a blanket she had used to cover Sherm when she had taken him away from Tabors Creek. She had sneaked him out and now she was, ironically and in a strange way, sneaking back in. She had the bag of money she started out with, although she had no idea how much was in it. Sherm had the house. If he could sell it, he'd get his money back. With that thought in mind, her conscience grew clear and she could relax a little bit.

During the darkest part of the night, Maggie dozed off for short periods of time, awakened by each peculiar sound she heard. On one occasion, she awoke to the noise of a screeching owl, which left her trembling and scared. Although she hadn't seen it, it flew close enough that she could hear the sound of its flapping wings. She had never felt so desperate and alone. Later there were the sounds of bobcats in the woods. She imagined their cries were getting closer and closer to the wagon as the night passed. "Oh God, what did I do? Please help me." She sat up and listened trying to hear any sound coming near the wagon until exhaustion forced her to sleep. Near morning she was again awakened by something that flew into her arm and startled her.

She screamed and sat up, wide awake this time. Too frightened to go back to sleep, she stayed awake and waited for the daybreak. As soon as there was enough light to see the ground, she took off again.

The sun was just on the horizon when Maggie pulled into Tabors Creek. Too frightened to go into town and undecided on what to do, she headed toward her house. *Where will I go*, she wondered. *Would Sherm hunt me here? Would he chance coming back to Tabors Creek? Even if he did, it wouldn't be today. He wouldn't even know yet I wasn't coming home*, she rationalized. She would be safe for at least one night. She needed rest, some sleep. There had only been moments of sleep last night. It would feel good to be back in her own home for just one night anyway.

*****

Sherm was delighted with himself. He had not only found out Ellen had been in Logan for the past two years going to nursing training, but he found out where she lived. If only he had been a day earlier, she would still have been right there in Logan. He laughed out loud when he remembered the conversation with Mrs. Ramson. "I'm her uncle," he had said. "I've been out of the area for a couple of years and I just found out she was somewhere in Logan goin' to nurses training. Fortunately, now I have found out where. I'm really happy for her – a smart thing for her to do. I was hoping to get down there and see her, but you say she's already gone, huh?"

"Yes, she left yesterday. I'm sorry you missed her."

"Would you have her home address? I could visit her there maybe this weekend," Sherm politely asked.

"I don't normally give that information out, but I'm sure she'd be disappointed if I didn't. Let me pull her chart and I'll get it for you."

"Thank you."

After she pulled Ellen's chart, she returned to the phone. "She lives in Lexington, Kentucky, at 356 Salem Street."

"Thank you very much, Mrs. Ramson."

*****

There was work to do at home before Sherm took off to find Ellen. From the Windham, he hurried home to take care of last minute details. In the house, he looked to be sure Maggie had finished washing the jugs before she left. He needed to fill them. She had already gone to work, as he expected. That was good. He needed the time alone to take care of the paperwork, count his money and make his last delivery this evening. Tomorrow he would leave early in the morning and head to Lexington. The bank had already closed for today. He would stop there on the way out of town, get his money and leave. After he found and shot Ellen and Bertie, he'd have to move fast. Probably, he'd just head south until he got to the nearest town and stop there until things cooled down. He couldn't come back to Ashland. They'd be hot on his tail. "Maggie's gonna spill her guts when she hears the news. She'll see I ain't comin' home and she'll be mad as hell. If I'd been smart, I'd have killed her today, but I wasn't thinking right," he said aloud. "The bitch. Wish I'd choked her." Maggie's outside shoes were sitting on the floor by the door. He kicked them across the room, then stormed out the door with two jugs in his hands.

Let 'em hunt, I don't give a Goddamn. They'll never find me. I've got plenty of money and I'll head south or anywhere else I damn well want to, he thought. *I can't wait to see the look on their faces when I find 'em. Bitches.*

He filled and capped the jugs and put them in the car. When he had emptied everything, he put out the fires under the pots and walked to the spot where he kept his money and papers. He opened the pit. The papers were there, but the money was gone. "Those God damned workers. They musta found this." With nothing he could do, he reached in the box for the key, but it too was missing. Sitting and staring at the spot where he had placed the key, he tried to think where he might have left it. He stood up and checked his pants pockets, already knowing he hadn't put it there. Assuming he had lost it, he hoped there was a spare at the bank. He ate, then left to make his delivery. He'd make the bank tomorrow.

*****

Maggie tied the horses behind the house. Even though Sherm wouldn't find her today, someone else might pass by. She went inside. Dust was everywhere. Sherm's clothes were laying on the floor. She couldn't stand the sight of them so picked them up and threw them out the back door. "I'll take care of that stuff another time." She walked into the bedroom. She sighed when she saw the dust and dirt. Too tired to care, she pulled the coverlet back and lay across the bed.

Bright sunshine drifting in the window awakened Maggie late in the afternoon. She was tired, dirty and hungry. There was nothing in the house to eat. What to do? She picked up the water bucket sitting on the stand beside the table and walked to the pump. She pumped for several minutes until the water began to pour. The water was a rusty brown from three years of non-use, but she continued to pump until the water finally became clear. She rinsed the bucket several times, then filled it for drinking and washing.

Back inside the house, being extremely thirsty, she drank water as she never had before. Then she built a fire and placed a pan of water on the top of the stove to heat for washing her bruised and sore body. What was she to eat though? Then she remembered, she had tossed a loaf of bread into her pillowslip that carried her belongings. Before she finished, she had eaten half the loaf of bread and drank much of the water.

Undecided on what to do, and still tired from the past events, Maggie lay back down and fell asleep. Tomorrow she would go into Tabors Creek and see the Sheriff.

*****

When Sherm awakened in the morning, Maggie wasn't in the bed. He yelled loudly for her, but she didn't answer. He noted her side of the bed hadn't been disturbed, which made him wonder if she'd come to bed at all. "Where the hell are you?" he yelled. When he got no response, he angrily stomped into the kitchen, but she wasn't there. "Goddamn it," he said looking around the room. Nothing had been disturbed and her shoes weren't by the door as usual. He opened the door to look outside and saw that the horses and wagon weren't there either. "Oh, Christ. That's where my money went. The bitch!" He pounded his fist on the wall. "It's a good God damn thing I put the rest in the bank." He opened the ice box and took out some milk. From a full bottle, he drank nearly half, then put it back inside. He quickly dressed, putting on his holster and revolver.

*****

The bank had just opened when Sherm arrived. Bank employee, Mildred Pensing was seated at the desk next to the wall of boxes. "Good morning," she said to Sherm.

"Yes, good morning. I need to get into my box and I've lost my key somewhere. I'm hopin' you got an extra one here."

"You're in luck, Mr. Peck. I recognize you, so I can open it for you. We keep a spare here for all the boxes, just in case that happens."

"I certainly appreciate that," Sherm said. He watched as Mildred Pensing unlocked the box for him. When she had finished, he stepped up and opened the door to the box. Instantly, he saw the leather pouch and the money were gone. He was enraged.

"Someone has been in this box," he shouted.

Mildred quickly walked to where he stood. His face was red and a very frightened Mildred backed up a few steps and stopped. "We don't open these boxes, Mr. Peck."

"I had a bag on top of my things and it's gone, Goddamn it. It's gone. Somebody got in here. Who the hell was it?" Sherm yelled. He violently slapped the wall.

Alarmed, Mildred began to back up towards the door.

Aware that the other employees would be coming in soon, Sherm knew he had to get his temper under control at once. He could be caught right here if he did something stupid like harm Mildred Pensing. He wanted to kill her, but couldn't, not now. Another time, maybe. "Was anyone in here besides me?"

"There was a lady with black hair, pulled up in a chignon yesterday about noon. She opened a box. I do believe it was that one," she answered. "I couldn't be real sure since I didn't watch real close."

"Why the hell did you let her into my box?"

"We don't let anyone into the boxes, Mr. Peck. She had a key to get in. We didn't furnish it."

Sherm didn't respond. He turned and walked out the door. *Where did she go? I'll find her. She's driving a wagon so she can't go too far. Where would she go?* He climbed into his car and drove away. He knew he had to find her or he'd never go anywhere. All of the money he had was in that bank box. *What to do?* He was desperate now. The only money he had left was what he got from last night's delivery. After a lot of thought, he knew he had to go to Lexington. *I'll find her and cut her tongue out.* He beat on the steering wheel with his fist as he drove.

*****

Sheriff Workman was in his office alone when she arrived. It was noon. As soon as he saw her enter, he stood up. "Maggie! Good God. Where the hell have you been? And what are you doin' here?"

Limping toward his desk, her hip aching, she began to cry. "My God, Sheriff, Sherm has found out and he's gonna' kill her. He said he'd kill her and her mother, just as soon as he found her. He got his gun and strapped it to his side and then he left."

"Slow down here. Slow down. Just a minute. You're talkin' 'bout Sherm Peck, I presume, aren't you?" he asked.

"Yes, yes. He's found out where Ellen is and he says he's gonna' kill her. And he'll kill me too if he finds me."

"Ellen? Where is Ellen?"

"She's down in Logan at a hospital there learnin' to be a nurse he told me. Said he was gonna' kill her just as soon as he made sure where she was," Maggie cried. "He will to. I know he will. When I left yesterday he was headed into town to make a telephone call and find out fer sure she was there."

"That son-of-a-bitch. Sit down, Maggie. I'll get you a cup of coffee, then you can tell me the whole story."

Sheriff Workman rushed to pour a cup of coffee and return to where Maggie sat. "Where are Bertie and the kids?" he asked.

"I don't know," Maggie said. "I don't know."

"I asked Sherm what hospital in Logan and he said there can't be more'n one hospital cause it's a small town."

"What in the hell were you doing with Sherm, Maggie?" Sheriff Workman finally asked.

"I don't know. It was a big mistake. He'll come after me to kill me when he knows I'm gone, I know that right now. I gave him all my money that I had when I left here with him, but he wouldn't give me back any of it, so I found his money and took it when I left. That's gonna' make him so mad he'll even come back here I think to get me, so I can't stay out there at my house. What am I gonna' do, Sheriff? You gotta help me."

"Because you left here with Sherm, makes you an accomplice, so you'll be in some trouble here too, Maggie. Course you comin' back here and helpin' us find him is gonna help you too. We'll work on that later, but for now, no, you can't be out there. We'll have to find you a place to stay where you can hide. You can't go out there until we know where he is and get him locked up. He has to be found. I don't think he'd come back here. Doubt even that he'd think you'd be here, but we need to make sure you're safe, just in case. We got no time to waste though. I've got to get on the phone and see what I can find out while I wait for Deputy Sheriff Bell to get back here from lunch. When he comes back, he'll get you to a place where you'll be safe. You can spend the time right here in one of the cells till we get you settled somewhere. We'll hide the wagon and take care of the horses until you can go home."

"Thank you, Sheriff. I'm hurtin' and tired. I just wanna lay down and rest somewheres where it's safe."

While Maggie waited, Sheriff Workman made his first phone call to the Sheriff's Office in Ashland, hoping they might capture Sherm before he left town.

His next telephone call was to the hospital in Logan. He spoke with the secretary at the desk who referred him to Mrs. Ramson. "Good evening, Mrs. Ramson. This is Sheriff Workman in Tabors Creek, West Virginia. I am trying to locate a young lady who I have been told is a nursing student there at your hospital."

"Are you looking for Ellen Potter, I suppose?" she asked.

"Yes, I am," Sheriff Workman replied. "How did you know?"

"Well, she's very popular. You're the second person today asking for her. Miss Potter was a nursing student here until just two days ago when she graduated. She is now a fine Registered Nurse, one of our best former students."

"That's quite an accomplishment. It's very important that I reach her. Do you happen to know who the other person was who was looking for her?"

"No, I don't have his name. I didn't meet him, you understand. He called to ask about her. Said he was her uncle and was looking for her. When he learned she was finished here, he asked for her address. Normally, that isn't something we give out, but he said he was hoping to get back in touch with her since he came back to town. He mentioned he'd been gone for awhile."

"Did you give it to him?" the Sheriff asked.

"I did indeed," Mrs. Ramson said.

Sheriff Workman was certain the caller had been Sherm. Someone sane needed to find Ellen before Sherm did.

"Please tell me where she lives. I need to contact her just as soon as possible.

"She lives at 356 E. Salem Street in Lexington, Kentucky."

"How long ago did you receive the other call concerning her?"

Mrs. Ramson hesitated, then asked, "What is the interest in her, may I ask?"

"Her life may be in danger, so I have to find her and find her quick. That's about all I can tell you right now."

"The other call was yesterday afternoon around 4:00 o'clock or so." She paused for a second, then continued. "Well, good luck to you, Sheriff. I do hope you reach her in time," Mrs. Ramson said. She really was unconcerned, however. She was void of sensitivity for anyone outside of her small realm, her walls. Her responsibility had ended the day Ellen had walked from the hospital, certificate in hand. She hung up the phone and casually continued writing a letter at her desk.

When he had the information on Ellen, Sheriff Workman hung up the phone, and immediately called both the U.S. Marshall's Office and the Lexington Police Station with the information. He prayed they'd beat Sherm to Ellen's home.

Looking through notes he'd taken as he listened to Maggie, Sheriff Workman found Doc Weide's name. "Tell me more about Doc Weide, Maggie."

"He was Sherm's doctor in Ashland. We went there together because Sherm's stomach was hurtin' him. The doctor told him he probably has an ulcer."

"He deserves more than an ulcer. He's gonna hang one of these days for shootin' the Feds here two years ago."

"I know Sheriff. I made a big mistake goin' with him, but I didn't know what else to do. I was afraid to say no to him," Maggie said.

"And you say Doc Weide is the one who had a picture of Ellen?"

"Yes," Maggie said. "He had been at the hospital where she was trainin' and took her picture."

"If you'll give me the spelling of the doctor's name, I'm gonna' give him a call and let him know just in case Sherm goes back there."

"Doc Weide is his name, Sheriff, but I don't know how to spell it," Maggie answered. "I'm not feelin' well, Sheriff. I need to lie down." Maggie dropped her head into her hands and seemed faint. Sheriff Workman led her to a cell and Maggie willingly walked in toward the bed. "Thank you, Sheriff. I just gotta get some rest." She lay down on the cot.

*****

With help from the telephone operator, Sheriff Workman was able to reach Doc Weide in his office. "Hello, Doctor Weide. This is Sheriff Workman from Tabors Creek, West Virginia. I'm calling you in reference to a man who I believe is a patient of yours. His first name is Sherm, and I'm not sure what last name he is using right now, but I'm sure whatever it is, it won't be the last name I have for him."

"Well, I don't have too many patients with the first name of Sherm, so I can pretty easily narrow it down. In fact, I can think of only two with that name off hand. What age is your guy?"

"He's probably 24," Sheriff Workman said.

"That's all I needed to know. One of my patients is twenty-four or about that and the other is in his sixties. So you must be speaking of Sherm Havard."

"Sherm Havard isn't the real name of our guy, of course, but the one you mention may well be the one we're lookin' for. If so, then he's using a name he concocted. I'm told each time he was seen in your office, he was accompanied by his female friend whose name is Maggie. Not sure if that's any help or not," the Sheriff said.

"That's the guy. I've heard him call her by name. Speaks pretty rough to her too, I might add. What about him?" Doc asked.

"I can't give you details right now, but if he calls you, please notify the police immediately. If he comes to your office, don't do anything that would light his fuse. He's a time bomb on a rampage and we're just not sure what he might do," Sheriff Workman said. "This is just a warning. I doubt that he has a reason to contact you, but if he does, you need to be prepared."

"Thanks Sheriff. I'll watch for him," Doc said.

"His real name is Sherm Peck, by the way."

"Sherm Peck. Oh my God, you're joking. Sherm Peck? I've seen his picture, back when he shot up the place there in Tabors Creek. I should have recognized him. Good God. Thanks, Sheriff. I think I'll double lock my doors tonight."

"Alright, Doc. Please let us know if you hear from him."

"I sure will. Thanks for the call." Doc Weide hung up the phone and checked each door and window to be sure all were locked.

Sheriff Workman waited until his Deputy arrived. After briefing him, he headed to Lexington.

*****

Sam was busy stocking the shelves behind the bar, expecting the evening crowd any time to start coming in slowly when his phone rang. "Hi Sam, this is George Weide."

"Hi Doc, how are you?"

"Well, I've had better days, that's for sure."

"What's up?" Sam asked.

"I just had a call from the Sheriff over in Tabors Creek, West Virginia. He's calling about a patient of mine."

"What patient?" Sam asked.

"Sherm Havard."

"Oh, yeah? What's he done?"

"Well, when I tell you his real name, you'll know the answer to that question."

"What's his real name?" Sam asked.

"Sherm Peck."

"Holy Shit. Are you sure?"

"Yeah, I'm sure. I just had the call. They're about to close in on him I think. You need to get rid of all your juice there at the bar before the Feds come following Sherm's footsteps. They'll tear your place apart if they do."

"Hell yes, they would. I'm sure that's not your only concern either."

"No, it isn't. I can't afford to have my name mixed up with anything to do with Sherm Peck, that's for damned sure," Doc said. "They can't know that I had anything to do with transporting that stuff to Florida. I should have known better. I was just enjoying that weekend sunshine down there. Course I love to fly too."

"Nothin' will come out of this mouth, Doc. You can be sure. If I were you though, I'd hurry over to the plane and make sure you didn't leave any telltales in there," Sam said.

"That's exactly where I'm headed."

"I have some here for you, so why don't I meet you there – I'll deliver it now and you can fly it down tomorrow."

"Sounds good to me."

*****

As soon as Sherm filled the car with gasoline, he left Ashland and headed for Lexington. There were a lot of miles to cover and the roads were muddy from heavy rains the previous day, but that was something Sherm wasn't able to consider. The rage he carried within was heavy like a load of steel, crushing reasoning and sensible decision-making. What had been kept pent inside him for the past two years was now at the edge of eruption. He was focused on one agenda – getting Bertie and Ellen for what they had done to him and to get what was left of his money they had taken.

There was Maggie too. He'd get her, somehow. She had his money – all that he had left. The more he thought about her, the more enraged he became. If he'd gotten rid of her like he had considered, he'd have his money now. That had been a big mistake. He wasn't quite sure how he'd kill Ellen and her mother; he just knew he had to do it. Probably, it would be easiest just to shoot them. And that might be his only choice. They'd fight him if they had the chance. That Bertie was strong as a horse too; he'd probably shoot her first. Then maybe he could play with Ellen for awhile, after he got the kids locked in a room or something. Had to consider that. Then he'd kill her. Maybe he'd choke her – watch her beg for help, after he screwed her. She'd been a good lay at one time. *The bitches. They need to die. They stole my money, my car, and left me with nothin'. They were glad I was gone. They'd be gladder yet if I was in jail.* After they were both dead, Sherm figured he'd search the house and find his money, what was left of it.

Nothin' he could do about the car they stole; no time to sell it. Now that he had another, he didn't need it, but could have used that money. *Wish to hell Maggie was there in Lexington. All my money. She's got all my money. Would she have gone to Ellen's?* Enraged, he pounded on the steering wheel. He'd find her too. Had to.

Rain began to fall after Sherm had been driving for a couple of hours. Before long, the heavy rain turned to a drizzle and the fog began to cover the ground. Thick fog moved in like rolling balls of cotton, making visibility near impossible. After he was unable to see the road any longer, Sherm had to pull over to the side. He stepped out of the car. "God damned son-of-a-bitchin' fog," he cursed. He walked around the car, kicked the right front tire, and laid his body across the hood banging lightly with his fist.

Not wanting to get wet, he retreated inside. He stayed there only a short time, but afraid to delay his trip, he decided to leave and try to find his way in the fog. Holding his head out of the window, Sherm tried desperately to see the road, but the soupy fog was impossible to see through. Still, he kept going. Luck stayed with him for a few miles, but then abruptly ended. He saw the rut in the road just seconds before he hit it. The car came to a sudden, dead stop, throwing him forward where his head smashed into the windshield. "Goddamn it!" he yelled, grabbing his head in his hand. He jumped from the car to see what damage he had done. The left rear wheel was deep in mud. "Oh, shit, I'll never get outta here," he yelled loudly. He walked around the other side to have a look. Just the one tire sat in the mud-filled hole, but it was obviously in a deep hole. Luckily, the windshield didn't break. Mumbling, Sherm got back inside the car. When he sat down, blood dripped onto his lap from his forehead. "Oh, Christ," he said as he took a rag from under the seat and wiped his head.

Several times Sherm tried to move the car forward and backward by revving the engine, but nothing would make it budge. He got back out and walked to the back of the car and began to push, but the car was too heavy for him alone. Exhausted and wondering what to do, he sat in the car for a short while. With nothing left to his imagination, he leaned back in the seat and fell asleep.

He slept for just a short time, but when he awoke, the fog had cleared and the sun was beginning to shine. He wanted to get into Lexington before dark, but there were still many miles to go and no way to get the car out. He walked through the woods looking for something to place on the road, under the tires. Wandering across a field and into a wooded area, he came across a deserted shack with no one around. Outside on the ground lay a pile of wood. Sherm picked up some of the boards and headed back to his car. Under each rear tire, he laid planks of wood, then got back into the driver's seat. He revved the engine and rocked the car back and forth by switching from reverse quickly back to first gear. After several attempts, the car jolted out of the hole and became free. Glad to be on the road, Sherm never looked back. Driving was slow, but he moved forward as quickly as he could.

When it grew dark, Sherm was leery about driving for fear of landing in another pothole in the middle of the night. The headlights weren't enough on this dark night to show how bad the road was. Passing through a very small community he stopped at a tiny café where he hoped to get something to eat and wait for early morning. The place appeared deserted, although an "Open" sign hung in the window and a light shone from inside at the back of the cafe. Rain began to pick up again slowly as Sherm stepped out of the car and hurried into the restaurant.

Inside sat four tables covered with red and white checkered oil cloths in front of a counter with three stools. The waitress, a heavy-set matronly woman, was the only other person in the café when he entered. "Hi honey," Sherm said.

"Well, now ain't you friendly!" She exclaimed.

"I have to be. I'm starvin' and I'm tired."

"I aim to please. You look like you been in a fight and lost with all that blood on your shirt. What the hell happened?"

"Just a scratch, that's all. Don't worry."

"Okay, honey, if you say so. Back to business. What you gonna' have?"

"What you got to offer?"

"We ain't got time for that now, do we?" The beaming woman spoke with sexual vibes, and her eyes rolling.

"I do if you do." They both laughed loudly.

"How about if I eat first," Sherm said.

"Okay. In that case, let's get back to my first question? What you gonna' have? I can fix you a mess of fried potatoes with gravy and biscuits – got some bacon fried too. Even got some ham I can fix you."

"Sounds good to me. I'll take whatever you fix. I'm hungry."

"You got it," the waitress answered. She walked to the back of the counter and into the kitchen.

Sherm took a seat and looked at the clock on the wall. The time was 9:00. "Damn," he said. "It's God damned late."

While the food was cooking, the waitress walked to the front. She put an LP record on the Victrola and turned to face Sherm. "I'm Erleen. What's your name and what the hell you doin' out on a night like this."

"Just call me Mac. I'm out here cause I have to be."

"You have to be?"

"I have some business in Lexington that I gotta take care of. How far is it from here?"

"Well, I'd guess you oughta make it in a couple of hours, I'd say," she said.

"Here's some music for you, Mac. I thought of this when you walked in the door."

From the music box the song "Ain't Misbehavin" blared loudly.

Tabors Creek

*****

When he finished eating, Sherm paid his bill.

"Got any extra time?" the waitress asked.

"Sure do." Sherm knew he couldn't go anywhere for at least a couple of hours. What better way to spend it? "I can't travel in this damned weather anyway. If you're thinkin' what I'm thinkin', might as well enjoy the time, don't you think?" Both of them smiled widely.

"You read my mind. I figured you wadn't goin' nowhere right now. Why don't you follow me," she asked as she headed toward the counter.

He followed her behind the counter, back through the kitchen, and into a bedroom behind the kitchen. "Is this gonna' be as good as the food?" Sherm asked.

She smiled. "Tell me later."

*****

Early in the morning and on the road again, Sherm's anger took control. He drove as fast as he could which wasn't nearly as fast as he wanted to go. The road was filled with ruts made worse by tonight's rain. *I gotta get there Goddamn it before Maggie spills her guts to the world, wherever she is.* Sherm shook off the drowsiness that tried to take over and pushed as hard as he could.

*****

Sheriff Workman ran to his car, anxious to get on the road to Lexington. He'd talked with the police in Ashland. Sherm had not been located. They feared he had already left Ashland. He wasn't at home and the house appeared empty. Lexington police were on their way to Ellen's house. They were also sending cars toward Ashland to try and intercede, just in case Sherm hadn't

277

reached Ellen's yet. Sheriff prayed that they reached Ellen and her family before Sherm. If Sherm left Ashland yesterday, then he could be in Lexington already – even before Lexington police had been notified. *Goddamn Maggie! Why didn't she come to me yesterday when she got into town?*

Sheriff knew it would take him hours to get to Ellen. Local police and the Feds would have been there and gone by the time he could get there. Still, he had to see her. He had to know. After Sherm was either dead or locked up, would she want him? Could she still love him? If only the police got there in time. "Damn you Maggie," he said aloud. "You shoulda come to me the minute you rode into town. We would have had a good chance of catchin' the bastard before he ever left Ashland." He slammed his fist against the steering wheel, angry at Maggie and worried for Ellen. Now Maggie had Sherm's money and it looked like she had it all from what she said. He couldn't go too far without that. He'd never find Maggie though since he'd surely never chance coming back to Tabors Creek. That meant he'd either have to rob a bank or get a job since he surely couldn't go back to Ashland. He'd know Maggie would tell the police now that she was out of the house. He'd kill the son of a bitch if he hurt Ellen. There was still that little thread of hope that he could make her his own when she was free.

*****

Sherm drove into Lexington, tired and hungry, but the rage he carried with him sustained him with a drive he couldn't get from any meal. He could eat later – after his job was done and he was on his way. He stopped at the first gas station he saw, needing gas and some directions. "Think it'll rain any more?" Sherm asked the gas station attendant.

"Well, them clouds up there don't look too promisin', for sure," the attendant replied. "What you doin' out in weather like this? Looks like you been in mud up to the hilt." He pointed to the muddy tires on Sherm's car.

"Yeah, them roads are pretty bad out there. I got some business to take care of here in Lexington today, but I'll be back home before the sun sets, if it ever comes out," Sherm lied.

"There's a pretty good little cafe down the road a piece, maybe about a mile or so from here where you could get yourself some breakfast. The food's real good and you're lookin' like a hungry man to me," he said, laughing loudly.

"Thanks, I might do that," Sherm said, although he had already decided there was no time for eatin'. He could do that later. Ellen and Bertie were his business. "Do you know where Salem Street is?"

"I sure do. It's only about two blocks from where I live. You just take the road you came in on and go in the same direction. It's only about ten blocks to Fourth Avenue where you turn right. You'll find Salem Street just a couple of blocks off of Fourth, on the right.

Sherm paid his bill for the gas and pulled out, then headed to Ellen's. It was still early, only 8:00 o'clock. He thought of Ellen. *She'll probably be up by now. Won't she be surprised to see me.* A big smile filled his face as he thought of her and the look she'd give him when she opened the door. He turned right on Fourth Street, then right again on Salem. The house on the corner had no house number. "Damn," he said as he tried to read the one on the house next door. Finally, he could read 504. He was close. After scanning numbers for half a block, he located it. He had found 356 Salem Street. "Not a bad lookin' house she got with my money," he said. He could feel his muscles tighten as he thought of her paying for the house with his money.

*****

Ellen had gotten up early this morning. Still in her bathrobe, she stood at the kitchen stove frying bacon for the family. The kids were sleeping. Bertie was setting the table, using her good arm.

"You alright with that, Mama?" Ellen asked.

"I'm fine. You just stop your worryin' about me. I can take care of myself. There's been worse things than a broken arm in my life."

"I was hopin' the kids would be up already, but looks like we're going to have to wake them here in a minute or two," Ellen said.

"We'll just wait until the last minute. They been so excited to have you home it was hard for them to go to bed early last night."

"I know and I wanted them up with me too. It's so good to be able to tuck them in bed at night." Ellen looked at her mother. "You know how much I missed that, Mama. It nearly ate my heart out."

"I know, honey. But it ended well. Soon we'll be outta here and no one will have our address. We'll be able to stop worrying about that bastard Sherm."

"Let's not think about it now. Let's have a nice breakfast with the kids. Give me just another minute or two and you can wake them."

*****

Sherm circled the house a couple of times looking for a good place to park the car. He had to be careful not to arouse suspicion with neighbors. Behind the house he noticed there was an alley. Perhaps he could park there. He drove around the block to have a better look. If he did that, he'd block the alley, so he decided that wasn't a good idea. After awhile, Sherm determined the best place to park was on the same side of the street as the house, but two houses away and in the shadow of a huge, old oak tree, which blocked the view from the house. When he finished his job, he would casually walk out of the house and get into his car and leave town. "I'll be gone before that bitch Maggie spills her God damned guts."

His gun lay on the floor in front of the seat. Picking it up, he placed it in his holster strapped underneath his jacket. Before leaving Ashland he had carefully loaded it and filled his pockets with extra ammo. When he stepped out of the car, Sherm saw that the house curtains were pulled shut so they wouldn't see him walk to the house. "Now ain't they accommodatin'. How sweet of the bitches," he said quietly as he walked toward the front steps. The first step creaked as he began to walk up. He didn't want them to come out lookin' to see who was there. He took hold of the railing and leaned on it gently to ease his weight on the next step, trying to be as quiet as possible. It worked. When he reached the porch, he looked around to be sure no one was outside or looking out a window who might see him enter. He slowly and quietly tried turning the front door knob, hoping it wasn't locked. It was locked. "Damn," he whispered. He stood there a minute. This was no time to make the wrong decision. Should he knock? Maybe he should walk around to the back door. It might be open. But it stood to reason that if the front door was locked, so was the back. He couldn't shoot off the lock. Neighbors would hear that.

*****

Ellen heard the knock on the door. "Oh, Mama. Someone is at the front door. It's probably Sarah. Could you get it, please."

"Sure," Bertie answered. "I'll invite her to stay for breakfast if she has time."

"Good. There's plenty for her too."

*****

It seemed like forever for someone to answer the door after he knocked. He stood there frozen, waiting, waiting. The door knob turned. The door opened. Bertie stood looking at a revolver pointed at her. She backed up slowly without saying a word. Sherm stepped inside and closed the door with his empty hand behind him. Quietly, Sherm said, "Call Ellen."

Bertie didn't move or say anything. Sherm poked the gun into her side. "Call her, now."

"Ellen, can you come here."

"What do you want, Mama? I'm fryin' the bacon."

"Come here, honey, please," Bertie called.

Hearing the urgency in her mother's voice, Ellen headed to the living room. When she saw Sherm, she gasped. "Oh my God. How did you find us?"

"Thought you were pretty God damned smart, didn't you?" Sherm said. He jabbed Bertie in the ribs with the gun. "Didn't you, you bitch?"

"Sherm, please. I'm beggin' you. Remember the kids are here," Ellen pleaded.

"Why didn't you think of that when you stole my car and my money?"

"We were just tryin' to survive, Sherm. That's all," Ellen said.

"Survive, my ass, you bitches stole my money and my car. That's not survivin'. That's thievin'."

"Put the gun down and we can talk," Bertie said.

"How shitin' dumb do you think I am, you pig."

"Sherm," Bertie said. "There was nothin' we could do. We had to leave. We had to."

"Where the hell is my money?"

"Everything we have is in the drawer in the bedroom. I'll get it all for you if you just leave us and don't hurt anyone," Bertie begged. "Please, Sherm. I beg you, don't hurt us."

"I'll go with you if that's what you want, Sherm," Ellen said.

Bertie looked at Ellen with a pleading look. "Ellen, please don't do that."

"Mama."

"Please, Ellen."

With the revolver pointed at Ellen, Sherm asked, "What the hell makes you think I'd want you. I don't want your ass anymore. Just give me my God damned money. I want it now," Sherm yelled.

Sherm pointed the gun at Bertie. "You're the one that probably drove my car, you God damned bitch, didn't you?"

"Sherm, I had to. We had no choice."

"I got none now either." He raised the gun. He shot as Ellen screamed.

"Mama." She ran to Bertie who lay crumpled on the floor. "Mama. Oh, my God, Sherm, look what you've done."

Sherm stood facing Ellen, with his back to the kitchen. "You're next, you whore. Who were you whorin' around with down in Logan?"

Ellen was kneeling beside her mother trying to get a pulse. Concern for her mother was overwhelming. For a split second, she forgot Sherm was there holding a gun pointed at her.

"Stand the hell up," he yelled.

Ellen stood and begged Sherm. "I need to tend to Mama, Sherm. Don't do this please."

Upstairs Mrs. Crossen had been listening to the morning radio show when she heard loud voices downstairs. She and Bertie had talked about Sherm recently and her thoughts went immediately to him. Could he be here? She began to tremble, fearing he might come upstairs. Then she remembered the kids. "Oh, those babies," she cried. The heat register located in her bathroom acted as a megaphone from the downstairs. She had never told Ellen and Bertie, nor had she ever tried to listen before, but this time she was frightened. She ran into the bathroom. On her knees, with her ear to the register, she heard Sherm yelling about the money. Then she heard Ellen pleading with him.

Finally, the gunshot. She knew then for sure. "Sherm. Oh, my God. It really is him. What should I do?" It took only a second to realize she had to act, not think. She hurried, as quietly as she could run, to the bedroom where she kept her rifle.

With her rifle in hand, she quietly crept down the inside stairs that led from her place into Bertie and Ellen's kitchen. She prayed they hadn't locked the door. She had asked them to leave it open for other reasons, but she never dreamed she'd need it for this. She had to keep calm. There was no time for making mistakes. Could she do it? She had to. *It'll take only one shot. Make sure it's a good one. Stop your shaking. He'll kill me if I make a mistake.* Slowly, slowly, she opened the door. It opened quietly. A prayer answered, she noted. She would thank God for that later. Standing behind Sherm, he couldn't see her point the gun at him.

"Put your God damned hands up. Get undressed. I'll kill you after we finish," Sherm yelled at Ellen.

Sally raised her rifle. *Aim slowly*, she told herself. *Don't make a mistake.* She fired before he knew she was there. Sherm fell. The frightened and crying children ran to her. She didn't allow them to look into the living room, but hurried them through the door and up the stairs. "Wait up there for me." Sure that Sherm was dead, she left Ellen tending to her mother and hurried upstairs. She quickly called the police.

*****

Sheriff Workman arrived in Lexington late in the evening. At the police station, he learned that Lexington police had arrived at Ellen's just minutes after Sherm had died. He also learned Ellen was alive and Bertie was in the hospital with a gunshot wound in her left shoulder. As quickly as he could get away, he left for the hospital. After locating her room number, Gordon hurried to Bertie's room.

"Hello Gordon," Ellen said. Standing up from Bertie's bedside, her eyes red from crying, she walked to him and put her arms around him. "It's nice to see you again."

"I'm really sorry, Ellen," Sheriff Workman answered. "It's good to see you too and I'm relieved to know you're okay.

"Thanks. It's not so good for Mama, but I'm prayin' she'll be alright."

Bertie lay sleeping, still under the effects of the anesthesia and pain medication. "She was in surgery for about four hours today," Ellen continued. "The doctor says she stands a good chance of recovering. Please pray for her. I'd be lost without her right now." Her eyes filled with tears.

Sheriff Workman saw the tears rolling down from Ellen's beautiful, though swollen, eyes and his heart ached for her.

"Please don't cry, Ellen. Let's just pray she gets better and she will, I'm sure. She's one strong lady. Both of you are in my mind."

"Thank you, Gordon. I'm sorry you came such a long distance. You must be very tired. Have a seat." She pointed to a straight chair in the room.

"Thanks. I think I will."

"Mama was shot in her left shoulder. She was in such pain. It was awful. I'm so thankful it's over. She just has to get better. Sherm never did like her no matter how hard she worked for all of us." With a hankie, Ellen wiped her eyes.

"It was worth the long drive just to see you, and I came only to see you, Ellen. As soon as I heard about Sherm, I called Lexington, hoping they might reach you before he did, but it wasn't soon enough. I worried all the way driving here." He paused and looked at her for a moment. She smiled, which gave him the courage to continue. "You know I've never stopped caring for you, Ellen. I doubt that I ever will."

"Please, Gordon. Let's don't go over that anymore. It only brings back the hurt."

"I know. I've been tryin' for the past two years to find you. Soon as I heard you left Tabors Creek, I started to look. I was pretty certain you were in Lexington, but didn't know where."

"There was a time I waited and waited for you and you were always gone. You never had time for me, Gordon."

"I know that now, Ellen. I was a fool. There's nothing else I can call it – just a fool. I guess I never thought you'd get tired of waiting and that was a big mistake. I don't want it to be too late now."

"But it is too late, Gordon. Too much has happened. Right now though my mind is on Mama," Ellen said. "I can't think about anything else."

"I just want to take care of you, that's all."

"No, Gordon, but I don't want to talk about it now, about things we've gone through. There's so much going on in my life right now. I guess you know I'm a nurse finally, so I'll be getting a job just as soon as I can. I understand what you're saying and it makes me feel sad, but everything has changed since we were together. It's not like it once was."

"That doesn't matter to me, Ellen."

"Please, Gordon. I must go. I will always care about you. I'd like to be your friend, if you will."

"If that's all I can have, then I'll take it, Ellen. I'm sorry for taking your time, but I thought it made sense to see you in person. I've loved you forever, even if you didn't realize it. You must know how much I've missed you. I hope you'll think about us and change your mind. I'll be stayin' tonight over at the police barracks, but I'll head back to Tabors Creek tomorrow. I won't take up any more of your time now. I just wanted to see you and make sure you and your mother, and the children too, are fine. Write to me if you will, or call me. I hope your mother gets well real soon."

Gordon walked from the room without looking back, the lead in his heart weighing him down. He knew this was the end.

Tabors Creek

*****

In the kitchen, Josh took an apple from the fruit bowl sitting on the stand beside the sink. "A great breakfast, Mom, thanks," he said. "You run the best restaurant in town, you know that?"

"You're buttering me up for something. What is it, Josh? What do you want?"

"Mom," Josh exclaimed. "I'm surprised at you. What makes you say that?" Both of them laughed loudly. Josh took a bite of the apple, humming to himself as he chewed.

Marsha Gibbons paused, looked at him, waiting for an answer. "Well, are you going to tell me?"

"Tell you what?"

"Come on now, Josh. You know what I'm talking about. What's on your mind? You're much too happy with yourself."

Josh grinned. "You always know everything, don't you Mom? Well, I've met a really nice lady. I've been leading up to telling you, but haven't figured quite how to say it yet. I'm invited to have supper with her and her mother this weekend."

"Joshua, I've known about this for a while now. I was just waiting for you to say something."

"Dad, huh?"

"That's right, Dad. He told me. We talked about it and we both think the same thing. We figure if you care about her, she must be a very nice girl and we wish you the best of luck."

"She is. She's very nice, and very pretty I might add. I suspect though that Dad never told you that she's been married before and has two children." Josh took a bite of the apple he held and waited for his mother to dissuade him because of that.

"Yes, of course he told me. Your dad and I don't have secrets, you should know that by now. I think the most important thing of all, Josh is that you both have the same feelings for each other. If she's the lovely lady you say she is, her children will probably be just like her and you'll love them too. Children mean extra work and more expenses, but a loving family is worth it all. I know; I have my own."

"Thanks Mom," Josh said. He put his arms around her and kissed her on the cheek. At the door, he called back inside as he stepped out, "See you in a little while."

Outside, Josh walked down a well-worn path around the side of the house, bordered by grass needing cut and headed toward the paddock and the track. Since early morning Brock Fegan had been running the brood of stabled horses in training, including Holiday's own Freedom. The air was warm this morning, the sky clear, with the exception of a few cotton-like, white, feathery clouds. Lilac trees at the side of the stable exuded a smell that searched for the flower-loving, unsuspecting soul. Catching Josh's eye and sense of smell, he sidetracked his walk toward the fragrant, purple flowers. After he pulled off a branch of blossoms, he headed to the track.

Scattered along the fence were daisies proudly holding their heads up soaking in the morning sun. In the distant field to the left of the track, rows of pink and white dogwood trees lit up in full, radiant bloom. Brock was on the far side of the track when Josh arrived. Riding Freedom, and seeing Josh at the fence, Brock rode over to where he stood when he reached the gate. "A beautiful day, huh?" Brock asked.

"Sure is. How's it going?"

"Great. With Phil's help, we've finished today's runs. I saved Freedom till last. By the way, there are just three of the horses we've trained that have made enough winning winter money to make Saturday's Derby. I've run them all against Freedom while they were here and he has outdone all of them every time he's run," Brock said. "Of course they've been gone for a couple of months now and being run by their respective jockeys I'm sure. Freedom's the only one who has made the 2.01 time for Derby distance."

"Well, I'd guess you had them pretty much at their peak, wouldn't you say?"

"I think so. I feel pretty confident."

"Have you heard if Dave Thompson has an entry?" Josh asked.

"Unfortunately, I've heard he's running Black N' Blue. That's a good horse. Damned good." He patted Freedom on the side. "Still think this guy's got the best chance though if Eddie keeps him on the inside. Just getting Eddie to do the right thing is the next step."

"Eddie's the best. You know that."

"I hope so."

"What do you mean, 'you hope so'? You ought to know so.'"

"Well, he's stubborn as hell; that's what I mean. He's gonna do it his way or no way."

"Aw, come on, Brock. Give him a break. He's gonna do what's right, don't worry about that."

"If you say so," Brock answered. "I sure as hell hope so. Freedom has the ability to take all three big ones. I heard there were 300 owners who nominated their horses this year. We weren't only lucky Freedom was one of the top 20 with the most money in the winter's biggest races, but he was second highest. Now that we made it to the Derby, I, for one, want to win it."

"Have you heard who was first?" Josh asked.

"Once again, unfortunately, it was Black N' Blue. That horse is good, as I said, and also that bastard Thompson will try whatever he can to take the Roses. We'll have to be on guard until Freedom gets far enough ahead of him that it won't matter. He's the only one I'm worried about. The others – they can't catch him. Freedom has more heart than all the rest put together."

"I'll talk to Eddie. He'll give whatever it takes to win. Stop your worrying."

"Are you finished with Freedom for now?" Josh asked.

"Yep. He's been out for half an hour already."

"I want to take him for a run out through the field – the last before he heads out to be a star."

Brock jumped down from Freedom's back. "Here you are." A smirk filled his face.

*****

In the field Josh reveled in the lush green of the fields. Everything was alive and more beautiful this time of year than any other. Josh allowed Freedom to trot at a moderate speed toward a stream running through the woods. He marveled at the beauty of this horse as they rode, the wind rustling through his mane of black hair. The strength of his strong legs boasted powerful muscles with each syncopated stride. "What a beauty you are," Josh said, thrilled to be riding on the back of a champion. At the edge of the stream he waited while Freedom drank from the running water. He ran his hand down Freedom's front flank. "You're a winner if you never run another race, my friend." As if he understood, Freedom raised his head, turned and nudged him in the arm.

Bushes of lavender bordered the woods around the stream for as far as Josh could see. Poppies were bursting with color next to the lavender and into the woods. Other scattered wild flowers in various colors could be seen among the trees. Another field nearby, bordered by a white board fence, was teeming with spring wheat, the tops of the wheat dancing in the wind as if keeping time to music. At a distance, he spotted a fox running from the wheat field into the woods. *A beautiful scene*, he thought.

Anticipation of his upcoming date with Ellen, Josh realized, was increasing his awareness and appreciation of everything around him. He forced himself to head back to the farm. In doing so, he took the long way back to delay the savoring of every feeling and sight he had at the moment. He allowed Freedom to run at his own pace, which this time was fast.

Josh lowered himself as low as he could behind Freedom's head and let him run.

Back at the barn, Josh led Freedom into the stable. With his favorite brush, he rubbed him down for several minutes. "How about some music while I finish rubbing you down, buddy. No dancing, though, you hear?" Josh laughed and Freedom threw his head in the air, tossing his mane. Josh walked to the radio sitting at the side of the stable and turned it on. A recording of Paul Whiteman's orchestra playing, *Ramona,* blared out. Josh began to hum the song as he looked into Freedom's feed bag; he then walked to a bin of oats. "How'd you like some of this, huh? You deserve a little treat after all that running."

Suddenly, the music stopped and the announcer began, "The manhunt for a long sought-after fugitive, Sherm Peck, ended just about an hour ago, right here in Lexington. Peck, who has been wanted for shooting two federal agents in Tabors Creek, West Virginia last July, was shot to death this morning in the home of his ex-wife, Ellen Potter, who lived at 356 Salem Street in Lexington. It appears he was shot by a neighbor who lived upstairs from where Mrs. Potter lived with her two children and her mother, Bertie Potter. We understand one of the two women was injured, but it's unknown at this point if it was Ellen Potter or her mother. As information is provided to us, we'll keep you informed." He continued, "In another incident, ….." Josh never heard what else was said, even though he didn't move. Fear and the possibility that Ellen had been shot had frozen him in place for a few seconds where he stood. "Oh my God, that's Ellen." He bolted toward the house. Inside, he called to his mother. "Mom, where are you?"

"I'm here," she called from upstairs.

"I'm headed into town," he yelled, then ran back outside and towards his car.

Hearing the door slam, Marsha looked out the upstairs window and called to Josh. "Where are you headed, Josh?"

Josh jumped into the car and raced down the road without looking back.

"I wonder what that was about," Marsha said.

*****

At Ellen's house, Josh parked the car and ran toward the house. Blocked by police, he wasn't allowed to enter. "What happened?" he asked.

"Sorry, we can't tell you anything. Listen to the news this evening."

"Who was shot?"

"Sorry, sir. As I said, we can't tell you anything." The policeman turned and walked away, ignoring the worried Josh.

Josh followed him, his voice getting louder with every sentence. "You don't understand. That's my girl in there. What's going on?"

"Sir, I'm sorry, but I can't tell you anything. You'll have to move along. Don't make any trouble."

Josh felt in shock as the policeman walked away from him.

Activity inside the house was evident through the windows, which Josh watched closely. He assumed they were probably taking pictures of the scene and doing paperwork. He stood on the sidewalk and waited for someone, anyone to come out of the house. He frantically rubbed his hands against each other fearing the worst.

*****

Sitting at Bertie's bedside, Ellen realized she was getting very hungry. She hadn't left her mother's room since early morning and it was now late evening. Bertie was sleeping soundly. A nurse, making rounds entered the room as Ellen was deciding what to do about supper. "My dear, you look exhausted. Have you eaten anything at all?" she asked.

"No, not yet. Too much happening. I hadn't any time to eat."

The nurse, dressed in her white, stiffly starched uniform with her hat proudly pinned to her hair moved to take Bertie's blood pressure. "Well, she's really quite sleepy, isn't she?"

"I think so," Ellen answered.

"Visiting hours will be over in just an hour. I doubt that she'll awake before then anyway. It might be good for you to go get something to eat and a good night's rest. You've had a pretty rough day."

"I hate to leave her though."

"I know how you feel, but I'll be here and I promise you I'll take good care of her. You go and get some rest." The nurse rested her arm on Ellen's shoulder.

"I think you're probably right. I am starving too. I didn't even get breakfast. That was when everything started."

The nurse shook her head in contempt. "You'll be alright, honey. Go get some rest. It's been one hell of a day."

"Thanks." Ellen took her mother's bag of clothes which she had worn in. She walked to the side of the bed. "I'll see you later, Mama." Bertie didn't move.

The fresh air felt good as Ellen walked down the street from the hospital. She was sad, but she was free. No more Sherm. Never again would she have to look over her shoulder to see if Sherm was behind her. She would never have to worry that he'd find her. She could stay here in Lexington. Or, she could go. She could do whatever she wanted to do. As soon as Bertie was healed, she would go to work. Even on this disaster day, she felt like skipping as she walked home.

*****

Josh waited for what seemed like forever, but still no one exited the house. He walked back to his car and sat down, hoping eventually someone would come out - anyone. Periodically, he got out of the car and walked the length of the block, then back again. Finally, as it began to get dark, he decided he had to give up and come back another time. He took one last walk down the block, to think through things before he gave up. As he walked, he saw another person crossing the street. He stopped. It looked like Ellen. He was probably just imagining it. He looked again. Could it be her? He waited while she walked into clear view. It was her! He ran as fast as he could. Caught off guard, she stopped, startled that someone was there. Then she saw Josh. The pent-up emotions of the day broke loose and she began to cry quietly. Josh put his arms around her and held her while she sobbed until her body shook. "I am so sorry, Ellen. So sorry."

Ellen wiped her eyes with the hankie she had in her hand. "How did you know?"

"I heard it on the radio."

"Thank you for being here. How long have you waited?"

"It's been a while, but no one would tell me who had been shot. I didn't know if you were hurt or not. So it must have been your mother? I'm so sorry Ellen, but I'm also thankful you are okay. How is your mother?"

"I think it's touch and go for a while yet. She was asleep when I left. She spent a long time in surgery. So you knew then she was shot."

"I knew someone had been shot, but that's all I knew. I didn't know which one of you, nor how bad it was."

"There was one bullet in her left shoulder. They were able to get the bullet out. Now she's just recovering from the shock and loss of blood."

"How about the kids? Are they alright and where are they?"

"They're just fine, Josh. Thanks for asking. Mrs. Crossen, our landlady, has them upstairs with her. She saved our lives, you know."

"I heard she did, yes."

"My Heavens, Josh. I can't tell you how happy I am that you're here."

"Well, I was anxious to meet the kids this weekend. Since I'm here though, why don't I take you inside and you get them with you before I leave," Josh asked.

"I'd like that, thanks."

*****

Inside, Mrs. Crossen was waiting with the children. Charlie came hurrying across the room with Neet right behind him. They hugged her, one on each side. "Are you home now?" Charlie asked.

"Mama is home and I'll be here to stay, don't you worry."

Josh watched as the two beautiful children hugged their mother. He could see and feel the love between Ellen and them. The security of both the children as they clung to their mother was very obvious. "Your children are as good looking as their mother, Ellen," Josh said.

"Thanks. I think so too. I mean I think they're good looking, period," she giggled.

"I liked the way I said it," Josh answered.

"Well, anyway, this is Charlie, my oldest. He's almost eight years old now and in the third grade when school begins again," looking at Charlie, on her right. "Neet is the youngest," she said turning to look at Neet on her left. "She'll be six in August."

"They're wonderful, Ellen. I'm glad to meet them."

"As bad as things are, the best thing is that we're finally free to enjoy ourselves and live without fear. I feel like a heavy burden has just been lifted. All I need now if for Mama to get well." Her eyes once again filled with tears.

"She will. Just have faith."

Josh turned to leave. "I'll be in touch with you, if I may. The big Derby race is on Saturday. I had planned to ask you to join us there, but of course I know better now. I hope you'll see me when I get back though."

"Thanks, Josh. I'll be listening to the radio. I don't even know your horse's number. Is this one you have trained?" Ellen asked.

"We have trained him, yes, and he's our horse. We own him."

"I guess there's a lot I don't know about you, huh?"

"Wait until next week," Josh said, grinning. Looking back and waving, he headed to his car.

*****

Josh and Hal Gibbons arrived in Louisville Thursday for the upcoming Derby. Jockey, Eddie Ellis, trainer, Brock Fegan, and exerciser, Tom Rowe had arrived Wednesday evening with Freedom who had been housed in the security area.

At 5:45 a.m. on Friday Eddie Ellis had Tom Rowe take Freedom to the track. Later at breakfast, the men sat in the clubhouse eating and discussing the day's events and plans. "How'd he do this morning on the track?" Hal asked.

"I stayed and watched while Tom exercised him," Eddie said. "He did great, really great. He backtracked back to the wire, stood around and looking pretty confident, surveyed the area. He was really taking it all in. What an ego he has – almost looked like he was practicing for parading around with the roses. He's one smart horse, I'll tell you. That and the heart he has for the race will be his fuel tomorrow."

"I think you're right about his ego. We've seen that," laughed Hal. "One thing is clear to me. When you look at

Freedom, you're looking at consistency with class, and I think he damn well knows it."

"You've got it exactly right, Hal. That's a good way to put it, 'consistency with class.' Yesterday he breezed through five-eighths in 1:00.40. And he was schooled in the paddock on Wednesday," Eddie said.

"Tell me something, Eddie," Josh said. "Have you and Brock reached an agreement on how to win this race?"

"What's he saying now?" Eddie gave a look of disgust. "We've talked of course. He needs to have a little more confidence in me. Believe me, Josh, I know what I'm doing."

"And I know you do. However, I just want to be sure you two are on the same wave length!"

"We're both in it to win, Josh. We often take different paths to get to the same place, but we get there, usually at the same time." With a wide smile, Eddie put his hands together under his chin as if in a prayer.

"Okay, pal. I'm leaving it in your hands. Just so you know what you're doing."

"Tell me more about this morning," Hal said.

"Well, he galloped a mile and a half. Later on this afternoon I plan to just walk him around a bit. He needs to get used to that. Don't want to overdo it though. Gotta keep him happy so that he makes us happy."

Everyone laughed. Hal shook his head, smiled and said. "We're at your mercy, Eddie, and I'm sure you'll see to it that tomorrow is a day we'll always remember."

*****

Eddie Ellis was nervous. He awakened early and dressed. After a light breakfast, he headed to the stables. Freedom was prancing around in his stable. "Good morning, fellow," Eddie said to him. "Are you ready for this big, wonderful day?" Freedom reared up, paddling both front hooves in front of him.

"That's a good enough answer for me. I knew you'd say that anyway. How about you and I take a walk around." He placed his exercise saddle on him and took him out the side of the barn, away from the crowd. No one would know who he was without his Derby gear on. In front of the stables, trainers, owners, and others were milling around. "Let's go see some of the crowd." On the track there were several horses warming up already. Eddie headed to the track. Fans hadn't started to arrive yet, a good time to let him run. At this point, Freedom was less known and therefore, a long shot to win. That wouldn't be true if the racing fans watched him in action today.

As expected, Freedom took a second longer than Eddie liked to get out of the gate, but on the track, nothing could catch him. On the far turn, Freedom's one-thousand pounds of muscle and speed was a streak of lightening, surprising even Eddie. "Okay, fellow, once is enough. Save it for later." Off the track, Eddie saw Dave Thompson watching the run. "Oh, shit," he said aloud. "Didn't want to see him yet." Brushing care aside, he headed back to the stable.

*****

By early afternoon the stands were filled with patrons and the excitement could be felt through the sound. The Jockey Club Stand was busy tending to ladies dressed as elegant as the affair and men in expensive wear. Most ladies wore fine dresses with hats to match. Some already held mint julep drinks in their hands. More than half of the men wore summer suits, straw hats, and shoes that exuded wealth as did the suits they wore. The others were generally dressed in white jackets and dark pants. Some watched the four races, which preceded the Derby. After each race, the track was manicured by trained track maintenance. Hal and Josh Gibbons had watched all of the races from their seats in the Grand Stand Dining Room.

Tabors Creek

*****

Eddie Ellis, weighing 115 pounds, sat astride Freedom. "You're dressed to win, I can tell," Eddie laughed as he patted his horse. A bridle made of leather straps held Freedom's bit and reins in place. He also wore the required blinders off to the side of each eye. On Freedom's back Eddie sat on a small leather patch on top of Freedom's number six cloth, which served as a saddle. A leather strap or girth stretched around Freedom's belly, which kept the saddle in place. On the bottom of Freedom's hooves were tiny, three-ounce aluminum shoes or plates. Eddie's bright red, silk shirt, perfectly matched Freedom's red number cloth.

Josh and Brock wandered down to where Eddie sat waiting. Seeing them, Freedom began to prance in place, waved his large mane back and forth, and nudged Josh in the arm when he reached them. "I see you, buddy. I see you," he joked. "We're expecting a lot from you." He rubbed his hand down Freedom's side.

"Well, you all set, Eddie?" Brock asked.

"Sure am."

"My best advice is, just keep him near the rail. He loves it there. I know you already know that, but this is just a reminder."

"Yep, I know."

"I'm hoping you get the "bird's seat," behind a couple of dueling horses. Save that peak speed for the last quarter of a mile, unless you get hung up beside Thompson's horse. If so, get around him and you're home. Watch him and watch him close. He may do anything to win," Eddie continued. "He's wearing number three, so he'll be loading with number thirteen. You'll be three horses apart at the starting gate, so that's good."

"Okay. Got it. Don't worry. We're in it to win it," Eddie said.

"One more thing," Brock said. "The three that we trained at Holiday are in there. Only number eight could give you a problem as I see it. That's Nick Costopoulos's horse, Easy Street, and he comes on in the last quarter of a mile. He's fast, but not as fast as Freedom."

"Thanks," Eddie said, without a smile.

"Good luck," Brock said.

"Good luck, Eddie," Josh said. Eddie reached to shake his hand.

Eddie headed toward the tunnel and onto the track. On the way, at the paddock, all of the jockeys dismounted, walked together, stopped and posed for pictures. They walked their horses around all of the people standing nearby so that the horses could hear the crowd and not be surprised by it. Freedom seemed to ignore all of the noise, but instead held his head high and appeared to pose for the cameras. The crowd around him loved it.

The group of proud horses paraded before the grandstands while the band played, "My Old Kentucky Home." The huge crowd stood and sang along with the band. Josh and his father sat in the expensive box seats that attract the wealthy, the famous, and the well-connected. When the song finished, the crowd of approximately 100,000 cheered, waved their programs and sipped their mint juleps. In their box seat, Josh and his father clinked their glasses together.

"To Freedom," Hal said.

"To Freedom," Josh toasted.

As exciting as it was, still Josh's thoughts wandered back to Ellen and her mother. He hoped her mother was healing. When he returned home, he knew he would spend all of his efforts in winning Ellen. It didn't matter that he didn't know her well. It didn't matter that she had two children. He only knew it felt right. She was warm and kind, as well as beautiful, and he was in love with her. Her love for him seemed to be there and her sincerity was obvious. He was thankful her values of him couldn't be based on his family's wealth and status. She believed him to be a horse trainer.

*****

In a short time all of the horses had headed for the starting gate. The crowd was ecstatic as the bugle sounded, announcing their entrance from the tunnel onto the track. "Well, here we go," Hal said. "I wonder what happened with Doc's horse? He must have decided not to go for it."

"Either that or he scratched," Josh answered.

"Right now, however, I have only one horse I really care about," Hal said.

"I heard there's one horse in there, Red Rider, who has never won a race, but he lost only by a nose in his last one and one-half mile run, so that's the only reason he's here," Josh said.

"Well, let's see what he can do here. Hopefully, not much," Hal said. "They say this is the most exciting two minutes in sports, and I think I know now what they mean." The excitement intensified as the jockeys and horses did their post parade around the track and into the chutes. In the chutes, the horses were raring to go, moving in and out of the chutes until the door behind them closed. When all the doors were shut, there was a few second's wait, and the bell rang.

The horses were out of the chute, each rider trying to make the others uncomfortable in their spot, while desperately racing to break out of the pack. Writer's Block took the lead out the starting gate and carried the field through quick early fractions of .22 for the quarter-mile. Black N Blue was next out of the pack with Freedom to his left. Eddie watched unbelieving when Blue's jockey was edging toward him as quickly as he could. Eddie held the reins tight and was able to move Freedom to the rail near the beginning. As the field was midway down the backstretch, Blue nudged Freedom. Eddie knew he'd have to move up or get rammed into the rail. In front of him Writer's Block held the spot Eddie wanted and needed. As much as he wanted to stay at the rail, Eddie knew he had to get away from the side of Blue. Although earlier in the race than he wanted, he pushed Freedom, who did what he was asked. He spurted to a two-length lead in front of Blue, followed by one length lead in front of Writers Block. He quickly moved back to the rail. He was in front, but it was early. Could he hold it? Behind him, Sarasota Sun trailed the field by six furlongs, Out Front moved up to second place and Blue fell behind to third. From next to last place, Hardly Ever slowly pulled away from the field and pulled in front of Blue. Eddie hung in on the rail, not realizing he was far ahead. On the last turn, Eddie gave one right-handed crack of the whip, and Freedom finished ahead of the field by 4-1/2 lengths for a record time of 2:01 2/5. Behind him came Out Front, trained at Holiday, in second place, with Hardly Ever finishing in third.

*****

Ellen left early in the morning for the hospital. Most of the night she had spent thinking about Gordon Workman and what she should do. She knew she had hurt him and it bothered her. She also needed to talk to him. He would be at the Police Station this morning before he left to go to Tabors Creek he had said. It would be best to go there before she went to the hospital. She hurried to get there before he was gone.

Inside the building, she asked for him. Luck was with her; he was still there.

"Good morning, Ellen," he said when he saw her. "I'm really glad you came."

"Good morning, Gordon. I'm glad to see you're still here. I was afraid I might miss you. I needed to talk to you if you have some time."

"I always have time for you, Ellen. You know that. I wasn't planning to leave actually until tomorrow morning. I changed my plans a bit."

"Can we go for a walk?"

"That's fine with me."

Tabors Creek

Outside, the two of them strolled down the street. The sun was out and the temperature was comfortable to walk. Flowers lined the yards of many of the homes. Street lamps held baskets of blue lobelia mixed with geraniums of red and white. It was a beautiful walk.

Ellen began. "There's something I've been wanting to tell you for a long time, but just never have. Sherm was always around and to be truthful, I was afraid to talk with you."

"I understand. What is it that you need to tell me?"

"I know you've met my children, even if you don't really know them."

"Yes, I have, although it's been a while since I've seen them. I know they're great kids. You're doing a fine job raising them, in spite of your circumstances."

"Well, I can't take the credit. If it weren't for my mother, I'd have been in lots of trouble," Ellen smiled faintly as she spoke.

"Yeah, I'd have to agree. Bertie's a really fine person, always has been as long as I've known her."

"Well, anyway, back to the point. I wanted to talk to you about what happened with you and me before I met Sherm."

"Alright," Gordon answered. He gazed at her longingly.

"I always thought you and I would end up being married."

"So did I, Ellen. You know I'd still like that."

"There's no need to talk about that anymore. Not now, please. Like I said before, too much has happened since then. But at the time, when I thought we'd be together I acted as if we were married, and that was wrong. I know that now, but I can't change it. I was young and didn't realize what could happen. Getting pregnant never entered my mind. I didn't have any idea I was pregnant when I met Sherm. I've tried to put it out of my thoughts, but I can't."

"You were pregnant?"

"Yes, Gordon, pregnant with Charlie, your son."

"My son?"

"Your son, Gordon. Charlie is your son. Look at him. He even looks like you."

Sheriff Workman stopped walking and stared at Ellen. "Are you serious? Tell me this isn't a joke."

"No, Gordon. It's no joke, I promise."

"I can't believe that. I'm shocked."

"Can't you tell how much he looks like you?"

"Well, now that you say it, yes, I guess I can. I can't believe this."

"I should have told you a long time ago, but as I said, I just couldn't. I'm free now. I don't have to be afraid anymore."

"I guess I ought to be mad that you didn't tell me, but I can't be. I'm just about the happiest guy in the world right this minute. Can I see him sometime?"

"Sure you can," Ellen said. "I think he'd love spending time with you now and then."

Sheriff Workman held his head in his hands. "It's hard to believe. If only I'd known, Ellen, I would have helped you."

"It just wasn't meant to be, Gordon. I have fallen in love with someone else now, so it truly wasn't meant for us. However, I can't go on denying you your son."

"I appreciate this more than you know, Ellen. Yesterday it seemed the world had come to an end. Today, you've brought it back again." He hugged her tightly.

"I need to get on to the hospital now, but I needed to talk to you before you left."

"Thank you," Ellen.

By the time they finished talking, the two of them were back to the Police Station. "I need to get on back to Tabors Creek tomorrow, Ellen. I'll call you sometime next week and make arrangements to get him when school is out for the summer. Maybe he could come spend a week or so in Tabors Creek. Would that be okay?"

"I think that would be great. Mama and me just might be able to bring him there. We'll see about that. I'll write to you and let you know."

"You've made me a happy man, Ellen. Thanks."

Sheriff Workman hugged Ellen and walked inside. She waved as she walked away.

*****

At the hospital Ellen sat holding her mother's hand. "How are you feeling, Mama?"

"I'm fine, honey. I'll be out of here in no time, wait and see." Bertie gave a slight smile as she talked.

"It's finally over, Mama. No more worrying and no more pain. We can walk down the streets now and smile at people without worrying about whether or not they recognize us. No more do we have to be afraid of who sees us or where we go. I know you feel so bad right now, but I'm so anxious for you to be well and start enjoying life again."

"I am too, Ellen."

But you've paid a heavy, heavy price for my mistakes and I'm so sorry," Ellen cried softly.

"You can stop talking like that right now. Don't you go blaming yourself, you hear me?" Bertie scolded. "I have never done anything in my life that anyone, including you, made me do. I have done what I wanted to do or what I needed to do, but never have I been made to do anything. I don't 'spect I ever will. I was with you because I wanted to be with you. It had nothing to do with what you had done. I wanted to be near you and my grandchildren. I was free to leave if I'd wanted to go. So you just stop thinking like that. Promise me that, will you?"

"Okay, Mama. I promise. Now that I'm home, you're going to get some relief. No more are you going to do those ironings like you've been doing. It's your time to rest."

"Don't you worry about me restin'. I'm old and tough."
She grinned and tried to laugh, but it hurt. She placed her hand
over her aching shoulder.

"Well, I'll agree. You are tough alright."

"This morning on the way here, I stopped and talked with
Sheriff Workman," Ellen said.

"Where was he?"

"He spent the night at the Police Station before he headed
back to Tabors Creek. In fact, he's spending two nights, he said."

"And what did he have to say?"

"I told him the truth, something which you didn't know
either."

"What's that, honey?" Bertie asked.

"I'm going to tell you because we will see him again in
the future, I'm sure."

"Land sakes, honey, tell me what it is you told him."

"Mama, Charlie is Gordon Workman's son, not Sherm's."

"Oh, my goodness. I never guessed that. For heaven's
sakes. Well, I should have guessed it. Come to think of it, he
looks like him. I'm glad you told me. You know Ellen, that's a
blessing in disguise. The boy will have someone to look up to
other than the man I thought was his father. It's the way it ought
to be."

"What a day this has been! First I wake up to an aching
shoulder and find out I've been hit. Then, I find this out. What's
next?" she joked.

"That's it. No more for today," Ellen said.

You know you've been here all day," Bertie said. "You
go home now with the kids. I'm going to do nothing but sleep.
It'll come easy today."

"Alright, Mama, I will. You do get some sleep. I'll be
back in the morning."

Ellen walked toward the door and looked back. Bertie's eyes
were already closed.

XI

Fall of 1932

All of the neighboring families gathered in the lawn of Hal and Marsha Gibbons' home at Holiday Farms. Josh Gibbons stood in front of the white grape arbor adorned with red roses and white gardenias as he waited for Ellen in her white bridal gown to walk out the front door of the Gibbons home. Bertie stood with Neet and Charlie next to the fountain filled with pink and white roses. The scent of the flowers filled the air with a delightful, pleasant aura that complemented the feeling that love and happiness were overwhelming in every person in attendance.

In the center of the fountain stood a three-foot, white, sculptured maiden allowing water to cascade from a watering can she held into the colorful flowers, terracing down to the lower level of the fountain. From there it fell to a lower bowl until it overflowed, creating a waterfall before it quietly recycled itself. Chairs were lined up under the large oak trees at the edge of the lawn.

Brock Fegan placed his arm around his wife, Kathy and leaned to whisper to her. "Reminds me of our day a few years ago, huh?"

"Yes, but it's been more than a 'few years'."

He hugged her tightly. "Doesn't seem like it."

Doc Weide stood next to Hal Gibbons. "Sure am happy for Josh," Doc said. "He picked a pretty woman."

"I think you're right, Doc."

"I knew it the first time I saw him look at her in the hospital."

"Sure glad you could make it today, Doc," Hal said.

"Wouldn't have missed it. Can't tell you how sorry I was to have to scratch at the Derby, but my Princess Angie had a sore foot. There was no way she could run."

"There's always next year," Hal said.

"I plan to be there. Congrats on Freedom's victory though."

As the group of guests talked and meandered the grounds, two violinists roamed the area playing music. Before long a hush fell over the crowd and all eyes went to the doorway of the house. Ellen stepped outside and gracefully ascended the stairs toward the crowd as everyone beamed. The violinists resumed their playing until she reached the side of Josh.

Tears filled his eyes when he took her hand. "You're beautiful," he said.

monap2005@comcast.net

Made in the USA
Columbia, SC
16 July 2018